Olla Podrida

by

Captain Marryat

Olla Podrida
by Captain Marryat

ISBN: 978-93-65785-43-2

Published by

DOUBLE 9 BOOKS

2/13-B, Ansari Road
Daryaganj, New Delhi – 110002
info@double9books.com
www.double9books.com
Tel. 011-40042856

ABOUT THE AUTHOR

Captain Frederick Marryat (an early innovator of the sea story) was a British Royal Navy Officer and novelist. He gained the Royal Human Society's gold medal for bravery, before leaving the services in 1830 to write books. He is mainly remembered for his stories of the sea, many written from his own experiences. He started a series of adventure novels marked by a brilliant, direct narrative style and an absolute fund of incident and fun. These have The King's Own (1830), Peter Simple (1834), and Mr. Midshipman Easy (1836). He also created a number of children's books, among which The Children of the New Forest (1847), a story of the English Civil Wars is a classic of children literature. A Life and Letters was processed by his daughter Florence (1872). He is recognized also for a broadly used system of maritime flag signalling known as Marryat's Code. Familiar for his adventurous novels, his works are known for their representation of deep family bonds and social structure beside naval action. Marryat died in 1848 at the age of fifty.

CONTENTS

Chapter One

April 3, 1835.

Reader, did you ever feel in that peculiarly distressing state of mind in which one oppressing idea displaces or colours every other, absorbing, intermingling with, empoisoning, and, like the filth of the harpy, turning every thing into disgust—when a certain incubus rides upon the brain, as the Old Man of the Mountain did upon the shoulders of Sinbad, burdening, irritating, and rendering existence a misery—when, looking around, you see but one object perched everywhere and grinning at you—when even what you put into your mouth tastes of but that one something, and the fancied taste is so unpleasant as almost to prevent deglutition—when every sound which vibrates in your ear appears to strike the same discordant note, and all and every thing will remind you of the one only thing which you would fain forget;—have you ever felt any thing like this, reader? If you have not, then thank God, by way of grace, before you out with your knife and fork and begin to cut up the contents of these pages.

I have been and am now suffering under one of these varieties of "Phobias," and my disease is a Politicophobia, I will describe the symptoms.

I am now in the metropolis of England, and when I walk out every common house appears to me to be the House of Commons—every lordly mansion the House of Lords—every man I meet, instead of being a member of society, is transferred by imagination into a member of the senate—every chimney-sweep into a bishop, and a Bavarian girl, with her "Py a proom," into an ex-chancellor. If I return home, the ring at the bell reminds me of a Peel—as I mount the stairs I think of the "Lobby"—I throw myself on the sofa, and the cushion is transformed into a woolsack—if a solitary visitor calls in, I imagine a public meeting, and call out chair! chair!—and I as often address my wife as Mr Speaker, as I do with the usual appellative of "my dear."

This incubus, like the Catholic anathema, pursues me everywhere—at breakfast, the dry toast reminds me of the toasts at public dinners—tea, of the East India charter—sugar, of the West India question—the loaf, of agricultural distress—and, as every one knows that London eggs are a lottery, according as they prove bad or good, so am I reminded of a Whig or

Tory measure. When the newspaper is brought in, I walk round and round it as a dog will do round the spot he is about to lie down upon. I would fain not touch it; but at last, like a fascinated bird who falls per force into the reptile's mouth, so do I plunge into its columns, read it with desperation, and when the poison has circulated, throw it away in despair. If I am reminded to say grace at dinner, I commence "My Lords, and gentlemen;" and when I seek my bed, as I light my taper, I move "that the House do now adjourn." The tradesmen's bills are swelled by my disease into the budget, and the checks upon my banker into supplies. Even my children laugh and wonder at the answers which they receive. Yesterday one brought me her book of animals, and pointing to a boa constrictor, asked its name, and I told her it was an *O'Connell*. I am told that I mentioned the names of half the members of the Upper and Lower House, and at the time really believed that I was calling the beasts by their right names. Such are the effects of my unfortunate disease.

Abroad I feel it even worse than at home. Society is unhinged, and every one is afraid to offer an opinion. If I dine out, I find that no one will speak first—he knows not whether he accosts a friend or foe, or whether he may not be pledging his bitter enemy. Every man looks at his neighbour's countenance to discover if he is Whig or Tory: they appear to be examining one another like the dogs who meet in the street, and it is impossible to conjecture whether the mutual scenting will be followed up by a growl or a wag of the tail; however, one remark will soon discover the political sentiments of the whole party. Should they all agree, they are so busy in abuse that they rail at their adversaries with their mouths full—should they disagree, they dispute so vehemently that they forget that they were invited to dinner, and the dishes are removed untasted, and the duties of the Amphytryon become a sinecure. Go to an evening party or a ball and it is even worse, for young ladies talk politics, prefer discussion to flirtation, and will rather win a partner over to their political opinions than by their personal charms. If you, as a Tory, happen to stand up in a cotillion with a pretty Whig, she taps you with her fan that she may tap your politics; if you agree, it is *"En avant deux,"* if not, a *"chassez croisée."* Every thing goes wrong—she may *set* to you indeed, but hers is the set of defiance, and she shakes her *wig* against your *Tory*. To *turn your partner* is impossible, and the only part of the figure which is executed *con amore* is *dos à dos*. The dance is over, and the lady's looks at once tell you that you may save your "oaths," while she "takes her seat."

I have tried change of scene—posted to watering places; but the deep, deep sea will not drown politics. Even the ocean in its roaring and commotion reminded me of a political union.

I have buried myself in the country, but it has been all in vain. I cannot look at the cattle peacefully grazing without thinking of O'Connell's tail, Stanley's tail, and a short-docked pony reminded me of the boasted little tail of Colonel Peel. The farm-yard, with its noisy occupants, what was it but the reality so well imitated by the members of the Lower House, who would drown argument in discord? I thought I was in the lobby at the close of a long debate. Every tenth field, every tenth furrow, (and I could not help counting,) every tenth animal, and every tenth step, reminded me of the Irish tithes; and when I saw a hawk swoop over a chicken, I thought of the Appropriation Bill—so I left the country.

I have tried every thing—I have been every where, but in vain. In the country there was no relaxation—in society no pleasure—at home no relief. England was disjointed, never to be united until it was dismembered—and there was no repose. I had my choice, either to go abroad, or to go mad; and, upon mature deliberation, I decided upon the former, as the lesser evil of the two. So I gave—I sold—I discharged—I paid—I packed up, and I planned. The last was the only portion of my multifarious duties not satisfactorily arranged. I looked at the maps, plied my compasses that I might compass my wishes, measured distances that I might decide upon my measures— planned, looked over the maps—and planned again.

Chapter Two

Well, as I said in my last chapter, I planned—and planned—but I might as well conjugate it, as many others assisted—it was I planned, thou plannedst, he planned, we planned, ye planned, and they planned—and what annoyed me was, that I could not help considering that "the whole house was in a committee," and without being able "to report progress." At first it was *decided upon* that we should proceed up the Rhine, and not leave off paddling until we had arrived at Manheim, at which town I fancied that I should at least be out of political distance. We read all about Manheim, found out that it was a regular-built town, with a certain number of inhabitants—with promenades, gardens, and a fine view of the Rhine. "So you're going abroad—where?" Manheim, was the reply, and all the world knew that we were bound to Manheim; and every one had something to say, or something that they had heard said, about Manheim. "Very nice place—Duchess Dowager Stephanie—very cheap—gay in winter—masters excellent"—were the variety of changes rung, and all was settled; but at last one unlucky observation raised a doubt—another increased—a third confirmed it. "A very dull place—German cookery bad for children—steam-boats from Rotterdam very bad, and often obliged to pass two nights on deck." A very influential member of the committee took alarm about the children being two nights on deck, and it was at last decided that to go up to Manheim by steam-boat at 4 pounds, 9 shillings a-head, and children at half-price was not to be thought of.

"I wonder you don't go to Bruges," observed a committee man; "nice quiet place—excellent masters—every thing so cheap—I once bought eighty large peaches there for two francs."

And all the children clapped their little hands, and cried out for Bruges and cheap peaches.

It was further submitted that it was convenient—you might go the whole of the way by water—and Bruges was immediately under consideration.

"If you go to Bruges, you will find it very dull," observed another; "but you'll meet Mrs Trollope there—now Brussels is very little farther, and is a delightful place;" and Brussels was also referred to the committee.

"You won't like Brussels—there is such a mixture, and house-rent is dear. Now I should recommend Spa for the summer—it is a most beautiful spot—and excellent company." And Spa was added to the list.

Then after a day or two came an Anti-Teutonic, who railed against Germany—and Germans—German towns, German travelling, and German *French*, which was detestable—German cookery, which was nothing but grease. "You may imagine," said he, "and so have many more, that Germany is more pleasant and less expensive than France; but they have been disappointed, and so will you be. Now, for a quiet place, I should recommend Saint Omer—only thirty miles from Calais—so convenient— and very pretty."

Saint Omer—humph—very quiet and retired—and no politics—and Saint Omer was occasionally canvassed.

"Saint Omer!" said another who called the next day, "you'll die of ennui. Go to Boulogne—it is delightful—you may be there as retired or as gay as you please."

Boulogne to be taken into consideration many inquiries made and all very satisfactory—good sands and excellent jackasses for the children.

"My dear friend, Boulogne is something like the King's Bench—at least most of the people only go there in preference. Every body will suppose that you've *levanted*. Pray don't go to Boulogne."

"Why don't you go by Southampton to Havre—there you'll have quiet and amusement—beautiful country about Honfleur—scenery up the Seine splendid; and then you can go up to Rouen by water, if you intend to go on to Paris."

Havre and Honfleur submitted to the committee.

But then came Dieppe, and Brest, and the environs of Paris, Versailles, Saint Germain, Passy, and other recommendations, in which every one particular place was proved incontestably to be more particularly suited to us than any other, and the committee sat for three weeks, at the end of which, upon examining the matured opinions of the last seven days, I found them to have fluctuated as follows:—

Monday morning, Manheim. Evening, Spa.

Tuesday morning, Bruges. Evening Brussels.

Wednesday morning, Saint Omer. Evening, Boulogne.

Thursday morning, Havre. Evening Honfleur.

Friday morning, Dieppe. Evening, Passy.

Saturday morning, Versailles. Evening, Saint Germain.

Sunday morning, Spa. Evening, Brussels.

The fact was, that there was a trifling difference of opinion in the committee—the great object appeared to be, and the great difficulty at the same time, to find a place which would suit all parties, that is to say, a place where there were no politics, plenty of gaiety, and cheap peaches.

Chapter Three

Paddle, paddle—splash, splash—bump, thump, bump. What a leveller is sea-sickness—almost as great a radical as death. All grades, all respect, all consideration are lost. The master may summon John to his assistance, but John will see his master hanged before he'll go to him; he has taken possession of his master's great coat, and he intends to keep *it*—*he* don't care for warning.

The nurses no longer look after the infant or the children, they may tumble overboard—even the fond yearnings of the mother at last yield to the overwhelming sensation, and it it were not for the mercenary or kind-hearted assistance of those who have become habituated to the motion of a vessel, there is no saying how tragical might be the commencement of many a party of pleasure to the Continent.

"O lauk, Mary, do just hold this child," says the upper nurse to her assistant; "I do feel such a *sinking* in my stomach."

"Carn't indeed, nurse, I've such a *rising*."

Away hurried both the women at once to the side of the vessel, leaning over and groaning heavily. As for the children, they would soon have been past caring for, had it not been for my protecting arms.

Decorum and modesty, next to maternal tenderness, the strongest feelings in woman, fall before the dire prostratiou of this malady. A young lady will recline unwittingly in the arms of a perfect stranger, and the bride of three months, deserted by her husband, will offer no resistance to the uncouth seaman, who, in his kindness, would loosen the laces that confine her heaving bosom.

As for politeness, even the *ancien régime* of the noblesse of France put it in their pockets as if there were a general chaos—self is the only feeling; not but that I have seen occasional traits of good-will towards others. I once witnessed a young lady smelling to a bottle of Eau de Cologne, as if her existence depended upon it, who handed it over to another, whose state was even more pitiable, and I was reminded of Sir Philip Sidney and the cup of water, as he lay wounded on the field of battle, "Thy necessity is greater than mine." And if I might have judged from her trembling lips and pallid countenance, it was almost an equal act of heroism. Paddle, paddle, splash, splash, bump, thump, bump—one would really imagine that the passengers were so many pumps, all worked at once with the vessel by the same hundred horse power, for there were an hundred of them about me, each as sick as a horse. "*Sic omnes,*" thought I.

I have long passed the ordeal, and even steam, and smoke, and washing basins, and all the various discordant and revolting noises *from those* who suffer, have no effect upon my nervous system—still was I doomed to torment, and was very sick indeed. For some time I had been watched by the evil eyes of one, whom the Yankees would designate, as *almighty ugly.* He was a thin, spare man, whose accost I could well have spared, for he had the look of a demon, and, as I soon found, was possessed with the demon of politics. Imagine what I must have suffered when I found out that he was a button-holder to boot. Observing that I was the only one who was in a state to listen, he seized upon me as his victim. I, who had fled from politics with as much horror as others have done from the cholera—I, who had encountered all the miseries of steam navigation, and all the steam and effluvia of close cabins, to find myself condemned with others "alike to groan—" what with King Leopold, and William of Nassau, and the Belgian share of the debt, and the French and Antwerp, and his pertinacious holding of my button. "Shall I knock him down," thought I; "he insists upon laying his hands upon me, why should I not lay my hands upon him?" But on second consideration, that would not have been polite; so I made other attempts to get rid of him, but in vain; I turned the subject to far countries—the rascal had been everywhere; at one moment he would be at Vienna, and discuss the German confederation—at another in South America, canvassing the merits of Bolivar and Saint Martin. There was no stopping him; his tongue was like the paddle of a steam-boat, and almost threw as much spray in my face. At last I threw off my coat, which he continued to hold in his hand by the third button, and threw myself into one of the cribs appropriated to passengers, wishing him a good night. He put my coat down in the crib beneath, and as he could no longer hold the button, he laid hold of the side of the crib, and continued his incessant clack. At last I turned my back to him, and made no answer, upon which he made a retreat, and when I awoke the next morning, I found that he was too ill to spout politics, although as he progressed, he spouted what was quite as bad.

Par parenthèse, he was a great liar, and as he drew a long bow when he was able to talk, so did he prove a long shot when he was sea-sick. Confound the fellow, I think I see him now—there he stood, a tall, gaunt misery, about the height of a workhouse pump, and the basin was on the floor of the cabin, nearly three feet from his two feet; without condescending to stoop, or to sit down, or to lift up the basin, so as to lessen the distance, he poured forth a parabola, "quod nunc describere" had just as well be omitted. I shall therefore dismiss this persecuting demon, by stating, that he called himself a baron, the truth of which I doubted much; that he was employed by crowned heads, which I doubted still more. On one point, however, I had little doubt, although he did not enter upon the subject, (and his tongue to a great degree confirmed it) that he was a *chevalier d'industrie*.

"I am rid of him, thank God," exclaimed I, as I went on deck to breathe a little fresh air, having lighted my cigar in the steward's berth as I ascended. The first objects which attracted my attention, were a young gentleman and lady, the former standing by the latter, who was sitting in a pensive position, with her elbow leaning on the gunnel. She was in deep mourning, and closely veiled.

"And how does the beautiful Maria find herself this morning?" said the young gentleman, leaning over her with his hand on the rail to support himself.

The beautiful Maria! How was it possible not to be attracted by such a distinguishing appellation? The beautiful Maria! I thought of Sterne's Maria, and the little dog with a string, and I trimmed my ear like a windsail in the tropics to catch the soft responding, and most assuredly, to my expectant imagination, melodious vibration of the air which would succeed.

At last there was a reply. "Oh! *tol, lol!*" And that in anything but a melodious voice. "Oh! *tol, lol!*" What a bathos! The beautiful Maria, whom in my imagination I had clothed with all the attributes of sentiment and delicacy, whom I had conjured up as a beau idéal of perfection, replies in a hoarse voice with, "Oh! *tol, lol!*" Down she went, like the English funds in a panic—down she went to the zero of a Doll Tearsheet, and down I went again into the cabin. Surely this is a world of disappointment.

Perhaps I was wrong—she might have been very beautiful, with the voice of a peacock; she might also have the plumage—but no, that is impossible—she must, from her sex, have been a peahen. At all events, if not very beautiful, she was very sick. I left the beautiful Maria screeching over the gunnel. If the young gentleman were to repeat the same question now, thought I, the beautiful Maria will hardly answer, "*Oh! tol, lol!*"

It was very cold on deck, blowing fresh from the East. I never heard any one give a satisfactory reason why a west wind should be warm, and an east wind cold in latitude 50 degrees N. It is not so in the tropics when the east wind follows the rarefaction occasioned by the sun. Yet, does not Byron say:—

"'Tis the land of the east, 'tis the clime of the sun."

Certainly our east winds are not at all poetical.

"Very cold, sir," said I, addressing a round-faced gentleman in a white great coat, who rested his chin and his two hands upon a thick cane. "You are fortunate in not being sea-sick."

"I beg your pardon, I am not fortunate. I am worse than sea-sick, for I want to be sea-sick and I can't. I do believe that everything is changed now-a-days, since that confounded Reform Bill!"

Politics again, thought I; what the devil has sea-sickness to do with the Reform Bill? Mercy on me, when shall I be at peace? "There certainly has been some change," observed I.

"Change, sir! yes, everything changed. England of 1835 is no more like merry England of olden time, than I am like Louis the Fourteenth—ruined, sir—every class suffering, sir—badly ruled, sir."

"Things are much cheaper."

"Much cheaper! Yes, sir; but what's the good of things being cheap when nobody has any money to purchase with? They might just as well be dear. It's a melancholy discovery, sir, this steam."

"Melancholy just now to those who are on board, and suffering, I grant."

"Pooh, nonsense! melancholy to those on shore, sir; the engines work while man looks on and starves. Country ruined, sir—people miserable—thrown out of employment, while foreigners reap the benefit; we sell them our manufactures at a cheaper rate; we clothe them well, sir, at the expense of our own suffering population. But is this all, sir? *Oh, no!*"

And here the gentleman dropped his chin again upon his hands, and looked very woeful indeed. After a few seconds, he resumed.

"We are dismembered, sir—ruined by faction. Society is disintegrated by political animosities; thousands have retreated from the scene of violence and excitement, to find peace and repose in a foreign land."

I nodded an assent.

"Ay, sir, and thousands will follow, withdrawing from the country its resources, circulating millions which enrich other nations, and avoiding their own share of the national burdens, which fall still heavier upon those who remain. But is that all, sir? *Oh, no!*"

This second "oh, no!" was pronounced in a more lugubrious note: he shook his head, and after a pause, he recommenced. "England is no longer priest-ridden, sir; but she is worse, she is *law-ridden*. Litigation and law expenses have, like locusts, devoured up the produce of industry. No man is safe without a lawyer at his elbow, making over to him a part of his annual income to secure the remainder. And then there's Brougham. But, sir, is that all? *Oh, no!*"

Another pause, and he continued. "I never grumble—I hate grumblers; I never talk of politics—I hate politics; but, sir, is it not the case, that madmen and fools have united to ruin the country? Is it not true, sir, that unable to rise by their talents, and urged by a wicked ambition, they have summoned main force, and the power of numbers to their assistance, and have raised a spirit which they cannot put down again? Is it not true, sir, that treason walks barefaced through the land, pointing to general destruction—to a violation of all rights, to anarchy, confusion, and the shedding of blood? is not reason borne down by faction, sir? but, sir, is that all? *Oh, no!*"

This last "oh, no!" was more melancholy than the preceding, but I considered that my companion must have nearly exhausted his budget of miseries, and was curious to ascertain what would come next.

"What, is there more, sir?" inquired I, innocently.

"More, sir. Yes, sir, plenty more. I ask you whether even the seasons have not changed in our unhappy country; have we not summer with unusual, unexampled heat, and winters without cold; when shall we ever see the mercury down below sixty degrees again? never, sir. What is summer but a season of alarm and dread? Does not the cholera come in as regularly as green peas—terrifying us to death, whether we die of it or not? Of what advantage are the fruits of the earth so bountifully bestowed— have they not all been converted into poisons? Who dares to drink a light summer wine now? Are not all vegetables abjured, peaches thrown to the pigs, and strawberries ventured upon only by little boys who sweep the streets, with the broom in one hand and the pottle in the other? Are not melons rank poison, and cucumbers sudden death? And in the winter, sir, are we better off? Instead of the wholesome frosts of olden days, purifying the air and the soil, and bracing up our nerves, what have we but the influenza, which lasts us for four months, and the spasmodic cough which fills up the remainder of the year? I am no grumbler, sir, I hate and abhor anything like complaining, but this I will say, that the world has been turned upside down—that everything has gone wrong—that peace has come to us unattended by plenty—that every body is miserable; and that vaccination and steam, which have been lauded as blessings, have proved the greatest of all possible curses, and that there is no chance of a return to our former prosperity, unless we can set fire to our coal mines, and re-introduce the small-pox. But, sir, the will of Heaven be done, I shall say no more; I don't wish to make other people unhappy; but pray don't think, sir, I've told you all. *Oh, no!*"

At this last "oh, no!" my companion laid his face down upon his knuckles, and was silent. I once more sought the deck, and preferred to encounter the east wind. "Blow, blow, thou wintry wind, thou art not so unkind," soliloquised I, as I looked over the bows, and perceived that we were close to the pile entrance of the harbour of Ostend. Ten minutes afterwards there was a cessation of paddle, paddle, thump, thump, the stern-fast was thrown on the quay, there was a rush on board of commissionnaires, with their reiterated cries accompanied with cards thrust into your hands, "Hôtel des Bains, Monsieur." "Hôtel Waterloo, Monsieur." "Hôtel Bellevue." "Hôtel Bedford, Monsieur." "Hôtel d'Angleterre," *ad infinitum*—and then there was the pouring out of the Noah's Ark, with their countenances wearing a most paradoxical appearance, for they evidently showed that they had had, quite enough of water, and, at the same time, that they required a great deal more. I looked at my children, as they were hoisted up from the ladies' cabin, one after another; and upon examination I decided that, with their smudged faces, the Hôtel des *Bains* would be the most appropriate to their condition; so there we went.

Chapter Four

Ostend, April 18, 1835.

I was confoundedly taken in by a rascal of a commissionnaire, and aware how the feelings of travellers are affected by the weather or the treatment they receive at any place they may pass through, I shall display the heroism of saying nothing about the place, except that I believe Ostend to be the most rascally hole in the world, and the sooner the traveller is out of it so much the better will it be for his purse and for his temper.

April 19.

It has been assumed as an axiom that every one in this world is fond of power. During our passage in the track-schuyt I had an evidence to the contrary, for as we glided noiselessly and almost imperceptibly along, a lady told me that she infinitely preferred the three-horse power of the schuyt to the hundred-horse power of the steam-packet. We arrived at Bruges, escaping all the horrors and difficulties of steam navigation.

House rent at Bruges is cheap, because one half of the houses are empty—at least that was the cause assigned to me, although I will not vouch for its being the true one. The reader may remember that this was the site of cheap peaches, but none met our sight, the trees not being yet in blossom. I ought to observe, for the satisfaction of the Foreign Bible Society, that at the hotel at Bruges I saw a book of their exportation lying on the chimney-piece in excellent preservation.

April 21.

As to what passed on our canal voyage to Ghent, I can only say that every thing passed us—for the roads were very heavy, the horses very lazy, and the boys still lazier—they rode their horses listlessly, sitting on them sideways, as I have seen lads in the country swinging on a gate—whereby the *gait* of the track-schuyt could not be styled a swinging pace. We did arrive at last, and thus ended our water carriage. At Ghent we went to the Hôtel Royal, from out of the windows of which I had a fine view of the belfry, surmounted by the Brazen Dragon brought from Constantinople; and as I conjured up times past, and I thought how the belfry was built and how the dragon got there, I found myself at last wandering in the Apocrypha of "Bel and the Dragon."

We went to see the picture by Van Eck, in the cathedral of Saint Bovin. The reader will probably wish to know who was Saint Bovin—so did I—and I asked the question of the sacristan: the reader shall have the benefit of the answer, "Saint Bovin, monsieur, il était un *saint*."

That picture of Van Eck's is worth a van full of most of the pictures we see: it was Van Eck who invented, and was indeed the father of painting in oil. It is a wonderful production.

Mrs Trollope says that people run through Belgium as if it were a mere railroad to other countries. That is very true—we did the same—for who would stop at Ostend to be swindled, or at Bruges to look at empty houses, or at Ghent, which is nothing but a Flanders Birmingham, when Brussels and King Leopold, and the anticipation of something more agreeable, were only thirty miles off. Not one day was our departure postponed; with post-horses and postilions we posted post haste to Brussels.

Chapter Five

April 22.

The Queen of Belgium "a fait un enfant." On the Continent it is always the wife who is considered as the faiseuse; the husband is supposed, and very often with justice to have had nothing to do in the matter—it certainly does appear to be optional on the part of the ladies, for they limit their family to their exact wishes or means of support. How different is it in England, where children will be born whether it is convenient or not! O Miss Martineau! you may talk about the "preventive check," but where is it? In England it would be as valuable as the philosopher's stone.

I think that the good people of Paris would do well, as they appear just now to have left religion in abeyance, to take up the manners and customs of the empire of the Nahirs, a Mahratta nation, which I once read about. In that country, as in heaven, there is no marrying, nor giving in marriage. All are free, and all inheritance is through the children of the sister; for although it is impossible to know who may be the father of any of the children, they are very certain that the sister's children must have the blood on the maternal side. What a good arrangement this would be for the Parisians—how many *pêchés à mortels* would they get rid of—such as adultery, fornication, etcetera,—by passing one simple law of the land. By-the-by, what an admirable idea for reforming a nation—they say that laws, now-a-days, are made to prevent crime: but if laws were enacted by which crime should no longer be considered as crime, what a deal of trouble might be saved.

The theatre is closed owing to the want of funds; the want of funds is owing to the want of honesty on the part of the manager having run away with the strong box, which was decidedly the very best box in the theatre.

April 26.

I went to see a species of Franconi, or Astley's: there is little variety in these performances, as there are only a certain quantity of feats, which can be performed either by the horses or the riders, nevertheless we had some novelty. We had the very best feminine rider I ever saw; she was a perfect female Centaur, looking part and parcel of the animal upon which she stood; and then we had a regularly Dutch-built lady, who amused us with a tumble off her horse, coming down on the loose saw-dust, in a sitting posture, and making a hole in it as large as if a covey of partridges had been husking in it for the whole day. An American black (there always is a black fellow in these companies, for, as Cooper says, they learn to ride well in America by stealing their masters' horses) rode furiously well and sprained his ankle—the attempt of a man in extreme pain to smile is very horrible—yet he did grin as he bowed and limped away. After that we had a performer, who had little chance of spraining her ankle: it was a Miss Betsey, a female of good proportions, who was, however, not a little sulky that evening, and very often refused to perform her task, and as for forcing the combined will of a female and an elephant to boot, there was no man rash enough to attempt it, so she did as little as she pleased, and it pleased her to do very little; one feat, however, was novel, she took a musket in her mouth, and fired it off with her trunk.

When I was in India I was very partial to these animals; there was a most splendid elephant, which had been captured by the expedition sent to Martaban; he stood four or five feet higher than elephants usually do, and was a great favourite of his master, the rajah. When this animal was captured there was great difficulty in getting him on board of the transport. A raft was made, and he was very unwillingly persuaded to trust his huge carcass upon it; he was then towed off with about thirty of the natives on the raft, attending him; the largest purchases and blocks were procured to hoist him in, the mainyards doubly secured, and the fall brought to the capstern. The elephant had been properly slung, the capstern was manned, and his huge bulk was lifted in the air, but he had not risen a foot before the ropes gave way, and down he came again on the raft with a heavy surge, a novelty which he did not appear to approve of. A new fall was rove, and they again manned the capstern; this time the tackle held, and up went the gentleman in the air; but he had not forgotten the previous accident, and upon what ground it is impossible to say, he ascribed his treatment to the natives, who were assisting him on the raft. As he slowly mounted in the air, he looked about him very wroth, his eyes and his trunk being the only portions of his frame at liberty. These he turned about in every direction as he ascended—at last, as he passed by the main channels, he perceived the half of a maintop-sail yard, which had been carried away in the slings, lying on the goose-necks; it was a weapon that suited him admirably; he seized hold of it, and whirling it once round with his trunk, directed the piece of wood with such good aim, that he swept about twenty of the natives off the raft, to take their chance with a strong tide and plenty of alligators. It was the self-possession of the animal which I admired so much, swinging in the air in so unusual a position for an elephant, he was as collected as if he had been roaming in his own wild forests. He arrived and was disembarked at Rangoon, and it was an amusement to me, whenever I could find time to watch this animal, and two others much smaller in size who were with him; but he was my particular pet. Perhaps the reader will like to have the diary of an elephant when not on active service. At what time animals get up who never lie down without being ordered, it is not very easy to say. The elephants are stalled at the foot of some large tree, which shelters them during the day from the extreme heat of the sun; they stand under this tree, to which they are chained by their hind legs. Early in the morning the keeper makes his appearance from his hovel, and throws the respective keys down to the elephants, who immediately unlock the padlocks of the chains, cast themselves loose, and in the politest manner return the keys to the keeper; they then march off with him to the nearest forest, and on their arrival commence breaking down the branches of the trees, selecting those which are most agreeable to their palates, and arranging them in two enormous faggots. When they have collected as much as they think they require, they make withies and bind up their two faggots, and then twist another to connect the two, so as to hang them over their backs down on each side, and having thus made their provision, they return home; the keeper may or may not be present during this performance. All depends upon whether the elephants are well trained, and have been long in servitude. Upon their return, the elephants pass the chains again round their legs, lock the padlock, and present the key as before; they then amuse themselves with their repast, eating all the leaves and tender shoots, and rejecting the others. Now when an elephant has had enough to eat, he generally selects a long bough, and pulling off all the lateral branches, leaves a bush at the end forming a sort of whisk to keep off the flies and mosquitoes; for although the hide of the elephant is very thick, still it is broken into crannies and cracks, into which the vermin insert themselves. Sometimes they have the following ingenious method of defending themselves against these tormentors—they put the end of their trunk down in the dust, draw up as large a quantity as they can, and turning their trunks over their heads, pour it out over their skin, powdering and filling up the interstices, after which they take the long branch I have before mentioned, and amuse themselves by flapping it right and left, and in all directions about their bodies, wherever the insects may settle.

And now for an instance of self-denial, which I have often witnessed on the part of my friend the large elephant. I have observed him very busy, flapping right and flapping left, evidently much annoyed by the persecution of the mosquitoes; by-the-by, no one can have an idea how hard the tiger-mosquito can bite. I will, however, give an instance of it, for the truth of which I cannot positively vouch; but I remember that once, when it rained torrents, and we were on a boating expedition, a marine who, to keep his charge dry, had his fore-finger inserted in the barrel of his musket, pulled it out in a great hurry, exclaiming to his comrade, "May I be shot, Bill, if one of them beggars ha'n't bit me right through the barrel of my musket." This *par parenthèse*, and now to proceed. As I said before, the elephant showed, by constant flagellation of his person, that he was much annoyed by his persecutors, and just at that time, the keeper brought a little naked black thing, as round as a ball, which in India I believe they call a child, laid it down before the animal with two words in Hindostanee—"*Watch it!*" and then walked away into the town. The elephant immediately broke off the larger part of the bough, so as to make a smaller and more convenient whisk, and directed his whole attention to the child, gently fanning the little lump of Indian ink, and driving away every mosquito which came near it; this he continued for upwards of two hours regardless of himself, until the keeper returned. It was really a beautiful sight, and causing much reflection. Here was a monster, whose bulk exceeded that of the infant by at least two thousand times, acknowledging that the image of his Maker, even in its lowest degree of perfection, was divine; silently proving the truth of the sacred announcement, that God had "given to man dominion over the beasts of the field." And here, too, was a brute animal setting an example of devotion and self-denial, which but few Christians, none indeed but a mother, could have practised. Would Fowell Buxton, surrounded by a host of mosquitoes, have done as much for a fellow-creature, white or black? not he; he would have flapped his own thighs, his own ears, his own face, and his own every thing, and have left his neighbours to take care of themselves; nor would I blame him.

As I am on the subject, I may as well inform my readers how and in which way this elephant and I parted company, for it was equally characteristic of the animal. The army was ordered to march, and the elephants were called into requisition to carry the tents. The quarter-master general, the man with four eyes, as the natives called him, because he wore spectacles, superintended the loading of the animals—tent upon tent was heaped upon my friend, who said nothing, till at last he found that they were overdoing the thing, and then he roared out his complaints, which the keeper explained; but there was still one more tent to be carried, and, therefore, as one more or less could make no difference, it was ordered to be put upon his back. The elephant said no more, but he turned sulky. Enough was as good as a feast with him, and he considered this treatment as no joke. Now it so happened that at the time the main street, and the only street of the town, which was at least half a mile long, was crowded to suffocation with tattoos, or little ponies, and small oxen, every one of them loaded with a couple of cases of claret, or brandy, or something else, slung on each side of them, attended by coolies, who, with their hooting, and pushing, and beating, and screaming, created a very bustling and lively scene. When the last tent was put on the elephant he was like a mountain with canvass on each side of him, bulging out to a width equal to his own; there was just room for him to pass through the two rows of houses on each side of the street, and not ten inches to spare; he was ordered by the keeper to go on— he obeyed the order certainly, but in what way—he threw his trunk up in the air, screamed a loud shriek of indignation, and set off at a trot, which was about equal in speed to a horse's gallop, right down the street, mowing down before him every pony, bullock, and coolie that barred his passage; the confusion was indescribable, all the little animals were with their legs in the air, claret and brandy poured in rivulets down the streets, coolies screamed as they threw themselves into the doors and windows; and at one fell swoop the angry gentle man demolished the major part of the comforts of the officers, who were little aware how much they were to sacrifice for the sake of an extra tent. With my eyes I followed my friend in his reckless career, until he was enveloped and hid from my view in a cloud of dust, and that was my farewell of him. I turned round, and observed close to me the quarter-master general, looking with all his *four eyes* at the effects of his inhumanity. But I have wandered some twenty thousand miles from Brussels, and must return.

Chapter Six

Brussels, May 5.

His Belgian Majesty, the Belgian ministers, Belgian ambassadors, Belgian authorities, and all the Belgian nobility and gentry, all the English who reside in Brussels for economy and quiet, and all the exiles and propaganda who reside here to kick up a row, have all left Brussels by the Porte d'Anvers. And all the Belgians who live at Brussels have shut up their shops, and gone out by the Porte d'Anvers. And the whole populace, men, women, and children, have gone out of the Porte d'Anvers. And all the infants have also gone, because the mothers could not leave them at home. And the generals, and their staffs, and the officers, and all the troops, and all the artillery, have also left Brussels, and gone out at the Porte d'Anvers, to keep the said populace quiet and in good order. So that there is no one left at Brussels, and Brussels must for one day take care of itself.

And now you of course wish to know why they have all left Brussels, and further, why they have gone through the Porte d'Anvers.

Because there is this day the commemoration of the inauguration of the *Chemin de Fer*, which has just been completed from Brussels to Malines, and which is on this day to be opened, that is to say, that three steam tugs, whose names are the Stephenson, the Arrow, and the Elephant, are to drag to Malines and back again in the presence of his majesty, all his majesty's ministers, all the ambassadors who choose to go, all the heads of the departments, and every body else who can produce a satisfactory yellow ticket, which will warrant their getting into one of the thirty-three omnibuses, diligences, or cars, which are attached to the said three steam-tugs, the Arrow, the Stephenson, and the Elephant. I shall go and see it—I will not remain at Brussels by myself, the "last man."

May 6.

It was a brilliant affair, and went off well, because the trains went on well. We were tugged through twelve miles of the most fertile pasture in the universe, the whole line of road so crowded with spectators, as to make evident the extreme populousness of the country. For the first mile it was one mass of people—and a Belgian crowd has a very agreeable effect, from the prevailing colours being blue and white, which are very refreshing, and contrast pleasantly with the green background. Every man had his blouse, and every woman her cap and straw bonnet; but if the Belgians look well *en masse*, I cannot say that they do so in detail: the men we do not expect much from, but the women are certainly the plainest race in the whole world—I will not except the Africans. In some of our men-of-war it was formerly the custom to have an old knife, which was passed from one to the other, as the men joined the ship, being handed to the ugliest man they could find; he held the knife until another came, more unfortunate in physiognomy than himself, when it was immediately made over to the last, who was obliged in his turn to retain it until he could discover some one even more unprepossessing. Following up this principle with the women of Belgium, and comparing them with other European states, they are most unequivocally entitled to hold the knife, and unless they improve by crossing the breed, I am afraid they will have it in their possession for centuries.

We arrived safe at Malines, and I was infinitely amused at the variety of astonishment in the five hundred thousand faces which we passed. In one rich meadow I beheld a crowd of Roman Catholic priests, who looked at the trains in such a manner as if they thought that they were "heretical and damnable," and that the Chemin de Fer was nothing but the Chemin d'Enfer. At Malines we all got out, walked to a stone pillar, where a speech was made to the sound of martial music, and we all got in again. And then to show the power of his engines, Mr Stephenson attached all the cars, omnibuses, and diligences together, and directed the Elephant to take us back without assistance from the other two engines. So the Elephant took us all in tow, and away we went at a very fair pace. It must have been a very beautiful sight to those who were looking on the whole train in one line, covered with red cloth and garlands of roses with white canopies over head, and decorated with about three hundred Belgian flags, of yellow, red, and black. However, the huge animal who dragged this weight of eighty tons became thirsty at Ville Vorde, and cast us off—it took him half an hour to drink—that is to say, to take in water, and then he set off again, and we arrived safely at Brussels, much to the delight of those who were in the cars and also of his majesty, and all his ministers, and all his authorities, and all the mercantile classes, who consider that the millennium is come, but very much to the disappointment of the lower classes, who have formed the idea that the *Chemin de Fer* will take away their bread, and who therefore longed for a blow-up. And Mr Stephenson having succeeded in bringing back in safety his decorated cars, has been *décoré* himself, and is now a Chevalier de l'Ordre Leopold. Would not the *Iron* order of the Belgian patriots have been more appropriate as a *Chemin de Fer* decoration?

It is impossible to contemplate any steam-engine, without feeling wonder and admiration at the ingenuity of man; but this feeling is raised to a degree of awe when you look at a locomotive engine—there is such enormous power compressed into so small a space—I never can divest myself of the idea that it is possessed of *vitality*—that it is a living as well as a moving being—and that idea, joined with its immense power, conjures up in my mind that it is some spitting, fizzing, terrific demon, who, if he could escape control, would be ready and happy to drag us by thousands to destruction.

And will this powerful invention prove to mankind a *blessing* or a *curse?*—like the fire which Prometheus stole from heaven to vivify his statue, may it not be followed by the evils of Pandora's fatal casket?

The lower classes of Belgium have formed an idea that the introduction of steam is to take away their bread. Let us examine whether there is not in this idea a degree of instinctive and prophetic truth.

The axiom of our political economists is, that the grand object to be sought and obtained is to produce the greatest possible results by the smallest possible means. The axiom, as an axiom by itself, is good; but the axiom to be opposed to it is, that the well-being and happiness of any state depends upon obtaining full employment for the whole industry of the people.

The population of Belgium is enormous. In England we calculate about eighteen hundred souls to the square league. In Belgium it amounts to three thousand eight hundred souls to the square league. Now it would be impossible for Belgium to support this population, were it not, in the first place, for her extensive manufactories, (for upon the cotton manufactories alone, in which steam is as yet but partially introduced, two hundred and fifty thousand souls depend for their existence,) and in the second place, from the subdivision of the land in small portions, arising from the laws of inheritance, which bar the right of primogeniture; the consequence of which is, that the major part of Belgium is cultivated by spade husbandry, and is in the very highest state of fertility. Nevertheless, the proportion of those who receive relief in Belgium from public institutions and private charities of all descriptions amounts even at present to *one in eight persons*. Now, allowing that the steam-engine should be generally introduced into this country, the consequence must be, that machinery will supply the place, and do the work of man. And what may be the result? that thousands will be thrown out of employment, and must be supported by the nation. When the population is so dense that there is not room for the labour of its present inhabitants, it is clear that the introduction of machinery can have but one effect—that of increasing pauperism. Are not, then, the Belgians right in thinking that it will deprive them of their bread?

That machinery has already had that effect to a certain degree in England cannot be denied; and not only our manufacturing, but our agricultural population, have been distressed from an adherence to the same principle, of obtaining the greatest possible results from the smallest possible means. The subdivision of land will do more to relieve the agricultural distress than anything else. At present large farms are preferred both by landlord and tenant, because a large farm can be cultivated with a fewer number of men and horses; but how does this act? It throws a certain quantity of labourers out of employ, who are supported in idleness. Is the sum gained by farmers by employing fewer men on large farms more than their proportion of the poor's rates paid for unproductive industry? That it may be more to the farmers is possible, as they shift a great part of the onus upon others; but to the nation it certainly is not—for the man who does not work must still be fed. May we not then consider the following propositions as correct?

That, producing the greatest possible results from the least possible means, is an axiom which can only hold good when it does not interfere with the industry of the people. That, as long as the whole population are employed, such powers become a benefit, and a source of extra wealth. But that, in proportion as it throws the population out of employment, so much the more does it prove an injury, and must finally lead to a state of things which must end in riot, anarchy, and confusion. *Quod est demonstrandum*—I hope it will not be in our time.

Chapter Seven

Antwerp.

Every one has heard of the cathedral at Antwerp and the fine pictures by Rubens—every one has heard of the siege of Antwerp and General Chassé, and how the French marched an army of non-intervention down to the citadel, and took it from the Dutch—and every one has heard how Lord Palmerston protocol-ed while Marshal Gerard bombard-ed—and how it was all bombard and bombast. The name of Lord Palmerston reminds me that conversing after dinner with some Belgians, the topic introduced was the great dearth of diplomatic talent in a country like England, where talent was in every other department so extremely prominent. It was not the first time that this subject had been canvassed in my presence by foreigners. Naturally envious of our general superiority, it is with them a favourite point of attack; and they are right, as it certainly is our weakest point. They cannot disparage our army, or our navy, or our constitution; but they can our climate, which is not our fault, but our misfortune; and our diplomacy, which is our fault, and has too often proved our misfortune also.

It certainly is the fact, that our diplomatic corps are very inferior, and this can arise but from one cause; the emoluments which have been attached to it having rendered admission into it an advantage eagerly sought by the higher classes as a provision for the junior branches of their families. Of course, this provision has been granted to those to whom government have felt most indebted for support, without the least regard to the important point as to whether those who were admitted were qualified or not; so that the mere providing for a younger son of an adherent to the government may have proved in the end to have cost the country millions from the incompetence of the party when placed in a situation requiring tact and discrimination. This evil is increased by the system of filling up the vacant appointments according to seniority—the exploded and absurd custom of "each second being heir unto the first." Should any man have proved, upon an emergency, that he was possessed of the highest talent for diplomacy, it will avail him nothing—he never, under the present system, will be employed—he cannot be admitted into the corps without having entered as a private secretary or attaché. It would be monstrous, unheard of; and the very idea would throw Lord Aberdeen on the one side, or Lord Palmerston on the other, into convulsions. Is it therefore to be wondered at our being so deficient in our diplomatic corps? Surely if any point more than another requires revision and reform, it is this; and the nation has a right to insist upon it.

It may be asked, what are the most peculiar qualities necessary in a diplomatist, taking it for granted that he has talents, education, and a thorough knowledge of the routine of business? The only term which we can give to this 'desideratum is' presence of mind—not the presence of mind required in danger, but that presence of *mind* which enables him, when a proposition is made, at once to seize all its bearings, the direction to which it tends, and the ultimate object (for that will always be concealed at first) which the proposer may have in view. Diplomatists, when they enter the field, are much in the situation of two parties, one defending and the other attacking a stronghold. Admissions are highly dangerous, as they enable the adversary to throw up his first parallels; and too often, when you imagine that the enemy is not one jot advanced, you find that he has worked through a covered way, and, you are summoned to surrender. It is strange that, at the very time that they assert that it would be impossible to employ those as diplomatists who have not been regularly trained to the service, officers in the army, and captains in the navy are continually so employed, and often under circumstances of vital importance. Now it would be supposed that the latter of all people they must be the most unfit; as, generally speaking, they are sent to sea, *as unfit for anything else.* But it appears that once commanding a frigate, they are supposed to be fit for everything. A vessel is ordered for "particular service," why so called I know not, except that there may be an elision, and it means "particularly *disagreeable* service." The captain is directed by the Admiralty to consider himself under the orders of the Foreign Office, and he receives a huge pile of documents, numbered, scheduled, and red-taped (as Bulwer says in his pamphlet), the contents of which he is informed are to serve as a guide for his proceedings. He reads them over with all their verbiage and technicalities, sighs for Cobbett's pure Saxon, and when he has finished, feels not a little puzzled. Document Number 4 contradicting document Number 12, and document Number 1 opposed to Number 66; that is, as *he* reads and understands English. Determined to understand them if possible, he takes a dose of protocol every morning, until he has nearly learnt them by heart, and then acts to the best of his knowledge and belief. And it is undeniable that, with very few exceptions, the navy have invariably given satisfaction to the Foreign Office when they have been so employed, and often under circumstances of peculiar difficulty. I have heard, from the best authority, that military men have also been equally successful, although they have not so often been called into "particular service." By the bye, particular service is all done at the same price as general service in his Majesty's navy, which is rather unfair, as we are obliged to find our own red tape, pens, ink, and stationery.

As I was walking on the glacis with a friend, he pointed out to me at a window an enormous fat man smoking his pipe, and told me that he had been in the Dutch service under William of Orange; but not being a very good hand at a forced march, he had been reduced with others to half-pay. He had not been many months in retirement when he went to the palace, and requested an audience of his Majesty, and, when admitted, stated that he had come to request that his Majesty would be pleased to put him again upon full pay. His Majesty raised many objections, and stated his inability to comply with his request; upon which the corpulent officer exclaimed, embracing with his arms as far as he could, his enormous paunch, "My God! your Majesty, how can you imagine that I can fill this big belly of mine with only my half-pay?" This *argumentum ad ventrem* so tickled King William, that he was put on *full pay unattached*, and has continued so ever since. The first instance I ever heard of a *man* successfully pleading as ladies do at the Old Bailey.

It is hard for a wanderer from childhood like me, to find out anything new or interesting. I have travelled too much and have seen too much — I seldom now admire. I draw comparisons, and the comparison drawn between the object before my eyes, and that in my mind's eye, is unfortunately usually in favour of the latter. He who hath visited so many climes, mingled with so many nations, attempted so many languages, and who has hardly anything left but the North Pole or the crater of Vesuvius to choose between; if he still longs for something new, may well cavil at the pleasures of memory as a mere song. In proportion as the memory is retentive, so is decreased one of the greatest charms of existence — novelty. To him who hath seen much, there is little left but comparison, and are not comparisons universally odious? Not that I complain, for I have a resource — I can fly to imagination — quit this every-day world, and in the region of fiction create new scenes and changes, and people these with new beings.

Moreover, there is still endless variety, endless amusement, and food for study and contemplation, in our own species. In all countries still the same, yet ever varying: —

"The proper study of mankind is man."

From which, I presume, we are to infer that it is time thrown away to study woman.

At the same party in which the conversation was raised relative to diplomacy, a person with whom I was, until that day, wholly unacquainted, was sitting by me, and as it happened, the name of one with whom I had long been on terms of intimacy was mentioned. "Do you know him?" said my neighbour, with a very peculiar expression. I replied that I had occasionally met him, for I thought there was something coming forward.

"Well, all I can say is, that he is rather a strange person."

"Indeed!" replied I; "how do you mean?"

"Why, they say, that he is of a very uncertain temper."

"Indeed!" continued I, with the same look of inquiry, as if demanding more information.

"Yes, yes, rather a dangerous man."

"Do you know him?" inquired I, in return.

"Yes; that is to say—not very intimately—the fact is, that I have avoided it. I grant that he is a very clever man—but I hear that he quarrels with everybody."

"Who told you so?" replied I.

Oh! he was not authorised to give the name of the person.

"Then," replied I, "allow me to say that you have been misinformed. I have been on intimate terms with that person for nearly twenty years, during which he never quarrelled with me or any one that I know of; although, I grant, he is not over civil to those whom he may despise. The only part of your communication which is correct is, that he is a very clever man, and our government are of the same opinion."

My neighbour was discomfited, and said no more, and I joined the general conversation. What may have been his cause of dislike I know not— but I have frequently remarked, that if a man has made himself enemies either from neglect of that sophistry and humbug, so necessary to enable him to roll down the stream of time with his fellows without attrition, if they can find no point in his character to assail, their last resort is, to assert that he is an uncertain tempered man, and not to be trusted.

This is the last, and although not the most empoisoned, still the surest shaft in the whole quiver of calumny. It does not exactly injure the character, but it induces others to avoid the acquaintance of the party so misrepresented.

It is rather singular, and perhaps I may have been fortunate, but in more than half-a-dozen instances I have found the very parties to whom this character has been given, although high-minded and high-spirited, the very antithesis to the character which has been assigned them. That some do deserve the character is undoubted—but there is no species of calumny to be received with such peculiar caution. It may be right to be on your guard, but it never should be the ground for a positive avoidance of the party accused. Indeed, in some degree, it argues in his favour, for it is clear that the whole charge they can bring against his character is an infirmity to which we are all more or less subjected; and he who looks for perfection in his acquaintance or his friends, will inevitably meet with disappointment.

Chapter Eight

Brussels.

I have lost all my memoranda! I cannot find them any where. Well—children are a great blessing when they are kept in the nursery—but they certainly do interfere a little with a papa who has the misfortune to be an author. I little thought, when my youngest girl brought me up a whole string of paper dolls, hanging together by the arms, that they had been cut off my memoranda. But so it was; and when I had satisfactorily established the fact, and insisted upon an inquisition to recover my invaluables, I found that they had had an auto-da-fé, and that the whole string of dolls, which contained on their petticoats my whole string of bewitching ideas, had been burnt like so many witches. But as the man said in the packet—"Is that all?" Oh, no!—they come rushing in like a torrent, bounding, skipping, laughing, and screaming, till I fancied myself like another Orpheus, about to be torn to pieces by Bacchanals (they are all girls), and I laid down my pen, for they drive all my ideas out of my head. May your shadows never grow less, mes enfans, but I wish you would not make such a cursed row.

The author and the author of existence do not amalgamate. That's a fact.

Their joyous countenances are answered by a look of despair—their boiling-water heat drives my thermometer down to zero—their confounded merriment gives me a confounded headache—their animal spirits drive me to vegetable spirits—their cup of bliss running over makes me also require a bumper—brandy restores the equilibrium, and I contrive to get rid of them and my headache about one and the same time.

Talking about brandy—one morning at two o'clock, about the witching time that ghosts do glide about in churchyards, as I was thinking whether it would not be better to go to bed instead of writing nonsense, in which opinion most of my readers may coincide with me, in stalked three young men who were considerably the worse for potation. There is a great deal of character in inebriety—at the same time that no estimate of character can be made from its effects; for we often find the most quiet men when sober to be the most choleric in their cups—but still is character, and much that is curious in witnessing its variety of effects. Now these young men were each drunk in a very different war—the first, in a way quite novel; for although he could preserve his equilibrium, and stare immensely, he had lost the power of speech; you saw his lips move, but no articulation or sound succeeded—the second was laughing drunk; everything that was said, either by himself or by any one else, was magnified into a pun or a *bon mot*—the third, with whom I had no previous acquaintance, was *politely* drunk. I presume the idea of intruding himself upon a stranger, at such an unseasonable hour, had produced that effect—but let me describe the scene.

"Ha, ha, ha! we come to you—ha, ha! capital. We want some brandy and water; and, ha, ha! we know you always keep a stock," said the second, seating himself in an armchair.

The first also took a chair, moved his lips for a few seconds, and then sat bolt upright, staring at the two candles; how many he counted I cannot pretend to say.

"Really," said Number Three, "we are—I'm afraid—taking a great liberty—a very great liberty; but—an apology is certainly due—if you will allow me to offer an apology for my two friends—will you allow me to introduce them?"

"Many thanks, but I have the pleasure of knowing *them* already."

"I really beg your pardon—it was quite unintentional on my part. I trust you are not offended? Will you allow me to introduce myself? I am Captain C—, of the —. Will you permit me to present my card, and to say how happy I shall be to make your acquaintance?" So saying, the third gentleman presented me with his card, and returned the card-case into his pocket.

"Capital!" cried Number Two. "Ha, ha, ha! what an excellent joke, ha, ha, ha! Now for the brandy-and-water."

This was soon produced, and although Number One had lost all articulation, he had still the power of deglutition; he filled his glass, sat up more erect, stared at the candles, and drank his grog; the other did the same, when Number Three again spoke.

"My dear Sir, I hope you will excuse the liberty, but my name is Captain C—, of the —. Will you allow me the honour of presenting my card, and of saying how proud I shall be to make your acquaintance?" So saying, he presented me another card, which I put aside with the first.

"Ha, ha, ha! what a good joke, to find you up. I said we should get brandy-and-water here; wasn't that capital?—ha, ha, ha, ha!"

I could not exactly see the joke of being kept up for perhaps two more hours, but I begged they would refill their glasses, as the sitting would be sooner ended one way or the other—either by the bottle being empty, or their falling under the table—I did not care which—when I was again addressed by Number Three.

"I really beg your pardon, but—I'm afraid I have been very remiss—will you allow me to introduce myself? I am Captain C—, of the —. Here is my card, and I cannot say how happy I shall be if I may have the honour of your acquaintance."

I bowed a third time, and received a third card.

"By heavens, I've finished my tumbler! Ain't that capital? Ha, ha, ha! famous fun;—and so has Alfred."

"Famous fun, indeed," thought I, as the contents of the bottle disappeared.

"And Alfred is going to help himself again; well, that is capital, ha, ha, ha!—ha, ha, ha!—ha, ha, ha, ha!"

Alfred, who was Number One, moved his lips, but like the frozen horn of Munchausen, sounds would not come out; he did, however, follow up the joke, by refilling his tumbler for the third time.

"Upon my honour, I've been very rude, I ought to apologise," said Number Three, again drawing out his card-case; "but will you allow me to offer my card? I am Captain C—, of the —, and I shall be most happy to make your acquaintance."

I bowed again, and received the fourth card.

Thus were the changes rung by numbers, one, two, and three, until I was tired out, two bottles more drank out, and I had received fifteen cards from my very polite friend, whom I had never seen before.

At four o'clock they all rose to depart.

"Upon my soul, I do believe I'm drunk," said Number Two; "capital joke—ha, ha, ha!"

Number One continued dumb, brandy had not thawed him; but he stared very hard at me, as much as to say, I would speak if I could.

Number Three put into my hand the sixteenth card, and made a rash attempt at a bow.

Having seen them fairly outside my door, I bolted it, saying with Shakespeare—

> "O! that a man
> Should put an enemy in his mouth
> To steal away his brains!"

I have been this morning to visit an establishment founded by two brothers, of the name of Van der Maelen. It comprehends natural history, botany, geography, and statistics, and they have, moreover, a lithographic press for maps and plates. It is a very curious, and very spirited undertaking. As yet, the whole has been effected by their own means, which are extensive, and without any assistance from government. How few people in this world employ their money so usefully! This establishment is but yet in its infancy, and the collections are not very valuable, although rapidly increasing, from the interest felt by every one in its welfare.

Of all collections of natural history, the fossil department is, to me, the most interesting; there is room for speculation and reflection, till the mind is lost in its own wanderings, which I consider one of the greatest delights of existence. We are indebted to the vast, comprehensive mind, and indefatigable labour of Cuvier, for the gleams of light which have lately burst upon us, and which have rendered what was before mere speculative supposition now a source of interesting and anxious investigation, attended with results that are as satisfactory as they are undeniable.

That there was a period when the surface of the earth was almost entirely covered with water—a state between chaos and order, when man was not yet created (for that then the world had not yet been rendered by the Almighty a fit receptacle for man), appears to be undoubted. Yet the principle of life had been thrown forth by the Almighty hand, and monsters had been endowed with vitality, and with attributes necessary for their existence upon an intermediate world.

These were the many varieties of the Ichthyosauri and the Plesiosauri, of whose remains we have now such abundant specimens—all animals of the lizard species; some supposed to have been supplied with wings, like the flying fish of the present day.

But imagine an animal of the lizard species, one hundred and twenty feet long—imagine such a monster—the existence of which is now proved beyond a cavil, by the remains, deeply imbedded in the hard blue lias rocks, and which remains are now in our possession. What a terrific monster it must have been! We look with horror at an alligator of twenty or thirty feet, but imagine an animal of that species extending his huge bulk to one hundred and twenty feet. Were they all destroyed when the waters were separated from the hand, or did they gradually become extinct when the earth was no longer a suitable habitation for them, and no longer congenial to those properties with which they had been endowed when ordered into existence by the Almighty power? The description of the Behemoth, by Job, has long been a puzzle to the learned; we have no animal of the present time winch will answer to it, but in many points, this description will answer to what may be supposed would be the appearance, the muscular power, and the habits of this huge denizen of a former world.

> "His force is in the navel of his belly.
> He moveth his tail like a cedar.
> His bones are as strong pieces of brass.
> His bones are like bars of iron.
> He lieth under the shady trees in the covert of the reeds
> and fens.
> The shady trees cover him with their shadow.
> The willows of the brook compass him about."

It may be a matter of deep surmise, whether all animals were created as we now find them, that is, whether the first creation was final—or how far the unerring hand has permitted a change to take place in the forms and properties of animals, so as to adapt them to their peculiar situations. I would say, whether the Almighty may not have allowed the principle of vitality and life to assume, at various epochs, the form and attributes most congenial to the situation, either by new formation or by change.

May not the monster of former worlds have dwindled down to the alligator of this—the leviathan to the whale? Let us examine whether we have any proofs in existing creation to support this supposition. We all know that the hair of the goat and sheep in the torrid zones will be changed into wool when they are taken to the colder climes, and that the reverse will also take place—we know that the hare and weazel tribes, whose security is increased from their colour so nearly approaching to that of the earth in temperate latitudes, have the same protection afforded to them when they are found in the regions of snow, by their changing to white— and we know that the *rete mucosum* of the African enables him to bear the exposure to a tropical sun, which would destroy an European. But this is not sufficient, we must examine further. Sir Humphry Davy has given us a very interesting account of a small animal found in the pools of water in the caves in Carniola; this animal is called the *Proteus Anguinus* or Syren: it is a species of eel with two feet—a variety only to be found in these caves—it lives in darkness, and exposure to the light destroys it. Now, here is an animal which we must either suppose to have been created at the universal creation—and that is to suppose that these caves and pools of water have also existed from the time of the creation—or that the principle of vitality has been permitted, at a later date, to take that form and those attributes congenial to its situation: it is a curious problem. Again, it is well known that in the continent of New Holland there are animals who have a property peculiar to that continent alone—that of a pouch or false stomach, to contain their young after their birth; it has been surmised that at one time the major part of that continent was under water, and that this pouch was supplied to them for the safety of their young; nor is this conjecture without strong grounds; if only the kangaroo and opossum tribes, which are animals peculiarly indigenous to that continent, were supplied with this peculiar formation, the conjecture would fall to the ground, as it might fairly be said that this property was only another proof of the endless variety in creation; but the most remarkable fact is, that not only the kangaroo and opossum, animals indigenous and peculiar to that portion of the globe, but that very variety of squirrel, rat, and mouse, which in every other respect are of the same species as those found in the other continents, are all of them provided with this peculiar false pouch to contain their young. Why, therefore, should all these have been supplied with it, if not for a cause? And the question now arises, whether at the first creation they had that pouch, or were permitted so far to change their formation, when the pouch became necessary for the preservation and continuation of these species? That these changes are the changes of centuries, I grant, and therefore are not likely to be observed by man, whose records or whose knowledge are not permitted to be handed down beyond a certain extent. Knowledge is not happiness; and when the accumulation has arrived to that height so as to render it dangerous, it is swept away by the all-wise and benevolent Creator, and we are permitted to begin again *de novo*. After all, what we term posterity is but a drop of water in the ocean of Time.

Chapter Nine

Brussels.

There are few people in Brussels, indeed in Belgium, who do not complain of the revolution; all that goes wrong is at once ascribed to this cause—indeed I was rather staggered by one gentleman, at Ghent, telling me very gravely that they had had no fat oxen since the revolution; but this he explained by stating that the oxen were fattened from the refuse of several manufactories, all of which had been broken up, the proprietors having quitted for Holland. The revolution has certainly been, up to the present time, injurious to both countries, but it is easy to foretell that eventually Belgium will flourish, and Holland, in all probability, be the sufferer. The expenses of the latter even now are greater than her revenue, and when the railroads of Belgium have been completed, as proposed, to Vienna, the revenue of Holland will be proportionably decreased from her loss of the carrying trade. It may be urged that Holland can also have her railroads—but she cannot: so large a proportion of her population find their support at present on the canals, that a railroad would be productive of the most injurious effects. It is true that she can lower her rates of carriage, but the merchant will save ten days of transport by the railroads, and this rapidity of communication will always obtain the preference.

But whatever may be the future prospects of Belgium, it is certain that, from the heavy expenses attending the support of so large an army, the retirement into Holland of most of the influential and wealthy commercial men, and the defection of almost all the nobility, at present she is suffering. Brussels, her capital, has perhaps been most injured, and is no longer the gay and lively town which it was under the dynasty of King William of Nassau. When the two countries were united, it was the custom of the Dutch court to divide the year between Brussels and the Hague; and as there was not only the establishment of the King, but also those of Princes William and Frederick (in fact three courts), as well as all the nobility of Holland and Belgium, there was an overflow of wealth, of company, and of amusement, which rendered Brussels one of the most delightful winter residences on the Continent: but this has now all passed away. The court of Leopold, in consequence of the radical party having the entire sway, is but a shadow, as nearly all the Belgian nobility have retired from it. The few who reside in town will not visit at the palace, and live in seclusion, receiving no company, and spending no money; the majority, however, have either removed from Brussels to their country seats, or have left the kingdom to spend their revenue amongst foreigners.

At present there are but few English here, it being no longer the scene of gaiety, and there are other reasons which gradually decrease the number. The fact is, that Brussels is not a very cheap residence. The duties on every thing are now enormous, and the shop-keepers prey upon the English as much as they can, having avowedly two prices, one for them and the other for the Belgians. There are very few amusements, and the people, since the revolution, are rude and bearish, imagining that by incivility they prove their liberty and independence. The other towns of Belgium are very dull and very cheap—Brussels is very dull and very dear. In another point, Brussels presents a contradiction to all the other capitals of Europe, in which you generally find the most polished manners, and the greatest beauty in the female sex, concentrated. At Brussels it is directly the reverse—the men are uncivil and the women plain: whereas in the Belgian provinces you will meet with civility and respect, and at Antwerp, Ostend, and most other provincial towns, fall in with many fine countenances, reminding you of the Spanish blood which has been for centuries mingled with that of the Low Provinces.

Nevertheless there are many advantages in Brussels: the communication with England is so rapid, and its situation so central, that it may be considered as the point from which travellers diverge on their various routes.

About the end of May the arrivals and departures from Brussels are constant; this stream continues to pour through the city for three months, after which, as the Belgians do not mix with the foreign residents, the latter are left entirely to their own resources for amusement. But the greatest objection to Brussels is, that the English have brought with them the *English feeling*. I hardly know how else to term it, but it certainly is a feeling peculiarly English, which has taken deep root within this last half century, and which has already produced much evil, and may eventually be productive of more serious results. I refer to the system of spending more money than you can afford, to enable you to hold a certain position in the scale of society.

For these last forty years, during which immense fortunes have been made in England, there has been a continued struggle of wealth against rank. *Parvenus*, as the aristocracy have been pleased to call them, have started up in every direction, vying with, and even eclipsing the nobility in lavish expenditure—in some instances, driving the aristocracy to spend more money than they could afford, and thereby impoverishing them; in others, forcing admittance into their circles. Wealth and public opinion have latterly gained the ascendency, and the aristocracy are now more looked up to on account of their large possessions than of their high birth. Now this has been nothing more than a demand for greater liberty and more extended rights on the part of the commoners of England, in proportion as they found themselves a more important body in the state. It has not been a case of Magna Charta, but it is still analogous; for they have demanded that the barrier raised between them and the aristocracy should be thrown down, as soon as they possessed all the advantages, with the exception of that nominal rank, the title too often conferred without discrimination on the one hand or claims on the other. As soon as a partial breach had been made in this barrier,—every one rushed for admittance, displaying wealth as their ticket of admission, and the consequence has been, that wealth has now become the passport into society; but another consequence has also ensued, which is, that to obtain entrance, almost everybody has been living and keeping up an appearance which has not been warranted by their means. Many have exceeded their incomes, and then sunk down into poverty; others have, perhaps, only lived up to their incomes; but in so doing, have disappointed those who, induced by the appearance of so much wealth, have married into the family and discovered that they have obtained wives with expensive ideas, and no money. But there have been other reasons which have induced some to live beyond their means—they have done it in the pure spirit of gambling. In England, credit, next to money, is of most value, and according to their supposed wealth, so did the parties obtain credit; an expenditure beyond their means was, therefore, with commercial men, nothing more than a speculation, which very often succeeded, and eventually procured to the parties the means of expenditure. It is well known that the income tax, in many cases, was paid double; commercial men preferring to give in their income at twice its real value, and pay the tax to that amount, that they might be supposed to possess more than they really had; indeed, as it was imagined that a man would evade so heavy an impost as much as possible, he was generally considered to be worth even more than what he himself had stated. It is from these causes that has arisen what I have called the English feeling, for display beyond the means, and which has made our countrymen look down upon those who cannot compete with them in expense. Let a married couple be ever so well connected—let them have talent, and every other advantage, it will avail them nothing, if they have not money, sufficient at least to keep a carriage, and not shock the mistress of a house by the sound of the rattling steps of a hackney-coach at her door; besides which, in our commercial country, the principle of barter, of *quid pro quo*, is extended even to dinner and evening parties—and the reason is obvious—when people live to the full extent, or even beyond their incomes, a little management is required. A dinner-party is so arranged, that the dinners received from others are returned to them, and they cannot afford to ask a couple who cannot give them a dinner in return, as they would fill up the places of others to whom a dinner is due, and who, if not asked then, must be at another time; and an extra dinner is an extra expense to be avoided. The English therefore, who have only moderate incomes, have the choice, either to live beyond their means, and leave their children unprovided for, or of being shut out from that society, to which every other is but the adventitious claim of wealth, they are entitled. The consequence has been that since the peace thousands and thousands have settled on the Continent, that they may make more display with a small income, and thousands more, with a much better feeling, to avoid expense, and lay by a provision for their children. Of course all these remarks are made with reservation, but with reservation, it may be said, that in England we have, or soon shall have, only two classes left, the extreme rich and the extreme poor, for the intermediate classes are gradually retiring to the continent, emigrating to Canada and America, or sinking down into the second class.

This is a most dangerous state of society, and, if carried to the extreme, has always proved ruinous to the state. Although the immense extent of the Roman empire may be asserted as the ultimate cause of its downfall, still that downfall was most certainly accelerated by the rottenness at the core, the system of patrons and clients having thrown all the wealth into the hands of a few. Are we not rapidly advancing to this state in England? The landholders are almost at the mercy of the fundholders, who, in fifty years' time, will probably have possession of the land as well as of the money. And should there be no check put to this disintegration of society, then must come what the radicals are now so anxious to obtain, the equitable adjustment—and in that case it is a problem how far that may not be really *equitable*; for society may, by degrees, arrive to a state so anomalous as to warrant that the few should be sacrificed for the benefit of the community at large.

Chapter Ten

Brussels, May 22.

Among the *lions* of Brussels, a dog was pointed out to me, as he lay on the pavement in front of the House of Assembly. It was a miserable looking cur; but he had a tale extra attached to him, which had magnified him into a lion. It was said that he belonged to a Dutch soldier, who was killed in the revolution, at the spot where the dog then lay, and that ever since (a period of four years) the animal had taken up his quarters there, and invariably lain upon that spot. Whether my informant lied, and the dog did not, I cannot pretend to say; but if the story be true, it was a most remarkable specimen of fidelity and ugliness. And he was a sensible dog, moreover; instead of dying of grief and hunger, as some foolish dogs have done, he has always dedicated an hour every evening to cater for his support, and then returns to pass the night on the spot. I went up to him, and when within two yards he thought proper to show his teeth, and snarl most dog-matically; I may therefore, in addition to his other qualities, state that he is an ill-natured dog. How far the report was correct, I cannot vouch; but I watched him three or four days, and always found him at his post; and after such strict investigation, had I asserted ten years instead of four, I have a prescriptive right, as a traveller, to be believed.

It is singular that it is only in England that you can find dogs, properly so called; abroad they have nothing but curs. I do not know anything more puzzling than the genealogy of the animals you meet with under the denomination of dogs in most of the capitals of Europe. It would appear as if the vice of promiscuous and unrestricted intercourse had been copied from their masters; and I have been almost tempted to take up the opinion, that you may judge of the morality of a capital from the degeneracy of the dogs. I have often, at Paris, attempted to make out a descent; but found it impossible. Even the late Sir G Naylor, with all the herald's office, stimulated by double fees, could not manage to decipher escutcheons obliterated by so many crosses.

I am very partial to dogs; and one of my amusements, when travelling, is to watch their meetings with each other; they appear to me to do everything but speak. Indeed, a constant observer will distinguish in dogs many of the passions, virtues, and rices of men; and it is generally the case, that those of the purest race have the nobler qualifications. You will find in them devotion, courage, generosity, good temper, sagacity, and forbearance; but these virtues, with little alloy, are only to be found in the pure breeds. A cur is quite a lottery: he is a most heterogeneous compound of virtue and vice; and sometimes the amalgamation is truly ludicrous. Notwithstanding which, a little scrutiny of his countenance and his peculiar movements will soon enable you to form a very fair estimate of his general character and disposition.

One of the most remarkable qualities in dogs is the fidelity of their attachments; and the more so, as their attachments are very often without any warrantable cause. For no reason that can be assigned, they will take a partiality to people or animals, which becomes a feeling so dominant, that their existence appears to depend upon its not being interfered with. I had an instance of this kind, and the *parties* are all living. I put up, for an hour or two, at a livery stables in town, a pair of young ponies. On my taking them out again, the phaeton was followed by a large coach-dog, about two years old, a fine grown animal, but not well marked, and in very poor condition. He followed us into the country; but having my establishment of dogs (taxes taken into consideration), I ordered him to be shut out. He would not leave the iron gates; and when they were opened, in he bolted, and hastening to the stables, found out the ponies, and was not to be dislodged from under the manger without a determined resistance. This alternate bolting in and bolting out continued for many days; finding that I could not get rid of him, I sent him away forty miles in the country; but he returned the next day, expressing the most extravagant joy at the sight of the ponies, who, strange to say, were equally pleased, allowing him to put his paws upon them, and bark in their faces. But although the ponies were partial to the dog, I was not; and aware that a voyage is a great specific for curing improper attachments, I sent the dog down the river in a barge, requesting the men to land him where they were bound, on the other side of the Medway; but in three days the dog again made his appearance, the picture of famine and misery. Even the coachman's heart was melted, and the rights and privileges of his favourite snow-white terrier were forgotten. It was therefore agreed, in a cabinet council held in the harness room, that we must make the best of it; and, as the dog would not leave the ponies, the best thing we could do, was to put a little flesh on his bones, and make him look respectable. We therefore victualled him that day, and put him on our books with the purser's name of Pompey. Now this dog proved, that sudden as was his attachment to the ponies, it was of the strongest quality. He never would and never has since left these animals. If turned out in the fields, he remains out with them, night as well as day, taking up his station as near as possible half way between the two, and only coming home to get his dinner. No stranger can enter their stables with impunity; for he is very powerful, and on such occasions very savage. A year or two after his domiciliation, I sold the ponies, and the parties who purchased were equally anxious at first to get rid of the dog; but their attempts, like mine, were unavailing, and, like me, they at last became reconciled to him. On my return from abroad, I re-purchased them, and Pompey of course was included in the purchase.

We are none of us perfect — and Pompey had one vice; but the cause of the vice almost changed it into a virtue. He had not a correct feeling relative to *meum* and *tuum*, but still he did not altogether steal for himself, but for his friends as well. Many have witnessed the fact of the dog stealing a loaf, or part of one, taking it into the stables, and dividing it into three portions, one for each pony, and the other for himself. I recollect his once walking off with a round of beef, weighing seventeen or eighteen pounds, and taking it to the ponies in the field — they smelt at it, but declined joining him in his repast. By-the-bye, to prove that lost things will turn up some day or another, there was a silver skewer in the beef, which was not recovered until two years afterwards, when it was turned up by the second ploughing. One day, as the ponies were in the field where I was watching some men at work, I heard them narrating to a stranger the wonderful feats of this dog, for I have related but a small portion. The dog was lying by the ponies as usual, when the servants' dinner-bell rang, and off went Pompey immediately at a hard gallop to the house to get his food. "Well, dang it, but he is a queer dog," observed the man, "for now he's running as fast as he can, to *answer the bell*."

Chapter Eleven

With all the faults of the Roman church, it certainly appears to me that its professors extend towards those who are in the bosom of their own church a greater share than most other sects, of the true spirit of every religion—charity. The people of the Low Countries are the most bigoted Catholics at present existing, and in no one country is there so much private as well as public charity. It is, however, to private charity that I refer. In England there is certainly much to be offered in extenuation, as charity is extorted by law to the utmost farthing. The baneful effects of the former poor laws have been to break the links which bound together the upper and lower classes, produced by protection and good will in the former, and in the latter, by respect and gratitude. Charity by act of parliament has dissolved the social compact—the rich man grumbles when he pays down the forced contribution—while the poor man walks into the vestry with an insolent demeanour, and claims relief, not as a favour, but as a right. The poor laws have in themselves the essence of revolution, for if you once establish the right of the poor man to any portion of the property of the rich, you admit a precedent so far dangerous, that the poor may eventually decide for themselves what portion it may be that they may be pleased to take; and this becomes the more dangerous, as it must be remembered, that the effect of the poor laws is *repulsion* between the two classes, from the one giving unwillingly, and the other receiving unthankfully. How the new Poor Law Bill will work remains to be proved; but this is certain, that much individual suffering must take place, before it works out the great end which it is intended to obtain.

That the Roman Catholic laity are more charitable is not a matter of surprise, as they are not subjected to forced contributions: but it appears to me that the Catholic clergy are much more careful and kind to their flocks than our own. Now, indeed, can it be otherwise, when even now, although so much reform in the Church has been effected, so many of our clergymen are pluralists and non-residents, expending the major part of the church revenue out of the parish, leaving to the curate, who performs the duty, a stipend which renders it impossible for him to exercise that part of his Christian duty to any extent?—for charity *begins* at home, and his means will not allow him to proceed much farther. That serious evils have arisen from the celibacy of the Roman clergy is true, for priests are but men, and are liable to temptation; but it is equally certain that when a Roman Catholic clergyman is a pure and pious man, he has nothing to distract his attention from the purposes of his high calling; and not only his whole attention is devoted to his flock, but his existence, if necessary, is voluntarily endangered. At the period of the cholera, there were many remarkable instances of this devotion to death on the part of the Roman priesthood, and as many, I am forced to say, of the Protestant clergy flying from the epidemic, and leaving their flocks without a shepherd. And why so? because the Protestant clergymen had wives and families depending upon them for support, and whose means of existence would terminate with their own lives. It was very natural that they should prefer the welfare of their own families to that of their parishioners. But in other cases not so extreme, the encumbrance of a family to a clergyman in England is very often in opposition to his duty. To eke out a scanty remuneration, he sets up a school or takes in pupils. Now if the duties of a clergyman consisted in merely reading the services on a Sunday, and christening, burying, and marrying, he might well do so; but the real duties of a clergyman are much more important. His duty is to watch over the lives and conduct of his parishioners, to exhort, persuade, and threaten, if necessary; to be ever among his flock, watching them as a shepherd does his sheep. And how can he possibly do this, if he takes charge of pupils?—he must either neglect his pupils or neglect his parish. He cannot do justice to both. As Saint Paul says to the bishops, "Although it is better to marry than burn, still it is better to be even as I am," unencumbered with wife and family, and with no ties to distract my attention from my sacred and important calling.

But the *public* charitable institutions abroad are much better conducted than those of England, where almost every thing of the kind is made a job, and a source of patronage for pretending pious people, who work their way into these establishments for their own advantage. It is incredible the number of poor people who are effectually relieved on the Continent in the course of the year, at an expense which would not meet the weekly disbursements of a large parish in England. But then, how much more judicious is the system! I know for a fact, that in the county where I reside, and in which the hard-working labourer, earning his twelve shillings a week, is quite satisfied if he can find sufficient *bread* for his family, (not tasting meat, perhaps, ten times during the whole year,) that those who were idlers, supported by charity, were supplied with meat three or four times a week; nay, even the felons and prisoners in the county gaol were better fed than was the industrious working man. And this is what in England is called charity. It is base injustice to the meritorious. But many of the charitable institutions in England, from mal-administration, and pseudo-philanthropy, have become very little better than establishments holding out premiums for idleness and hypocrisy.

Among the institutions founded by Roman Catholics and particularly deserving of imitation, that of the Soeurs de la Charité appears to be the most valuable. It is an institution which, like mercy, is twice blessed—it blesses those who give, and those who receive. Those who give, because many hundreds of females, who would otherwise be thrown upon the world, thus find an asylum, and become useful and valuable members to society. They take no vows—they only conform to the rules of the sisterhood during the time that they remain in it, and if they have an opportunity, by marriage or otherwise, of establishing themselves, they are at free liberty to depart. How many young women, now forced into a wretched, wicked life, would gladly incorporate themselves into such a society in England; how many, if such a society existed, would be prevented from falling into error!

It is well known, that to support a large community, the expenses are trifling compared to what they are when you have the same number of isolated individuals to provide for. A company of two or three hundred of these sisters living together, performing among themselves the various household duties, washing, etcetera, and merely requiring their food, would not incur the same expense in house rent, firing, and provisions, as thirty or forty isolated individuals. Soldiers in barracks are even well fed, housed, and clothed, at a much less expense than it costs the solitary labourer to eat his *dry bread* in his own cottage; and the expenses of such communities, if once established, would very soon be paid by their receipts.

It would be a double charity, charity to those who would willingly embrace the life, and charity to those who might require their assistance. It is well known how difficult it is to obtain a sick nurse in London. It is an avocation seldom embraced by people, until they are advanced in years, and all feeling has been dried up by suffering or disappointment. Those who undertake the task are only actuated by gain, and you can expect but eye-service. Not being very numerous, and constantly in demand, they are overworked, and require stimulants in their long watchings. In fact, they drink and dose—dose and drink again.

But how different would it be if the establishments, which I have referred to, were formed! those who are wealthy would send for one of the sisters when required, and if the illness were tedious, her services could be replaced by another, so that over-fatigue might not destroy watchfulness and attention to the patient. You would at once feel that you had those in your house in whom you could confide. If your means enabled you, you would send a sum to the funds of the charity in return for the service performed, and your liberality would enable them to succour those who could only repay by blessings. A very small subscription would set afloat such a charity, as the funds would so rapidly come in; and if under the surveillance of the medical men who attended the hospitals, it would soon become effective and valuable. I trust if this should meet the eye of any real philanthropist who has time to give, which is more valuable than money, that he will turn it over in his mind:— the founder would be a benefactor to his country.

Chapter Twelve

May 25.

"A man cannot die more than once," is an old apothegm, and it would appear bold to dispute it; but still there are lives within lives, such as political lives, literary lives, etcetera, and there is also such a thing as being dead in the eye of the law; so that it is evident that a man can die twice, that is, once professionally or legally, and once naturally.

I presume, like all other scribblers, I must meet my literary death, that is, when I have written myself down, or have written myself out. I have no objection, for I am very weary of my literary existence, although authors are not so in general; on the contrary, they can perceive in themselves no sign of decay when it is apparent to every body around them. Literary decay is analogous to the last stage of a consumption, in which you believe you are not going to die, and plan for the future as if you were in perfect health. And yet to this complexion must all authors come at last. There is not a more beautiful, or more true portrait of human nature, than the scene between the Archbishop of Grenada and Gil Blas, in the admirable novel of Le Sage. Often and often has it been brought to my recollection since I have taken up the pen, and often have I said to myself, "Is this homily as good as the last?" (perhaps homily is not exactly the right term my writings.) The great art in this world, not only in writing, but in everything else, is to know when to leave off. The mind as well as the body must wear out. At first it is a virgin soil, but we cannot renew its exhausted vigour after it has borne successive crops. We all know this, and yet we are all archbishops of Grenada. Even the immortal Walter Scott might have benefited by the honesty of Gil Blas, and have burnt his latter homilies; but had he had such an unsophisticated adviser, would he not, in all probability, have put him out by the shoulders, wishing him, like the venerable hierarch, "a little more taste and judgment."

Since I have been this time abroad, I have made a discovery for which all prose writers ought to feel much indebted to me. Poets can invoke Apollo, the Muses, the seasons, and all sorts and varieties of gods and goddesses, naked or clothed, besides virtues and vices, and if none of them suit, they may make their own graven image, and fall down before it; but we prose writers have hitherto had no such advantage, no protecting deity to appeal to in our trouble, as we bite our pens, or to call upon to deliver us from a congestion of the brain. Now being aware that there were upwards of three hundred and fifty thousand canonised saints on the Roman calendar, I resolved to run through the catalogue, to ascertain—if there was one who took prose authors under his protection, and to my delight, I stumbled upon our man. By-the-bye, Tom Moore must have known this, and he has behaved very ill in keeping him all to himself. But I must introduce him. It is the most holy, and the most blessed, Saint Brandon. Holy Saint Brandon inspire me, and guide my pen while I record thy legend! In the first place, let me observe that our patron saint was an Irishman, and none the worse for that, as Ireland has had as good saints as any in the calendar. And it is now clear that he does protect us prosaic writers, by the number of reporters and gentlemen of the press which have been sent over from the sister kingdom. But to proceed.

Saint Brandon, it appears, was a reading man, and amused himself with voyages and travels; but Saint Brandon was an unbeliever, and thought that travellers told strange things. He took up the Zoology of Pliny, and pursued his accounts of "Antres vast, and men whose heads do grow beneath their shoulders." He read until his patience was exhausted, and, in a fit of anger, he threw the manuscript into the flames. Now this was a heavy sin, for a man's book is the bantling of his brain, and, to say the least, it was a literary-infanticide. That very night an angel appeared to him, and as a penance for his foul crime (in the enormity of which every author will agree with the angel), he was enjoined to *make the book over again*, no easy task in those days, when manuscripts were rare, and the art of book-making had not been invented. The sinner, in obedience to the heavenly mission, goes to work; he charters a vessel, lays in provisions for a seven years' voyage, and with a crew of seven monks, he makes sail, and after going round the world seven times, during which the world went round the sun seven times, he completed his task in seven volumes folio, which he never published, but carried his manuscript away with him to prove that he had performed his penance. For this miraculous voyage—and certainly with such a ship's company, it was a miracle—he was canonised, and is now the patron saint of all prose authors, particularly those whose works are measured by the foot-rule.

And now that I have made known to my fraternity that we also have a saint, all they have to do is to call upon him six or seven times, when their brains are at sixes and sevens. I opine that holy Saint Brandon made a very *hazard-ous* voyage, for it is quite clear that, in the whole arrangement, it was—*seven's the main.*

Chapter Thirteen

En route, May 26.

Passed Waterloo—was informed that two days before the Marquis of Anglesey had arrived there, and stayed a short time to visit the cemetery of his leg; a regular family visit of course, as all the *members* were present.

May 27.

Slept at Namur. The French are certainly superior to us in the art of rendering things agreeable. Now, even in the furnishing of a common apartment, there is always something to relieve the eye, if not to interest you. I recollect when I was last in London, in furnished apartments, that as I lay awake in the morning, my eye caught the pattern of the paper. It was a shepherdess with her dog in repose, badly executed, and repeated without variation over the whole apartment. Of course I had nothing to do but to calculate how many shepherdesses and dogs there were in the room, which, by counting the numbers in length and breadth, squaring the results, and deducting for door and windows, was soon accomplished. But how different was the effect produced by the paper of the room in which I slept last night! It was the history of Dunois, the celebrated bastard of France, who prays in his youth that he may prove the bravest of the brave, and be rewarded with the fairest of the fair. This was not the true history, perhaps, of Dunois; but I am drawing the comparison between the associations and reminiscences conjured up by this decoration in opposition to the dull and tasteless recapitulation of the English manufacture. From the latter I could not extract a bare idea, except that shepherdesses are, as a race, extinct, and that Lord Althorp had taken the tax off shepherds' dogs, by way of a bonus, to relieve a distressed capital of some hundred millions, to which the agricultural interest had very properly replied, "Thank you for nothing, my Lord;" but from the sight of the French paper what a host of recollections started up at the moment! The mind flew back to history, and was revelling in all the romance of chivalry, from King Arthur and his Knights, to the Field of the Cloth of Gold.

"Yet, after all," thought I, at the end of a long reverie, "divest chivalry, so called, of its imposing effect, examine well into its nature and the manners of the times, and it must be acknowledged that the modern warfare has a much greater claim than the ancient to the title of chivalry. In former times men were cased in armour of proof, and, before the discovery of gunpowder, had little to fear in a *mêlée*, except from those who, like themselves, were equally well armed and equally protected, and even then only from flesh wounds, which were seldom mortal. The lower classes, who served as common soldiers, were at the mercy of the mounted spearsmen, and could seldom make any impression upon their defences. In those days, as in the present, he who could command most gold carried the day, for the gold procured the steel harness, and a *plump* of spears brought into the field was more than equal to a thousand common men. He who had the best tempered armour was the most secure, and that was it be only procured by gold. He who could mount and case in iron the largest number of his followers was the most powerful, and, generally speaking, the most lawless. Divest chivalry of its splendour, which threw a halo round it, and it was brutal, and almost cowardly. Single combats did certainly prove courage; but even in them, skill, and more than skill, personal strength, or the best horse, decided the victory. In fact, although not the origin, it was the upholder of the feudal system, in which might was right; and we may add, that the invention of gunpowder, which placed every man upon a level, if not the cause of, certainly much assisted to break up the system. How much more of the true spirit of chivalry is required in the warfare of the present day, in which every man must stand for hours to be shot at like a target, witnessing the mowing down of his comrades, and silently filling up the intervals in the ranks made by their deaths, exposed to the same leaden messengers; a system of warfare in which every individual is a part of a grand *whole*, acting upon one concerted and extended plan, and forced a hundred times to exhibit the passive and more perfect bravery of constancy, for once that he may forget his danger in the ardour of the charge! When shall we learn to call things by their right names?"

Liege, May 28.

Our landlord is a most loyal man, but there is a reason for it. Leopold took up his quarters at this hotel in his way to Spa. In every room we have upon every article of *fayence*—"Leopold, with the Genius of Belgium crowning him with laurels, while Truth is looking on." Every plate, every dish, is impressed with this proof print of loyalty. But this is not all, as the man said in the packet, "Oh, no!" All the wash-hand basins, jugs, and every other article required in a bed-chamber, have the same loyal pattern at the bottom. Now it appeared to me, when I went to bed, that loyalty might be carried too far; and what may have been intended as respect, may be the cause of his Majesty being treated with the greatest disrespect; and not only his sacred Majesty, but the glorious Belgian constitution also. As for poor Truth, she is indeed said to sojourn at the bottom of a well; but in this instance, it would, perhaps, be as well that she should not be insulted—I am wrong, she always is, and always will be, insulted, when she appears in the purlieus of a court, or in the presence of a king.

After all, mine is a strange sort of Diary. It is not a diary of events, but of thoughts and reminiscences, which are thrown up and caught as they float to the surface in the whirlpool of my brain. No wonder!—events are but as gleanings compared to the harvest of many years, although so negligently gathered into store. I have been puzzling myself these last two hours to find out what a man's brain is like. It is like a kaleidoscope, thought I; it contains various ideas of peculiar colours, and as you shift them round and past, you have a new pattern every moment. But no, it was not like a kaleidoscope, for the patterns of a kaleidoscope are regular, and there is very little regularity in my brain, at all events.

It is like a pawnbroker's shop, thought I, full of heterogeneous pledges; and if you would take anything out, experience stands at the counter, and makes you pay her compound interest, while many articles of value are lost for ever, because memory cannot produce the duplicate.

And then I compared it to almost every thing, but none of my comparisons would hold good. After all, thought I, I have been only playing at "What are my thoughts like?" which is a childish game; and how can I possibly find out what my brain is like, when my brain don't choose to tell? So I rose, and opening the window, lighted my cigar, and smoked myself into a reverie, as I watched the smoke ascending from the chimneys of the good town of Liege.

And this is the city which travellers pass through, describing it as a mere manufacturing town, thought I. A city which has, in its time, produced a greater moral influence upon society than any other in existence—a city that has led the van in the cause of religion and liberty. Liege presents a curious anomaly among the states of Europe. It is the only town and province, with the exception of Rome, which has been, for centuries, ruled by the clerical power. But be it recollected, that at the very period that Christianity was offering up her martyrs at the blood-stained arena of the Coliseum, it was from Liege (or rather Tongres, for Liege was not then built) that she was spreading wide her tenets, unpersecuted and unrestrained, for she was too far removed from idolatry and imposture to be regarded. The province of Liege was the cradle of the Christian faith. From the earliest records there were bishops at Tongres; and it was about five hundred years after Christ, that Saint Monulphe, the reigning bishop, founded the city of Liege. From that time until the French Revolution, this town and these fertile provinces had always remained under clerical authority.

Although these prince-bishops proved that, upon necessity, they could change the crosier for the coat of mail, still, as by endowments and benefactions they increased their revenues, so did they, by the mildness of their sway, induce thousands to settle in their territory; and to increase their population (which was to increase their wealth), they first granted to their citizens those privileges and liberties, which have, upon their precedent, been obtained by force or prayers by others. The very boast of the English of the present day, that *every man's house is his castle*, was the sacred grant of one of the bishops to the citizens at Liege, long before the feudal system had been abolished in our island.

I may also observe, for it is to be gained from the chronicles of this province, that the time at which it may be said that the primitive Christian church first fell into error, appears to have been about one thousand years after the death of our Saviour. And as I thought of all this, and a great deal more, and smoked my cigar, I felt a great deal of respect for the good old city of Liege; and then I wandered back to the country I had passed through the day before, excelling in all lovely scenery. I had seen it before, but it was many years ago; and it may be seen many times without the least degree of satiety. I do not know any scenery which raises up such pleasurable sensations as that of the Valley of Meuse, taking it the whole way from Namur to Liege, and from Liege to Spa. It is not so magnificent as the Rhine, to which it bears a miniature resemblance. It is not of that description creating a strong excitement, almost invariably succeeded by depression; but it is of that unchanging and ever-pleasing, joyous description, that you are delighted without being fatigued, and have stimulus sufficient to keep you constantly in silent admiration without demanding so much from the senses as to weary them. If I could have divested myself from the knowledge that I was in motion, and have fancied that the scene was moving past, I could have imagined myself seated at one of our large theatres, watching one of Stanfield's splendid panoramas. But the lighted end of my cigar at last approximated so near to my nose, that I was burnt out of my reverie; I took the last save—all whiffs, tried to hit an old woman's cap with the end of it, as I tossed it into the street, and retreated to the diurnal labour of shaving—of all human miseries, certainly, the "unkindest cut of all"— especially when the maids have borrowed your razor, during your absence, to pare down the apex of their corns.

Chapter Fourteen

Liege.

I have been reading the "Salmonia" of Sir Humphry Davy: what a pity it is that he did not write more! there are so many curious points started in it. I like that description of book, which, after reading a while, you drop it on your knee, and are led into a train of thought which may last an hour, before you look for the page where you left off. There are two cases argued in this work, which led me into a meditation. The one is, a comparison between reason and instinct, and the other, as to the degree of pain inflicted upon fish by taking them with the hook. Now it appeared to me, in the first question, what has been advanced is by no means conclusive, and although it is the custom to offer a penny for your thoughts, I shall give mine for nothing, which is perhaps as much as they are worth, (I say that, to prevent others from making the sarcastic remark), and in the second question, I think I can assist the cause of the lovers of the *gentle* art of angling—why *gentle*, I know not, unless it be that anglers bait with *gentles*, and are mostly *gentle*-men.

But before I attempt to prove that angling is not a cruel sport, I must first get rid of "reason and instinct." Of reason most undoubtedly a philanthropist would reply, "Be it so;" nevertheless, I will argue the point, and if I do not succeed, I have only to hedge back upon Solomon, and inquire, "If man was born to misery as the sparks fly upwards, why are not the inferior classes of creation to have their share of it?"

I do not think that any one can trace out the line of demarcation between reason and instinct. Instinct in many points in wonderful, especially among insects, but where it is wonderful, it is a blind obedience, and inherited from generation to generation. We observe, as in the case of the bees, that they obey the truest laws of mathematics, and from these laws they never have deviated from their creation, and that all animals, as far as their self-defence or their sustenance is concerned, show a wonderful blind obedience to an unerring power, and a sagacity almost superior to reason. But wonderful as this is, it is still but instinct, as the progenitors of the race were equally guided by it, and it is handed down without any improvement, or any decay in its power. Now if it could be asserted that the instinct of animals was only thus inherited from race to race, and could "go no farther," the line of demarcation between reason and instinct would at once be manifest, as instinct would be blindly following certain fixed laws, while reason would ever be assisted by memory and invention. But we have not this boasted advantage on the side of reason, for animals have both memory and invention, and, moreover, if they have not speech, they have equal means of communicating their ideas. That this memory and invention cannot be so much exercised as our own, may be true, but it is exercised to an extent equal to their wants, and they look no further; that is to say, that if any want not prepared for, or anything should take place interfering with their habits and economy, instinct will enable them to meet the difficulty. There is nothing more wonderful than the application of mechanical power by ants. No engineer could calculate with greater nicety, and no set of men work together with such combination of force. After they have made ineffectual attempts to remove a heavy body, you will observe them to meet together, consult among themselves, and commence an entire new plan of operations. Bees, also, are always prepared to meet any new difficulty. If the *sphinx atropos*, or death's head moth, forces its way into the hive, the bees are well known, after having killed it with their stings, to embalm the dead body with wax—their reason for this is, that the body was too large for them to remove through the passage by which it entered, and they would avoid the unpleasant smell of the carcass. It may be argued, that instinct had always imparted to them this knowledge; but if so, they must have had a fresh accession of instinct after they had been domiciled with men: for it is well known that the hole in the tree, in which the wild bees form their cells, is invariably too small to admit any animal larger than themselves, and the bodies of such sized animals they could remove with as much ease as they do the bodies of their own dead.

I could cite a hundred instances, which would prove that animals have invention independent of the instinct handed down from generation to generation. I will, however, content myself with one instance of superior invention in the elephant, which occurred at Ceylon. Parties were employed felling timber in the forests of Candia, and this timber, after having been squared, was dragged to the depôt by a large party of elephants, who, with their keepers, were sent there for that purpose. This work was so tedious, that a large truck was made, capable of receiving a very heavy load of timber, which might be transported at once. This truck was dragged out by the elephants, and it was to be loaded. I should here observe, that when elephants work in a body, there is always one who, as if by common consent, takes the lead, and directs the others, who never refuse to obey him. The keepers of the elephants, and the natives, gave their orders, and the elephants obeyed; but the timber was so large, and the truck so high on its wheels, that the elephants could not put the timber in the truck according to the directions given by the men. After several attempts, the natives gave up the point, and retiring to the side of the road as usual, squatted down, and held a consultation. In the meantime, the elephant who took the lead summoned the others, made them drag two of the squared pieces to the side of the truck, laid them at right angles with it, lifting one end of each on the truck, and leaving the other on the ground, thus forming the inclined plane. The timber was then brought by the elephants, without any interference on the part of the keepers or natives, who remained looking on, was pushed by the elephants with their foreheads up the inclined plane, and the truck was loaded. Here then is an instance in which the inventive instinct of the animal—if that term may be used—was superior to the humbler reasoning powers of the men who had charge of them.

That animals have the powers of memory as well as man, admits of no dispute. In elephants, horses, and dogs, we have hourly instances of it: but it descends much lower down—the piping bullfinch, who has been taught to whistle two or three waltzes in perfect concord, must have a good memory, or he would soon forget his notes. To detail instances of memory would therefore be superfluous; but, as it does occur to me while I write, I must give an amusing instance how the memory of a good thrashing overcame the ruling passion of a monkey, which is gluttony, the first and only instance that I ever saw it conquered.

I had on board a ship which I commanded, a very large Cape baboon, who was a pet of mine, and also a little boy, who was a son of mine. When the baboon sat down on his hams, he was about as tall as the boy was when he walked. The boy having tolerable appetite, received about noon a considerable slice of bread and butter, to keep him quiet till dinner-time. I was on one of the carronades, busy with the sun's lower limb, bringing it in contact with the horizon, when the boy's lower limbs brought him in contact with the baboon, who having, as well as the boy, a strong predilection for bread and butter, and a stronger arm to take it withal, thought proper to help himself to that to which the boy had been already helped. In short, he snatched the bread and butter, and made short work of it, for it was in his pouch in a moment. Upon which the boy set up a yell, which attracted my notice to this violation of the articles of war, to which the baboon was equally amenable as any other person in the ship; for it is expressly stated in the preamble of every separate article, "All who are in, or belonging to." Whereupon I jumped off the carronade, and by way of assisting his digestion, I served out to the baboon monkey's allowance, which is, more kicks than halfpence. The master reported that the heavens intimated that it was twelve o'clock; and with all the humility of a captain of a man-of-war, I ordered him to "make it so;" whereupon it was made, and so passed that day. I do not remember how many days it was afterwards that I was on the carronade as usual, about the same time, and all parties were precisely in the same situations,—the master by my side, the baboon under the booms, and the boy walking out of the cabin with his bread and butter. As before, he again passed the baboon, who again snatched the bread and butter from the boy, who again set up a squall, which again attracted my attention. Looked round, and the baboon caught my eye, which told him plainly that he'd soon catch what was not "at all *my eye;*" and he proved that he actually thought so, for he actually put the bread and butter back into the boy's hands. It was the only instance of which I ever knew or heard of a monkey being capable of self-denial when his stomach was concerned, and I record it accordingly. (Par parenthèse:) it is well known that monkeys will take the small-pox, measles, and I believe the scarlet fever; but this poor fellow, when the ship's company were dying of the cholera, took that disease, went through all its gradations, and died apparently in great agony.

As, then, invention and memory are both common to instinct as well as to reason, where is the line of demarcation to be drawn; especially as in the case of the elephants I have mentioned, superior instinct will invent when inferior reason is at fault? It would appear, if the two qualities must be associated, that, at all events, there are two varieties of instinct: blind instinct, which is superior to reason, so far that it never errs, as it is God who guides; and inventive instinct, which enables the superior animals to provide for unexpected difficulties, or to meet those which memory has impressed upon them. But if we examine ourselves, the difficulty becomes even greater—we have decidedly two separate qualities. We are instinctive as well as reasonable beings; and what is inventive instinct but a species of reason, if not reason itself?

But although I say that it is hardly possible to draw the line of demarcation, I do not mean to say that they are one and the same thing; for instinct and reason, if we are to judge by ourselves, are in direct opposition. Self-preservation is instinctive; all the pleasures of sense, all that people are too apt to consider as happiness in this world; I may say, all that we are told is wrong, all that our reason tells us we are not to indulge in, is *instinct*.

Such are the advantages of being reasonable beings in *this world*; undoubtedly, we have a right to claim for ourselves, and deny to the rest of the creation, the enjoyments of the next. Byron says:—

"Man being reasonable, must get drunk."

That is to say, being reasonable, and finding his reason a reason for being unhappy, he gets rid of his reason whenever he can. So do the most intellectual animals. The elephant and the monkey enjoy their bottle as much as we do. I should have been more inclined to agree with Byron, if he had said:—

Man being reasonable, must *go to the devil.*

For what are poor reasonable creatures to do, when instinct leads them to the "old gentleman;" and reason, let her tug as hard as she pleases, is not sufficiently powerful to overcome the adverse force.

After all, I don't think that I have come to a very satisfactory conclusion. Like a puppy running round after his own tail, I am just where I was when I set out; but, like the puppy, I have been amused for the time. I only hope the reader will have been so too.

And now, my brethren, I proceed to the second part of my discourse, which is, to defend anglers and fly-fishers from the charge of cruelty.

It is very true that Shakespeare says, "The poor beetle that we tread on, in mortal sufferance, feels a pang as great as when a giant dies;" and it is equally true that it is as false as it is poetical.

There is a scale throughout nature, and that scale has been divided by unerring justice. Man is at the summit of this scale, being more fearfully and wonderfully made, more perfect than any other of the creation, more perfect in his form, more perfect in his intellect; he is finer strung in his nerves, acuter in his sympathies; he has more susceptibility to pleasure, more susceptibility to pain. He has pleasures denied to, and he has pains not shared with him by, the rest of the creation. He enjoys most, and he suffers most. From man, the scale of creation descends, and in its descent, as animals are less and less perfect, so is meted out equal but smaller proportions of pleasure and pain, until we arrive to the Mollusca and Zoophyte, beings existing certainly, but existing without pleasure and without pain—existing only to fill up the endless variety, and add the links to the chain of nature necessary to render it complete. The question which naturally will be put is, "how do you know this? it is assertion but not proof." But arguments are always commenced in this way. The assertion is the *quid*, the *est demonstrandum* always comes afterwards. I handle my nose, flourish my handkerchief, and proceed.

Man is the most perfect of creation. What part of his body, if separated from the rest, can he renew? No part, except the hair and the nail. Reproduction can go no further. With the higher classes of animals, also, there is no reproduction: but even at this slight descent upon the scale, we may already point out a great difference. Although there is no reproduction, still there are decided proofs of inferiority; for instance, a hare or rabbit caught in a trap, will struggle till they escape, with the loss of a leg; a fox, which is carnivorous, will do more; he will *gnaw* off his own leg to escape.

Do they die in consequence? no, they live and do well; but could a man live under such circumstances? impossible. If you don't believe me, gnaw your own leg off and try. And yet the conformation of the Mammalia is not very dissimilar from our own; but man is the more perfect creature, and therefore has not the same resources.

I have hitherto referred only to the *limbs* of animals; I will now go further. I had a beautiful little monkey on board my ship. By accident it was crushed, and received such injury that the backbone was divided at the loins, and the vertebra of the upper part protruded an inch outside of its skin. Such an accident in a man would have produced immediate death; but the monkey did not die; its lower limbs were of course paralysed. The vertebra which protruded gradually rotted off, and in six weeks the animal was crawling about the decks with its fore feet. It was, however, such a pitiable object, that I ordered it to be drowned. Now, if we descend lower down in the scale until we come to the reptiles and insects, we shall find not only that the loss of limbs is not attended with death, but that the members are reproduced. Let any one take a spider by its legs, it will leave them in your hands that it may escape. Confine the animal under a glass, and in a few weeks it will have all its members perfect as before. Lizards are still more peculiar in their reproduction. I was at Madeira for many months, and often caught the lizards which played about the walls and roofs of the out-houses; and if ever I caught a lizard by the tail, he would make a spring, and leave his tail in my hand, which seemed to snap off as easily as would a small carrot. Now the tail of the lizard is longer than its body, and a continuation of the vertebrae of the back. I soon found out that lizards did not die from this extensive loss, but, on the contrary, that their tails grew again. Even the first week afterwards, a little end began to show itself, and in about two months the animal had reproduced the whole. What I am about to say now will probably be considered by some as incredible; they are, however, at full liberty to disbelieve it. One day I was looking out of the window with the late Tom Sheridan, who lived in the same house, and we observed on the roof of the out-house a lizard with two tails, but neither of them full grown; and we argued that, at the time the animal lost his tail, he must have suffered some division of the stump. Being at that time a naturalist, i.e. very cruel; I immediately caught a lizard, pulled off his tail, notched the vertebra, and turned him loose again. Our conjectures were right; the animal in two or three weeks had two tails growing out like the one we had seen. I repeated this experiment several times, and it always appeared to succeed; and all the two-tailed lizards were called mine.

Now this power of reproduction increases as you descend the scale; as an instance, take the polypus, which is as near as possible at the bottom of it. If you cut a polypus into twenty pieces, without any regard to division, in a short time you will have twenty perfect polypi.

Now the deductions I would draw from these remarks are—

That the most perfect animals are least capable of reproduction, and most sensible of pain.

That as the scale of nature descends, animals become less perfect, and more capable of reproduction.

Ergo—they cannot possibly feel the same pain as the more perfect.

Now with respect to fish, they are very inferior in the scale of creation, being, with the exception of the cetaceous tribe, which class with the Mammalia, all cold-blooded animals, and much less perfect than reptiles or many insects. The nervous system is the real seat of all pain; and the more perfect the animal, the more complicated is that system: with cold-blooded animals, the nervous organisation is next to nothing. Most fish, if they disengage themselves from the hook, will take the bait again; and if they do not, it is not on account of the pain, but because their instinct tells them there is danger. Moreover, it is very true, as Sir H. Davy observes, that fish are not killed by the hook, but by the hooks closing their mouths and producing suffocation. How, indeed, would it otherwise be possible to land a salmon of thirty pounds weight, in all its strength and vigour, with a piece of gut not thicker than three or four hairs?

Upon the same grounds that I argue that fish feel very little comparative pain, so do I that the worm, which is so low in the scale of creation, does not suffer as supposed. Its writhings and twistings on the hook are efforts to escape natural to the form of the animal, and can be considered as little or nothing more. At the same time I acknowledge and, indeed, prove, by my own arguments, that it is very cruel to *bob for whale*.

To suppose there are no gradations of feeling as well as of perfection in the animal kingdom, would not only be arguing against all analogy, but against the justice and mercy of the Almighty, who does not allow a sparrow to fall to the earth without his knowledge. He gave all living things for our use and our sustenance; he gave us intellect to enable us to capture them: to suppose, therefore, at the same time, that he endowed them with so fine a nervous organisation as to make them undergo severe tortures previous to death, is supposing what is contrary to that goodness and mercy which, as shown towards us, we are ready to acknowledge and adore.

I cannot finish this subject without making a remark upon creation and its perfectibility. All *respectable* animals, from man down to a certain point in the scale, have their lice or parasites to feed upon them. Some wit, to exemplify this preying upon one another, wrote the following:—

"Great fleas have little fleas,
And less fleas to bite them,
These fleas have lesser fleas,
And so—*ad infinitum*."

This, however, is not strictly true. Parasites attach themselves only to the great. Upon those they can fatten. Having your blood sucked, is therefore, a great proof of high heraldry and perfectibility in the scale of creation. If animals were endowed with speech and pride like man, we might imagine one creature boasting to another, as a proof of his importance.

"And I, too, also have my louse!"

Chapter Fifteen

Liege, May 30th.

What strange meetings take place sometimes! I recollect once, when I was sitting at a *table d'hôte*, at Zurich, being accosted by a lady next to me, and being accused of having forgotten her. I looked with all my eyes, but could not discover that I had ever seen her before. At last, after allowing me to puzzle for some time, she said: "Sir, you and I met at dinner four years ago, at Mr K—'s house in Demerara." It was very true; but who would have thought of running his memory over to South America, to a cursed alluvial deposite, hatching monthly broods of alligators, and surrounded by naked slaves, whilst out of the window before him his eye rested upon the snow-covered mountains of Switzerland, and he breathed the pure air of William Tell and liberty. This morning I fell in with an acquaintance whom had not seen for years, and him also I did not recollect. I am very unfortunate in that respect, and I am afraid that I have very often given offence without intending it; but so imperfect is my memory of faces, that I have danced with a lady in the evening, and the next day have not known her, because she was in a bonnet and morning dress. Sometimes the shifts I am put to are quite ludicrous, asking all manner of questions, and answering those put to me at random, to find out some clue as to who my very intimate friend may be. They ought not to be angry at my forgetting their names, for sometimes, for a few minutes, I have actually forgotten my own. It does, however, only require one clue to be given me, and then all of a sudden I recollect every thing connected with the party. I remember one day as I was passing Whitehall, somebody came up, wrung my hand with apparent delight, and professed himself delighted to see me. I could do no other than say the same, but who he was, and where I had seen him before, was a mystery. "I am married since we parted," said he, "and have a fine little boy." I congratulated him with all my heart. "You must come and see me, and I will introduce you to Mary."

"Nothing would give me more pleasure;" but if he had only called his wife Mrs So-and-so, I should have a *clue*. "Let me see," said I, "where was it we parted?"

"Don't you recollect?" said he, "At the Cape of Good Hope."

But I was still mystified, and after putting several leading questions, I found myself quite as much in the dark as ever. At last I asked him for his card, that I might call upon him. He had not one in his pocket. I pulled out my tablets, and he took out the pencil, and wrote down his address; but that was of no use to me.

"Stop, my good fellow, I have so many addresses down there, that I shall be making some mistake; put your name down above it."

He did so, and when I saw the name every thing came fast like a torrent into my recollection; we *had been* very intimate, and he was fully justified in showing so much warmth. I could then talk to him about old scenes, and old acquaintances; so I took his arm, and went forthwith to be introduced to his Mary. The knowledge of this unfortunate failing makes me peculiarly careful not to avoid a person who appears to know me; and one day a very absurd scene took place. I was standing on some door steps close to the Admiralty, waiting for a friend, and there was another gentleman standing close to me, on the pavement. A third party came up, extending his hand, and I immediately took it, and shook it warmly, — although who my friend was, I was, as usual, very much puzzled to find out. Now it so happened that the hand which I had taken was extended to the gentleman standing by me, and not to me; and the party whose hand I was squeezing looked me in the face and laughed. I did the same, and he then gave his hand to the right party, and walked off. As, however, we had said, "How d'ye do?" we had the politeness to say, "Good-by;" both taking off our hats on the broad grin.

I *was* observing, that I here met with a person whom I could not recollect, and, as usual, I continued to talk with him, trusting to my good fortune for the clue. At last it was given me. "Do you recollect the little doctor and his wife at Bangalore?" I did, and immediately recollected him. As the story of the doctor and his wife has often made me laugh, and as I consider it one of the best specimens of *tit for tat*, I will narrate it to my readers. I have since been told that it is not new — I must tell it nevertheless.

A certain little army surgeon, who was stationed at Bangalore, had selected a very pretty little girl out of an invoice of young ladies, who had been freighted-out on speculation. She was very fond of gaiety and amusement, and, after her marriage, appeared to be much fonder of passing away the night at a ball than in the arms of her little doctor. Nevertheless, although she kept late hours, in every respect she was very correct. The doctor, who was a quiet, sober man, and careful of his health, preferred going to bed early, and rising before the sun, to inhale the cool breeze of the morning. And as the lady seldom came home till past midnight, he was not very well pleased at being disturbed by her late hours. At last, his patience was wearied out, and he told her plainly, that if she staid out later than twelve o'clock, he was resolved not to give her admittance. At this, his young wife, who, like all pretty women, imagined that he never would presume to do any such thing, laughed heartily, and from the next ball to which she was invited, did not return till half-past two in the morning. As soon as she arrived, the palanquin-bearers knocked for admittance; but the doctor, true to his word, put his head out of the window, and very ungallantly told his wife she might remain all night. The lady coaxed, entreated, expostulated, and threatened; but it was all in vain. At last she screamed, and appeared to be frantic, declaring that if not immediately admitted, she would throw herself into the well, which was in the compound, not fifty yards from the bungalow. The doctor begged that she would do so, if that gave her any pleasure, and then retired from the window. His wife ordered the bearers to take her on her palanquin to the well; she got out, and gave her directions, and then slipped away up to the bungalow, and stationed herself close to the door, against the wall. The bearers, in obedience to her directions, commenced crying out, as if expostulating with their mistress, and then detaching a large and heavy stone, two of them plunged it into the water; after which, they all set up a howl of lamentation. Now the little doctor, notwithstanding all his firmness and *nonchalance*, was not quite at ease when he heard his wife express her determination. He knew her to be *very entêtée*, and he remained on the watch. He heard the heavy plunge, followed up by the shrieks of the palanquin-bearers. "Good God," cried he, "is it possible?" and he darted out in his shirt to where they were all standing by the well. As soon as he had passed, his wife hastened in-doors, locked, and made all fast, and shortly afterwards appeared at the window from which her husband had addressed her. The doctor discovered the *ruse* when it was too late. It was now his turn to expostulate; but how could he "hope for mercy, rendering none?" The lady was laconic and decided. "At least, then, throw me my clothes," said the doctor. "Not even your slippers, to protect you from the scorpions and centipedes," replied the lady, shutting the "jalousie." At day-light, when the officers were riding their Arabians, they discovered the poor little doctor pacing the verandah up and down in the chill of the morning, with nothing but his shirt to protect him. Thus were the tables turned, but whether this *ruse* of the well ended well,—whether the lady reformed, or the doctor conformed,—I have never since heard.

Chapter Sixteen

Liege, June 2.

The academy or college established at Liege in 1817 is very creditable to the Liegeois. Much has been done in fifteen years: the philosophical apparatus, collections of minerals and natural history, are all excellent for instruction, although the minerals are not very valuable. The fossils found in the Ardennes are very interesting, and ought to be a mine of wealth to the Liegeois, as by exchanging them they might soon have a valuable collection. It is a pity that the various museums of Europe do not print catalogues, not of their own collections only, but also of the duplicates which they can part with, so that they may be circulated, not only among the national collections, but also among private cabinets; by so doing they would all become more perfect. It is currently reported that more duplicates have been allowed to perish in the cellars of the British Museum than would have furnished all the cabinets in Europe. It may be replied, that other cabinets had nothing to offer in exchange; but that is only a surmise: and even if they had not, they should have been presented to other institutions abroad. Science ought not to be confined to country or people: it should be considered as universal.

To the college is annexed a botanical garden. There is nothing I dislike more than a botanical garden. I acknowledge the advantages, perhaps the necessity, of such institutions; but they always appear to me as if there was disarrangement instead of arrangement. What may be called order and classification seems to me to be disorder and confusion. It may be very well to class plants and trees for study, but certainly their families, although joined by man, were never intended to be united by God. Such a mixture in one partition, of trees, and shrubs, and creeping plants, all of which you are gravely told are of one family. I never will believe it: it is unnatural. I can see order and arrangement when I look at the majestic forest-trees throwing about their wild branches, and defying the winds of heaven, while they afford shelter to the shrubs beneath, which in their turn protect and shelter the violets that perfume all around. This is beautiful and natural—it is harmony; but in a botanical garden every thing is out of its place. The Scripture says, "Those whom God hath joined let no man put asunder;" may we not add, Those whom God hath sundered let no man presume to join. I felt as I looked at the botanical garden as if it were presumptuous and almost wicked, and as it was on the banks of the Meuse, I sat down on the wall and recovered myself by looking at the flowing river, and thinking about utility and futility, "and all that sort of thing and everything else in the world," as poor Matthews used to say,—and there I sat for an hour, until my thoughts revolved on the propriety of going back and eating my dinner,—as Mrs Trollope used to do when she was in Belgium.

As I was walking about in the evening, I perceived a dirty little alley illuminated with chandeliers and wax candles. There must be a ball, thought I, or some gaiety going on: let us inquire. "No, sir," replied a man to whom I put the question, "it's not a ball,—it is a Monsieur who has presented to an image of the Virgin Mary which is up that court, a petticoat, which, they say, is worth one thousand five hundred francs, and this lighting-up is in honour of her putting it on." The race of fools is not extinct, thought I. I wonder whether, like King Ferdinand, he worked it himself. Belgium is certainly at this present the stronghold of superstition.

Chapter Seventeen

June 3.

Went to Harquet's manufactory of arms, and was much amused. They export all over the world, and the varieties they make up for the different markets are astonishing. They were then very busy completing an order for several thousand muskets for the Belgian troops, which load at the breech and fire off without locks or priming. They showed me a fowling-piece on the same principle, which they fired off under water. But the low prices of the arms astonished me. There were a large quantity of very long fowling-pieces with the *maker's* name at *Constantinople*, for the Turkish gentlemen, at thirty francs each: a common musket was fourteen francs. I perceived in a corner a large number of muskets, of infamous workmanship, and with locks resembling those awkward attempts made two hundred years back. I asked what they were for. They were for the South American market, and made to order, for the people there would use no others: any improvement was eschewed by them. I presume they had borrowed one of the Spanish muskets brought over by Pizarro as a model, but, at all events, they were very cheap, only eight francs each. God help us, how cheaply men can be killed now-a-days!

It is very seldom that you now meet with a name beginning with an X, but one caught my eye as I was walking through the streets here. *Urban Xhenemont, négociant.* I perceive there are still some to be found in Greece; the only one I know of in England is that of Sir Morris Ximenes, who, I presume, claims descent from the celebrated cardinal. The mention of that name reminds me of the songs of the improvisatore, Theodore Hook, and his address in finding a rhyme for such an awkward name as Ximenes. Few possess the talent of improvising. In Italy it is more common, because the Italian language admits the rhyme with so much facility; but a good improvisatore is rare even in that country. There was a Dutchman who was a very good improvisatore, a poor fellow who went about to amuse companies with his singing and this peculiar talent. One day a gentleman dropped a gold Guillaume into a glass of Burgundy, and told him if he would make a good impromptu, he should have both the wine and the gold:

without hesitation he took up the glass, and suiting the action to the word, sang as follows: —

> "Twee Goden in een Glas,
> Wat zal ik van maken?
> K' steek Plutus in myn tas,
> K slaak Bacchus in myn Kaken."

Which may be rendered into French as follows: —

> "Quoi! deux dieux dans un verre,
> Eh bien! que vais-j'en faire?
> J'empocherai Plutus,
> J'avalerai Bacchus."

The gentleman, who gave me this translation, also furnished me with a copy of extempore French verses, given by a gentleman of Maestricht, who was celebrated as an improvisatore. They certainly are very superior. He was at a large party, and agreed to improvise upon any theme given him by five of those present in the way of *Souvenir*. The first person requested the souvenir of *early youth*.

> "Vous souvient-il? Amis de ma jeunesse,
> Des beaux momens de nos fougueux exploits?
> Quand la raison sous le joug de l'ivresse,
> Essaye en vain de soutenir ses droits.
> Ce tems n'est plus, cet âge de folie,
> Où tout en nous est pressé de jouir:
> Mes bons amis, du printemps de la vie
> Gardons toujours le joyeux *souvenir*."

The next party requested a souvenir of the conscription, many of them, as well as the poet, having been forced into the army of France.

> "Vous souvient-il? que plus tard, sous les armes
> Plusieurs donons, désignés par le sort,
> Loin des parents; versant d'amères larmes,
> Allaient trouver ou la gloire ou la mort.
> Ces jours de deuil par milliers dans l'histoire
> Ne viendront plus, sur nous s'appesantir
> Amis, volons an temple de Mémoire
> Effaçons-en le sanglant *souvenir*."

The third party requested a souvenir of his "first love."

"Vous sonvient-il? de cet enfant de Guide
Fripon rusé, volage et séducteur;
Qui par les yeux d'une beauté timide,
D'un trait de feu veut nous frapper au coeur.
Du sentimens que sa flèche fit naître,
Et que la mort peut seul anéantir,
Eternissons le ravissant bien-être,
En conservant un si beau *souvenir*."

The fourth proposed as a theme, the morning of his marriage.

"Vous souvient-il? du jour ou l'hyménée
Vint nous dicter ses éternelles loix,
En attachant à notre destinée
L'objet sacré de notre premier choix.
Solennité qui par des voeux nous lie,
De saints devoirs chargeant notre avenir,
Solennité que le vulgaire oublie
Nous te gardons en pieux *souvenir*."

The last party desired him to wind up with *friendship*.

"Quel souvenir puis-je chanter encore,
Après celui né dans la volupté?
Il en est un que le tems corrobore,
C'est le premier élan de l'amitié.
Eh! qui de nous n'a pas dans sa jeunesse,
Livré son coeur à ses charmes puissants,
Sainte Amitié, jusqu'à dans la vieillesse,
Console-nous des ravages du tems."

I should imagine that after the gentleman had finished all this, he must have been pretty well out of breath.

About four miles from Liege is the celebrated manufactory of Seraing, belonging to Messrs Cockerell. It is beautifully situated on the banks of the Meuse, and was formerly the summer palace of the Prince Archbishop. But it is not only here that you observe these symptoms of the times— all over France you will perceive the same, and the major portion of the manufactories have the arms of princes or nobles emblazoned over the façade, while the interiors, which once were the abode of refinement and luxury, are now tenanted by artisans and appropriated to utility. The utilitarian system was, however, more fully exemplified before the Belgian revolution, for William of Nassau was, in fact, a partner of Mr Cockerell.

Mr Cockerell, the father, who is now dead, came over from England before the peace, bringing with him either the machinery for spinning cotton, or the knowledge necessary for its construction, so jealously guarded by our manufacturers. He established himself at Liege, and soon gained patrons. The firm has now three or four manufactories at Liege besides the one at Seraing. Large as was the bishop's palace, it has been increased to about three times its original size: it reminds me more of Portsmouth yard than any other place. The number of workmen employed in this manufactory alone is between fourteen and fifteen hundred. They make every variety of steam engines, and not only supply this country, but Prussia, Austria, France, and even Russia. People talk of Mr Cockerell having done much mischief to his country by furnishing foreigners with the machinery which enabled us to undersell them. I doubt it very much: I consider that the sooner other countries are enabled to compete with us to a certain extent, the better it will be for England. At present we are in an unhealthy state, and chiefly arising from the unlimited use of machinery. Let us lose that advantage, and, if not richer, at all events we shall be much happier. We are now suffering under a plethora of capital at the same time that we are oppressed with debt. As for Mr Cockerell, it may be very well to cry out about patriotism, but the question is, would not every other man have done the same? Had he not a right to bring his talents to the best market? and before he is accused of having had no regard for his country, it may first be fairly asked, what regard had his country shown for him?

Chapter Eighteen

Spa, June 10.

Here we are, and for a time at rest. Rest! no, the wheels of the carriage may rest, even the body for a time may rest, but the mind will not. We carry our restlessness with us wherever we go. Like a steam-engine, the mind works, and works, and works, sometimes, indeed, with less rapidity of motion; but still it goes on, goes on in its ever-continued labour; waking or sleeping, no repose; until the body, which is the mechanical part of the engine, is worn out by constant friction, or the steam of the mind is exhausted. And people tell you, and believe that there is rest in the grave. How can that be? The soul is immortal and cannot exist without consciousness. If not conscious, it does not exist; and if conscious, it must work on, even beyond the grave, and for ever. To assert that there is rest in the grave, is denying the immortality of the soul. And what a contemptible, base slave the body is to the soul! I was going to say that he could not call his soul his own; but that would be a Catachresis, and I hate and abominate every thing which begins with *cat*. It is singular that they are all unpleasant, or unlucky, or unsafe; for instance—

	remind you of
Cat-acombs	death, funerals, and mummies.
Cat-alogue	sale of effects, some poor devil done up.
Cat-aplasm	a boil poulticed.
Cat-aract	sore eyes, Sam Patch, and devastation.
Cat-arrh	head stuffed, running of the glands.
Cat-echism	equally unpleasant in youth and marriage.
Cat-egorical	argument, which is detestable.
Cat-erpillars	beasts who foul nature.
Cat-erwaul	horrid variety of love.
Cat-gut	street music, hurdy-gurdy.
Cat's-paw	a calm, with a prize in sight.

As for a cat itself, I cannot say too much against it; and it is singular, that the other meanings of the single word are equally disagreeable; as to *cat* the anchor, is a sign of *going to sea*, and the *cat* at the gangway is the worst of all.

Five o'clock in the morning,—the sun has not yet appeared above the hills, but the mist is rising gradually. The bell of the church in front of my window is tolling;—it ceases; and the pealing of the organ, with the chanting of the priests, comes distinct and clear upon my ear, as the notes of the bugle over the still water, from some dashing frigate in the Sound, beating off at sunset. How solemn and how beautiful is this early prayer! The sun is rising, the mists of the night are rolling off, and the voices and music resound at the same time to heaven. The church is full, and many remain outside, uncovered, and kneeling in humility. But who comes here, thought I, as a man in a shabby coat walked to within a few yards of the church door, and laid down his burden, consisting of a drum, a fiddle, a roll of canvass, a chair, and a long pole. This is a curious stock in trade, methinks; how in the name of all the saints do you gain your livelihood? This was soon ascertained. A minute before the mass was over, he fixed his pole upright in the ground, hung his canvass on it, and unrolled it, displaying a picture divided in six compartments. He then hung his fiddle to his button, took his drum, and putting his chair close to his pole, stood upon it, giving a long, but not loud roll of his drum, which he repeated at intervals, to attract attention. He had taken his station with judgment; and as the people came out of church, he had soon a crowd about him, when he commenced with crossing himself, and then continued to explain the legend which was attached to his pictures on the canvass. I could not hear all, but still I could understand enough to fill up the rest. It was the wonderful cure performed by a certain saint; and as he told the story, he pointed to the different compartments with his fiddlestick, for he had laid aside his drum as soon as he had collected an audience. Now and then he crossed himself devoutly, and at last informed the crowd around him that he had the very prayer, and the very remedy which had been prescribed. He then played his fiddle, singing the prayer in a solemn chaunt; and then he pulled out of his pocket a packet of little books and little boxes. They are only one halfpenny each; and all that is necessary is, that they should touch the figure of the saint on the canvass, to be imbued with the necessary virtue. He sells them rapidly; each time that he puts them to the canvass crossing himself, and insisting that the party who purchases shall do the same. He takes his fiddle again, and sings the history of the saint, pointing with his fiddlestick to the compartments of the picture as he goes on; and now he pulls out more little books and more boxes; and how fast they purchase them! The stock in trade in his own possession is certainly of little value; but he possesses a fruitful mine in the superstition of others. Ah, well! Are not those inside the church setting him the example of mixing up religion with quackery?

Spa is beautifully situated, between abrupt hills covered with verdure; the walks cut in these hills are very beautiful, and much pains have been taken to render the place agreeable;—no wonder, when we recollect how many crowned heads have visited the place: but the sun of Spa has set, probably never to rise again; for whatever may be the property of its waters, to be frequented, a watering-place must be fashionable. There are many causes for its desertion. One is, the effects of the Belgian revolution. During the time that Belgium was attached to the Netherlands, the king, with the prince and princess of Orange, came here almost every year, bringing with them, of course, a great number of the nobility; but now the nobility have deserted the court; and when Leopold came here, no one followed. He was disgusted, and remained but a few days. The Prussians used also to resort very much to Spa; but the king of Prussia finding that so many young men were ruined at the gaming-tables, and so much distress occasioned by it, with a most fatherly despotism, has refused all the officers permission to visit Spa, and has forbidden the medical men to recommend the waters. The Russians also flocked in great numbers to Spa; but the emperor, although very indifferent about their losing their money, is very particular about his subjects gaining revolutionary opinions; and Spa being in a revolutionary country, has been condemned: they may just as well ask to go to Siberia, for that would probably be their route; and lastly, there is one more cause which, these two last seasons, has had a powerful effect, neither more nor less than a certain book, called the *"Bubbles of the Brunnen."* I say for the last two seasons, for its influence will not extend to a third, as hundreds and hundreds who have gone to the Baths with the intention of passing this season, have already returned in disgust. A word upon this.

When Sir George Head published his "Bubbles," he set people almost as mad as they were during the great "Bubble Mania;" and like all the mining and other associations, they have proved but bubbles at last. It is said that one hundred and thirty-five thousand passports were taken out last year to go up the Rhine, by people who wished to see the pigs go through their daily manoeuvres, to an unearthly solo on the horn, and to witness the decapitation of the Seltzer-water bottles, which were condemned as traitors. Now, so large an influx of people to these German watering-places could have but one effect; that of a glorious harvest to the innkeepers, and those who had lodgings to let. The prices, at these places, have now become so enormous, that three florins have been asked for a single bed, and everything else has risen in the same proportion. The reaction has now begun to take place, and every day and every hour we have carriages returning through Liege, and other towns, from these watering-places, the occupants holding up their hands, quite forgetting the pigs and bottles, and only exclaiming against extortion, and everything German. They have paid too dear for their whistle, as Franklin used to say; the bubble has burst, and they look with regret at their empty purses. And yet, all that Head said in his amusing book was true. He rambled through a verdant and unfrequented lane, and described what he felt as he stopped to pick blackberries. An immense multitude have followed him, the green lane has been beaten down into a high road, and, as for blackberries, they are only to be procured at the price of peaches in May.

And now let us reflect whether the bubble will not also burst with the Germans. Formerly they were contented with moderate profits, and received their visitors with humility and thankfulness. Now, that they have suddenly made large profits, they have become independent and unceremonious; and, like most people, because they have reaped a golden harvest for two years, they anticipate that it will continue. The value of property at these places has risen, speculations have been entered into on a large scale, provisions and the necessaries of life have become dear; new houses are building against time, and the proprietors smoke their pipes with becoming gravity, calculating upon their future gains. But the company will fall off more and more each succeeding year, although the speculations will continue; for people always find a good reason for a bad season, and anticipate a better one the next. At last, they will find that they are again deserted, and property will sink in value to nothing; the reaction will have fully taken place, prices will fall even lower than they were at first; honesty and civility will be reassumed, although, probably, the principal will have been lost. Thus will the bubble burst with them, as it has already with deserted Spa.

But when all idle people shall have visited all the bubbling fountains of Germany, where are they to go next? There are some very nice springs in Iceland not yet patronised; but although the springs there are hot, the Springs, vernally speaking, are cold. I can inform travellers where they will find out something new, and I advise them to proceed to the boiling springs at Saint Michael's, one of the Western isles, and which are better worth seeing than all the springs that Germany can produce. I will act as *guide de voyage*.

When you land at Saint Michael's, you will find yourself in one of the dirtiest towns in the world, and will put up at one of the worst hotels; however, you will have to pay just as dear as if lodged at the Clarendon, and fed at the *Rocher de Cancale*. The town contains many inhabitants, but more pigs. German pigs are not to be compared to them. You must then hire donkeys and ascend to the mountains, and after a hot ride, you will arrive at a small valley in the centre of the mountains, which was once the crater of a volcano, but is now used by nature as a kettle, in which she keeps hot water perpetually boiling for those who may require it. There you will behold the waters bubbling and boiling in all directions, throwing up huge white columns of smoke, brought out in strong relief by the darker sides of the mountains which rear their heads around you. The ground you tread upon trembles as you walk; you feel that it is only a thin crust, and that in a moment you may sink into the vast cauldron below, and have a hot bath without paying for it. Continue along the valley, and you will find lakes of still, deadly-cold water, with hot springs at their verge, throwing the smoke over their surface, while they pour in their boiling water as if they would fain raise the temperature; depositing sulphur in cakes and crystals in their course. And in another spot there is a dark, unfathomable hole, called the Devil's Mouth: you approach it, and you hear low moanings and rumblings, as if nature had the stomach-ache; and then you will have a sudden explosion, and a noise like thunder, and a shower of mud will be thrown out to a distance of several yards. Wait again; you will again hear the moans and rumblings, and in about three minutes the explosion and the discharge will again take place; and thus has this eternal diarrhoea continued ever since the memory or tradition of man.

Yet, upon this apparently insecure and dangerous spot have been erected houses and baths, and it is resorted to by the fashionables of Saint Michael's, who wish, by its properties, to get rid of certain cutaneous disorders: for the whole air is loaded with sulphurous vapour, as the eternal pot keeps boiling.

Observe the advantages of this place:— you may have a bath as hot as you please, as cold as you please, or you may have a mud *douche*, if you have that buffalo propensity; and then you will have to rough it, which is so delightful; you will find little or nothing to eat, and plenty of bedfellows in all their varieties, a burning sun, and a dense atmosphere, and you will be very delighted to get back again, which, after all, is the *summum bonum* to be obtained by travel.

Not very far from this valley of hot water there is another valley, containing four small lakes, and in those lakes are found the most beautiful gold and silver fish, perhaps, in the world. How they came there, Heaven only knows; but I mention this because there is a curious coincidence. These lakes are known by the name of the Quadre Cidade, or four cities. Now, if my readers will recollect, in the "Arabian Nights," there is a story of a valley with four lakes, which were once four cities, and that in these lakes were fish of various beautiful colours, who were once the inhabitants. If I recollect right, when the fish were caught and put into the frying-pan, they jumped up and made a speech; (so would fish now-a-days, if they were not mute;) and the story is told by a prince, whose lower extremities are turned into black marble, very convenient, certainly, if he dined out every day, as he had only his upper toilet to complete. This coincidence appeared to me to be very curious, and had I had time and opportunity I certainly should have fried four of these unfortunate fish, to ascertain whether they were of the real breed spoken of in the Arabian Tales, of the authenticity of which no one, I presume, will venture to doubt.

Chapter Nineteen

Spa, July 15.

What a curious history might be afforded by Spa and its gaming tables! When Spa was in its glory, when crowned heads met and dukes were forced to remain in their carriages for want of accommodation, when it was the focus of all that was *recherché* and brilliant, for Spa was so before the French revolution, the gaming tables were a source of immense profit; and to whom do you imagine that a great portion of the profits belonged? — to no less a person than the most sacred and puissant prince, the Bishop of Liege, who derived a great revenue from them. But it would appear as if there was a judgment upon this anomalous secular property, for these gaming-tables were the cause of the Prince Bishop losing all, and being driven out of his territories. There were two gaming establishments at Spa, the Redoubt in the town, and the Vauxhall about a quarter of a mile outside of it. The Redoubt is a fine building, with splendid ball-rooms and a theatre, but you must go *through the gaming-rooms* to enter either the ball-room or the theatre. The Vauxhall has no theatre, but the rooms are even more spacious; but when Spa was at its zenith, even these two immense edifices were barely sufficient for the company. Both these establishments were under the same proprietors, and it so happened that the English nobility, who were always a very strong party here, were displeased with the conduct of the lessees, and immediately raised funds for the building of a second Vauxhall. The bishop ordered the building to be discontinued, but, as by the privileges granted by former bishops, this was a violation of the rights of the Liegeois, his order was disregarded, and the Vauxhall now known by the name of *the Vauxhall,* was finished. When finished, the bishop would not permit it to be opened, but his commands being disregarded, he came down with two hundred soldiers and two pieces of cannon and took possession. This created a revolution, and the bishop was ultimately obliged to fly his territory and seek assistance. The Prussians marched an army into the city, and there was apparent submission, but as soon as they quitted, the insurrection again took place, and the bishop was forced again to solicit aid from the Austrians, for Prussia would no longer interfere. Metternich, who was so fond of legitimacy that he considered the gaming-tables a legitimate source of revenue to the apostle, marched in an Austrian army, and hundreds were slaughtered that the bishop might obtain his rights. Such was the state of affairs when the French revolution broke out and convulsed Europe, and the province of Liege was among the very first to receive with open arms the *bonnet rouge* and to join themselves with France, and thus did the bishop lose his beautiful province for ever. As far as Liege was concerned, the French revolution proved a blessing. It certainly was a disgraceful finale to an ecclesiastical power, which, as I have before mentioned, had formerly led the van in the march of Christianity and liberty.

But it appears that the clergy are fated to have an interest in these gaming-tables, the stipend of the English resident clergyman being, even now, paid out of their profits; for when Belgium was made over to the Netherlands, King William assumed his right to the bishop's former share of the profits of the tables, and of course brought as many people down here as he could to *lose their money*, as he pocketed his *thirds*. Since the revolution, Leopold is in King William's shoes, but there are little or no profits, as Spa is deserted and the expenses of the establishments are great. Perhaps there is no spot of ground in Europe—I will not except Paris—where so much money has been lost by gaming as at Spa. I was walking with a friend who pointed out to me a small pavilion in a garden. "There," says he, "the Prince of Orange, who played very deeply, lost to a Spanish gentleman those very jewels that were pretended to be stolen. It was well got up in the papers, but that is the real truth." How far it may be the truth or not, I cannot pretend to say, and only know that in Spa you cannot pick your teeth without all the world knowing it, and that this is fully believed at Spa to be the real truth of the disappearance of the splendid jewels of the princess, which have since been redeemed from the Spanish gentleman, who now resides at the Hague.

Gaming has always been held up in abhorrence as a vice; but it is rather a passion strongly implanted by nature, and abhorrent from the dreadful effects produced by its overpowering influence, than a vice *per se*. Life itself is a lottery, and the best part of our life is passed in gambling. It is difficult to draw the line between gambling and speculation, for every speculation is a gambling transaction. Is not the merchant a gambler? in fact, is not every venture an act of gambling? As for the Stock Exchange, it is the very worst species of gambling. All we can say is, that gambling may be legitimate or otherwise; that is, there are species of gambling which may enrich the individual if he is fortunate, but whether it enriches him or not, at all events it is beneficial to the community at large. A merchant speculates—he sends out manufactures of every description: he fails, and is ruined: but the artisans have procured employment for their industry, and, although the merchant fails, the community at large has benefited. This is legitimate gambling; but do people in business stop there? No: they will agree to deliver so many thousands of casks of tallow or tons of hemp at such and such a time and at a certain price, whatever the price may then be. They cannot complete their engagement, and they are ruined; but in this instance, which is simply termed speculation, we have quite as much gambling as if the money were at once laid down on the table, and the chances decided in an hour instead of so many months. But there is this difference, that this party does not injure his character by such a transaction, whereas, if he lost his money at the gaming-table he would. The English are, with the exception of the Americans, the most gambling nation under heaven; naturally so, because they are the greatest mercantile nation. The spirit of gambling is innate, and when directed into the proper channel it becomes enterprise. It is doubtless a great moral error on the part of a government to encourage vice with the view of increasing the revenue, but, at the same time, there is no tax so well laid on as that which is imposed on vice. Again, there are certain propensities in man which cannot be overcome, and which, if attempted to be wholly eradicated by legal enactments, would occasion more evil still. All that a judicious government can or should attempt to effect is, to restrain them within proper bounds, to regulate them, and as much as possible to keep them out of sight, that the virus may not extend. It is well known, that certain houses are licensed by the magistrates, because, it being impossible to eradicate the vice, they can do no more than to separate it, that it may not be communicated to the healthier part of the community. Now upon this principle, which is the true principle of sound legislation, I have often thought that it was a great error in our legislature when they consented to put down the public lotteries in England. I am convinced that they were beneficial, acting as safety-valves to the gambling spirit of the nation, and that their prohibition has been productive of much crime and misery. The spirit of gambling cannot be eradicated; it ought, therefore, to be kept within due bounds. There was one great advantage in the English lottery; it was drawn but once a year, and those who purchased the tickets were content to remain quiet until their success was made known. The chances, although very distant, of so high a prize, satisfied the spirit of gambling; if they lost, they purchased again, and waited patiently for another year, trusting to be more fortunate. Now, although they gambled, they did not acquire the *habit* of gaming. What has been the consequence since the lotteries have been abolished? that there are hells of every description established throughout the metropolis, from those which admit the stake of a shilling, to Crockford's splendid Pandemonium; and those who were formerly content with a lottery ticket, now pass their evenings away from their families, and ruin themselves in a very short time. The lottery never ruined any one. The sum staked might be large for the circumstances of the parties, but it was a yearly stake, and did not interfere with the industry, the profits, or the domestic happiness of the year. One half the tradesmen who now appear in the "Gazette," have been ruined by frequenting the low hells with which the metropolis abounds. From the above considerations, I do not think it was advisable to abolish the lotteries.

The next question is one upon which I hesitate to offer an opinion; but it is worthy of consideration how far it may be advisable to license and tax gaming-houses. Were it possible to put them down altogether, the question need not be discussed; but it is impossible. Has any magistrate ventured to interfere with Crockford's, where it is well known that the highest gaming is carried on every night? Are you not permitted to walk through the club at any hour of the day? Do they not have the tables exposed to the view of every one? Yet who has interfered, although you find that the smaller hells are constantly broken in upon, and the parties had up to the police-office? Are not the laws made for all? Is that an offence in the eyes of government in a poor man which is not one in the rich? Yet this is the case: and why so? Because the rich will game, and the government cannot prevent them. Has not a man a right to do as he pleases with his own money? You legalise the worst of gambling on the Stock Exchange, for a man can there risk what he cannot pay: you cannot control the gaming of the race-course, and yet you would prevent a man from gambling after his own fashion. You wink at the higher classes ruining themselves, and you will not permit the middle classes. Now the consequence of not having licensed tables is, that you have no control over them, and the public, who will play, are the dupes of rascals who cheat in every way: whereas, if a certain number were licensed and controlled, those who play would have a better chance, and the licensed tables taxed by government would take care to put down all others who were not. We must legislate for society as it is, not as it ought to be; and, as on other points, we have found it necessary to submit to the lesser evil of the two, it is a question whether in this also we might not do better by keeping within due bounds that which it is impossible to prevent.

I was amused with an anecdote told me to-day. An Englishman and a Frenchman arrived at Spa in the same diligence. They both took up their quarters at the same hotel, but from that moment appeared to have no further intimacy.

"Do you see that fellow?" would the Englishman say, pointing at the Frenchman, "I know him, and he's a confounded rogue. I recommend you to be shy of him."

"Voyez-vous cet Anglais?" said the Frenchman as the Englishman passed by. "Gardez-vous en bien; c'est un coquin supérieur."

Thus did they continue to warn the company of each other, until the close of the season, when one fine day they both went off together in the diligence, leaving all their debts unpaid, and their trunks and portmanteaus for the benefit of the landlord of the hotel, who, on opening them, found them to contain nothing but stones and rubbish. This was a new species of holy alliance, but the *ruse* was by no means ill advised. When you hear a man constantly proclaiming the roguery of another, you are too apt to give him credit for honesty in his own person. Thus, with those whom each party associated and dealt with, they obtained a credit for honesty, which enabled them to succeed in their roguish endeavours.

Chapter Twenty

Ostend.

From Spa to Liege, from Liege to Brussels, from Brussels to Ostend, how detestable it is to go over the same ground again and again! only to be imposed upon and cheated again and again. What a weary world this is, and what a rascally one! How delightful a little honesty would be, by way of a change! Of all the rascality spread like butter on bread over the surface of the globe, certainly the butter lies thicker on the confines of each territory. There is a concentration of dishonesty at the ports of embarkation and debarkation. Take London when you land from a steam-boat, or Dover, or Calais, or Ostend. It is nothing but a system of extortion or over-reaching. And why so? because in the hurry, the confusion, the sickness, and the ignorance of what is right, everything that is wrong can be practised with impunity. These preyers upon mankind at the confines, remind you of the sharks in India, who always ply *in the surf*, where their motions cannot be seen, and the unwary are invariably their prey. I have knocked three down already, and one would imagine they would hasten for redress; but they will not, for that would take hours, and during these hours they will lose the opportunity of making their harvest, so they get up again, and pocket the affront, that they may not lose time in filling their pockets. Talking about roguery, there was a curious incident occurred some time back, in which a rascal was completely outwitted. A bachelor gentleman, who was a very superior draftsman and caricaturist, was laid up in his apartments with the gout in both feet. He could not move, but sat in an easy chair, and was wheeled by his servant in and out of his chamber to his sitting-room. Now a certain well-known vagabond ascertained the fact, and watched until the servant was sent upon a message. The servant came out of the front door, but left the area door open, communicating with the kitchen. Down went the vagabond, entered the kitchen, and walked up stairs, where, as he anticipated, he found the gentleman quite alone and helpless.

"I am sorry, sir, to see you in this situation," said the rogue; "you cannot move, and your servant is out."

The gentleman stared.

"It is excessively careless of you to leave yourself so exposed, for behold the consequences. I take the liberty of removing this watch and these seals off the table, and putting them into my own pocket; and, as I perceive your keys are here, I shall now open these drawers, and see what suits my purpose."

"Oh! pray help yourself, I beg," replied the gentleman, who was aware that he could do nothing to prevent him.

The rogue did so accordingly; he found the plate in the sideboard drawer, and many other articles which suited him, and in about ten minutes, having made up his bundle, he made the gentleman a very low bow, and decamped. But the gentleman had the use of his hands, and had not been idle; he had taken an exact likeness of the thief with his pencil, and on his servant returning soon after, he despatched him immediately to Bow Street with the drawing, and an account of what had happened. The likeness was so good, that the man was immediately identified by the runners, and was captured before he had time to dispose of a single article purloined. He was brought to the gentleman in two hours afterwards, identified, the property found on him sworn to, and, in six weeks, he was on his passage to Botany Bay.

Chapter Twenty One

London, November.

We have the signs of the times here. I peep through the fog and see quite enough to satisfy me that the prosperity is but partial. Money in plenty, but lying in heaps—not circulated. Every one hugs his bag, and is waiting to see what the event may be. Retrenchment is written up as evident as the prophetic words of fire upon the walls of Belshazzar's palace—*To let—to let—to let*. Leave London in any direction, and you find the same mystical characters every one hundred yards of the road. This beautiful villa, this cottage ornée, this capital house with pleasure-grounds, this mansion and park—all—all to let. It is said that there are upwards of seven thousand of these country seats to let within twelve miles of the metropolis. Again, look at the arms of the carriages which still roll through the streets, and you will perceive that if not with a coronet or supporters, nine out of ten have the widow's *lozenge*. And why so? because they belong to the widows of those who died in the times of plenty, and who left them large jointures upon their estates. They, of course, can still support and even better support, the expense; but the estates now yield but sufficient to pay the jointure, and the incumbent swallows up the whole. And where are the real owners of the properties? At Paris, at Naples, at Brussels, if they can afford to be in a Capital—if not, dispersed over Belgium, Switzerland, and Italy—retrenching in other countries, or living more comfortably upon their incomes. How many millions, for it does amount to millions, are now spent on the continent, enriching the people of other countries, and in all probability laying up for those countries the sinews for another war to be directed against England! How much of wretchedness and starvation has been suffered in our own country within these few years, which, if our people had not been living abroad, might never have been felt! Where are the élite of our aristocracy? Where are our country gentlemen who used to keep open house at their estates, disseminating their wealth and producing happiness? All driven abroad—society disjointed—no leader of fashion to set the example, by luxurious entertainments, of disseminating that wealth which ultimately finds its way into the greasy pocket of the labourer or mechanic. Shops opened late and closed early. Gin palaces, like hell, ever open to a customer. The pulse of London hardly beats—it is perceptible, but no more. Nothing is active but the press, and the pressure from without. But who would remain ten days in London in the month of November, when he can go away, without he had serious thoughts of suicide? Candles at high noon, yellow fogs, and torches in mid-day, do not suit me, so I'm off again to a purer atmosphere.

Chapter Twenty Two

Yesterday I fell in with two old friends, who, from a mere "truant disposition," joined perhaps with a little good will towards me, came over to Spa. As soon as their arrival had been announced, I went to them, and at their request joined their dinner. After our first greetings, B—, who not only appears, but really is, a man of fashion, in the best sense of the term, wanted his snuff-box. It was in his bed-room, and his bed-room was locked by the servant, who had taken the key and gone out. The consequence was, that B— had to wait some time, and until the man came back. I have always had a great aversion to a valet when constantly moving about on the Continent, as a single man; and, although I do not now, as I used to do when a midshipman, brush my own clothes and black my own shoes, yet I like independence, in every thing, and infinitely prefer doing anything myself, to being waited upon; for, generally speaking, it is the master who waits and not the man.

"I wonder you bother yourself with such a travelling appendage, B—," observed I, giving him a pinch of snuff to quiet his impatience. "I have never lately travelled with one."

"My dear fellow—the comfort of it—you have no idea. It would be impossible to get on without one."

"Quite impossible," observed W—, my other acquaintance.

"I have been brought up in a school in which the word impossible has been erased from the language."

"Well, but the comfort of it. When you arrive, dirty and dusty, your portmanteau opened, all your articles of dress laid out."

"I can do all that myself sooner than he can; and, as I must wait till it be done, I may as well do it myself."

"Yes, so you may, but then the security; every thing locked up, which, in a strange hotel, is so necessary."

I lock my own room, and know where to find the key when I come in.

"Very likely; but still it is impossible to travel comfortably without a valet."

"Quite impossible," rejoined W—.

"Be it so," replied I; "we differ in opinion. All I can say is, that necessary as a valet is when stationary, he is a nuisance when you travel *en garçon*."

The conversation dropped, and we sat down to dinner; the time passed away, as it always does, when old friends, who respect and like each other, meet, after an absence of some months. After dinner we smoked cigars; and, as the evening advanced, there were none left on the table. B— rang the bell for his servant to procure others; the servant had gone out and was no where to be found, and for *security* had locked the bed-room door and taken the key with him. So we drank our claret, and waited for his return. "Thinks I to myself"—but I said nothing. At last, we waited till past twelve o'clock; but the gentleman's gentleman was no where to be found. B— was angry with the man, W— had thrown himself on the sofa. He wished to go to bed after a long day's travel; but his key was also, for security, in the valet's pocket, who had been searched for every where without success. B— begged me not to remain out of politeness; but I did remain not out of politeness, but of *"malice,"* as the French term it. "I had too much pleasure in their company to think of leaving them;" and we continued to sip brandy-and-water. At last, three o'clock came, B— was out of all patience, W— snoring on the sofa, and I, quite delighted. The sun should have poured his beams upon us before I would have gone away. The bell was rung, but in vain, for the waiters would wait no longer. It was proposed to send for a menuisier to pick the lock; but how was one to be found at three o'clock in the morning? At last the valet, drunk and reeling in his morning jacket, entered the room. "The keys the keys!" demanded B— in wrath.

"The key!" roared W—, who had woke up.

"I have them," replied the valet, with a most knowing leer, facetiously smiling. "I have them—all safe—all right, gentlemen. Here they are," continued the man, pulling them out, and presenting them as if he had done a very clever thing. "Here they are, you see."

The man was too tipsy to be expostulated with, and the gentlemen took their keys in silence. "And now," said I, "gentlemen, I wish you a very good night. You have fully established the extreme *comfort* of a travelling valet, and the impossibility of doing without one." It was a glorious victory, although to get *out* of the house I had to open a window and leap from it, and to get *into* my own house at that hour was even more difficult.

Chapter Twenty Three

I have been reading Jesse's "Gleanings." Is he quite correct? I have my doubts. In one point I certainly do not agree with him, in his favourite opinion of cats. I do, however, know an instance of misplaced affection in a cat, which, although it does not add to the moral character of the race, is extremely curious for more reasons than one, and as it happened in my own family, I can vouch for its authenticity. A little black spaniel had five puppies, which were considered too many for her to bring up. As, however, the breed was much in request, her mistress was unwilling that any of them should be destroyed, and she asked the cook whether she thought it would be possible to bring a portion of them up by hand before the kitchen fire. In reply, the cook observed that the cat had that day kittened, and that, perhaps, the puppies might be substituted for her progeny. The experiment was made, two of the kittens were removed, and two puppies substituted. The cat made no objections, took to them kindly, and gradually all the kittens were taken away, and the cat nursed the two puppies only. Now, the first curious fact was, that the two puppies nursed by the cat were, in a fortnight, as active, forward, and playful, as kittens would have been: they had the use of their legs, barked, and gambolled about; while the other three, nursed by the mother, were whining and rolling about like fat slugs. The cat gave them her tail to play with, and they were always in motion; they very soon ate meat, and long before the others they were fit to be removed. This was done, and the cat became very inconsolable. She prowled about the house, and on the second day of tribulation fell in with the little spaniel, who was nursing the other three puppies.

"O ho!" says Puss, putting up her back, "it is you who have stolen my children."

"No," replied the Spaniel, with a snarl, "they are my own flesh and blood."

"That won't do," said the cat, "I'll take my oath before any justice of peace that you have my two puppies."

Thereupon issue was joined, that is to say, there was a desperate combat, which ended in the defeat of the spaniel, and the cat walking proudly off with one of the puppies, which she took to her own bed. Having deposited this one, she returned, fought again, gained another victory, and redeemed another puppy. Now it is very singular that she should have only taken two, the exact number she had been deprived of. Does this not prove to a certain extent the power of calculating numbers in animals? and does not the precocity of the two puppies brought up by the cat, infer there is some grounds for the supposition that with the milk is imbued much of the nature and disposition of the mother? A few experiments made on these points would be interesting, and we should have a new science, that of *lacteology*, to add to craniology, in our nurture and rearing of the species.

This reminds me of a singular fact, little known. The Burmahs, who are disciples of Gaudma, equally with the inhabitants of Pegu and Syriam, whose country they have conquered, worship the White Elephant, who is considered as a god. There have been but three white elephants since the foundation of the Burmah dynasty by Alompraa. The first one is dead, and I have one of his teeth carved with figures, which was consecrated to the great Dagon Pagoda. The second now *reigns*—he is attended by hundreds, wears a howdah, or cloth, studded with precious stones; which is said to be worth a million of money. He also wears his bangles or armlets on each leg, and fares sumptuously every day. White elephants are very scarce; the colour is occasioned by a disease in the animal, a species of leprosy. Any elephant hunter in these countries, who is fortunate enough to capture a white elephant, is immediately created a noble, and advanced to high honour and wealth. The third white elephant, of which I am about to speak particularly, and who may be considered as the heir apparent, was taken a few months previous to our declaring war against the Burmahs. He was very young; his mother had been killed, and he yet required partial nourishment. He was brought to Rangoon, established in one of the best houses in the place, and an edict was sent forth from the capital, ordering that twenty-four of the most healthy young married women should be dedicated to his wants, and if they fell off in powers of nourishment, be replaced by others. This was considered an honour—for were they not nursing a *God*? Major Canning, the political agent, who went to see this curious spectacle, described it to me as follows: "The animal was not above three feet and a few inches high, its colour was a dirty grey, rather than white; it was very healthy, playful, and in good spirits. When I went into the room, which was very spacious, and built of teak-wood, the twenty-four nurses were sitting or lying on mats about the room, some playing at draughts and other games, others working. The elephant walking about, looking at them, and what they were doing, as if he understood all about it. After a short time, the little deity felt hungry, and, with his trunk he pushed some of the women, but to annoy him they would not yield to his solicitations. When he became angry, and was too rough for them, they submitted, and he put his trunk round their waists in the most affectionate manner, while he was supplying himself." I did not see the animal myself, as immediately that they heard of our arrival at the mouth of the river, they despatched him under a strong guard to a place of security. But I should like to ascertain hereafter, whether his nurture made him a more reasonable being than are elephants in general.

How one's thoughts fly away over time and space! What a rush of incidents crowd into my memory, merely from having mentioned this circumstance of the white elephant. I did once intend to have written a narrative of what passed during our sojourn in that country, for I saw more of the inhabitants than most people; but others have forestalled me, and it is now too late. Nevertheless, it will perhaps amuse the reader, if, without entering into the military details, I mention a few of the operations and scenes which then occurred. It shall be so then, and we will discourse a little about the Burmahs.

An Armenian merchant who resided there told me a story one day which was curious. The King of Pegu was possessed of the most splendid ruby in the world, both as to size and colour. This was well known; it was the boast of the nation. When the Burmahs subdued the kingdom of Pegu, the old king with all his family were taken prisoners, vast treasure was also captured, but the great ruby was not to be found, notwithstanding the torture and beheading of thousands. With the usual barbarity of these countries, the old king, a miserable paralytic little man, was stripped naked and confined in an iron cage, which I saw when I was at Rangoon. In this confinement he lived for ten or twelve years, every festival day being brought out and exposed to the derision of the populace. At last he died, and his body was thrown out to be devoured by the dogs and birds of prey. One of the soldiers who assisted to drag the body out of the cage, turned it over with his foot, and perceived that his right hand grasped a hump of *damma*, (a sort of pitch,) which curiosity induced the Burmah to force out with the point of his spear. This had been observed before, but the Burmahs, who are very superstitions and carry about them all sorts of charms, imagined it to be a charm for his paralysis or palsy with which he was afflicted, and therefore had allowed him to retain it. But when the Burmah took it up, the weight of it convinced him that it was not all damma: he examined it, and found that it was the great ruby of the Pegu kingdom which had been lost, and which the old man had for so many years, in a state of nudity and incarceration, held in his left hand. I asked one of the Burmah chiefs whether this ruby now in the possession of the King of Ava was so fine as represented: his answer was in truly Eastern hyperbole—"Dip it in the Irrawaddy," said he, (that is, an enormous river seven hundred miles long and in many parts several miles broad,) "and the whole water will turn to blood."

I have said that the Burmahs are very superstitious: they have a great variety of charms which they wear about their persons, but there is one custom of theirs which is very singular. They polish rubies; that is, without cutting them in *facettes*, but merely the stone, whatever its primitive shape, is rubbed down on every side until it is perfectly smooth. They then make an incision in the flesh, generally the arm or leg, put in the ruby and allow the skin to heal over it, so that the stone remains there. Soldiers and sailors in search of plunder will find out any thing, and this practice of the Burmahs was soon discovered; and after the assault and carrying of a stockade, you would see the men passing their hands over the bodies, and immediately they felt a rising in the limb, out with their knives and cut in for the rubies. Indeed, the plunder was more considerable than might be imagined, for every Burmah carried all his wealth about his person.

Another singular custom arising from their superstition prevails among this people. The king has a corps denominated *Invulnerables*, whose ranks are filled up in this manner:— when a criminal is condemned to death for certain offences, such as robbery, he is permitted to challenge as an *invulnerable*. This is proved by his standing at a certain distance from several men who fire at him with ball. Should he not be wounded or killed, he is pronounced an invulnerable and enrolled in the corps. In every stockade we attacked, there were always one or two of these men, and they really appeared to believe in their own powers. They generally stood above the timbers of the stockade, dancing and capering as the boats advanced, and continued their extravagance amidst a shower of bullets, exposing their persons in a most undaunted manner. There was one fellow who, dressed in a short red jacket, and nothing else except the cloth round his loins, who was well known to our men; they called him *Happy Jack*, from the capers which he used to cut, and somehow or another it was his good fortune never to be hit, at least, not that we know of, for taking stockade after stockade, at every fresh attack there was Happy Jack to be seen capering and shouting as usual, and never ceasing to expose himself until the troops had landed and were about to scale the fortress. It was quite amusing to hear the men shout out with laughter, "By heavens, there's Happy Jack again." I hope he is alive at this moment; at all events, he deserves to be.

Chapter Twenty Four

Spa.

Yes, now Spa is agreeable: we have no *redoubte* open with fools losing their money, no English *passants* looking after amusement, no valetudinarians drinking the *poupon*, no Spa boxes crowding every window: we are now as a Spa should be, a *coterie* of houses in a ravine, surrounded by the mountains of the Ardennes, crowding and shoving up together in mutual protection against the deep snow and the forest wolves. There is something new in this: most of the houses are shut up; the shop-windows are all bare; the snow is two feet deep in the streets; the mountains on every side are white; the icicles hang upon the leafless boughs, and the rivulets are enchained. All is one drear blank; and except the two-horse diligence which heaves slowly in sight three or four hours past its time, and the post, (which is now delivered at nine o'clock instead of noon); there is no such thing as an arrival: the boys slide upon their little sledges down the hills; the cattle are driven home; the church clock strikes; and unless we are enlivened by the crowd assembled round the countryman, who appears with the carcass of a wolf which he has been fortunate enough to kill, we are all quiet, monotony and peace: in fact, Spa, now that it is a desert, has become to me, at least agreeable.

They say, this hard winter promises plenty of wolves; if so, I recommend those who are fond of excitement come here. Indeed, it will be profitable, for if they are active huntsmen, they can pay their expenses. A dead horse costs little, and in Spa, as they give very little to the horses to eat in summer, and nothing at all in the winter, they die fast. You have only to drag the carcass to an outhouse at a little distance from the town, and with your rifle watch during the night. The wolves will come down to prey upon the carrion, and it is hard if you do not kill your couple during the night, and then you are rewarded by the commune. I do not know what the price is now, but when the King of Holland was in possession of Belgium it was one hundred francs for a male, and three hundred francs for a female wolf. Now a brace a night, four hundred francs, or sixteen pounds, is not a bad night's earning: in Spa it would keep a half-pay officer for three months. There is a curious story here, proving the sagacity of a wolf which came down an hour before dusk into the town, and made off with a child of two years old in her mouth. The cry was raised, and the pursuit immediate. After following her track for many miles, she gained upon them, it became quite dark, and the people returned homewards, melancholy at the fate of the poor child. When they were about half way back, they heard the wail of an infant, and, guided by it, they arrived at a thick bush, where they found the child alive and unhurt. The wolf, finding that her pursuers gained upon her, had deposited the child there, intending to return and make a meal of it upon a more favourable opportunity.

We have had nothing to excite us within these last few days but the death and burial of an old curate. He died in all the odour of sanctity three days ago, and was buried yesterday. He was not loved or even liked, for he wanted that greatest of all gifts—charity. His situation was worth, with offerings, six thousand francs a year,—a large sum in this country: but he did not give to the poor; he exacted from them, and they religiously obeyed him, no one killing a pig or anything else without a present of part of it to the curate. When the old man was told that he could not live, the ruling passion still governed him. He sent for a person to dispose of for him the sundry pieces of pork which he had gathered as presents, then took the extreme unction, and died. His will is not known, but he is supposed to be very rich, and whether he leaves his wealth to some nephews, or to support a hospital here which is at present without funds, is a question of some interest. He was buried in great parade and procession, followed by hundreds holding candles. He was dressed in his best, and every one said that he never looked so clean or so well in his life. He was carried on an open *brancard*, with his canonical hat on his head, the snow fell fast and settled on his face and clothes, but he felt it not. The funeral was as cold as his charity, the thermometer being exactly 130 below the freezing point. Except the procession of the dead curate and of a dead wolf, we have had nothing to interest us for the last ten days.

But I promised to talk about the Burmahs. There have been two or three accounts of the military movements, but there has been no inquiry or examination into the character of the people, which, in my opinion, is of more importance than is generally supposed; for although the East India Company may imagine that they have done with the Burmahs, it is my conviction that the Burmahs have not done with them, and even I may live to witness the truth of my assertion.

It certainly is a point of some interest to ascertain from whence the Burmah nation originally came: that they are not aborigines, I think most certain. They are surrounded by the Cochin Chinese, the Chinese, and the Hindoos, all races of inferior stature and effeminate in person, with little or no beard. Now the Burmahs are a very powerful race, very muscular in their limbs, possessing great strength and energy: generally speaking, I should say, that they are rather taller than Europeans. They have the high cheek bones of the Tatar, but not the small eyes; they have strong hair and beards, and certainly would remind you of a cross between the Jew and the Tatar. This is singular; and it gave the idea to some of those who are fond of indulging in theory, that they might be the remnants of that portion of the Jews who, when permitted to leave Babylon, instead of going east with the others, bent their course to the westward and were never spoken of afterwards. But the only props they had to this argument were the appearance of the people, the weight in silver being called the *tekel* or shekel, and the great pagoda having the name of the *Dagon* pagoda. At least I heard of no more to support the argument but those three, which can hardly be sufficient, although the coincidence of the two words is singular.

The Burmahs are semi-barbarous: but this term must be used in the most favourable light; because, surrounded on every side by people who are wedded to their own customs, the Burmahs have a liberality and a desire to improve, which is very remarkable. I never met with any Burmah, not even a lad, who could not read and write; they allow any form of religion to be made use of, and churches of any description to be built by foreigners, but they do not like missionaries making converts of their own people; for as the king is the head of the religion, conversion is a breach of allegiance. One of the missionaries had an audience with the king, and demanded permission to make proselytes. The king replied that the missionary might convert as many as he pleased, but that he would cut all their heads off afterwards. The missionary had not much trouble, when this answer was made known, in counting the heads of his proselytes. In their own religion, which is Budhism, the Burmahs appear to be very relax; it is too absurd for the energy of their minds. Those who enter the priesthood wear a yellow dress; but if a priest at any time feels disposed to quit his profession, he is at liberty so to do. All he has to do is to throw off his yellow garment; but at the same time he can never resume it. The Burmahs are superstitious about charms, but are not superstitious on religious points. In fact, there is very little religion among them, and had we, at the close of the war, instead of demanding a crore of rupees, insisted that they should embrace Christianity, the king would have given the order, and the whole nation would have nominally been Christians. I once asked a Burmah soldier what was his idea of a future state. His idea of bliss was singular—"I shall be turned into a buffalo, and shall lie down in a meadow of grass higher than my head, and eat all day long, and there won't be a single mosquito to annoy me." While on the subject of religion, I may here observe, that at the capture of Rangoon I entered a Chinese temple, the altar-piece, if I may use the term, was the

Ganesa of the Hindoos, but not seated on the lotus leaf, but on the Chinese rat. On each side of this were two little candelabras, formed of the Egyptian ibis, holding the oil cups in its beak. I also found the Hounyman, or monkey god of the Hindoos, and Budhist figures. I once observed some sepoys playing and laughing at a bronze image they had picked up at the pagoda of Syriam, and on examining it, I was surprised to find that it was a figure of the Egyptian Isis, with her hand raised, and her person in the position described as the correct one when blessing the world. The art of embalming appears to be known to the Burmahs, and is occasionally practised by the priests. At the capture of the old Portuguese fort at Syriam, I found, not far from it, a sort of canopied shed, decorated with carving, cut paper, and tinsel, and supported by four pillars, like a bedstead. Below lay the body of a priest, embalmed and gilt. I intended to have brought this home, but before I arrived there, I found one of my marines, a graceless dog without religion or any other good quality, very busy hammering the mummy to pieces with the butt end of his musket. I was very angry, and ordered him to desist. In excuse, he replied that it was an abominable molten image, and it was his duty, as a *good Christian*, to destroy it—the only evidence of Christianity ever witnessed on that fellow's part. On examination, I found that the body had been wrapped in sundry clothes, and, like the ark of Noah, pitched within and without: over the clothes was a coat of damma, then of chunam, and lastly it was gilt; the head of the mummy was fictitious, and formed of a cocoa-nut, the real skull being where, in the mummy, would have appeared to have been the breast of the body. It did not smell much, but there were a great many small scarabei inside, and it was so mutilated that I did not remove it. The Burmahs are cleanly in their houses, which generally are raised from the ground a few feet, so as to allow the pigs; which are the scavengers of the town, to walk under. They have houses of brick, or stone and mortar, such as the custom-house at Rangoon, and one or two others; but the most substantial houses are usually built of thick teak plank. The smaller houses and cottages are built of bamboo, the floors and walls being woven like wicker-work: the cleanliness and the beauty of these houses when new are very remarkable, and what is still more so, the rapidity with which they are built. I have known an officer order a house to be built of three rooms, with doors and windows to each, and of a comfortable size, and three or four Burmahs will complete this house in a day, and thatch the roof over. In another point, the Burmahs show a degree of civilisation, which might be an example to the northern Athens—to every house there is a very neat and clean cloaca.

The government, like all in Asia, is most despotic; and the people have the faults which are certain to be generated by despotism—but not to that degree which might be expected. They have their hereditary nobility, and the orders of it are very clearly defined. They consist of gold chains, worn round the neck, with four plates or chased bosses dividing them; the lowest order wears the bosses linked together by three chains, the next highest in degree with six, the next nine, and the last and highest order has twelve; the king only wears twenty-four chains. The use of gold and silver, as drinking cups, etcetera, is only permitted to the nobility. They are very clever in chasing of metals, and they have a description of work in glass and enamel, quite their own, with which they decorate the temples, houses of the priests, and coffers containing the sacred volumes. Their ornamental writings in the Pali language, a variety of the Sanscrit, known only to the priests, are also very beautiful—especially that upon long leaves of ivory. Upon the whole, their manufactures are superior to all around them, except perhaps the Chinese.

The women are small, and delicately formed, in proportion to the men; they are not shut up, but go where they please; their dress is becoming; they braid the hair with flowers, and they are much fairer than would be supposed. Those who keep much within doors are nearly as white as Europeans. They have a singular custom of putting a patch of white chunam on the cheek bone, something in opposition to the black patches which used formerly to be worn by our belles; and it is intended to show how near they approach to white. Indeed, when the men of the lower class, who are exposed all day to the sun, remove their garments, it is singular to witness how many shades lighter they are in that part of their bodies which is covered up. Usually, the men have but one wife, but occasionally there are supernumeraries.

The laws of the Burmahs appear to be good, but, as in all despotic countries, they are not acted upon, unless it please the ruler. Slavery of a certain species is allowed. Should one man be in debt to another, and is summoned before the chief; if he states his inability to pay, he is asked how many children he has, and according to the debt, so are his children given in bond slavery to his debtor, who writes off a certain sum every year until they are free. If he has no children, his wife, or himself perhaps, will be bonded in the same manner. But in this case, where ill-treatment can be proved, the bondage will be removed; and further, any person so bonded, may at his or her wish remove to the service of another master, provided they can find one who will pay to the debtor the amount still due, and thus finish the time of servitude under one whom they like better. These bonds are all in writing, and must be produced. Some of our military officers released several of the young women from their slavery.

Sitting down in your presence, is, among the Burmese, a mark of respect. Every poor man who is sent for, immediately drops down on his hams in the corner of the room, or at the portal. The use of the cocoa, or betel nut, is universal among the men, but not so common with the women until they grow old. The consequence is, that the teeth of the men are quite black and decayed, while those of the young women are very good.

The most remarkable feature in the character of the Burmahs is their *good temper*; I think they are the most even-tempered race, ever met with. They are always gay, always content under any privation. I had, as will be seen hereafter, more opportunities of seeing into the character of this people than others had, for we mixed with them in amity for some weeks. They are very fond of marionettes, and puppet playing, and are very amusing mimics. They work very hard, and with the greatest cheerfulness. They have a high respect for the English, or the white faces, as they call us; and the superiority of our warlike instruments, and our ships, *was* a subject of wonder, and, at the same time, of most careful examination. They perceive how far they are behind us, and are most anxious to improve. From this reason, joined to others, it was a pity that we ever made war with the Burmahs; they had made an easy conquest of those around them, and were satisfied with their supposed superiority, but now they are not, for they are active and enterprising, fond of war, and will not be content until they have improved their system. Twenty years hence we shall find the Burmahs a much more formidable nation than they are at present, for they have every quality necessary to become the first nation in the East: indeed, when we consider with what weapons they defended themselves, and the nature of the warfare, it is not a little to their credit that they held out for nearly three years against the power of Great Britain.

Chapter Twenty Five

February, 1836.

The Burmahs are decidedly a brave nation: the government being despotic, their rulers are cruel, but the people are not. I state this, as cowardice and cruelty usually go hand in hand. Good temper and generosity are the prominent features in their character—excellent materials to work upon in judicious hands. I witnessed acts of courage at the early part of the war, before the Burmahs found out how impossible it was to cope with our superior arms, which were most surprising, and which excited our admiration. They are peculiarly a warlike nation; indeed, they are fond of war. Every man is a soldier, and when ordered out to join the ranks, obeys without receiving any pay, providing his own arms. This fact, at once, establishes that they are inclined to war. Their aims generally consist of a double-handed sword, a weapon of great force, and very large spears; but every one will possess a musket if he can, and if it has not a lock, he will fire it with a match. It is in this point that the Burmahs are so deficient in aims: we used to consider it a very courageous act to venture to fire off a Burmese musket, they were in such a wretched condition: and to crown all, every man *makes his own gunpowder*. Now it may be easily imagined what stuff this must be; as, previous to an expected combat, each Burmah sits down and composes the article to the best of his knowledge and belief. The consequences are, that when these muskets do go off (and it is ten to one they do not), it is again ten to one that the bullet falls short, from the inefficacy of the powder. There is another singular fact, and one which proves that they have been used to muskets but a short time: it is, that they have no bullet-moulds or leaden bullets. All their bullets are of iron, hammered as round as they can hammer them at the forge; of course the windage produced by this imperfect shape, occasions it to deviate much from its intended direction.

The guns on their stockades and war-boats are equally defective from bad powder, and the hammered iron bullets. It is difficult to know where they could have collected such a curious assemblage. Sometimes you will fall in with a small brass piece of exquisite Spanish manufacture, at others you will find them of the strangest forms that can be conceived. I rather think they were purchased, or taken as a part of the duties on vessels trading to Rangoon. I recollect once at the first taking of a stockade, we knocked off the trunnions of an old iron gun, and left it there as useless. The Burmahs reoccupied the stockade, and we had to take it a second time, when we found that they had most ingeniously supplied the want of trunnions with iron hoops and rivets, and the gun was fired at us before we entered. At another time, we entered a stockade which had kept up a brisk fire for a few minutes, and to our surprise found that they had made *wooden* guns, very well bound and braced with iron hoops. Of course these guns would not fire more than two or three shots each, as the touch-holes became inflamed, and were soon so large as to render the guns unserviceable; but I mention these points, to prove the perseverance of these people, and the efforts they made in their own defence. After the first campaign it is true that they deserted, and the levies were made by force; but the reason of this, for I inquired into it, was not that they had any objection to fight, but that, fighting without pay, they wanted to go home and put the seed into the ground, as otherwise their wives and families would starve.

The Burmah war-boats are very splendid craft, pulling from eighty to one hundred oars; the Burmahs manage them very dexterously, and will pull them from seven to eight miles an hour. They have a war-boat dedicated to the Deity, which brought intelligence that saved the nation at the time of the war with the empire of Pegu, in a space of time so short, as almost to appear incredible.

As I before observed, the gun mounted on the boat's bow is of little effect, but their spears are really formidable. At a night attack upon some of our vessels, anchored off a stockade which they wanted to regain, I had an evidence of the force with which they are thrown. The sides of the vessels were covered with them, sticking out like porcupine's quills, and they had entered the plank with such force, that it required a very strong arm to pull them out again. We lost some men by them; the effect of a hundred spears hurtling through the air at the same time was singularly appalling to our men, who were not accustomed the sound, especially during the night. I heard several of the sailors observe afterwards that they "did not like that at all," and I am sure they would have infinitely preferred to have been met with fire-arms. Some of these spears were sixteen feet long, with an iron head, sharp at both sides, weighing from twelve to fourteen pounds. I have seen bows and arrows in the possession of the Burmahs, but never have observed that they used them in their conflicts with us. They appeared to despise them. The system of warfare and defence pursued by these people, is undoubtedly excellent for the peculiarities of the country. Their stockades are usually built of any thick teak timber, or rather squared trees, which are much too strong to be penetrated by any other than battering cannon, and, in consequence, were invariably carried by escalade. Some of them are built of bamboos, running from a foot to two feet in diameter. These are equally strong, with the peculiarity that if you fire cannon at them the bamboos yield, admit the shot, and then close again. If these stockades are not close to the river side, they usually have a deep ditch round them, and are further protected by what was more serious to us than the escalading, which were abbatis of pointed bamboos, stuck in a slanting direction in the ground. The slight wounds made by these bamboos brought on lock-jaw, and too often terminated fatally. In the attacks upon us at Rangoon they made their approaches with some degree of military skill, throwing up trenches as they advanced. Their fire-rafts on such a rapid river were also formidable. They have wells of petroleum up the country: their rafts were very large, and on them, here and there, were placed old canoes filled with this inflammable matter. When on fire, it blazed as high as our maintop, throwing out flames, heat, and stink quite enough to drive any one away.

I have mentioned their mode of warfare and their deficiencies, to prove that if the Burmahs had been as well provided with every species of arms equal to our own, the country would not have been so soon subjugated as it was. Their system of defence was good, their bravery was undoubted, but they had no effective weapons. I strongly suspect that they will, now that they have been taught their inferiority, use every means to obtain them; and if so, they will really become a formidable nation. As one proof of their courage, I will mention, that at every stockade there is a look-out man, perched on a sort of pole, about ten feet or more clear of the upper part of the stockade, in a situation completely exposed. I have often observed these men, and it was not till the cannonade had fairly commenced on both sides, that they came down, and when they did, it was without hurry; indeed, I may say, in a most leisurely and indifferent manner. Of their invulnerables and their antics I have already spoken.

In countries governed despotically, life is not so much valued as it is in others. The very knowledge that it may be taken in a moment at the will of the rulers, renders even the cowardly comparatively indifferent. Having been accustomed from our earliest years to anticipate an event, when it actually arrives we meet it with composure and indifference. The lad in England who is brought up to thieving, and who is continually reminded by his parents, that he *must be hung* before he is twenty goes to the gallows when his turn comes with much *sang froid*. So it is in a despotic country, where the people witness the heads of their companions roll on the ground, and surmise how soon their own turn will come. I had more than one evidence of this during my stay. In one instance I wished to obtain information from a prisoner, but could extract none. He had been sitting between the carronades on deck for twenty-four hours, and some of the men or officers had given him a bowl of grog and a couple of cigars, with which he was busy when I interrogated him. As he professed ignorance, I told him that if he would not give me the desired information, I should take his head off; and I sent for the serjeant of marines, who appeared with two of his party, and with his drawn sword. We called him out from between the guns, but he begged through the interpreter to be allowed to finish his grog, to which I consented: when that was done, he was again ordered out, but requested leave to finish about an inch of cigar which remained in his mouth. To which I also acceded, not being in a particular hurry to do that which I never intended to do. During all this the man was perfectly composed, and did not show the least alarm at his approaching fate. As soon as the cigar was finished, he bound his long hair up afresh, and made preparation. I again asked him if he would tell, but he pleaded ignorance, and stepped forward, went down on his knees and took off the cloth from about his loins, which he spread on the deck to receive his head, and then putting his hands on the deck, held it in the position to be cut off. Not a muscle trembled, for I watched the man carefully. He was, of course, remanded, and the sailors were so pleased with him, that he went on shore with more grog and more tobacco than he had probably ever seen in his life.

The Burmahs have, however, a means of extracting information from spies, etcetera, which I never saw practised by them, although it was borrowed from them by us. It was in our own quarter-master-general's office that I witnessed this species of torture, so simple in its operation, and apparently so dreadful in its effects. It consists in giving one single blow upon the region of the heart, so as to stop for some seconds the whole circulation. The way by which this is effected is as follows:— the man— the Burmahs are generally naked to the waist—is made to sit down on the floor; another man stands behind him, and leaning over him, takes a very exact aim with his sharp bent elbow at the precise spot over his heart, and then strikes a blow which, from its being propelled so very mechanically, descends with increased force.

The effect appears dreadful; the dark hue of the sufferer's face turns to a deadly white; the perspiration bursts out from his forehead, and he trembles in every limb. I never witnessed such apparent agony. These blows repeated three or four times, will unman the most resolute, and they will call for death as a favour.

There is one point which must not be overlooked by the Indian government, and which, connected with what I have already mentioned, makes the Burmese nation more formidable; it is, the great contempt they have for the sepoys. And what is equally true, the fears which the sepoys have of them. The Burmahs are only afraid of the white faces, as I shall very soon establish. They despise the sepoys, although they are so well armed. Now, that the sepoys are good troops, there can be no doubt; they have proved it often; but, at the same time, they are not, as some of the Indian officers have asserted in my presence, the best troops in the world, and preferable to Europeans. That they are much easier to control, and that they excel in discipline, I grant, because they are never intoxicated; but they have, in the first place, very little stamina, and are, generally speaking, a small and very effeminately built race. Still they have fought well—very well; but they never fought well against the Burmahs; and for this simple reason,—that superstition is more powerful than courage, and subdues it. The sepoys are very superstitious, and had the idea, which was never eradicated, that the Burmahs were *charmed men*, and they never went out against them willingly, even when they were headed by the English troops. As for the Burmahs' contempt of them, it was notorious. I have myself seen one of the Burmah prisoners at Rangoon lift up a piece of timber that six of the sepoys could hardly have moved, and throw it down, so as to make it roll at the feet of the sepoy guard who watched him, making them all retreat several paces, and then laugh at them in derision. But we had many more decisive proofs. The Burmahs had stockaded themselves about seven miles from Rangoon, and it was determined to dislodge them. Colonel S—, who was very partial to the native troops, was ordered on this service, and he requested particularly that he might have no troops but the sepoys. Sir A Campbell did not much like to consent, but, as the stockades were not higher than breastworks, and the Burmahs not in very great force, he eventually yielded to the Colonel's arguments. Fifteen hundred sepoys were ordered out, and the Colonel went on his expedition. The Burmahs had good intelligence that there were no European troops, and when the sepoys arrived, they did not wait to be attacked, but attacked the sepoys, and put them completely to the rout. One half of the sepoys were said to be killed; the others came back to Rangoon in parties of ten or twelve, and in the utmost consternation and confusion. Sir A Campbell was, of course, much annoyed, and the next day a European force was despatched against the Burmahs. On their arrival they witnessed a dreadful and disgusting scene. A long avenue had been cut in the wood, and on each side of it were hung by the heels, at equal distances, shockingly mutilated, the naked bodies of the seven hundred and fifty sepoys killed. The Burmahs did not, however, attempt to resist the European force, but after a few shots made their retreat. Now, this is a very important fact: and it is a fact which cannot be denied, although it has not been made known. In India there is a nominal force of three hundred thousand men; but they are scattered over such a vast extent of territory, that, allowing they could be made disposable, which they could not, it would require many months before they could be collected, and if the Burmahs despise the sepoys, and the sepoys dread the Burmahs, the only check against the latter will be the European troops; and of them how many can be called out. Not ten thousand, at the very utmost; and the difficulty of collecting them was well known at the commencement of the Burmah war. There certainly is a great difference between attacking others in their own territories, and defending ourselves; but if the Burmahs could hold out against us, as they did, for nearly three years, without arms to cope with us, what might be the consequence if they were supplied with arms and officers by any other nation? We have now a footing in the country, and it must be our object to prevent the ingress of any other, and to keep the Burmahs as quiet and as peaceable as we can. But our very intercourse will enlighten them by degrees, and we have more to dread from that quarter than from all the hordes of Russia or Runjeet Sing, and the whole disaffection of India.

As I have more to say relative to the Burmahs, I will, in my next chapter, enter into a short narrative of the expedition to Bassein. It was a bloodless one, although very important in its results: and circumstances occurred in it which will throw much light upon the character of the nation.

Chapter Twenty Six

It was not until many months after the war had been carried on, that Sir Archibald Campbell found himself in a position to penetrate into the heart of the Burmah territory, and attempt the capital. He wanted almost every thing, and among the rest reinforcements of men; for the rainy season had swept them off by thousands. At last, when determined to make the attempt, he did it with a most inadequate force; so small that, had the Burmahs thought of even trenching up and barricading the roads at every half mile, he must have been compelled, without firing a shot, to have retreated. Fortunately, he had an accession of men-of-war, and his river detachment was stronger than he could have hoped for. I do not pretend to state the total force which was embarked on the river or that which proceeded by hand, communicating with each other when circumstances permitted, as the major part of the provisions of the army were, I believe, carried up by water. The united river force was commanded by Brigadier Cotton, Captain Alexander, and Captain Chads; the land forces, of course, by Sir A Campbell, who had excellent officers with him, but whose tactics were of no use in this warfare of morass, mud, and jungle.

It will be proper to explain why it was considered necessary to detach a part of the forces to Bassein. The Rangoon river joins the Irrawaddy on the left, about one hundred and seventy miles from its flowing into the ocean. On the right of the Irrawaddy is the river of Bassein, the mouth of it about one hundred and fifty miles from that of the Irrawaddy, and running up the country in an angle towards it until it joins it about four hundred miles up in the interior. The two rivers thus enclose a large delta of land, which is the most fertile and best peopled of the Burmah provinces, and it was from this delta that Bundoola, the Burmah general, received all his supplies of men. Bundoola was in the strong fortress of Donabue, on the Bassein side of the river, about half way between where the Rangoon river joined it on the left, and the Bassein river communicated with it a long way farther up on the right. Sir A Campbell's land forces were on the left of the river, so that Bundoola's communication with the Bassein territory was quite open; and as the river forces had to attack Donabue on their way up, the force sent to Bassein, was to take him in the rear and cut off his supplies. This was a most judicious plan of the General's, as will be proved in the sequel. Major S—, with four or five hundred men in three transports, the Larne, and the Mercury, Hon. Company's brig, were ordered upon this expedition, which sailed at the same time that the army began to march and the boats to ascend the river.

On the arrival at the mouth of the river we found the entrance most formidable in appearance, there being a dozen or more stockades of great extent; but there were but two manned, the guns of the others, as well as the men, having been forwarded to Donabue, the Burmahs not imagining, as we had so long left that part of their territory unmolested, that we should have attempted it. Our passage was therefore easy; after a few broadsides, we landed and spiked the guns, and then, with a fair wind, ran about seventy miles up one of the most picturesque and finest rivers I was ever in. Occasionally the right lines of stockades presented themselves, but we found nobody in them, and passed by them in peace. But the river now became more intricate, and the pilots, as usual, knew nothing about it. It was, however, of little consequence; the river was deep even at its banks, over which the forest trees threw their boughs in wild luxuriance. The wind was now down the river, and we were two or three days before we arrived at Bassein, during which we tided and warped how we could, while Major S— grumbled. If the reader wishes to know why Major S— grumbled, I will tell him—because there was no fighting. He grumbled when we passed the stockades at the entrance of the river because they were not manned; and he grumbled at every dismantled stockade that we passed. But there was no pleasing S—; if he was in hard action and not wounded, he grumbled; if he received a slight wound, he grumbled because it was not a severe one; if a severe one, he grumbled because he was not able to fight the next day. He had been nearly cut to pieces in many actions, but he was not content. Like the man under punishment, the drummer might strike high or strike low, there was no pleasing S—: nothing but the *coup de grace*, if he be now alive, will satisfy him. But notwithstanding this mania for being carved, he was an excellent and judicious officer. I have been told he is since dead; if so, his Majesty has lost one of the most devoted and chivalric officers in his service, to whom might most justly be applied the words of Hotspur, — "But if it be a sin to covet honour, I am the most offending soul alive." (See note 1.)

As I before observed, the branches of the trees hung over the sides of the river, and a circumstance occurred which was a source of great amusement. We had a little monkey, who had been some time on board, and was a favourite, as usual, of the ship's company. The baffling winds very often threw us against the banks of the river, near which there was plenty of water; and when this was the case, the boughs of the trees were interlaced with the rigging of the ship. This unusual embracing between nature and art gave Jacko the idea of old times when he frolicked in the woods, and unable to resist the force of early associations, he stepped from the top-sail yard to the branch of a large tree, and when the ship had hauled off clear, we found that Jacko had deserted. We lamented it, and ten minutes afterwards, thinking no more about him, we continued our course up the river. About an hour had elapsed, during which we had gained upwards of a mile, when again nearing the bank on that side, we heard a loud chattering and screaming. "That's Jacko, sir," said one of the men, and others expressed the same opinion. We manned the jolly-boat, and sent it on shore towards the place where the noise was heard. The monkey did not wait till the bow of the boat touched the shore, but springing into it when some feet off, he took his seat very deliberately on the stern, and was pulled on board, where immediately he flew up the side, caressing every one he met. The fact was, that Jacko had found several of his own race in the woods, but, like all wild animals, they immediately attacked one who had worn the chains of servitude, and Jacko had to fly for his life. We very often interlaced the rigging with the boughs after that, but the monkey remained quiet on the booms, and showed not the slightest wish to renew his rambles.

I think it was on the third day that we arrived below the town of Naputah, which was defended by a very formidable stockade, commanding the whole reach of the river. The stockade was manned, and we expected that it would be defended, but as we did not fire, neither did they; and we should have passed it quietly, had not S— grumbled so much at his bad luck. The next day we arrived at Bassein, one of the principal towns in the Burman Empire. Here again the Major was disappointed, for it appeared that, on hearing of the arrival of the expedition at the entrance of the river, the people had divided into two parties, one for resistance, the other for submission. This difference of opinion had ended in their setting fire to the town and immense magazines of grain, dismantling the stockades, and the major part of the inhabitants flying into the country. The consequence was, that we took possession of the smoking ruins without opposition.

It was soon observed that the people were tired of the protracted war, and of the desolation occasioned by it. They wanted to return to their wives and families, who were starving. But up to this time the chiefs had remained faithful to Bundoola, who had amassed stores and provisions at Bassein, intending to retreat upon it, should he be driven out of the fortress of Donabue; and as long as he held that fortress, receiving from Bassein his supplies of men and of provisions. The Burmahs were so unwilling to fight any longer, that they were collected by armed bands, and made prisoners by the chiefs, who sent them up as required; and many hundreds were still in this way detained, enclosed in stockaded ground, and watched by armed men, in several towns along the river. An expedition was first despatched up the river, to its junction with the Irrawaddy, as there was a town there in which was the dockyard of the Burmahs, all their war boats, and *canoes* of every description being *built* at that place. They ascended without difficulty, and, after a little skirmishing, took possession of the place, burnt all the boats built or building, and then returned to Bassein.

Of course, we had then nothing to do: Major S—'s orders were to join Sir A Campbell, if he possibly could; which, with much difficulty, he ultimately effected. We must now return to the Irrawaddy expedition sent up at the same time that Sir A Campbell marched by land, and our expedition went up the Bassein river.

This force arrived at Donabue before we had gained Bassein. It found a most formidable fortress, or rather, three fortresses in one, mounting a great number of guns, and, as I before observed, held by Bundoola, the commander of the Burmah forces, in whom the Burmah troops placed the greatest confidence. I speak from hearsay and memory, but I believe I am correct when I state that there were not less than ten thousand men in Donabue, besides war elephants, etcetera. Now the river force did not amount in fighting men certainly to one thousand, and they were not in sufficient strength to attack a place of this description, upon which every pains had been taken for a long while to render it impregnable. The attack was however made, and the smaller stockade of the three carried; but when they had possession of the smallest stockade, they discovered that they were at the mercy of the second, and in a sort of trap. The consequence was, defeat—the only defeat experienced by the white troops during the whole war. The troops were re-embarked, and the boats were obliged to drop down the river clear of the fire of the fort. I believe two hundred and fifty English troops were left dead in the stockade, and the next day their bodies, crucified on rafts, were floated down among the English boats by the triumphant Bundoola. In the meantime a despatch had been sent to Sir A Campbell, who was in advance on the banks of the river; stating that the force afloat was not able to cope with the fortress, the real strength of which no one had been aware of. The consequence was, that Sir A Campbell retraced his steps, crossed the river, and attacked it in conjunction with the flotilla, Sir A Campbell taking it in the rear. After some hard fighting, in which the elephants played their parts, the troops gained possession, and Bundoola having been killed by a shell, the Burmahs fled. Now it was very fortunate that the expedition had been sent to Bassein, for otherwise the Burmahs would have fallen back upon that place, which held all their stores, and would thus have been able to continue in the rear of Sir A Campbell, as he advanced up the river. But they had heard of the destruction and capture of Bassein, and consequently directed their flight up the river towards the capital. We were in possession of all these circumstances shortly after we had taken possession of Bassein; and although the death of Bundoola and taking of Donabue had dispirited the Burmahs, yet there were many chiefs who still held out, and who, had they crossed with their troops to the Irrawaddy, would have interrupted the supplies coming up, and the wounded and sick who were sent down. We had, therefore, still the duty of breaking up these resources if possible. Having ascertained who the parties were, we sent a message to one of the weakest to say, that if he did not tender his submission, and come in to us, we should attack him, and burn the town to the ground.

The chief thought it advisable to obey our summons, and sent word that he would come in on the ensuing day. He kept his promise: about noon, as we were sitting in the verandah of a large *Sammy* house (a sort of monastery), which we had taken possession of, we were informed that he had arrived. The token of submission on the part of the Burmahs is, presenting the other party with *wax candles*. If a poor man has a request to make, or favour to ask of a great man, he never makes it without laying a small wax candle at his feet. Neither do they approach the Rayhoon and Mayhoon without this mark of respect.

Some time after this, one of the chiefs who had submitted took up his quarters at Bassein; and his little daughter, about eight or nine years old, was very fond of coming to see me, as I generally made her little presents. She became very much attached to me, but she never appeared without a little wax candle, which she dropped at my feet before she threw herself into my lap.

In the present instance, the chief first made his appearance, and having come within a few feet, sat down as a *mark of respect*. He was followed by six more, who each carried about two pounds of wax candles, tastefully arranged in a sort of filigree work of coloured papers. After these came about fifty men, carrying large baskets full of vegetables and fruit, which they poured out on the floor before us, and then walked away and squatted at a distance. A few words of ceremony were then exchanged, and the friendship cemented over a bottle of brandy and some wine; which, notwithstanding the use of spirituous liquors is against their religion, and forbidden by the government, they did not object to. Before he left I made him a present in return, and he went away delighted with the gift. Several more of the minor chiefs afterwards came in, and the same formalities were gone through; but there were three of the most important who would not make their appearance; one, the chief of Naputah, the town which we had passed, which did not fire at us from the stockades, and two others down at another large arm of the river, who had many men detained for the service of the army if required, and who were still at open defiance. All these three were gold chatta chiefs, that is, permitted to have a gold umbrella carried over their heads when they appeared in public.

After waiting a certain time for these people to send in their submission, we sent word down to the chief of Naputah, that we should visit him the next day, threatening him with the consequences of not complying with our request. Accordingly we weighed in the Larne, and dropped down the river till we were abreast of the town and stockade, which was about thirty miles distant from Bassein. Our broadside was ready; but as we were about to fire, we perceived that boats were manning, and in about five minutes the chief of Naputah, in his own war-boat, accompanied by about twelve others, and a great many canoes, pulled off from the shore and came alongside. He made his submission, with the usual accompaniments, and we were soon very good friends. We gave him a beautiful little brass gun, which ornamented our poop, and he went away very well pleased. We here had an opportunity of witnessing the dexterity with which they handle their boats. They really appeared to be alive, they darted through the water with such rapidity. Many of the Burmahs remained on board, examining every part of the vessel and her equipment; and soon they were on the best of terms with the seamen and the few troops which I had on board to assist us, for we were very short manned. We had gained intelligence that there were some guns sunk in a creek, about three miles from Bassein, and we had despatched a boat to look for them, having the assurance of a chief who was at Bassein that the people were peaceable and well-disposed. By some mistake, the boat went up the wrong creek, and pulled many miles into the country, without finding the spot pointed out by marks given. At night they were at the mercy of the Burmahs, who came to them to know what they required. The Burmahs told them that they had mistaken the creek, but were very kind to them, giving them a good supper, and passing the night among them, playing their marionettes. The next day they showed them their way, and when they came to the guns, the Burmahs dived, and made ropes fast, and brought them up for them, sending a message that they would come and see the *Great Water-dog* (meaning me) the next day.

We remained two days at anchor, off the town of Naputah, waiting for this boat, as it was our intention to go down the river, and attack the two other gold chatta chiefs, if they did not send in their submission. On the second day the chief came on board to ask us if we would attend a Nautch which he gave that evening in compliment to us; but requested that we would not bring all our people, as it would frighten his own. Although it was not pleasant to trust ourselves on shore in the night, in the midst of so large a force, yet, anxious to make friends with him, we thought it advisable to accept the invitation in the manner he desired. I replied, "that I would only bring on shore a few officers, and my usual attendants of six marines without arms." At eight o'clock some of the officers and I went on shore: it was quite dark, but we found the chief at the landing-place ready to receive us. The marines had their bayonets, and the officers had pistols concealed in case of treachery, and the first lieutenant kept a good look out, with the broadside of the ship all ready at the first flash of a pistol, but these precautions were unnecessary; the chief took me by the hand and led me up to his house, in front of which had been erected a sort of covered circus, brilliantly lighted up with oil in cocoa-nut shells, and round which were squatted several hundred Burmahs. He took us all to the raised verandah of the house, which was fitted up for the ceremony, where we found his wife, and all his attendants, but not his daughter, who was said to be very handsome. As soon as we had taken our seats the Nautch commenced. About twenty men struck up a very barbarous kind of music, in which the bells and drums made the most noise. After a few minutes of discordant sound, the play began. The actors were in a sort of costume, and appeared quite at home in their parts. The story consisted in the attempts of a young prince to obtain the hand of a young princess; and the dialogue was constantly interrupted by an actor who appeared to be a looker-on, but who made his remarks upon what passed, so as to excite bursts of laughter from the audience. He was the Jack Pudding, or wit of the piece, and several of his jokes were not very delicate. At all events, he was the Liston of the company, for he never spoke nor moved without creating a laugh. The play ended very curiously; after the prince had gained the princess, they had a procession, in which they made an imitation of a ship, out of compliment to us; and then built a little house on the stage with singular rapidity, to the door of which they conducted the youthful couple, closed it, and then the play was over. In the meantime *pickled tea* (which is a great compliment and excessively nasty) was handed round to us, and we all partook of it, taking it out with our fingers; but we could not swallow it, so it remained like a quid of tobacco in our cheeks until we had an opportunity of getting rid of it.

The purser had had the foresight to put a couple of bottles of wine, and one of brandy, in the pockets of the marines, which were now produced, while the band continued to play, and wrestling was introduced. We asked the chief to join us, but he refused; he handed down a sort of picture, in which was represented the white elephant, pagodas, etcetera, and told us that he was not only the war chief, but the head of the religion at Naputah, and that it would not be right that he should be seen by his people transgressing the laws. In the meantime his daughter, who did not come out to us, was very anxious to know what sort of people we were, and she sent for one to be brought in to her. My clerk was the favoured party. She examined him very closely, pulled his dress about, made him bare his legs, to see how white they were, and then dismissed him. The clerk reported her as very handsome, and quite as white as he was; splendidly dressed; and with an air of command, which showed that she was aware of her importance.

We staid about two hours longer, and then we rose to go away. The chief walked with us down to the boats, and we were not sorry to find ourselves on board again; for the population was much more numerous than we had imagined, and had any treachery been attempted, we must have fallen a sacrifice.

Chapter Twenty Seven

Expedition to Bassein continued

May, 1836.

Although on friendly terms with the chief of Naputah, he was a person of such weight in that part of the country, that it was advisable, if possible, to identify him with us, so that he should never again fall off, and oppose us, in the contingency of a reverse, on the Irrawaddy. The next day we sent for him, informing him that it was to make him a present in return for his civility the day before. But before we handed the present to him, we stated our intention of dropping down the river to reduce the two gold chatta chiefs who still held out; and that, as we did not exactly know where their towns were situated, we wished for some of his people to go with me. To this first proposition, after some hesitation, he consented. We then pointed out that our men were not accustomed to work in the sun, and were often ill; that, as we were now friends, we wished him to allow me some of his boats to assist the ship in the river. To this also he consented. In fine, we brought forward our last proposition, which was, that he should supply us with six or eight war-boats, well manned, and that we would pay the men and officers at the same rate per day as we paid our own men; stating the sum we would give, and that, if he was really sincere in his friendship and goodwill, we expected not to be refused. Now, among the Burmahs who were with him, there were many whose relations were detained to join the army; a consultation ensued; the chief was pressed by his own people, and, at last, gave his consent. We then presented him with the piece of plate, upon which his eyes had constantly been turned, and he went away, promising us that the men and boats should be alongside by daylight the next morning.

This chief adhered to his promise, and we weighed anchor the next day, and made sail down with the war-boats, and three or four despatch-canoes, pulled by four or five men. These little canoes, when put to their speed, dashed through the water at such a rate, that they threw off from each bow one continued little fan-shaped *jet-d'eau*, which had a very beautiful appearance, the sunbeams forming them into rainbows. As for our Burmah force, they were at one time pulling against the vessel sailing; at others, hanging on, and the people climbing about the rigging, and ascending the masthead of the vessel; but they soon all congregated to the stand of muskets, for that was the great object of attraction. In the afternoon we had ball practice with the small arms; and the Burmahs were, much to their delight, permitted to fire. It is surprising how exact they were in their aims, considering the little practice they must have had. Bad as all the muskets are which are served out to the ships of war, I really believe that there was not a Burmah who would not have laid down every thing he possessed, except his life, to have obtained one. One of them, when he was permitted to take a musket, looked proudly round, and said, with a smile of joy, "Now I'm a man!"

The next day we arrived at the branch of the river where one of the chiefs held out. At daylight our own boats were manned, and with the Burmah boats ranged in line, made an imposing appearance, which was very necessary, for at that time we were so short-handed, that we could not send away more than forty men—a force so small, that, had the Burmahs opposed to us seen it advance, they would probably have tried their strength with us. As it was, we pulled into the stockaded town in a line, the despatch-boats flying across us backwards and forwards like porpoises before the bows of a ship running down the trades: not that they had any messages to carry, but merely to show their own dexterity. When we had advanced to within a quarter of a mile, a boat came out and communicated with one of the despatch-boats, saying that the Burmahs would not fight if we did not attack them, and that they would deliver up the men detained, and their chief as a prisoner. We agreed to these terms, landed, took possession of the chief with his gold chatta, correspondence with Bundoolah, etcetera, and took him on board. On this occasion, we would not trust the Burmahs employed with muskets; it was too soon; they had only their own swords and spears.

The chief was a fine tall man with a long beard. Like all Burmahs, he took his loss of liberty very composedly, sitting down between the guns with his attendants, and only expressing his indignation at the treachery of his own people. We were very anxious to know what had become of the guns of the dismantled stockade, which were said to be in his possession, but he positively denied it, saying that they had been despatched in boats across to the Irrawaddy. Whether this were true or not, it was impossible to say; but, at all events, it was necessary to make some further attempts to obtain them, so we told him, that if he did not inform us where the guns were, by the next morning his head would be taken off his shoulders. At this pleasant intelligence he opened his betel-bag and renewed his quid. The next day he was summoned forth to account for the said guns, and again protested that they had been sent to Donabue, which I really believe was false, as they were not taken out of the stockade until after Donabue was in the possession of Sir A. Campbell: it was therefore judged proper to appear to proceed to extremities; and this time it was done with more form. A file of marines was marched aft with their muskets, and the sergeant appeared with his drawn sword. Sand was strewed on the deck in front of the marines; and he was led there and ordered to kneel down, so that his head, if cut off, would fall where the sand was strewn. He was again asked if he would tell where the guns were concealed, and again stated that they were at Donabue; upon which he was desired to prepare for death. He called one of his attendants and gave him his silver betel-box, saying, "Take this to my wife, — when she sees it she will know all." I watched him very closely; his countenance was composed, but, as he bent forward over the sand, the muscles of his arms and shoulders quivered. However, as it is not the custom to cut off people's heads on the quarter-deck of his Majesty's ships, we very magnanimously reprieved him, and he was afterwards sent a prisoner to Calcutta. But that he had the guns, we discovered afterwards, which adds to his merit.

Having succeeded in this attempt, we made sail for the stockade of the other chief, and arrived there that evening. As he was supposed to be greater in force than the other, we decided upon an attack in the dark, when he would not be able to distinguish of what our force was composed; and this . time we gave muskets to our Burmah comrades. The attack was successful, we obtained possession, and the chief fled, but our Burmahs pursued him nearly two miles, made him prisoner, and brought him aboard. As he immediately tendered his submission, which the other would not do, he was released the next day.

We had done all our work, and having employed the Burmahs for a few days more in destroying the stockades at the entrance of the river, they were paid and discharged from his Majesty's service. They would not, however, quit us; but, so long as we remained in the river they continued to hang on to the ship, and discovered three guns which had been sunk, which they weighed and brought on board.

I have entered into this short narrative, as it will give some idea of the character of these people. The government is despotic, cruel, and treacherous, but the people are neither cruel nor treacherous: on the contrary, I think they would make most excellent and faithful soldiers; and it is singular to find, surrounded by natives who have not the slightest energy of mind or body, a people so active, so laborious, and so enterprising as the Burmahs. The English seamen are particularly partial to them, and declared they were "the best set of chaps they had ever fallen in with." They admitted the Burmahs to their messes, and were sworn friends. I forgot to say, that when the chiefs sent in their submissions, at first, among other presents, they sent *slaves*, usually females, which was rather awkward. But not wishing to affront them, I begged that the slaves sent might be children, and not grown up, as we had no accommodation for them. The consequence was, that I had quite a young family when I left the river, which I distributed at Rangoon and the presidencies on my return. For if they were only bond-slaves, which I suppose they were, it was a kindness to have them educated and taken care of. We lost one little fellow, that was a great favourite with the men; he was about three years old, and could speak English. He had been christened by the sailors Billy Bamboo, and was quite as amusing as the monkey. The poor little fellow died very suddenly, and was much regretted by all on board.

I certainly do think that we may eventually find the Burmahs to be the most powerful enemy that we shall have to contend with in India; and, at the same time, I cannot help giving my opinion as to the ridiculous fear we entertain of the Russians ever interfering with us in that quarter. That the extension of the Russian empire has been a favourite object through many of her dynasties, is true: but it is so no longer: they have discovered that already their empire is too extensive; and hardly a year passes but they have outbreaks and insurrections to quell in quarters so remote that they are scarcely heard of here. That Russia might *possibly* lead an army through our Indian possessions, I admit; but that she never could hold them if she did do so, is equally certain; the conquest would be useless to her, after having been obtained at an enormous sacrifice. The fact is, the Russians (with the exception of the Emperor Paul) never had any intention of the kind, and *never will attempt it*: but they have discovered how very alive we are to the possibility, and how very jealous and anxious we are on the subject, and it is possible that they have made demonstrations in that direction to alarm us; but I think myself, that the great object of Russia in these advances has been to force a channel for trade, which in her present situation she is to the south of her extensive empire nearly deprived of. Notwithstanding the outcry which has so often been raised against the Russian empire, it has always appeared to me that *our natural ally* is Russia; as for an alliance with France it is morally impossible that two rival nations like us can continue very long at peace; our interests are separate and conflicting, and our jealousy but sleeps for the moment. We have been at peace with France many years, and have not yet succeeded in making a satisfactory commercial treaty with her; neither will any of the other Continental powers permit our manufactures to enter, with the exception of Russia, who not only takes them, but returns to us what is most valuable for our marine.

Why, then, this outcry against the ambition of Russia? nothing but tirades against *Russian* ambition. Does France show no ambition? Does America show no ambition? Have we no ambition ourselves? Why this constant suspicion and doubt against a power whose interest it is to be closely allied to us, and who can always prove a valuable aid in case of emergency? — simply because Russia wishes to have an opening to the Black Sea. And this is very natural; her northern ports are closed nine months in the year, and therefore her navy and mercantile marine are almost useless. She has no outlet, no means of raising either. Does she, then, ask too much? Is a great empire like Russia to be blocked up, her commerce and navy crippled, for the want of an outlet? She does require the opening of the Black Sea; it is all that she requires. She never will remain quiet until she obtains it; and obtain it sooner or later she certainly will; and in my opinion she is perfectly justified in her attempts. What would be the consequence if she succeeded? — that, if we were wise enough to continue on terms of amity with Russia, who has invariably extended the hand of friendship to us, and has I believe never failed in her treaties, we should have a balance of power to us very important. Whose navies shall we in future have to contend against? — those of France and America; for it is certain that whenever we go to war with France, America will back her, and their navies will be united. At present, the navy of America is not very large, but it can soon be made so; and we should not be sorry to have the navy of Russia on our side, to balance against the two which will always be opposed to us. It is, therefore, our interest to *assist* Russia in the object she has in view, and to keep up a firm alliance with her. It is the interest of France to excite jealousies between Russia and this country; and her emissaries have been but too successful, at the very time that France has, contrary to all treaty, and exclaiming against *Russian* ambition, seized upon Algiers, and is now playing her game, so as if possible to command the whole of the Mediterranean. The very strides which France has made in that quarter should point out to us the propriety of opening the Black Sea for Russia, so as to restore the balance of power in that future site of contention. I repeat that we are blind in every way to our own interests, in not uniting ourselves firmly by an alliance, offensive and defensive, with Russia; and that by so doing, we should be the greatest gainers; for with France we must never expect more than a *hollow truce,* concealing for the time her jealousy and thirst for revenge, — a truce during which her secret efforts to undermine us, will be still carried on as indefatigably as ever, and which must only be considered as a mere feint to recover her breath, before she again renews her frenzied efforts to humiliate England, and obtain universal dominion.

Chapter Twenty Eight

London, June, 1837.

To one who has visited foreign climes, how very substantial everything appears in England, from the child's plaything to the Duke of York's column! To use a joiners phrase, everything abroad is comparatively scamp-work. Talk about the Palais Royale, the Rue Richelieu, and the splendour of the Parisian shops—why, two hundred yards of Regent-street, commencing from Howell and James's, would buy the whole of them, and leave a balance sufficient to buy the remainder of the French *expositions*. But still, if more substantial and massive, we are at the same time also heavy. We want more space, more air, more room to breathe, in London; we are too closely packed; we want gardens with trees to absorb the mephitic air, for what our lungs reject is suitable to vegetation. But we cannot have all we want in this world, so we must do without them.

What wealth is now pouring into the country! and, thank God, it is now somewhat better expended than it was in the bubble mania, which acted upon the plethora certainly, but bled us too freely and uselessly. The rail-road speculators have taken off many millions, and the money is well employed; for even allowing that, in some instances, the expectations of the parties who speculate may be disappointed, still it is spent in the country; and not only is it affording employment and sustenance to thousands, but the staple produce of England only is consumed. In these speculations—in the millions required and immediately produced, you can witness the superiority of England. Undertakings from which foreign governments would shrink with dismay are here effected by the meeting of a few individuals.

And now for my commissions. What a list! And the first item is—two Canary birds, the last having been one fine morning found dead: nobody knows how; there was plenty of seed and water (put in after the servant found that they had been starved by his neglect), which, of course, proved that they did not die for want of food. I hate what are called pets; they are a great nuisance, for they will die, and then such a lamentation over them! In the "Fire Worshippers" Moore makes his Hinda say—

> "I never nursed a dear gazelle,
> To glad me with its soft black eye,

But when it came to know me well
And love me—it was sure to die."

Now Hinda was perfectly correct, except in thinking that she was peculiarly unfortunate. Every one who keeps pets might tell the same tale as Hinda. I recollect once a Canary bird died, and my young people were in a great tribulation; so to amuse them we made them a paper coffin, put the defunct therein, and sewed on the lid, dug a grave in the garden, and dressing them out in any remnants of black we could find for weepers, made a procession to the grave where it was buried. This little divertissement quite took their fancy. The next day one of the youngest came up to me and said, "Oh, papa, when will you die?"—A strange question, thought I, quite forgetting the procession of the day before.—"Why do you ask, my dear?"—"Oh, because it will be such fun burying you."—"Much obliged to you, my love."

There is much more intellect in birds than people suppose. An instance of that occurred the other day, at a slate quarry belonging to a friend, from whom I have the narrative. A thrush, not aware of the expansive properties of gunpowder, thought proper to build her nest on a ridge of the quarry, in the very centre of which they were constantly blasting the rock. At first she was very much discomposed by the fragments flying in all directions, but still she would not, quit her chosen locality; she soon observed that a bell rang whenever a train was about to be fired, and that, at the notice, the workmen retired to safe positions. In a few days, when she heard the bell, she quitted her exposed situation, and flew down to where the workmen sheltered themselves, dropping close to their feet. There she would remain until the explosion had taken place, and then return to her nest. The workmen, observing this, narrated it to their employers, and it was also told to visitors who came to view the quarry.

The visitors naturally expressed a wish to witness so curious a specimen of intellect; but, as the rock could not always be ready to be blasted when visitors came, the bell was rung instead, and, for a few times, answered the same purpose. The thrush flew down close to where they stood; but she perceived that she was trifled with, and it interfered with her process of incubation: the consequence was, that afterwards, when the bell was rung, she would peep over the ledge to ascertain if the workmen did retreat, and if they did not, she would remain where she was, probably saying to herself, "No, no, gentlemen; I'm not to be roused off my eggs merely for your amusement."

Some birds have a great deal of humour in them, particularly the raven. One that belonged to me was the most mischievous and amusing creature

I ever met with. He would get into the flower-garden, go to the beds where the gardener had sowed a great variety of seeds, with sticks put in the ground with labels, and then he would amuse himself with pulling up every stick, and laying them in heaps of ten or twelve on the path. This used to irritate the old gardener very much, who would drive him away. The raven knew that he ought not to do it, or he would not have done it. He would soon return to his mischief, and when the gardener again chased him (the old man could not walk very fast), the raven would keep just clear of the rake or hoe in his hand, dancing back before him, and singing as plain as a man could, "Tol de rol de rol; tol de rol de rol!" with all kinds of mimicking gestures. The bird is alive now, and continues the same meritorious practice whenever he can find an opportunity.

Chapter Twenty Nine

June, Steam-boat Princess Victoria.

It certainly appears that the motion of a steam-vessel produces more nausea than that of a sailing-vessel; and people appear to suffer in some degree in proportion to the power of the engines. This may be accounted for by the vibration of the vessel increasing in the same ratio.

We are now in a vessel of two hundred and fifty horse power, and the consequence is that the passengers are as sick as two hundred and fifty horses. The effect of the vibration of the after part of the vessel amounts to the ridiculous.

When dinner was put on the table, we had no occasion for a bell to announce it, for every glass on the table was dancing to its own jingling music. And when the covers were taken off, it was still more absurd— everything in the dishes appeared to be infected with Saint Vitus's dance. The boiled leg of mutton shook its collops of fat at a couple of fowls which figured in a sarabande round and round their own dish,—roast beef shifted about with a slow and stately movement—a ham *glisséed croisée* from one side to the other—tongues wagged that were never meant to wag again— bottles reeled and fell over like drunken men, and your piece of bread constantly ran away and was to be pulled back into its proper place. It was a regular jig-a-jig—a country-dance of pousette, down the middle, and right and left.

The communication of motion was strange; the whole company seated on long forms were jig-a-jigging up and down together—your knife jigged and your fork jigged—even the morsel which was put into your mouth gave one more jump before it could be seized. However, we jigged it to some purpose; for, in eighteen hours and a half, we passed from London to Antwerp.

The English are naturally great *voyageurs*: the feeling is inherent from our insular position. I have been reflecting whether I can recollect, in my whole life, ever to have been three months in one place, but I cannot, nor do I believe that I ever was—not even when sent to school; for I used to run away every quarter, just to see how my family were—an amiable weakness, which even flogging could not eradicate. And then I was off to sea; there I had my wish, as Shakespeare says, borne away by "the viewless winds, and blown with restless violence about the pendent world," north, south, east, and west; one month freezing, the next burning; all nations, all colours,— white, copper, brown, and black; all scenery, from the blasted pine towering amidst the frost and snow, to the cocoa-nut waving its leaves to the sea-breeze. Well, "homekeeping youths have homely wits," says the same author; and he has told more truth than any man who ever wrote. I certainly did hear of one young man who did not gain much by travelling; he was a banker's clerk, and obtained three months' vacation to go on the Continent. He landed at Ostend, and the next day found himself in the track-schuyt that is towed by horses, from Bruges to Ghent. The cabins were magnificent, velvet and gold the down cushions luxurious, the dinner and breakfast sumptuous, the wine excellent, the bed-rooms comfortable, and the expense moderate. Moreover, the motion was imperceptible. What could a man wish more? He arrived at Ghent, and could not make his mind up to quit this barge; so he returned in her to Bruges, and then back again to Ghent; and thus he continued between the two towns, backwards and forwards, until the three months' leave had expired, and he was obliged to return to the desk. I have never yet made up my mind whether this personage was a wise man or a fool.

But, until the opening of the Continent, the English were only voyageurs, not travellers; and that, after having been so long debarred, they should be desirous of visiting the various portions of Europe, is not only natural but praiseworthy; but that they should make the Continent their residence— should expatriate themselves altogether, is, to me, a source of astonishment as well as of regret.

The excuse offered is the cheapness. It is but an excuse, for I deny it to be the fact: I have visited most places, with and without a family; and I will positively assert, not for the benefit of others who have already expatriated themselves, but as a check to those who feel so inclined, that they will discover too soon that, at less expense, they can command more good living and substantial comforts in England, than in any part of the Continent they may fix upon as their habitation.

Let us enter a little into the subject. First, as to the capitals, Paris, Brussels, etcetera.

Let it first be remembered that we have no longer war prices in England, that almost every article has fallen from thirty-five to fifty per cent. It is true that some tradespeople who are established as fashionable keep up their prices; but it is not absolutely necessary to employ them, as there are those equally skilled who are more moderate. But even the most fashionable have been obliged, to a certain degree, to lower their prices; and their present prices, reduced as they are, will most assuredly die with them.

Everything will, by degrees, find its level; but this level is not to be found at once. Should peace continue, ten years from this date will make a great alteration in every article, not only of necessity, but of luxury; and then, after having been the dearest, England will become the cheapest residence in the world. House rent in the capitals abroad is certainly as dear, if not dearer than it is in England. There are situations more or less fashionable in every metropolis; and if you wish to reside in those quarters, you pay accordingly. It is true that, by taking a portion of a house, you to a certain degree indemnify yourself;—a first, second, or third story, with a common staircase loaded with dirt and filth; but is this equal to the comfort of a clean English house, in which you have your own servants, and are not overlooked by your neighbours? If they were to let out houses in floors in England as they do in Paris and elsewhere, a less sum would be demanded. You may procure a handsome house in a fashionable quarter, well furnished, in London, for 300 pounds per annum. Go to the Place Vendôme, or those quarters styled the English quarters, at Paris, and which are by no means the most fashionable quarters, and you will pay for a handsome front floor 700 francs per month; so that for one floor of a house in Paris you will pay 336 pounds per annum, when in London you will obtain the whole house for 300 pounds. The proprietor of the Paris house, therefore, receives much more by letting his floors separate than the English do. The common articles of necessity are as dear, if not dearer abroad; the *octroi* duty upon all that enters the barriers raising the price excessively. Meat at Paris or Brussels is as dear as in London, and not so good; it is as dear, because they charge you the same price all round, about 5 pence per pound, independent of its inferiority and the villainous manner in which it is cut up. Our butchers only butcher the animal, but foreign butchers butcher the meat. Poultry is as dear; game much dearer; and so is fish. Indeed, fish is not only dear, but scarce and bad. Horses and carriages are quite as dear abroad, in the capitals, as in London. Clothes are in some respects cheaper, in others dearer, especially articles of English manufacture, which are more sought after than any others.

Amusements are said to be cheaper; but, admitting that, the places of amusement are oftener resorted to, and in consequence as much money is spent abroad as in England. It is true that there are an immense number of theatres in Paris, and that most of them are very reasonable in their charges for admission; but be it recollected that there are not above three of them which are considered fashionable, if even respectable; and there the prices are sufficiently high. If people went to Sadler's Wells, the Coburg, Victoria,

Queen's Theatre, Astley's, and other minor theatres in London, as they do to the Theatres Saint Martin, Gymnase, et Variétés at Paris, they would find no great difference in the prices.

What then is there cheaper? Wine. I grant it; and, it is also asserted, the education of children. We will pass over these two last points for the present, and examine whether living is cheaper on the Continent, provided you do *not* hive in any of the capitals.

That at Tours and other places in the south of France, at Genoa, at Bruges, in Belgium, you may live cheaper than in London, I grant; but if any one means to assert that you can live cheaper than in the country in England, I deny it altogether. People go abroad, and select the cheapest parts of the Continent to live in. If they were to do the same in England, they would find that they could live much cheaper and much better; for instance, in Devonshire, Cornwall, and Wales, and, indeed, in almost every county in England.

The fact is, it is not the cheapness of the living which induces so many people to reside abroad. There are many reasons; and as I wish to be charitable, I will put forward the most favourable ones.

In England, we are money-making people, and we have the aristocracy of wealth as well *as* the aristocracy of rank. It has long been the custom for many people to live beyond their incomes, and to keep up an appearance which their means have not warranted. Many, especially the landed proprietors, finding their rentals reduced from various causes, have been necessitated to retrench. They were too proud to put down their carriages and establishments before the eyes of those who had perhaps looked upon them with envy, and whose derision or exultation they anticipated. They therefore have retired to the Continent, where a carriage is not necessary to prove that you are a gentleman. Should those return who have emigrated for the above reasons, they would find that this striving for show is hardly perceptible now in England. Those who have remained have either had sense enough, or have been forced by circumstances, to reduce their expenditure.

Another cause is the easy introduction into what is called good society abroad on the Continent, but which is in reality very bad society. Certainly there are a sufficient number of Counts, Viscounts, and Marquesses to associate with; but in France high birth is not proved by titles, which are of little or no value, and do not even establish gentility. This society may certainly be entered into at a much less expense than that of England, especially in the metropolis; but, depend upon it, there is a species of society dear at any price.

With respect to education of children, that boys may receive advantage from a Continental education I admit; but woe be to the mother who intrusts her daughter to the ruin of a French *Pension*!

In England there are many excellent schools in the country, as cheap and cheaper than on the Continent: but the schoolmasters near London, generally speaking, are ruining them by their adherence to the old system, and their extravagant terms. The *system* of education on the Continent is certainly superior to that of England, and the attention to the pupils is greater: of course there are bad schools abroad as well as in England; but the balance is much in favour of those on the Continent, with the advantage of being at nearly one-half the expense. A great alteration has taken place in modern education; the living languages and mathematics have been found to be preferable to the classics and other instruction still adhered to in the English schools.

I have always considered, and have every reason to be confirmed in my opinion, that the foundation of all education is mathematics. Every thing else may be obtained by rote, and without thinking; but from the elements of arithmetic up to Euclid and algebra, no boy can work his task without thinking. I never yet knew a man who was a good mathematician who was not well-informed upon almost every point; and the reason is clear— mathematics have prepared his mind to receive and retain. In all foreign schools this important branch of education is more attended to than it is in England; and that alone would be a sufficient reason for me to give them the preference. In point of morals, I consider the schools of both countries much upon a par; although, from the system abroad of never debasing a child by corporal punishment, I give the foreign schools the preference even in that point.

I consider, then, that boys are better educated abroad than in England, and acquire much more correctly the living languages, which are of more use to them than the classics. So much I can say in favour of the Continent; but in every other respect I consider the advantage in favour of England. Young women who have been brought up abroad I consider, generally speaking, as unfitted for English wives; and that in this opinion I am not singular, I know well from conversation with young men at the clubs and elsewhere. Mothers who have returned with their daughters full of French fashions and ideas, and who imagine that they will inevitably succeed in making good matches, would be a little mortified and surprised to hear the young men, when canvassing among themselves the merits of the other sex, declare that "such a young lady may be very handsome and very clever, but she has received a *Continental education*, and that won't do for them." Many mothers imagine, because their daughters, who are bold and free in their manners, and talk and laugh loud, are surrounded by young men, while the modest girl, who holds aloof, is apparently neglected, that their daughters are more admired; but this is a great mistake. Men like that boldness, that coquetry, that dash, if I may use the term, because it amuses for the time being; but although they may pay attention to women on that account, marrying them is quite another affair. No: the modest retiring girl, who is apparently passed by, becomes the wife; the others are flattered before their faces, and laughed at behind their backs. It certainly is unmanly, on the part of our sex, to behave in this manner, to encourage young women in their follies, and ruin them for their own amusement; as Shakespeare says:—

"Shame to him whose cruel striking
Kills for faults of his own liking."

But so it is, and so it will be so long as the world lasts, and mankind is no better than it is at present.

If then, as I have asserted, there is so little to be gained by leaving a comfortable home, what is the inducement which takes so many people abroad to settle there? I am afraid that the true reason has been given by the author whom I now quote. Speaking of the French metropolis, she says—

"I have been lately trying to investigate the nature of the charm which renders Paris so favourite a sojourn of the English.

"In point of gaiety (for gaiety read dissipation) it affords nothing comparable with that of London. A few ministerial fêtes every winter may perhaps exceed in brilliancy the balls given in our common routine of things; but for one entertainment in Paris at least thirty take place *chez nous*. Society is established with us on a wider and more splendid scale. The weekly *soirées*, on the other hand, which properly represent the society of this place, are dull, meagre, and formal to the last degree of formality. There is no brilliant point of reunion as at Almack's,—no theatre uniting, like our Italian Opera, the charm of the best company, the best music, and the best dancing. Of the thousand and one theatres boasted of by the Parisians, only three are of a nature to be frequented by people of consideration, the remainder being as much out of the question as the Pavilion or the Garrick. Dinner parties there are none; water parties none; *déjeûners*, unless given by a foreign ambassadress, none. A thousand accessories to London amusements are here wanting. In the month of May, I am told, the public gardens and the Bois de Boulogne become enchanting. But what is not charming in the month of May? Paris, perhaps, least of all places; for at the commencement of the month every French family of note quits the metropolis for its country seat, or for sea or mineral bathing. Foreigners and the mercantile and ministerial classes alone remain. What, then, I would fain discover, constitutes the peculiar merit of inducing persons uninstigated by motives of economy to fix themselves in the comfortless and filthy city, and call it Paradise? Alas! my solution of the problem is far from honourable to the taste of our absentees. *In Paris people are far less amenable than in London to the tribunal of public opinion*; or, as a lady once very candidly said to me, 'One gets rid of one's friends and relations.'"

Indeed, there are so many petty annoyances and vexatious of life attendant upon residents abroad, that it must require some strong motives to induce them to remain. Wherever the English settle they raise the price of everything, much to the annoyance of the *rentiers* and respectable people of the place, although of advantage to the country generally. The really highbred and aristocratic people will not associate with the English, and look upon them with any feeling but good will. With regard to servants, they are invariably badly served, although they pay two or three times the wages that are paid by the inhabitants, who, in most places, have made it a rule never to take a domestic that has once lived in an English family; the consequence is that those engaged by the English are of the worst description, a sort of *pariahs* among the community, who extort and cheat their employers without mercy. If not permitted so to do, they leave them at a minutes warning; and you cannot go to any foreign colony of English people without listening to very justified tirades of the villany of the servants. Upon the same principle, there are few places abroad where the tradespeople have not two prices; one for the English, and the other for the inhabitants.

I was in company with an English lady of title, who gave me a very amusing instance of the insolence of the Belgian servants. She had a large family to bring up on a limited income, and had taken up her abode at Brussels. It should be observed that the Belgians treat their servants like dogs, and yet it is only with the Belgians that they will behave well. This lady, finding her expenses very much exceeding her means, so soon as she had been some time in the country, attempted a reformation. Inquiring of some Belgian families with whom she was acquainted what were the just proportions allowed by them to their servants, she attempted by degrees to introduce the same system. The first article of wasteful expenditure was bread, and she put them upon an allowance. The morning after she was awoke with a loud hammering in the saloon below, the reason of which she could not comprehend; but on going down to breakfast she found one of the long loaves made in the country nailed up with tenpenny nails over the mantelpiece. She sent to inquire who had done it, and one of the servants immediately replied that she had nailed it there that my lady might see that the bread did not go too fast.

There is another point on which the English abroad have long complained, and with great justice,—which is, that in every litigation or petty dispute which may appear before a smaller or more important tribunal, from the Juge de Paix to the Cour de Cassation, the verdict invariably is given against them. I never *heard* an instance to the contrary, although there may have been some. In no case can an Englishman obtain justice; the detention of his property without just cause, all that he considers as law and justice in his own country, is overruled: he is obliged to submit to the greatest insults, or consent to the greatest imposition. This is peculiarly, observable at Paris and Brussels, and it is almost a *jour de fête* to a large portion of the inhabitants when they hear that an Englishman has been thrown into prison. It must, however, be acknowledged that most of this arises not only from the wish of the rentiers, or those who live upon their means (who have these means crippled by the concourse of English raising the price of every article), that the English should leave and return to their own country; but also from the number of bad characters who, finding their position in society no longer tenable in England, hasten abroad, and, by their conduct, leave a most unfavourable impression of the English character, which, when Englishmen *only travelled*, stood high, but, now they reside to economise, is at its lowest ebb; for the only charm which the English had in the eyes of needy foreigners was their lavishing their money as they passed through the country, enriching a portion of the community without increasing the prices of consumption to the whole.

As a proof of the insolence to which the English are subjected, I will give the reader a verbatim copy of a letter sent to me by a friend not more than a year ago. I have heard of such a circumstance taking place in France, but then the innkeeper was a Chevalier of the Legion of Honour; but this case is even more remarkable. Depend upon it, those who travel will find many a Monsieur Disch before they are at the end of their journey. I will vouch for the veracity of every word in the letter:—

"Wisbaden, July 3, 1836.

"My Dear —, As you kindly said that you would be glad to hear of our progress when any opportunity offered of writing you a letter, I now avail myself of some friends passing through Brussels to let you know that thus far we have proceeded in health and safety; but whether we shall complete our project of wintering in Italy seems more and more doubtful, as I believe the cholera to be doing its work pretty actively in some of the states we propose to visit; and a gentleman told me yesterday, who has lately left the country, that the Pope is so glad of an excuse to keep heretics out of his dominions, that he has never taken off the quarantine: so that, under any circumstances, we must vegetate in some frontier hole for a fortnight before we can be admitted; a circumstance in itself sufficiently deterring, in my opinion. Besides which, what with the perplexity of the coinage, and the constant attempt at pillage which we have already met with, and which, I am told, is quadrupled on the other side of the Alps, such a counterbalance exists to any of the enjoyments of travelling, that I am heartily weary of the continual skirmishing and *warfare* I am subjected to;—warfare indeed, as at Cologne I was *called out*. The story is too good to be lost, so I will tell it for your amusement and that of our friends at Brussels; moreover that you may caution every one against Mons. Disch, of the Cour Imperiale:— We had *marchandéed* with Madame Disch for rooms, who at last agreed to *our* terms; but when the bill came, she changed her *own*. We remonstrated, and the bill was altered; but Mons. Disch made his appearance before I could pay it, insisting on the larger sum, saying his wife had no business to make a bargain for him. I remonstrated in vain, and Mrs — commenced most eloquently to state the case: he was, however, deaf to reason, argument, eloquence, and beauty. At last I said, 'Do not waste words the matter, I will pay the fellow and have done with him, taking care that neither I nor my friends will ever come to his house again,' at the same time snatching the bill from his hand when he demanded, in a great fury, what I meant by that; exclaiming, 'I am Germans gentlemans,—you English gentlemans, I challenge you—I challenge you.' Although somewhat wroth before this. I was so amused that I laughed in the rascal's face, which doubled his rage, and he reiterated his mortal defiance; adding,—'I was in London last year; they charge me twelve—fourteen shillings for my dinner at coffee-house, but I too much gentlemans to ask them take off one farding. I challenge you—I challenge you.' I then said, 'Hold your tongue, sir; take your money and be off.' 'Me take money!' replied he; 'me take money! No, my servant take money; I too much gentlemans to take money.' Upon which the waiter swept the cash off the table, handed it to his master, who immediately sacked it and walked off."

I certainly have myself come to the conclusion that the idea of going abroad for economy is most erroneous. As I have before observed, the only article, except education, which is cheaper, is wine; and I am afraid, considering the thirsty propensities of my countrymen, that is a very strong attraction with the nobler sex. If claret and all other French wines were admitted into England at a much lower duty, they would be almost as cheap in England as they are in foreign capitals; and, as the increased consumption would more than indemnify the government, it is to be lamented that it is not so arranged.—Formerly we shut out the French wines, and admitted those of Portugal, as our ancient ally; but our ancient ally has shown any thing but good-will towards us lately, and we are at all events under no further obligation to support her interests. Let us admit French wines in bottles at a very low duty, and then England will be in every respect as cheap, and infinitely more comfortable as a residence than any part of the Continent. The absentees who are worth reclaiming will return; those who prefer to remain on the Continent are much better there than if they were contaminating their countrymen with their presence. How true is the following observation from the author I before quoted on her return from abroad:—

"Home, home at last. How clean, how cheerful, how comfortable! I was shown at Marthien the shabby, dirty-looking lodgings where the — are economising, in penance for the pleasure of one little year spent in this charming house! Poor people! How they must long for England! how they must miss the thousand trivial but essential conveniences devised here for the civilisation of human life! What an air of decency and respectfulness about the servants! what a feeling of homeishness in a house exclusively our own! The modes of life may be easier on the Continent,—but it is the ease of a beggar's ragged coat which has served twenty masters, and is twitched off and on till it scarcely holds together, in comparison with the decent, close-fitting suit characteristic of a gentleman."

Chapter Thirty

Brussels.

Authors, like doctors, are very apt to disagree. Reading, the other day, a very amusing publication, called the "Diary of a Désennuyée," some passages in it induced me to fall back upon Henry Bulwer's work on France. Among his remarks upon literary influence in that country, he has the following:—

"A literary Frenchman, whom I met not long ago in Paris, said to me that a good-natured young English nobleman, whom I will not name, had told him that dancers and singers were perfectly well received in English society, but not men of letters.

"'Est il possible qu'on soit si barbare chez vous?'"

He subsequently adds:— "To be known as a writer is certainly to your prejudice.

"First, people presume you are not what they call a gentleman; and the grandfather who, if you were a banker or a butcher, or of any other calling or profession, would be left quiet in his tomb, is evoked against you."

Mr Bulwer then proceeds with a variety of argument to prove that literary men are not *Maecenased* by either the government or aristocracy of Great Britain. He points out the advantages which the French literati have from their Institute, the ennoblements, the decorations, and pensions which they receive; and certainly makes out a strong case.

The author of the "Diary" would attempt to deny the statements of Mr Bulwer; but, in the very denial, she admits all his points but one—to wit that they are not so well received by the aristocracy in England as they are in France.

She says—

"What does Henry Bulwer mean by the assertion that literary men are more eagerly welcomed in society here than in England?

"They occupy, perhaps, a more independent and honourable position, are less exposed to being lionised by patronising dowagers, and more sure of obtaining public preferment; but, with the exception of Mignet and Mérimée—who are courted for their personal merits and official standing rather than for their literary distinctions—I have scarcely met one of them. To the parties of the ministers of the *Grand Referendaire*, and other public functionaries, artists and men of letters are admitted as part of a political system; but they are not to be found—like Moore, Rogers, Chantrey, Newton, and others—in the boudoirs of the *élite*, or the select fêtes of a Devonshire House.

"The calling of '*un homme de lettres*' is here, however, a profession bearing its own rewards and profits, and forming an especial and independent class. In common with the artists they look to ennoblement in the Academy, and under the existing order of things have been richly endowed with places and pensions."

It appears then, in France, that to the parties of ministers, etcetera, they are admitted as a part of the political system; and further, that they have been festered by the government, by being ennobled and richly endowed with places and pensions. Therefore, upon his opponent's own showing, Henry Bulwer has made out his case. In another part of the same work there is the following amusing passage, in advice given by a lady of fashion to her protégée upon entering into London society.

"'Pore over their books as much as you please, but do not so much as dip into the authors,' said she, when I proposed an introduction to one of the most popular authors of the day. 'These people expend their spirit on their works—the part that walks through society is a mere lump of clay, like the refuse of the wine-press after the wine has been expressed.' In conversing with a clever author you sometimes see a new idea brighten his eye or create a smile round his lip; but for worlds he would not give it utterance. It belongs to his next work, and is instantly booked in the ledger of his daily thoughts, value 3 shillings 6 pence. The man's mind is his mine; he can't afford to work it gratis, or give away the produce."

If we are to draw any inference from this extract, it is, that although some noblemen do extend their patronage to literary men, at all events the general feeling is against them. I must say that I never was more amused than when I read the above sarcasm. There is much truth in it, and yet it is not true. In future when I *do* say good things, as they call them, in company, I shall know precise value of my expenditure during the dinner or evening party by reckoning up the three-and-sixpences. One thing is clear, that if an author say half a dozen good things, he fully pays for his dinner.

In the "Student," Edward Bulwer makes some remarks which range in opposition to the author of the above "Diary." In arguing that most authors may be known by their works, he says—

"Authors are the only men we really do know; the rest of mankind die with only the surface of their character understood."

It appears, then, that people have no excuse for being disappointed in authors; when they meet them in company they have but to read their works, and if they like the works they must live the authors. Before I proceed I must be permitted to make a remark here. An author's opinion given as his own will allow the public to have an insight into his character and feelings, and the public are justified in forming their opinions of an author upon such grounds. But it too often happens that the public will form their opinion of an author from opinions put by him into the mouths of the characters drawn in a work of fiction, forgetting that in these instances it is not the author who speaks, but the individuals which his imagination has conjured up; and that the opinions expressed by these creatures of his brain, although perfectly in keeping with the character, and necessary to produce that *vraisemblance* which is the great merit of fiction, may be entirely opposed to the real sentiments of the author. The true merit of fiction, and that which is essential to its success, is the power of the author at the time that he is writing to divest himself, as it were, of himself, and be for the time the essence of the character which he is delineating. It is therefore a great injustice to an author to accuse him of being an infidel because his infidel character is well portrayed, particularly as, if he is equally fortunate in describing a character which is perfect, the public do not ever give him the credit for similar perfection. That is quite another affair. Again, Edward Bulwer says, in opposition to the poverty of the *mine*:—

"A man is, I suspect, but of a second-rate order whose genius is not immeasurably above his works,—who does not feel within him an inexhaustible affluence of thoughts, feelings, and invention, which he never will have leisure to embody in print. He will die and leave only a thousandth part of his wealth to posterity, which is his heir."

I like to bring all in juxtaposition. There is excitement in making mischief, and that is the reason why people are so fond of it. Still, the question at issue ought to be fairly decided; and, as in case of arbitration, when the disputants cannot agree, a third party is called in by mutual consent, I shall venture to take upon myself that office, and will fairly argue the point, as there is more dependent upon it than, upon the first view, the question may appear to merit.

If we turn back to the last century, in what position shall we find authors?—looking up to patrons among the aristocracy, and dedicating their works to them in panegyrics, fulsome from their obsequiousness and flattery. At that period the aristocracy and the people were much wider apart than they are at present.

Gradually the people have advanced; and, as they have advanced, so have the authors thrown off the trammels of servitude, and have attacked the vices and follies as well as the privileges of those to whom they once bowed the knee.

The advancement of the people, and the lowering of the aristocracy, have both been effected through the medium of the press. The position of authors has been much altered. Formerly we behold such men as Dryden, Otway, and many others (giants in their days), humbling themselves for bread. Now we have seldom a dedication, and of those few we have the flattery is delicate. The authors look to the public as their patrons, and the aristocracy are considered but as a part and portion of it. These remarks equally hold good with respect to the government. Authors are not to be so easily purchased as formerly; they prefer writing in conformity with public opinion to writing for government, because they are better remunerated. Now, if it will be recalled to mind that in the rapid march of the people, in their assertion of their right to a greater share in the government of the country, in the pointing out and correcting of abuses, and in the breaking down of all the defences which have gradually yielded in so many years, it is the authors and the press who have led the van, and that in these continual inroads the aristocracy have been the party attacked, — it is no wonder that there has arisen, unwittingly perhaps on the part of the aristocracy, a feeling against the press and against authors in general.

The press has been, and will probably for a long while continue to be, the enemy of the aristocracy; and it is hardly reasonable to expect that the aristocracy should admit the enemy within its camp. For, be it observed, whether a man write a political pamphlet or a novel, he has still the same opportunity of expressing his sentiments, of flattering the public by espousing their opinions; and as a writer of fiction, perhaps, his opinions have more effect that as a pamphleteer. In the first instance, you are prepared to expect a political partisan; in the latter, you read for amusement, and unconsciously receive the bias. For one who reads a political pamphlet (by-the-by, they are generally only read by those who are of the same way of thinking as the author) there are hundreds who read through a work of fiction, so that the opinions of the latter are much more widely disseminated. Now, as most works are written for profit as well as reputation, they are naturally so worded as to insure the good-will of the majority, otherwise they would not have so extensive a sale. The majority being decidedly liberal, every work that now appears more or less attacks the higher orders. When, therefore, a gentleman who has been well received in the best society ventures upon writing a work, it is quite sufficient to state that he is an author (without his book being read) to occasion him to *"lose caste"* to a certain degree. Authors have been the enemies of the higher classes. You have become an author—consequently you have ranked yourself with our enemies. Henry Bulwer, therefore, is right where he asserts that "to be known as an author is to your prejudice among the higher classes."

Having made these observations to point out that the aristocracy and the press are at variance, let us now examine into the merits of authors, as mixing in society. And here I think it will be proved that it is more their misfortune than their fault that there should be a prejudice against them. They are overrated before they are seen, and underrated afterwards.

You read the works of an author—you are pleased with them, and you wish to become acquainted with the man. You anticipate great pleasure— you expect from his lips, in *impromptu*, the same racy remarks, the same chain of reasoning, the same life and vigour which have cost him so many hours of labour and reflection, or which have been elicited in his happiest moods, and this from a person who comes, perhaps, almost a total stranger into a large company. Is this fair or just to him? Did you find any of your other friends, at first meeting, play the fiddle to a whole company of strangers? Are not authors as reserved and shy as other people—even more so? And yet you ask them, as if they were mountebanks or jugglers with a certain set of tricks, to amuse the company. The very circumstance of being aware that this is expected of him makes the man silent, and his very anxiety to come up to your expectations takes away from his power.

The consequence is, that you are disappointed, and so are the company, to whom you have announced that "Mr So-and-So" is to meet them. Had you become intimate with this person you would perhaps have found the difference, and that he whom you pronounced as so great a failure, would have turned out equally amusing. At the same time there is some truth in the remarks of the "Désennuyée" that "some authors will not let out their new ideas, because they require them for their books." But, as Bulwer observes, they must be but second-raters, as the majority of authors are.

In many instances they are punsters; but punning is not a standard of authorship; or, perhaps, there may be other second-rate authors present, and if so, they know that they are in the company of literary pickpockets.

To prove that this remark of the "Désennuyée" can only apply to second-rate authors, let us examine into the conversational powers of those who are first-rate. And here I can only speak of those whom I have known— there may be many others. Where could you find such conversationists as Coleridge, Charles Lamb, Sir John Malcolm, and many others, who are now gone? And among those in existence, I have but to mention Croker, Theodore Hooke, Professor Wilson, Bulwer, Lockhart, the Smiths, and, in the other sex, Lady Blessington, Lady Morgan, Mesdames Somerville, Austin, and Jameson.

Now these are all first-rate authors in their various styles; and I can challenge any one to bring forward an equal number out of the whole mass who are so powerful or delightful in society. And there is still more to be said in favour of authors. I know many whose conversation is superior to their writings; I will not name them as they, perhaps, would not consider this to be a compliment but it fully tends to disprove the remarks of the "Désennuyée" as to authors of talent reserving their thoughts for their hooks, for, on the *contrary*, when in company, they generally take the lead. Still, there is a difference arising from the variety of temperament: some, accustomed to mix constantly in society, will be indifferent whether they are acquainted with the parties present or not; others, more retiring, require to feel at their ease, and it is only in small coteries, and among friends, that their real value can be appreciated. Theodore Hooke is a proof of the former, the late Charles Lamb was of the latter. Some shine most when they have no competitors; others are only to be brought out when other men of talent are in company, and, like the flint and steel, their sparks are only to be produced by collision.

If I might be permitted to offer an opinion to the authors themselves, it would be, not to mix in general company, but confine themselves to their own friends. They would stand much higher in reputation if they adhered to this plan; above all, let them avoid what the author of the "Désennuyée" terms those "Skinnerian lion feeds" given by those who have no talent to appreciate, and who, to fill their menagerie, will mix you up with foreign swindlers, and home-bred ruffians. This is most humiliating and has certainly injured the fraternity.

I have but one more remark to make. Authors in England have little to expect from the Government and the aristocracy. Pensions and honours have been given, but until Sir Robert Peel set a more worthy example, they were bestowed for the support of political opinions, not as a reward of talent. That the aristocracy, with but a few exceptions, have not fostered talent, is most true; and they are now suffering from their want of judgment. They have shut their doors to authors, and the authors have been gradually undermining their power. To what extent this may be carried, it is impossible to say; but one thing is certain, that the press is more powerful than either king or lords, and that, if the conflict continue, the latter must yield to the influence of the former, who will have ample retaliation for the neglect to which they have been subjected.

What a superiority there is in England over France, and every other nation, in the periodical and daily press, especially in the latter! Take up the "Constitutionnel," or "Journal des Débats" at Paris, and then look at the broad double sheets of the "Times" and other morning papers, with the columns of information and original matter which they contain. Compare the flimsy sheets, bad printing, and general paucity of information of the continental daily press, with the clear types, rapid steam power called into action, the outlay, enormous expenditure, and rapid information obtained by our leading journals from all quarters of the globe. I have looked with astonishment and admiration at the working of the "Times" newspaper by its beautiful steam-engine; it is one of the most interesting sights that can be beheld.

Nothing but the assistance of steam could, indeed, enable the great daily newspapers to accomplish their present task. When the reader calls to mind that the debates in the House are sometimes kept up till two or three o'clock in the morning; that the reporters, relieved every twenty minutes, have to carry all their communications to the office; that all this matter has to be arranged, put in type, and then worked off; and that, notwithstanding this, the double sheet of matter is on thousands and thousands of tables by nine o'clock the next morning, it is really wonderful how it can be accomplished. Saturday night appears to be the only night on which those connected with these immense, undertakings can be said to have any repose from year's end to year's end. What a life of toil what an unnatural life must theirs be, who thus cater during the hours of darkness for the information and amusement of the mass who have slept soundly through the night, and rise to be instructed by the labour of their vigils! It can be effected in no other country in the world. It is another link in the great chain of miracles, which proves the greatness of England.

The editors of these papers must have a most onerous task. It is not the writing of the leading article itself, but the obligation to write that article every day, whether inclined or not, in sickness or in health, in affliction, distress of mind, winter and summer, year after year, tied down to one task, remaining in one spot. It is something like the walking a thousand miles in a thousand hours. I have a fellow-feeling for them, for I know how a monthly periodical will wear down one's existence. In itself it appears nothing—the labour is not manifest nor is it the labour—it is the continual attention which it requires. Your life becomes as it were the magazine. One month is no sooner corrected and printed than on comes the other. It is the stone of Sisyphus—an endless repetition of toil—a constant weight upon the mind—a continual wearing upon the intellect and spirits, demanding all the exertion of your faculties, at the same time that you are compelled to do the severest drudgery. To write for a magazine is very well, but to edit one is to condemn yourself to slavery.

Magazine writing, as it is generally termed, is the most difficult of all writing, and but few succeed in it; the reason of which is obvious—it must always be what is termed "up to the mark."

Any one who publishes a work in one, two, or three volumes, may be permitted to introduce a dull chapter or two: no one remarks it; indeed, these dull chapters allow the mind of the reader to relax for the time, and, strange to say, are sometimes favourable to the author. But in magazine-writing these cannot be permitted; the reader requires excitement, and whether the article be political or fictitious, there requires a condensation of matter, a pithiness of expression (to enable you to tell your story in so small a space), which is very difficult to obtain. Even in continuations the same rule must be adhered to, for, being read month after month, each separate portion must be considered as a whole and independents of the other; it must not therefore flag for one minute. A proof of this was given in that very remarkable production in "Blackwood's Magazine," styled "Tom Cringle's Log." Every separate portion was devoured by the public—they waited impatiently for the first of the month that they might read the continuation, and every one was delighted, oven to its close, because the excitement was so powerful. Some time afterwards the work was published in two volumes, and then, what was the consequence?—people complained that it was overcharged—that it was too full of excitement—gave no repose. This was true; when collected together it had that fault—a very good one, by the by, as well as a very uncommon one; but they did not perceive that until it was all published together. During the time that it came out in fragments they were delighted. Although, in this instance, the writing was overcharged, still it proved, from the popularity it obtained when it appeared in the magazine, what force and condensation of matter is required in writing for periodicals.

Chapter Thirty One

I am grave to-day; it is the birth-day of one of my children—a day so joyful in youth, in more advanced life so teeming with thought and serious reflections. How happy the child is—and it is its happiness which has made me grave.

How changed are our feelings as we advance in life!—Our responsibility is increased with each fleeting year. In youth we live but for ourselves—self predominates in every thing. In mature age, if we have fulfilled the conditions of our tenure, we feel that we must live for our children. Fortunately, increase of years weans us from those selfish and frivolous expenses which youth requires, and we feel it little or no sacrifice to devote to our children the means which, before, we considered so important to the gratification of our pride and our ambition. Not that we have lost either our pride or our ambition, but they have become centred in other objects dearer to us than ourselves—in the race springing up—to whom we shall leave our names and worldly possessions when our own career is closed.

Worn out with the pursuit of vanity, we pause at a certain age, and come to the conclusion that in this life we require but little else than to eat, drink, prepare for a future existence, and to die.

What a miserable being must an old bachelor be!—he vegetates, but he cannot be said to exist—he passes his life in one long career of selfishness, and dies. Strange, that children, and the responsibility attached to their welfare, should do more to bring a man into the right path than any denunciations from holy writ or holy men! How many who might have been lost, have been, it is to be hoped, saved, from the feeling that they must leave their children a good name, and must provide for their support and advancement in life! Yes, and how many women, after a life so frivolous as to amount to wickedness, have, from their attachment to their offspring, settled down into the redeeming position of careful, anxious, and serious-minded mothers!

Such reflections will rise upon a birth-day, and many more of chequered hopes and fears. How long will these flowers, now blossoming so fairly, be permitted to remain with us? Will they be mowed down before another birth-day, or will they be permitted to live to pass through the ordeal of this life of temptation? How will they combat? Will they fall and disgrace their parents, or will they be a pride and blessing? Will it please Heaven to allow them to be not too much tempted, not overcome by sickness, or that they shall be severely chastised? Those germs of virtue now appearing, those tares now growing up with the corn—will the fruit bring forth good seed? will the latter be effectually rooted up by precept and example? How much to encourage! and how much to check! Virtues in excess are turned to vice—liberality becomes extravagance—prudence, avarice—courage, rashness—love, weakness—even religion may turn to fanaticism—and superior intellect may, in its daring, mock the power which granted it. Alas! what a responsibility is here. A man may enjoy or suffer when he lives for himself alone; but he is doubly blest or doubly cursed when, in his second stage, he is visited through his children. What a blessing is our ignorance of the future! Fatal, indeed, to all happiness in this world would be a foreknowledge of that which is to come. We have but to do our duty and hope for the best, acknowledging, however severe may be the dispensation, that whatever is, or is to be, is right.

How strange, although we feel in the midst of life we are in death, that mortals should presume to reduce it to a nice calculation, and speculate upon it! I can sell my life now to an annuity-office for twenty years' purchase or more, and they will share a dividend upon it. Well, if ever I do insure my life, I hope that by *me* they will lose money, for, like every body else in this world, I have a great many things to do before I die. There was but one man I ever heard of who could lie down and die, saying, "Now, Lord, let thy servant depart in peace." I have no warning yet, no screw is loose in this complex mechanism; and yet, this very day, a chimney-pot may fall on my head, and put an end to all my calculations.

It is right that the precarious tenure of our existence should not be wholly forgotten, but certainly was never intended that it should be borne on the mind, for, if we had ever in our memory that we may die this very hour, what a check there would be to all energy, and enterprise, and industry. Who would speculate with the anticipation of large returns upon some future day, if he did not calculate upon living to receive them? We should all stop to say *Cui bono*? If it were not that our hopes support us, not only support us in all reasonable, but even unreasonable calculations, the world would be at a stand-still. No, no! we have our duty to perform towards our God; but we are also enjoined to perform our duty towards our neighbour. The uncertainty of life is to be remembered as a check to our worldly passions, but not as a drag-chain to our worldly career.

Chapter Thirty Two

En route, August, 1837.

There is a great art in packing property, and in it our profession are fortunately adepts. A midshipman, for instance, contrives to put every thing at the bottom of his chest. No very easy matter to pack up and arrange a carriage full of children, two birds, and a spaniel puppy—in all, twelve living beings with all their appendages, down to the birds and dogs' tails. As for packing up a dog, that is impossible; the best way is to pack it off. Canary birds travel very well in the carriage lamps, in the summer time, when they are not lighted; and I mention this as a hint to those who travel with such indispensable appendages; independent of their being out of the way, their appearance behind the glass is a source of great amusement to those who are standing by where you change horses.

Stopped at Saint Frond, and asked what was to be seen. Nothing here but churches and monks. One of the little girls, three years old, looked with avidity at the Virgin Mary, three feet high, in gold brocade. The old verger observing this, led her nearer to it, ascribing her admiration probably to piety, when, to his horror, she screamed out, "*Quel jolie poupée!*" Solomon says, "Out of the mouths of babes shall ye be taught wisdom." The old man dropped her hand, and looked as if he would have lighted the faggots had she been bound to the stake, as she, in his opinion, deserved.

The perseverance of Belgian beggars is most remarkable, and equally annoying. The best way is to take out your purse, and pretend to throw something over their heads; they turn back to look for it; and if you keep pointing farther off, you distance them. On the whole, I consider that it is much more advisable not to give to beggars, than to relieve them. Begging is demoralising, and should be discountenanced in every country. If children are brought up to whine, cry, and humiliate themselves as in Belgium, that feeling of pride and independence in early youth, which leads to industry in after life, is destroyed. And yet, the aged and infirm would appear to be proper objects of charity. In many cases, of course, they must be; but to prove how you may be deceived, I will state a circumstance which occurred to me some years ago.

I was driving up the road with a friend. He was one of the pleasantest and most honest men that nature ever moulded. His death was most extraordinary: of a nervous temperament, ill health ended in aberration of intellect. At that time Lord Castlereagh had ended his life of over-excitement by suicide; the details in the newspapers were read by him, and he fancied that he was Lord Castlereagh. Acting precisely by the accounts recorded in the newspapers, he went through the same forms, and actually divided his carotid artery, using his penknife, as had done the unfortunate peer. Peace be with him! To proceed. I was driving in a gig, a distance of about forty miles from town, on the Northern Road, when, at the bottom of a steep hill, we fell in with a group who were walking up it. It consisted of a venerable old man, with his grey locks falling down on his shoulders, dressed as a countryman, with a bundle on a stick over his shoulders; with him were a young man and woman, both heavily burdened, and five children of different sizes. The appearance of the old man was really patriarchal, and there was a placidity in his countenance which gave a very favourable impression. For a short time they continued breasting the hill on the pathway: when about one-third up, the old man crossed the road to us, as our horse was walking up, and taking off his hat, said, "Gentlemen, if not too great a liberty, may I ask how far it is to —?" mentioning a town about twelve miles off. We told him, and he replied, "That's a long way for old legs like mine, and young legs of tired children." He then informed us that they had lost their employment in the country, and that, with his son and daughter, and their children, he had gone to town to procure work, but had been unsuccessful, and they were now on their return. "God's will be done!" continued he, after his narrative, "and thankful shall we be to find ourselves at our cottages again, although twelve miles is a weary bit of road, and I have but a few halfpence left; but that will buy a bit of bread for the poor children, and we must do as we can. Good morning, and thank'ye kindly, gentlemen."

Now there was no begging here, certainly, except by implication. The effect, however, of his narrative was to extract a crown out of our pockets, which was received with a shower of blessings on our heads. We drove off, observing how difficult it was to know how to select real objects of charity, and flattering ourselves that alms in this instance were worthily bestowed. My readers will agree with me, I have no doubt.

It so happened that, about ten days afterwards, I was driving on the Dover Road, in the same gig, and in company with the same gentleman, when we came to the bottom of Shooters Hill. Who should we fall in with but the very same party, the venerable old man, the young people, and the children trudging up the pathway. The same plan of proceeding was observed, for, although we recognised them immediately it appeared that they did not recognise us. We allowed the old fellow to tell his tale, as before; it was just the same. He first took off his hat, and inquired the distance to

—; and then entered into the same narrative, only changing the place of abode, and ending with his few halfpence to buy bread for the children. I let him finish, and then I did not, as before, give him a crown, but I gave him a cut across his face with the whip, which made him drop his bundle, put his hands up to it; and we left him, stamping with pain in the middle of the road, till we were out of sight. A young rogue I can easily pardon, but an old one, on the verge of the grave, is a proof of hardened villainy, which admits of no extenuation. After giving him this *cut direct*, we never met again.

To return to Saint Frond.—In the last church we visited we had a scene. A woman was in the confessional; the priest, with a white handkerchief up to conceal his face, and prevent what he said being overheard, attracted the attention of the children, who demanded an explanation. Children ask so many questions. "Do you think she has been very wicked? Will he forgive her?" Before I could offer my opinion upon this important subject, the woman gave a loud scream, and fell back from the confessional in a fit. The priest rose, the handkerchief no longer concealed his face, and he appeared to be burning with indignation. She was carried out of the church, and the priest hastened up the aisle to the vestry. What had she done? At all events, something for which it appeared there was no absolution.

Aix-la-Chapelle—alas! What did we care for the tomb of Charles the Great, and his extensive dominions, his splendour and power? We had lost something to us of much more importance—a carpet bag; not that the carpet bag was of much value, for it was an old one, nor the articles which it contained, for they were neither new nor of much worth; but we lost in that carpet bag an invaluable quantity of comfort, for it contained a variety of little absolute necessaries, the loss of which we could not replace until our arrival at Cologne, to which town all our trunks had been despatched. The children could not be brushed, for the brushes were in the carpet bag; they could not be combed, for the combs were in the carpet bag; they were put to bed without nightcaps, for the night-caps were in the carpet bag; they were put to bed in their little chemises, reaching down to the fifth rib or thereabouts, for their night-clothes were in the carpet bag: not only the children, but every one else suffered by this carpet bag being absent without leave. My boots burst, and my others were in the carpet bag; my snuff-box was empty, and the canister was in the carpet bag; and the servants grumbled, for they had smuggled some of their things into the carpet bag.

It would appear that everything had been crammed into this unfortunate receptacle. Had we lost a jewel-case, or a purse full of money, it would have been a trifle compared to the misery occasioned by this jumble up of every day conveniences of little value, showing how much more comfort depends upon the necessaries than the luxuries of life. I may add, now that I read what I have written, that this carpet bag increased in dimensions to a most extraordinary compass for several weeks afterwards. Everything that was missing was declared by the servants to have been in the carpet bag, which, like the scape-goat of the Jews, wandered in the wilderness, bearing with it all the sins of all the nurses and every other domestic of the family.

On our road, the landlord of an inn put the following printed document into my hands, which I make public for the benefit of those who are sportsmen without being landholders.

> " *Comfortable Inn* .—The proprietor of the Red House, at Burgheim, on the road from Aix-la-Chapelle to Cologne, pleasantly situated in the middle of the town, opposite the Post-Office and Post-House, has the honour of recommending himself to travellers. The 'Galignani's Messenger' and other newspapers are taken in. The English, German, and French languages spoken. Having excellent preserves of game in the neighbourhood, he is happy to inform travellers that he can provide them with good sports in wild boar, deer, and hare hunting, and wild duck and partridge shooting. Horses and carriages of all descriptions supplied for excursions in the neighbourhood.
>
> " *AJ Hons* ."

Prussia.—I fear that our political economists are running after a shadow, and that their reciprocity system will never be listened to. It is remarkable, that, after subsidising this and other powers to break up the continental system established by Napoleon for the expulsion of English manufactures and the consequent ruin of England, now that the world is at peace, these very powers who, by our exertions and our money, have been liberated from their thraldom, have themselves established the very system of exclusion which we were so anxious to prevent. A little reflection will prove that they are right. The government of a country ought never, if possible, to allow that country to be dependent upon any other for such resources as it can obtain by its own industry. We, ourselves, acted upon this principle when we established the silk manufactories in Spitalfields; and it is the duty of every government to do the same.

The indigenous productions of the soil may fairly be admitted on a system of reciprocity and exchange, but not articles of manufacture, of which the raw material is to be obtained by all. For instance, the lead, and iron, and tin of Great Britain, the wines of other countries, are all articles to be exchanged or paid for by those who have not mines of those metals, or do not possess vineyards. Further than this reciprocity cannot go, without being injurious to one, if not to both parties.

Three of the carriage-wheels defective! Add this to the carpet bag, and people will agree in the trite observation that misfortunes never come single. This is not true; they do come single very often, and when they do, they are more annoying than if they come in heaps. You growl at a single mishap, but if you find that Fortune is down upon you and attempts to overload you, you rise up against her with indignation, snap your fingers, and laugh at her. The last mishap brought consolation for all the others; if we had not so fortunately found out the defects in the wheels, we might have broken our necks the next day, especially, as some amateur took a fancy and helped himself to our *sabot*. I only wish he may be shod with it for the remainder of his days.

It is curious how the ignorant and simple always rise or depreciate others, whatever their rank may be, to their own levels, when they talk of them. I listened to one little girl telling a story to another, in which kings, queens, and princesses were the actors.

"And so," said the queen to the princess, "what a very pretty doll that is of yours!"

"Yes, your majesty; papa bought it for me at the bazaar, and gave 5 shillings 6 pence for it," etcetera.

This reminded me of the sailors telling stories on board of a man-of-war, who put very different language into the mouth of royalty.

"Well," says the king, "blow me tight if I'll stand this. You must buckle-to as fast as you please, Mrs Queen."

"I'll see you hanged first, and your head shaved too," answered her majesty in a rage, etcetera, etcetera. What queens may say in a rage it is impossible to assert; but to the seamen this language appeared to be perfectly regal and quite correct.

Some people form odd notions of gentility. A cabman took up a well-dressed female, who made use of expressions which rather startled him, and he observed to a friend of his, a hackney-coachman, that he had no idea that the higher classes used such language.

"Pooh! pooh!" replied the coachman, "she warn't a lady."

"I beg your pardon," replied the cabman, "a real lady, *hat and feathers*!"

Cologne.—This is a regular Golgotha—the skulls of the Magi, *par excellence*, and then the skulls of Saint Ursula and her 11,000 virgins. I wonder where she collected so many! Saint Ursula brought a great force into the field, at all events, and, I presume, commands the right wing of the whole army of martyrs. I went into the golden chamber, where there are some really pretty things. The old fellow handed us the articles one after another, but I observed that there were many things which I had seen when here before, which were not presented to view, so I looked into the cabinet and found them. They were crystal vases, mounted with gold and precious stones. One had the thigh-bone of Saint Sebastian; another, part of the ulna of Saint Lawrence; and a third a bit of the petticoat of the Virgin Mary. I handed them out to the ladies, and asked him why he did not show us those as he used to do before. The old man smiled and turned the corners of his mouth down, as if to say, "Its all humbug!" Relics are certainly at a discount, even among the Catholics.

I question whether the Bridge of Boats at Cologne don't pay better than any other in the whole world, although by no means the handsomest; the stream of passengers on it all day is as strong and as wide as the Rhine itself. As for Cologne, the best thing that could happen to it is to be burnt down. Narrow streets, badly ventilated, badly drained; your nose is visited with a thousand varieties of smell as you pass along; and the Eau de Cologne in the gutters is very different in savour from that which you buy in the bottles.

We had a pleasant passage from Cologne to Coblentz, and from thence to Mayence, because we had pleasant company. It is singular, but it is a fact, that you go on board a steamboat to avoid fatigue, and each night you are more tired than if you had travelled by land. You go to avoid dust and heat; the first is exchanged for blacks out of the funnel, and you are more dirty than if you had travelled twice the distance; and the heat is about the same; in these points you certainly gain nothing. The expense of these Rhine steamboats is very great. By a calculation I made—to travel by post, five persons in a carriage, from Cologne to Strasburg—you will expend 200 and odd francs less than by the steam conveyance. In time you certainly lose by steam, as you are four days and a half going to Strasburg, and by land carriage it is half the distance, being only forty-five posts.

Neither do you save trouble; for the steam-boats being changed every evening, you have to take your luggage on shore, shift it from one to the other, and, at the very time that you are least inclined to do anything, independent of an enormous expense which you ought not to pay, but cannot well resist.

Now, as you really gain nothing in the above points, it is at least to be supposed that you gain in the picturesque; but this is not the case: and I have no hesitation in asserting that those who go up the Rhine are generally disappointed, although they do not like to say so. They expect too much.—

The vivid descriptions, the steel engravings, have raised their anticipations too high; and they find that the reality is not equal to the efforts of the pen and pencil. Several of the passengers acknowledged to me that they were disappointed; and I must confess that I hardly knew the Rhine again. When I travelled up the Rhine by land I thought it beautiful; but in a steam-boat it was tame.

This was observed by others, besides myself, who had ascended both by steam and by the road running close to the banks; and the reason was simple. When you travel by land you have the whole breadth of the Rhine as a foreground to the scenery of the opposite bank, and this you lose by water; and the bank you travel on is much more grand from its towering above you, and also from the sharp angles and turns which so suddenly change the scenery. Abruptness greatly assists the picturesque: the Rhine loses half its beauty viewed from a steam-boat. I have ascended it in both ways, and I should recommend all travellers to go up by land. The inconveniences in a steam-boat are many. You arrive late and find the hotel crowded, and you are forced to rise very early (as Mayence at three o'clock in the morning), which, with a family, is no trifle. The only part of the Rhine worth seeing is from Cologne to Mayence; below Cologne and above Mayence it is without interest; and although between these two places the steam-boats are well served, above Mayence everything is very uncomfortable, and you are liable to every species of exaction.

If I were to plan a tour up the Rhine for any friends, I should advise them not to go by the Rotterdam steamer; it is a long voyage and without interest, and with many inconveniences; but start in the steamer to Antwerp, go up to Brussels by the rail-road; from thence you will start for Cologne by the route of Namur and Liege through Waterloo; and I rather expect that many will prefer the banks of the *Meuse* to the Rhine. I know nothing more beautiful than the road from Namur as far as Chaude Fontaine, although compared to the Rhine it is on a miniature scale. From Liege to Aix-la-Chapelle, and from thence to Cologne. Go up the Rhine by land as far as Mayence, and then you may do as you please. When you are coming back, descend by the steam-boats; for then you go with the stream and with great rapidity, and arrive in good time at the towns where they stop. You will then have seen the Rhine by land and by water.

At present the bubble is at its height; but it will burst by-and-by. The English are lining the banks of the Rhine with gold, and receive insult and abuse in exchange. I have been much amused with a young countryman who has come up in the steamer with me. Not able to speak a word of French or German, he is pillaged every hour of the day; but if he could speak, he has no idea of the value of his money. He pulls out his purse, and the waiters help themselves—very *plentifully*, I may safely add. What he has come for it is difficult to say: not for the picturesque, for he slept the whole time between Cologne and Mayence—that is, all the time that was not occupied by eating and drinking. His only object appears to be to try the Rhenish wines. He has tried all upon the *Wein Presen*. He called for a bottle of the best; they gave him one not on the *carte*, and charged him exactly one pound sterling for the bottle. He is a generous fellow; he sits at the table with his bottle before him, and invites every man to partake of it. And he found plenty on board who were willing to oblige him.

"Capital wine, an't it?" said he to a Frenchman who drank his wine, but did not understand a word of English.

"A votre santé, Monsieur," replied the Frenchman.

"I say, what wine do you call it?"

"C'est exquis, Monsieur," replied the Frenchman.

"Eskey, is it? You, waiter, bring us another bottle of eskey."

Chapter Thirty Three

To continue.—Should travellers think it advisable to proceed upon the Rhine, so far as Mayence, let them be careful how they venture to proceed farther. I did so, out of curiosity to know what the features of the Rhine were, after it had lost its character for magnificence; and I will now detail my progress. At Mayence you are shifted into a smaller steamer, with less power, upon the principle that there being but a few passengers, their comforts do not require so much attention; for, as the Rhine becomes more rapid as it narrows, upon any other principle the power of the engine should have been greater. I must caution the reader not to believe what is told them by the steam-packet company.

Barbers were once considered liars *par excellence*, but I am inclined to give the preference to these new associations. The features of the Rhine change immediately that you leave Mayence; the banks are low, and the river is studded with numerous islands, all of which, as well as the greatest proportion of the banks, are covered with osiers. Still, there is a great beauty in the Rhine even there; the waving of the osiers to the strong breeze, the rapidity of the current, the windings of the river, the picturesque spires of the village churches, or the change of scenery when the river pours through forests, lining each bank as the vessel slowly claws against the rapid stream, are by no means uninteresting; of course we did not arrive at Leopoldshaffen at the hour stated by the people at the office, but we did arrive late at night, and took up our quarters at a small auberge in the above village, which is not marked down in the maps, but which has post-horses and diligences to convey passengers to Carlsruhe. Notwithstanding the assertion at the packet-office, that we were to be in one day to Leopoldshaffen, in one day more to Strasburg, we found there was no steamer until the day after the morrow, and that we must wait one day more if we did not choose to go to Carlsruhe. The females, being fatigued, preferred remaining where they were. We sauntered about and amused ourselves quietly. The next day, we found the steamer had arrived, and that instead of her ascending in one day to Strasburg, it would take a day and a half, and that we must pass the night aboard without the least accommodation—not very pleasant, with a carriage full of young children. We embarked on board the steamer, which was a miserable small vessel, with an engine of bad construction, and very small power; and with this we were to oppose the most rapid part of the Rhine.

In every other point the vessel was equally ill found: they had a very small stock of provisions, bad wine, and none of those comforts provided for the passengers in the other vessels. To crown all, another family with children (of whom more hereafter) had taken their passage. The steward told us, that never expecting so many people on board going up to Strasburg, he was totally unprepared; and so it eventually appeared.

We started, and soon found out that the power of the engines was quite disproportionate to the object in view. The Rhine now assumed a more desolate character. For miles and miles not a village nor even a solitary town to be seen; the Hartz mountains forming a blue opaque mass in the distance; the stream rapidly passing through narrow and deep channels, leaving one half of the bed of the river dry. At times we passed very dangerous straits, where the waters boiled and eddied over reefs of rocks, and were often obliged to force our way by keeping within a foot of steep and muddy banks, where trees torn up, and hanging by the roots, proved how violent must be the current when the river is increased by the melting of the mountain snow.

Our progress was, as it may be imagined, most tedious; at no time did we advance above a mile and a half per hour; sometimes we did not gain a hundred yards in the same time, and occasionally we were swept back by the current, and had to lose still more ground, while they increased the power of the engine at the risk of explosion. The consequence was, that when the day closed, the conducteur gave his opinion, that instead of being at Strasburg by eleven or twelve o'clock the next day, we should not arrive till four or five o'clock: we anchored within a yard of the bank, and prepared to pass the night how we could.

Our party consisted of seven, with two nurses. The other party consisted of four grown-up females, one male, four boys, an East African negro, and a *cowskin*; the latter was a very important personage, and made a great noise during the passage. The gentleman was apparently one of those who denominate themselves eclectic: he paid very little attention to what was going on; a peaceable sort of man, whose very physiognomy said "any thing for a quiet life:" one of the ladies was his wife, and two others, virgins of some standing, apparently his sisters; the other lady, a bilious-looking sort of personage, and happy in being the mother of four very fine boys, as great pickles as ever lived; these she kept in order with the assistance of the negro and the cowskin, the use of the latter occasioning such evident marks of astonishment and horror to *our* little ones, as not to be at all satisfactory to the lady in question, who appeared not averse, had she dared, to have given them a taste of it. The youngest and the youngest but one of the boys were the two sufferers; the youngest had a regular dozen administered every half hour. The two eldest were more particularly under the care of the negro, who used his fists, I presume because they wore corduroys, and, as Hood says, did not care for "cut behind." We had not been in the vessel two minutes before there was a *breeze*. I heard the negro expostulating as follows: — "You very foolish boy, what you mean? who ever heard of putting new cloth cap into water to catch fish?" This was the first offence. I must say that the coercion used did not appear to originate from any feeling of regard for the children, for they were allowed to climb, and push, and run over the sky-lights, and over the engine, and I every moment expected that some of them would be provided for either by the cog-wheels or the river Rhine.

It was evident at once, not only from the above accessories, but from the Chinese trunks which contained their luggage, that they were an Indian importation, and their behaviour subsequently proved it, beyond all doubt, even if they had not made it known—not by talking to us, but by talking at us, for they evidently did not consider that we were sufficiently respectable to be admitted into their society, even in the short intercourse of fellow-travellers.

I cannot here help making an observation relative to most of the people who come from India. They are always dissatisfied, and would gladly return. The reason is very obvious; they at once lose their rank and consequence, and sink down to the level which they are entitled to in English society. In India the rank of the servants of the Company takes precedence; but whatever their rank or emolument may be in India, they are still but servants of a company of merchants, and such rank is not, of course, allowed in England. Accustomed to unlimited sway and control over a host of fawning slaves, and to that attention as females—which, where females are not very plentiful, is most sedulously paid—accustomed to patronise the newcomers, who, of course, feel grateful for such well-timed civility and hospitality—in short, accustomed to rank, splendour, wealth, and power—it is not surprising that, upon their return to England, when they find themselves shorn of all these, and that their station in society is far more removed from the apex, they become sullen and dissatisfied. Of course, there are many who have been resident in India, where family and connections insure them every advantage upon their return to their native country; but it must be recollected that the greater proportion of those who return consists of those who were of low origin, and who have obtained their appointments in reward for the exertions of their parents in behalf of their patrons in parliamentary returns, etcetera, and of young females who have (with their face as their fortune) been shipped off to India upon a matrimonial speculation. Now, however high in rank they may have, in the course of many years' service, arrived to in India, when they return they are nobodies; and unless they bring with them such wealth as to warrant their being designated as nabobs, their chance of admittance into the best society is very small indeed.

I have said that they *talked* at us, and not to us. The gentleman was civil, and would have conversed, but he was immediately interrupted and sent off on a message; and, for a quiet life, he gave it up. The system of talking at people always reminds me of the play of the "Critic," in which it is asked why, if "he knows all this, it is necessary to tell him again?" Simply because the audience do not; so, the party in question were the actors, and we were the audience to be informed. The conversation between the adults run as follows:—

"You recollect how polite Lord C— was to us at —?"

"To be sure I do."

"Lady D— told me so and so."

"Yes, I recollect it very well."

"What a nice man the Honourable Mr E— is!"

"Yes, that he is."

"How very intimate we were at — with Lady G—."

"That we were."

And so on, during the whole of the day, much to our edification. How contemptible, how paltry is such vanity! But with their indulgence of it for our amusement, the cow-skin, and a scanty dinner, we got through the first day, during which two or three occasional patronising questions or remarks were thrown at our heads, and then they reverted to their own assumed exclusiveness. The night, as may be supposed, was anything but comfortable to those in the cabin; but I shall not dwell upon what, if fairly narrated, would be a very pretty sketch of human nature.

We were to arrive the next day at five o'clock in the afternoon, but we toiled on; and the sun at last went down, and we found ourselves with the steeple of Strasburg a long way off. We again anchored, and had to pass another night in this miserable vessel and delightful company. The detention, of course, made our fellow-passengers more cross; and could I have obtained possession of the cowskin, I would certainly have thrown it overboard. The captain sent a man on shore to procure us something to eat, for the steward declared himself bankrupt. The next forenoon we arrived at the bridge of boats between Kehl and Strasburg; and thus was finished our tedious and unpleasant voyage, of which I have given a description as a warning to all future travellers. Our fellow-passengers did once condescend to address and inform us that they had left England (a party of ten people) only to pay a visit to some friends in Switzerland—an expensive sort of trip, and which did not appear at all consistent with the fact that they were travelling without a carriage or female servants. Be it as it might, we separated without so much as a salutation or good-bye being exchanged.

Much of the picturesque on the Rhine is destroyed by the vineyards, which are, in reality, the most unpoetical things in landscape scenery, being ranged up the sides of the mountains in little battalions like infantry. It is remarkable in how shallow and how very poor a soil the vine will grow. At Saint Michael's, they dig square holes in the volcanic rocks, and the vines find sustenance. At the Cape of Good Hope the Constantia vineyards are planted upon little more than sand. I dug down some depth; and could find nothing else. The finest grapes grown in Burgundy are upon a stratum of soil little more than a foot deep, over schistus slate quarries, and the soil itself composed chiefly of the *débris* of this soft rock.

We know that the vegetable creation has a sort of instinct as well as the animal and it appears to me that there are different degrees of instinct in that portion of nature as well as in the other. A vine, for instance, I take to be a very clever plant, and both apple and pear-trees to be great fools. The vine will always seek its own nourishment, hunting with its roots through the soil for the aliment it requires; and if it cannot find it where it is planted, it will seek, in every direction and to a great distance, to obtain it. It is asserted that the famous vine at Hampton Court has passed its roots under the bed of the river, and obtains aliment from the soil on the other side; but an apple or pear-tree will take no such trouble—it will not even avoid what is noxious. Plant one of these trees in the mould three or four feet above the marl or clay; so long as the roots remain in the mould, the tree will flourish, but so soon as the tap root pierces down to the marl or clay below the mould, the tree will canker and die. To prevent this, it is the custom to dig first down to the marl and put a layer of tiles upon it, which turn the roots of the trees from a perpendicular to a horizontal direction, and then they do well; but leave the tree without assistance, and the fool will commit suicide, blindly rushing to its own destruction; while the vine will not only avoid it, but use every exertion to procure what is necessary for its continuing in health and vigour. The vine is therefore certainly the more intellectual plant of the two.

Chapter Thirty Four

Strasbourg.

There certainly is an impulse implanted in our natures to love something; our affections were never intended to lie in abeyance, and if they cannot be placed upon the other sex or our own children, they still seek something as an object. This accounts for old bachelors being fond of their nephews and nieces, for blood relationship has nothing to do with it; and for old ladies, who have not entered into wedlock, becoming so attached to dogs, cats, and parrots. Sometimes, indeed, the affections take much wilder flights in the pursuit of an object, and exhibit strange idiosyncrasies; but still it proves by nature we are compelled to love something. I have been reflecting how far this principle may not be supposed to pervade through the universe, and whether we cannot trace it in the inferiors of the animal creation: whether we cannot trace a small remnant of Paradise in the beasts who enjoyed it with man, as well as in man himself. It is well known that animals will take very strong and very strange attachments towards other animals. It is, perhaps, more apparent in domestic animals, but is not that because they are more brought together and more under our immediate eye? in some instances, as in the case when maternal feelings are roused, the strongest antipathies and habit will be controlled. A cat losing her kittens has been known to suckle a brood of young rats, but in this case I consider instinct to have been the most powerful agent; wild beasts confined in cages show the same propensity. The lion secluded in his den has often been known to foster and become strongly attached to a dog thrown in to him to be devoured; but there never was an instance of a lion or any other wild beast, which had a female in the same den or even a companion of its own species, preserving the life of any other living creature thrown in to him. This feeling occasions also the production of Hybrids; which in a wild state could never take place. There is not, probably, a more ferocious or ill-tempered animal than the bear when it is grown up; it is subdued by fear, but shows no attachment to its keeper; yet, the other day I fell in with a remarkable narration proving the feeling I have referred to, actuating even this animal. A proof of the bad feeling of a bear is fully established by the fact that, although Martin, as the old bear is called in the Jardin des Plantes, at Paris, had been confined in his fosse nearly twenty years, during which time not a day passed that he was not well fed by the people who amused themselves in the gardens, when a man fell into his pit, he immediately destroyed him. It does, however, appear, that all bears are not so ill-tempered as Monsieur Martin. Leopold, Duke of Lorraine, had a bear confined by a long chain, near the palisades below the glacis. Some poor Savoyard boys, who had emigrated as they still do, with the hopes of picking up some money to take back with them, had taken shelter in an out-house daring a severe snow storm. One of them who was numbed with the cold, thought that he would try if he could not find some warmer berth, and in seeking this, as the snow fell fast, he at last crawled nearly exhausted into the kennel of the bear. Instead of tearing the lad to pieces, the bear took him in his fore paws, and pressed him to his shaggy warm coat till he was quite recovered. A bear generally receives you with open arms, whatever may be his ultimate decision; but in this instance it was favourable. The poor little boy finding himself in good quarters, went fast asleep; the next morning he sallied forth to obtain some victuals if he could, but without success. Cold and hunger drove him again to the kennel of the bear, who not only was delighted to see him, but had actually laid aside a portion of his supper for the boy's use. The amicable arrangement continued for some days, and the bear, at last, would not touch his victuals till the boy's return. This peculiar friendship was at last discovered, and the story narrated to the Duke, who sent for the boy, and took care of him, admitting him into his own household. The narrator observes that the boy died a year or two after this unusual occurrence had taken place. I have no doubt but that many more instances might be brought forward by others to establish my supposition. To us, all wild animals of the same species appear to be much alike in disposition, because we have not an opportunity of examining and watching them carefully, but I should rather imagine, that as we can perceive such a manifest difference in temper between individual horses and dogs and other animals who are domesticated, that the same difference must exist in the wild species, and that, in fact, there may be shades of virtue and vice in lions, tigers, bears, and other animals; and that there does exist in animals as well as in man, more or less according to their natural dispositions, a remnant of those affections which in the garden of our first parents were so strongly implanted as to induce the lion to lie down with the lamb. "God is Love," says the Scriptures; before the devil found his way to this earth all was love, for God only was there. Now man struggles between the two principles of good and evil. When his nature was changed, so was that of animals; but the principle not being extinct in man, why should not a portion still remain in the rest of the creation, who with him were permitted to inhabit the garden of Eden, and whose savage natures were not roused until with man they were driven from that abode of peace?

The most affectionate animal that I know of is the common brown Mongoose: it is a creature between the squirrel and the monkey, with all the liveliness but without any of the mischief of the latter. Unfortunately they will not live in our country, or they would supersede the cat altogether; they are very clean, and their attachment is beyond all conception to those who have not seen them. They will leap on their master's shoulder, or get into his bed, and coil their long bushy tails round his neck like a boa, remaining there for hours if permitted. I recollect one poor little fellow who was in his basket dying—much to the grief of his master—who, just before he expired, crawled out of his straw and went to his master's cot, where he had just sufficient strength to take his place upon his bosom, coil his tail round his neck, and then he died.

Hares and rabbits are also very affectionate. One of my little girls had one of the latter, which she brought up in the house. He grew very large, and was domesticated just like a dog, following you everywhere, in the parlour and up into the bed-room; in the winter lying on the rug before the fire on his side, and stretching out his four legs as unconcerned as possible, even refusing to go away if you pushed him. As for the cat, she durst not go near him. He thrashed her unmercifully, for he was very strong; and the consequence was that she retired to the kitchen, where he would often go down, and if she was in his way drive her out. The hare and rabbit, as well as the deer tribe, defend themselves by striking with their fore paws, and the blow which they can give is more forcible than people would suppose. One day when I was in a cover, leaning against a tree, with my gun in my hand, I presume for some time I must have been in deep thought, I heard a rustling and then a squeak on the other side of the tree; I looked round the trunk, and beheld a curious combat between two hares and a stoat. The hares were male and female, and had their leveret between them, which latter was not above six weeks old. The stoat—a little devil with all its hair, from the tip of its nose to the end of its tail, standing at end—was at about two yards distance from them, working round and round to have an opportunity to spring upon the leveret, which was the object of its attack. As it went round so did the hares face him, pivoting on a centre with the young one between them. At last the stoat made a spring upon the leveret. He was received by the hares, who struck him with their fore feet such blows as I could not have believed possible; they actually resounded, and he was rolled over and over until he got out of distance, when he shook himself and renewed his attacks. These continued about ten minutes, and every time he was beaten off; but, at every spring, his teeth went into the poor little leveret; at last it gave its last squeak, turned over on its side, and died, the father and mother still holding their relative situations, and facing the stoat. The latter showed as much prudence as courage; for so soon as he perceived that the leveret was dead, he also walked off. The hares turned round to their young one, smelt at it apparently, pushed it with their noses, and shortly after, as if aware that it was past all defence, hopped slowly away; they were hardly out of sight in the bushes when back came the stoat, threw the leveret, twice as big as himself, over his shoulders, and went off with his prize at a hard gallop, reminding me, in miniature, of the Bengal tiger carrying off a bullock. All the actors in the drama having gone off; I walked off, and shortly after both barrels of my gun went off, so the whole party disappeared, and there's an end of my story.

If an elephant were not so very unwieldy, and at the same time so very uncertain in his temper, he is the animal who has the most claims from affection and intelligence to be made a pet of; but an elephant in a drawing-room would be somewhat incommodious; and, although one may admit a little irritability of temper in a lap-dog weighing three pounds, the anger of an elephant, although he expresses himself very sorry for it afterwards, is attended with serious consequences. There is something very peculiar about an elephant in his anger and irritability. It sometimes happens that, at a certain season, a wild elephant will leave the herd and remain in the woods alone. It is supposed, and I think that the supposition is correct, that these are the weaker males who have been driven away by the stronger, in fact, they are elephants crossed in love; and when in that unfortunate dilemma, they are very mischievous, and play as many fantastic tricks as ever did any of the knights of the round table on similar occasions in times of yore.

I was at Trincomalee; an elephant in this situation had taken possession of the road at some leagues distant, and, for reasons best known to himself, would not allow a soul to pass it. He remained *perdu* in the jungle till he saw somebody coming, and then he would burst out and attack them. It is the custom to travel in palanquins from one part of the island to another, as in all parts of India. If some officer or gentleman was obliged to proceed to Colombo or elsewhere, so soon as the palanquin came towards him, out came the elephant; the native bearers, who knew that it was no use arguing the point, dropped the palanquin and fled, and all that the occupant could do was to bundle out and do the same before the elephant came up, otherwise he had little chance of his life, for the elephant immediately put his knees in the palanquin and smashed it to atoms. Having done this, he would toss the fragments in the air in every direction, at the same time carefully unfolding all the articles contained in the palanquin for the occupants use—shirts, trowsers, boots, bottles, books, undergoing a most rigid examination, and after that being rendered to fragments. If the cooley who had the charge of the bag of letters made his appearance, he was immediately pursued until he gave up the whole correspondence, official or private. The bag was opened, every letter was opened one by one, and then torn in fragments and tossed to the winds. In this way did he keep possession of the road, stopping all communication for several weeks, until it was his sovereign will and pleasure that people might receive their letters and travel across the country as before. Now what an unaccountable freak was this! It was like the madness of a reasonable being. If I recollect right, it was when Captain Owen was on the east coast of Africa, some of his party who landed were attacked by elephants, who threw them down on the ground and, instead of killing them, as might have been expected, and would have given them no trouble, they drew up a large quantity of mud in their trunks and poured it into their mouths so as to nearly to suffocate them, and then left them. On another occasion, they put their fore feet on their limbs, so as to pinch and bruise them severely in every part of their bodies, but avoided their bones so as not to fracture one. Now this was evidently two species of torture invented by the elephants, and these elephants in a wild state. There certainly is something very incomprehensible about these animals.

The lion has been styled the king of beasts, but I think he is an usurper allowed to remain on the throne by public opinion and suffrage, from the majesty of his appearance. In every other point he has no claim. He is the head of the feline or cat species, and has all the treachery, cruelty, and wanton love for blood that all this class of animals have to excess. The lion, like the tiger and the cat, will not come boldly on to his prey, but springs from his concealment. It is true that he will face his assailants bravely when wounded, but so will the tiger.

In my opinion, the horse is the most noble of all animals, and, I am sorry to say, the most ill-used, at least in England; for I do not recollect a single instance of having seen a horse ill-treated on the Continent. In fact, you hardly ever see a horse on the Continent that is not in good working condition: you never meet the miserable, lame, blind, and worn-out animals that you do in England, which stumble along with their loads behind them till they stumble into their graves. If any one would take the trouble to make friends with their horses, they would be astonished at the intelligence and affection of this noble animal; but we leave him to our grooms, who prefer to use force to kindness. At the same time, I have observed, even in colts, very different dispositions; some are much more fond and good-tempered than others; but let them be what they will as colts, they are soon spoiled by the cruelty and want of judgment of those who have charge of them in the stable. The sympathy between the Arab and his horse is well known: the horse will lie down in the tent, and the children have no fear of receiving a kick; on the contrary, they roll upon, and with him: such is the result of kindness. And I can now give a proof of the effects of the contrary, as it was, in this instance, what may be termed *malice prepense* in the animal. The horses used in the West Indies are supplied from the Spanish Main; they are from the Andalusian stock originally, partly Arab and barb. These horses are taken by the lasso from the prairies, and are broken in as follows:— They head them down to the sea beach, saddle and bridle them for the first time, and mount them with a pair of spurs, the rowels of which are an inch long. So soon as the animal plunges and attempts to divest himself of his rider, he is forced into the sea, and there he is worked in and out of his depth till he is fairly worn out and exhausted. This is repeated once or twice till they are submissive, and then they are sent off as broke-in horses to the West India Islands. A friend of mine had a very beautiful animal, which he had purchased from one of these ships. He had not bought him more than a week before he took the bit in his mouth, and ran away with the black boy who was exercising him. The boy lost his seat and fell, and the horse, for a hundred yards, continued his career; and then it stopped, turned round, and galloped up to the boy, who was still on the ground, and never ceased kicking him till the poor fellow's brains were scattered in the road. Now this was evidently determination for revenge.

Chapter Thirty Five

Strasbourg is full of the pomp and circumstance of war. Being one of the keys of France, it has a garrison of ten thousand men, and the drums and bands play from morning to evening, much to the delight of the children, at all events. It is a well-built town, although the houses are most of them of very ancient date, with three stories of *mansardes*, in their high-peaked roofs. I am rather partial to the Alsatian character; it is a combination of French, Swiss, and German, which make a very good cross. Not being in any particular hurry, I have remained here ten days, and I will say for Strasbourg, that it has many recommendations. It is lively and bustling; the walks outside the ramparts are beautiful, and living is very reasonable. It has, however, the reputation of being a very unhealthy place, and, I am afraid, with truth. It is singular that the beautiful cathedral, although it has already suffered so much by lightning, has not yet been fitted with a conductor. There was a meeting of the dignitaries some years back; some argued in favour and some against it, and it ended in neither party being persuaded, and nothing being done. I met another Englishman here, to whom the question might so properly be put, "What the deuce are you doing here?" An old worthy, nearly seventy, who, after having passed his fair allowance of life very happily in his own country, must, forsooth, come up the Rhine, without being able to speak a word of French, or any other language but his own. He very truly told me that he had just begun to see the world at a time that he should be thinking of going out of it. He honoured me with the office of interpreter as long as he stayed, and I was not sorry to see him booked for the steam-boat, all the way to the London Custom House stairs.

There is one remarkable point about the town of Strasbourg, which is, that the Protestants and Catholics have, I believe always, and do now, live in a state of amity which ought to be an example to others. In running over the history of the town, I do not find that they ever persecuted each other; but if they have not persecuted each other, I am shocked to say that they have not spared the Jews. At the time of the plague, they accused the Jews of having occasioned it by poisoning the wells, and only burnt alive *two thousand of them at once*! I wonder when the lightning struck the cathedral they did not drown two thousand more in the Rhine—strange Christianity! when smitten by the hand of God, to revenge themselves by smiting their fellow-creatures. I had to call upon a Professor here upon some business;

he amused me very much; he fancied that he could speak English: perhaps he might have been able to do so at one time, but if so, he had forgotten it, but he did not think he had. I addressed him in French, and told him my business. "Sir, you speak English?"—"Yes," replied I. "Then, Sir, I tell you that—" Then he stopped, pondering and perplexed for some minutes, without saying a syllable. "Speak French, Sir," said I; "I perceive that you have forgotten a word in our language;" and I then put another leading question to him, to which he replied, "Yes, I recollect that very well, and I—" Then another dead pause for the verb. I waited a minute in perfect silence, but his memory was as treacherous as he was obstinately bent upon talking English, and then I again spoke to him, and he replied, "That is true, that you must—" Then he broke down again, and I broke up the conference, as I really could not wait until he formed English words, and he was evidently resolved that he would speak in no other language. Fortunately, it was no business of my own, but a commission from another, which ended in an omission, which, perhaps, did quite as well.

This morning I strolled into a small *débit de tabac*, to fill my box, and it being excessively warm, was not sorry to sit down and enter into a conversation with the young woman who attended upon the customers. I asked her, among other questions, if the shop was hers. She replied, "That she had hired the license." This answer struck me, and I inquired if she could obtain a license for herself. She replied, "No, unless," said she, laughing, "I should marry some old *estropié* who has been worn out in the service." She then informed me of what I was not aware which is, that instead of giving pensions to the old militaires, they give them, and them only, the licenses for selling tobacco. They may either carry on the trade themselves, or may lease out their licenses to others, for as much as they can obtain for it per year.

I perceive that the Gallic cock now struts on the head of the staff, bearing regimental colours, instead of the eagle of Napoleon. They certainly have made the cock a most imposing bird, but still a cock is not an eagle. The couplets written upon this change, which was made by Louis Philippe, are somewhat sarcastic:—

> "Le vaillant coq Gaulois,
> Grattant sur le fumier,
> A fait sortir le roi
> Louis Philippe Premier;
> Qui par juste reconnoissance
> Le mit dans les armes de France."

Did not sleep very comfortably this night; there were too many of us in the bed, and all of us bits of philosophers. I am a bit of a philosopher myself, and surely fleas cannot be considered more than very little bits. All French fleas are philosophers, it having been fairly established by a French punster that they belong to the *secte—d'Epicure (des piqueurs)*.

The English who go up the Rhine to Switzerland generally proceed on the German side. Few pass through Alsace or German France, and those who do, take the shortest route, by which they avoid Colmar. As I took the longest in preference, I shall in few words point out the features of the country. You pass through the valley of the Rhine, which is flat and fertile to excess, the only break in the uniformity of the country being the chain of Vorges mountains, distant about eight miles on your right, and the occasional passage of the dry bed of a winter torrent from the mountains. The cathedral at Colmar is well worth seeing. In outward architecture it is not very remarkable, but its painted windows are quite as fine as those of Strasbourg; and, in one point, it excels all the cathedrals I have seen, which is the choir, handsomely carved in oak, and with good pictures let into the panels. It is in better taste, more solid, and less meretricious in its ornaments, than any I know of. It has also a very fine pulpit, the whole of which, as well as the steps and balustrade leading up to it, is of fine marble. At Colmar, the eye will be struck with the peculiarity of architecture in some of the old buildings; it very often is pure Saracenic. The roads being excellent, we arrived in good time at Basle.

Once more in Switzerland; I have more pleasure now in revisiting a country which has left pleasant reminiscences in my mind, than in passing through one hitherto unexplored. In the latter case, I am usually disappointed. When we revisit those spots in which our childhood was passed, how invariably do we find that the memory is true to what the place appeared to us when children, and hardly to be recognised when our ideas and powers of mind have been developed and enlarged in proportion with our frames. Is it possible? thought I, when I returned, after a lapse of fifteen years, to the house of my childhood out of mere curiosity, for my family had long quitted it. Is this the pond which appeared so immense to my eyes, and this the house in my memory so vast? Why it is a nutshell! I presume that we estimate the relative size of objects in proportion to our stature, and, as when children, we are only half the size of men, of course, to children, everything appears to be twice the size which it really is. And not only the objects about us, but everything in the moral world as well. Our joy is twice the joy of others, and our grief, for the moment, twice as deep: and these joys and griefs all for trifles. Our code of right and wrong is equally magnified: trifles appeared to be crimes of the first magnitude, and the punishments, slight as they were, enough to dissolve our whole frame into tears until we were pardoned. Oh dear! all that's gone, as Byron says—

"No more, no more, O never more on me,
The freshness of the heart shall fall like dew."

The cathedral at Basle is nearly one thousand years old, which is a ripe old age, even for a cathedral. I believe that it is only in Switzerland, and England, and Holland, that you find the Protestants in possession of these edifices, raised to celebrate the Catholic faith.

I met here a very intelligent Frenchman who has resided many years in the town. One of the first questions I put to him was the following:

For more than twenty years Switzerland has been overrun with English and other visitors, who have spent an enormous sum of money in the country: what has become of all this money?

He replied that I might well ask the question.

"They have no banks in Switzerland; and, although land exchanges owners, still the money does not leave the country. We have here," he said, "a few millionaires, who do lend their money in France upon good securities; but except these few, they do nothing with it. The interest of money is so low, that I have known it lent by one of the rich people at two-and-a-half per cent; and the Swiss in general, in preference to risking what they can obtain for so small a premium, allow it to remain in their chests. There is, at this present moment more bullion in Switzerland than in any other country in Europe, or, perhaps, than in all the countries in Europe. A Swiss is fond of his money, and he does not use it; the millionaires that we have here, make no alteration in their quiet and plain state of living." He then continued, "At this moment, those who can afford to spend their money at Basle are retrenching, not from motives of economy, but from feelings of ill will. The burghers, who have country seats, to which they retire during the summer, have abandoned them, and if any one wished to settle in this canton, they might purchase them for half their value. The reason is, that there has been a difference between the town burghers and the country people. The canton wanted a reform bill to be passed, in which they have not succeeded. They required a more equitable representation—the country people amount to about forty thousand, the town of Basle to only ten thousand; and the town of Basle, nevertheless, returns two-thirds of the council, which governs the canton, to which the people who live in the country have raised objections. Hence the variance; and to punish the country people by not spending their money among them, the burghers have abandoned their country houses."

It may not, perhaps, be generally known, that at the time of the three days at Paris, there was an *émeute* in Switzerland, in which the aristocracy were altogether put down; and in Berne, and some other cantons, the burghers' families, who, on pretence of preventing the aristocracy from enslaving the count, had held the reins of power for so long a period, were also forced to surrender that power to those who had been so long refused participation in it. This was but the natural consequence of the increase of wealth in the country: those who before had remained quiet, feeling themselves of more consequence, insisted upon their rights; and the usual results were, that the administration of the government changed hands; but although this might be considered as an advantage gained, still it was but a change, or rather an admission of those who had become wealthy to a participation of the advantages connected with the exercise of authority; a change beneficial to a few, but to the *masse*, productive of no real advantage. At Berne, to be a member of the government, is considered as a certain source of wealth, a convincing proof that the interests of those who hold the reins are not neglected; and that in a republic it is as difficult to insure to the people their legitimate rights, as under any other form of government. And so it will be as long as the world turns round; man is everywhere the same exacting, selfish, preying creature; and his disposition is not to be changed.

The Helvetic Republic is, in fact, nothing but an aggregation of petty despotisms—leniently administered, I grant; but still nothing but despotisms. Those who are in power, or connected with those in power, are the only portion of the community who can amass large sums; and thus the authority is handed down from one to the other within certain limits, which it but rarely transgresses, something very nearly approximating to the corporations in England.

In Switzerland, the working man remains the working man, the labourer the labourer, almost as distinct as the Indian castes the nobles are crushed, and the haughty burgh rules with all the superciliousness of vested right.

I have always held a "respublica" as only to exist in theory or in name. History has proved the impossibility of its retaining its purity for half a century. What the American Republic may be, it is impossible to say, until one has been in the country, and discovered what its advocates have been careful to conceal. The Americans had a great advantage in establishing this system of government; they had nothing to overthrow, nothing to contend with. They all started fair, and their half century is now nearly complete. Time will prove whether it be possible in this world to govern, for any length of time, upon such a basis. Mr Cooper, in his work on Switzerland, is evidently disappointed with his examination into the state of the Helvetic Republic; and he admits this without intending so to do.

At Soleure I saw nothing very remarkable, except a dog with a very large goitre on his neck, a sight which I never had witnessed before, during the long time that I wandered through Switzerland.

On our way to Berne, to divide the day's travelling more equally, we stopped at a small village, not usually the resting-place of travellers, and I there met with a little bit of romance in real life, which Sterne would have worked up well, but I am not sentimental. The house, to which the sign was the appendage, struck me, at first entering, as not having been built for an *hôtellerie*; the rooms were low, but large, and the floors *parquetté*; here and there were to be seen remains of former wealth in pieces of *marquetterie* for furniture, and clocks of *ormolu*. There were some old prints, also, on the walls, very superior to those hung up usually in the auberges of the continent, especially in a village auberge. When the supper was brought up, I observed that the silver forks and spoons were engraved with double arms and the coronet of a marquis. I asked the female who brought up the soup, from whence they had obtained them? She replied, rather *brusquement*, that she supposed they had been bought at the silversmith's, and left the room as if not wanting to be questioned. The master of the auberge came up with some wine. He was a tall, fine, aristocratical-looking man, about sixty years of age, and I put the question to him. He replied that they belonged to the family who kept the inn. "But," said I, "if so, it is noble by both descents?" "Yes," replied he, carelessly, "but they don't think anything of that beer." After a few more questions, he acknowledged that they were the armorial bearings of his father and mother, but that the family had been unfortunate, and that, as no tithes were allowed in the country, he was now doing his best to support the family. After this disclosure, we entered into a long discussion relative to the Helvetic Republic, with which I shall not trouble my readers. Before I went, I inquired his name from one of the servants, and it immediately occurred to me that I had seen it in the list of those twenty-six who are mentioned as the leaders of the Swiss who defeated the Burgundians, and whose monument is carved in the solid rock at Morat. Two engravings of the monument were in the rooms we occupied, and I had amused myself with reading over the names. I am no aristocrat myself, heaven knows! and if a country could be benefited, and liberty obtained, by the overthrow of the aristocracy, the sooner it is done the better; but when we see, as in Switzerland, the aristocracy reduced to keeping village inns, and their inferiors, in every point, exerting that very despotism of which they complained, and to free the people from which, was their pretence for a change of government, I cannot help feeling that if one is to be governed, let it be, at all events, by those who, from the merits of their ancestors and their long-held possessions, have the most claim. Those who are born to power are not so likely to have their heads turned by the possession of it as those who obtain it unexpectedly; and those who are above money-making are less likely to be corrupt than those who seek it. The lower the class that governs, the worse the government will be, and the greater the despotism. Switzerland is no longer a patriarchal land. Wealth has rolled into the country; and the time will come when there will be a revolution in the republic. Nothing can prevent it, unless all the cantons are vested into one central government, instead of so many petty oligarchies, as at present, and which will eventually tire out the patience of the people.

I parted from my noble host, and will do him the justice to say that his bill was so moderate, compared to the others paid in Switzerland, that I almost wished that all the inns in the cantons were held by the nobility— that is, provided they would follow his example. His wine was excellent, and I suspect was laid in long before the sign was hung up at the door.

From Soleure to Berne the whole road was lined with parties of troops ordered in that direction: every man of them was drunk, cheering, and hooting, and hallooing at us as we passed. As for the peasant girls they met on the road, I really pitied them. At last we have arrived at Berne. The Bernese have chosen a most appropriate symbol in their heraldic crests of the bear, and, as if they had not a sufficient quantity inside of their towns, they keep four in the ditch outside.

What a difference between the *tables d'hôte* in Germany and in Switzerland! I always prefer the *table d'hôte* when it is respectable, for nothing is more unpleasant than remaining in a hotel shut up in your own room; the latter may be more dignified and aristocratic, but it is not the way to see the world; one might as well be in England, and, indeed, had much better. A *table d'hôte* is a microcosm: you meet there all nations, people of all professions—some idle, some busy travelling on important matters, others travelling for amusement. You are unfortunate if you do not fall in with one clever man at least, and you are quite sure to meet with a fool, which is almost as amusing. When I survey a *table d'hôte* I often think of the calenders who had all come to spend the *Ramadhan* at Bagdad, and their histories; and I have thought that Grattan might make a very good series of Highways and Byways if he could obtain the history of those who meet at this general rendezvous. The *tables d'hôte* in Germany are excellent, properly supplied, and very moderate. I cannot say so of those in Switzerland. The fondness of the Swiss for money betrays itself in everything, and instead of liberality at the *table d'hôte*, we have meanness. The dinner itself is dearer than in Germany, and not half so good; but what is the most unexcusable part of our host's conduct is, that he half serves his guests, as Sancho was served at Barataria; for instance, as is usually the case, the viands are put on the table and then removed to be carved; two ducks will make their appearance at one end, two chickens at the other; are removed, and only one of each is cut up and handed round, the others are sent away whole to be re-dressed for some great man who dines in his own room. This has been constantly the case since I have been here. It may be asked, why we do not remonstrate? In the first place, I prefer watching my host's manoeuvres; and in the next, although I might get my duck, my host would charge me the whole value of it when he sent in his bill.

The French Ambassador could not have taken a better step to bring the Swiss to their senses than threatening them with a blockade. It would have been ruin to them. All the golden harvests would have been over, their country would have been deserted, and their Ranz des Vaches would have been listened to only by the cows. As the French minister expected, the councils fumed and vapoured, the officers drew their swords and flourished them, and then—very quietly pocketed the affront that they might not be out of pocket. What a pity it is that a nation so brave and with so many good sterling qualities, should be, as it would appear, so *innately* mercenary! There never was a truer saying than "Point d'argent, point de Suisse."

Chapter Thirty Six

Geneva.

Twenty years have made a wonderful alteration in the good sober puritanical city of Geneva. The improvement from the new buildings which have been erected is so great, that I could hardly recognise the old city of Geneva in her dress. It was an old friend with a new face, for as you enter the town, all the new buildings and streets meet your view. As far as it has proceeded (for there is much left yet to be finished), the new portion of Geneva is finer than any portion of Paris, upon an equal space of ground. But what surprised me more was to read the *affiches* of the *Comédie*. A theatre in Geneva! When I was last here, a theatre was considered by the good people as criminal to the highest degree. I inquired where the theatre was to be found, and it was all true—there *was* a *theatre*. I then made more inquiries. It appeared that Mammon had seduced the puritans of Geneva. People would not winter at Geneva; it was so dull—no amusements; and as soon as the snow was knee deep at Chamouny, they all ordered horses and flew away to Paris or Italy. This affected the prosperity of the good citizens, and they talked among themselves; but no one of the Town Council would propose a theatre, until it was discovered, by private communicasion, that they were unanimously agreed,—then the proposition was started and carried. But there are many concomitants attending a theatre, and with the theatre many other innovations have crept in; so that in a few years Geneva will be no better than Paris. When I was last here, Science was the order of the day. There were many celebrated men residing in the town, but they are all gone to their forefathers. Every branch of Natural History had its *savant*; but, above all, Mineralogy was the most in vogue. But Mineralogy has been superseded lately, by her eldest sister Geology, who, although not so pretty, has been declared more interesting and profound. Still Mineralogy is the more scientific, although Geology is the more speculative. In the education of children, I know no study which so enlarges the mind or gives a habit of research and application, as that of Natural History; it is amusement and instruction so happily blended, that it never tires. Perhaps, the natural cupidity of our natures assists, as the knowledge of every new specimen is for the most part accompanied by the *possession* of the specimen and an addition to the collection. Moreover, it is a tangible study; not a nomenclature of things, but each substance is in your hand to be examined.

The arrangement and classification gives a habit of neatness and order, and children are taught to throw nothing away until its value is known. Every child should be made acquainted with Natural History; and where the specimens can be obtained, and there is room for them, they should be allowed to have a collection, such as minerals, corals, shells, and plants; for these sciences, amusing in themselves, will gradually impel them to the others more abstruse, as every branch of Natural Philosophy is intimately connected with them. The mind will ever be active, and if not interested in rational pursuits, it will fly off to the sensual.

They have a very excellent plan in Switzerland, in many of the boys' schools, of all the scholars setting off together on a pedestrian tour of some weeks. You will meet a whole school of thirty or forty urchins, with their knapsacks on their shoulders, attired in blouses, trudging away from town to town, and from mountain to mountain, to visit all the remarkable peculiarities of the country.

This is a most excellent method of relaxing from study, and invigorating the mind at the same time that it is allowed to repose. Neither is it so expensive as people would imagine. One room will hold a great many school-boys, where the mattresses are spread over the floor: and I saw them make a very hearty breakfast upon bread and cheese and three bottles of wine, among about forty of them. Why should not the boys about London set off on a tour to the lakes or elsewhere, in the same way—every year changing the route. They then would see something of their own country, which few do before they are launched in life, and have no time to do afterwards. I have never seen the lakes; in fact, I know nothing of my country, although I have scoured the world so long. I recollect that my father, who had never seen the Tower of London, was determined every year that he would go and see it; but he never could find time, it appears, for he died without seeing it at last. I did, however, make the observation, that if Geneva had backslided so far as to permit a theatre, there was a feeling that this innovation required being carefully opposed. When I was at Geneva before, there was no theatre, but neither were there shops which dealt exclusively in religious tracts and missionary works. I observed on this my second arrival, that there were a great many to serve as a check to the increasing immorality of the age.

I have referred to the change of twenty years, but what a change has been effected in about three hundred years, in this very country. Read what took place in these cantons at about the date which I have mentioned. I have been reading the chronicles. Observe the powers assumed by the bishops of that period; they judged not only men but brutes; and it must be admitted that there was some show of justice, as the offending parties, being dumb themselves, were allowed lawyers to plead for them.

How the lawyers were paid, has not been handed down; and it appears that the judgments were sometimes easier pronounced than carried into execution.

At Basle, in the year 1474, it appears that a cock was accused of the enormous crime of having laid an egg: he was brought to trial and condemned to be burnt alive, as a warning to all cocks not to lay eggs, from which it is well known would have been hatched a cockatrice or basilisk.

In 1481, cockchafers committed great ravages in the Grisons. The Bishop of Coire condemned them all to transportation, and a barren valley was assigned to them as their future residence. Whether the cockchafers obeyed his Lordship's orders, is not handed down to posterity.

Some years afterwards the river Aar was infested with leeches, who spoilt all the salmon. The Bishop of Lausanne excommunicated the whole tribe of leeches in a solemn procession to the river; and it is dreadful to reflect, that this excommunication remains upon their heads even unto this day. Also next door, in France, in 1386, a sow was arraigned for having eaten a young child, and condemned to be hanged; to add to the disgrace of her punishment, she was dressed *in man's clothes*.

About the same period rats were extremely mischievous, and in consequence were summoned to appear before my Lord the Bishop. But the rats had a good lawyer, who first asserted that the rats, being dispersed in all the neighbouring villages, had not had time to collect together, and make their appearance; and that a second and a third summons would be but an act of justice. They were, therefore, again summoned after the performance of mass on Sunday in each parish. Notwithstanding the three summonses, the rats did not appear in court, and then their defender asserted, that in consequence of the affair having been made so public by the three summonses, all the cats were on the look-out, and therefore his clients dare not make their appearance without all the cats were destroyed. The consequence of this difficulty was, that the rats were not punished for contempt of court.

I have often thought that it is a great pity that agricultural associations in England do not send over a committee to examine into the principle upon which they build and load carts and waggons on the Continent.

It is a point on which we are very unenlightened in England. The waste of wood in the building, and the wear and tear of horses, is enormous. We have yet many things to learn in England, and must not be ashamed to profit from our neighbours. One horse will do more work on the Continent, especially in France and Switzerland, from the scientific principles upon which their vehicles are built, and the loads are put on, than three horses will accomplish in England. The inquiries of the committee might be extended much if they went to the Agricultural Association at Berne; they would discover many things which have not yet entered into their philosophy. I doubt very much whether the four-course shift of Norfolk, where farming is considered the most perfect, is not more expensive and more exhausting to the land, than the other systems resorted to on the Continent; that is, that it is not that which will give the greatest possible returns at the minimum of expense. I have before observed how very seldom you see a horse out of condition and unfit for work on the Continent; one great cause must be from their not being racked and torn to pieces by overloading; and notwithstanding which, the loads they draw are much heavier than those in England. I have seen a load of many tons so exactly poised upon two wheels, that the shaft horse neither felt his saddle nor his belly-band.

One great cause of the ill usage of horses in England is the disgraceful neglect of the public conveyances of all kinds. If an alteration was to be made in the regulations of hackney coaches and cabs, we should no longer have our feelings tortured by the spectacles of horse misery which we daily meet with. There are plenty of commissioners for hackney coaches, and it is a pity that they had not something to do for the money they receive, or else that they were abolished and their duty put into the hands of the police. It may appear a singular remark to make, but I cannot help thinking that there would be a good moral effect in the improvement of hackney coaches. There are a certain class of people in London, to whom these vehicles are at present of no use. I refer to those who have a sufficient independence, but who cannot afford to keep their carriages, and who, by the present system of social intercourse, are almost shut out of society, or are inclined to spend more money than prudence would dictate. In all other capitals, the hackney coaches are clean and respectable, and in some instances as good as a private carriage; and besides that, they have a superior kind of carriage for evening parties, which renders the expense of a private carriage unnecessary. There certainly may be some excuse made for those who dislike hackney coaches pulling up at their doors, when we look at the disgusting turn-outs of the London stands, at one time filled with drunken men and women, at others carrying diseased people to the hospital, or dead bodies to the Surgeons' Hall. An English hackney coach is a type of misery, as regards the horses' outsides, and a *cloaca* within; you know not, when you step into it, whether you are not to encounter disease and death. It may be said that there are such vehicles as glass coaches, as they are termed; but those are only to be hired by the day, and become very expensive. The arrangements of these vehicles should be under the police: every coach and cab should be examined, at the commencement of the year, as to its appearance outside as well as its cleanliness inside. The horses should be inspected, and if not in fair working condition, and of a certain height, the license should be refused. And there should be a superior class allowed at certain stands, who are entitled to demand a higher fare. This would not only be a boon to the public, but a much greater one to the poor horse, who would not drag out his lengthened misery as he does now. When there was no longer any means of selling a poor brute, to whom death was a release, he would be put out of his misery. It would also be a great improvement if the Numbers were put inside instead of out, as they are abroad; and if *every* description of vehicle, if well fitted, were licensed.

Chapter Thirty Seven

The Hôtel des Bergues is certainly a splendid establishment; many people winter at this hotel in preference to going to a pension, which is, with the best arrangements, disagreeable, for you are obliged to conform to the usages and customs, and to take your meals at certain hours, hungry or not hungry, as if it were a pension of school-boys and girls, and not grown up people. The price demanded is the same as at the pensions, viz 200 francs, or 8 pounds per month, which includes everything but wine and fuel. The establishment is certainly very well conducted. There is a salon, next to the table d'hôte, large enough to hold 200 people, well warmed and lighted, handsomely carpeted, with piano, books, prints, newspapers, card tables, etcetera. Indeed, there is everything you wish for, and you are all independent of each other, I was there for two or three days, and found it very pleasant; I was amused with a circumstance which occurred. One of the company, a Russian, sat down to the piano, and played and sang. Every one wished to know who he was, and on inquiring, it was a Russian prince. Now a prince is a very great person where princes are scarce, as they are in England, although in Russia, a prince, where princes are plenty as blackberries, is about on a par with an English baronet.

He was a very honest off-hand sort of personage, and certainly gave himself no airs on account of his birth and rank. Nevertheless, the English ladies, who were anxious that he should sing again, made a sort of deputation to him, and begged the honour of his highness favouring them with a song, with every variety of courtesy and genuflexion.

"Oh yes, to be sure," replied his highness, who sat down and played for an hour, and then there was so much thanking, complimentary acknowledgement of condescension on his part, etcetera, and the ladies appeared so flattered when he spoke to them. The next day it was discovered that a slight mistake had occurred, and that, instead of being a prince, he had only come to Geneva along with a Russian prince, and that the real prince was in his own room upstairs; upon which not only he fell himself at least 200 per cent, but, what was really too bad, his singing fell also; and many who had been most loud in his praises began to discover that he was not even a prince of musicians, which he certainly was.

We had a good specimen of the independence and familiarity of Swiss servants on the occasion of this gentleman's singing; they came into the salon, and mixed almost with the company that they might listen to him; and had they been ordered out, would, in all probability, have refused. An American, with whom I was conversing, observed that in *his* country such conduct on the part of servants, notwithstanding what had been said by English travellers on the subject, would never have been permitted. I have fallen in with some odd characters here.

First, what would be considered a curiosity in England—a clergyman of the Church of England with mustachios! What would the Bishop of London say?—and yet I do not see how, if a clergyman choose to wear them, he could be prevented. He has good authority to quote; Calvin wore them, and so, I believe, did Luther.

Secondly, with a personage who is very peculiarly disorganised when he drinks too much. His wife, a most amiable quiet lady, is the party whose character is attacked. As soon as Mr — is in his cups, he immediately fancies that his wife is affected with the liquor, and not himself, and he tells everybody in a loud whisper his important secret. "There now, look at Mrs —, one of the best women in the world; an excellent wife and mother, and at most times as lady-like as you would wish to see: but look at her now—you see she's quite drunk, poor thing; what a pity, isn't it, that she cannot get over her unfortunate propensity; but I am afeard it's no use. I've reasoned with her. It's a sad pity, and a great drawback to my happiness. Well, hang sorrow—it killed a cat. Don't notice what I've told you, and pass the bottle."

I believe that the English are better acquainted with geography than other nations. I have been astonished at the ignorance on this point I have found in foreigners who otherwise were clever and well-informed men and women. When the Marquis de Claremont Tonnère was appointed to the office of Minister of the Marine and Colonies, upon the restoration of the Bourbons, a friend of mine had an audience with him, and it was not until a very angry discussion, and a reference to the map, that he could persuade the minister that Martinique was an *island*. However, in this instance we had nearly as great an error committed in our own Colonial office, which imagined that the Dutch settlement of Demerara upon the coast of South America, and which had fallen into our hands, *was* an island; indeed, in the official papers it was spoken of as such. A little before the French Revolution, a princess who lived in Normandy determined upon a visit to her relations in Paris; and having a sister married to a Polish nobleman, she determined to take Poland in her way. To her astonishment, instead of a day to two, her voyage was not completed under four months.

I have heard it often asserted, that you should not build your house so as to look at a fine prospect out of your windows, but so as to walk to view it at a short distance. This may be true with the finest prospects in other countries, but not so in Switzerland, where the view never palls upon the eye, from the constant changing which occurs in the tinting of the landscape. You may look upon the Lake of Geneva every day, and at no one day, or even portion of the day, is the effect the same. The mountains of Savoy are there, and change not their position: neither does the Lake; but at one time the mountains will appear ten miles nearer to you than they will at another. The changing arising from refraction and reflection is wonderful. Never did I witness anything finer than the Lake of Geneva at the setting of yesterday's sun. The water was calm and glassy as a mirror, and it reflected in broad patches, like so many islands dispersed over it, every colour of the rainbow. I cannot attempt to describe it; the effect was heavenly, and all I could say was, with the Mussulman, "God is great!"

Chapter Thirty Eight

In this world we are so jealous of any discovery being made, that innovation is immediately stigmatised as quackery. I say innovation, for improvement is not the term. The attempt to improve is innovation, the success of the experiment makes it an improvement. And yet how are we to improve without experiment? Thus we have quackery in everything, although not quite so severely visited as it formerly was by the Inquisition who would have burnt alive him who asserted that the sun did not go round the earth, but the earth round the sun. In medicine, quackery is the most frequently stigmatised. We know but little of the human frame as far as medicine is to act upon it. We know still less of the virtues of various plants which will effect a cure. We are acquainted with a few but there are hundreds equally powerful, the properties of which we are ignorant of. Could we add to medical science the knowledge of the African negroes and Indians, which they so carefully conceal from us, our pharmacopoeia would be much extended. When metallic medicines were first introduced into general use by a physician, an ancestor of mine, and the wonderful effect of them established by the cures, the whole fraternity was up in arms, and he was decried us a quack; notwithstanding which, the works he wrote have gone through twenty five editions, and the doses prescribed by him are to this day made use of by the practitioners.

The fact is, that although the surgical knowledge of the day is very perfect, the medical art is still in its infancy. Even the quackeries which fail should not be despised, for they have proved something, although they could not be perfected. Animal magnetism, for instance: it failed, but still it discovered some peculiar properties, some sympathies of the human body, which may hereafter give a clue to more important results. The great proof of the imperfection of medical science is the constant change made by the profession itself. One medicine is taken into favour, it is well received every where, until the faculty are tired of it, and it sinks into disgrace. Even in my time I have seen many changes of this sort, not only in medicine, but in diet, etcetera.

What medical men would have thought of prescribing fat bacon for delicate stomachs twenty years ago? Now it is all the vogue; breakfast bacon sold in every quarter of the metropolis. Either this is quackery, to use their own term, or twenty years ago they were very ignorant, for their patients received positive injunctions to avoid all fat and greasy substances.

Thus do the regular practitioners chop and change about, groping in the dark: but the only distinction is, that all changes made by the faculty are orthodox; but any alteration proposed out of the pale of MD, is an innovation and a quackery.

That we have every where ignorant men, who are *de facto* quacks, I admit; but still that term has been as liberally applied to the attempts of scientific and clever persons to improve the art of medicine. Even homoeopathy must not be totally rejected until it has had a fair trial. It has one merit in it, at all events, that you take less physic.

I consider the continual appearance of new quacks on the horizon a sure proof of the low state of our medical knowledge. The more so as these quacks, although they kill, do effect very remarkable cures. Do not regular practitioners kill also? or rather, do not their prescriptions fail? If a quack cures, they will tell you that it was by mere accident. I suspect that there is more of accident in the practice than the faculty are ready to admit; and Heaven knows they so change about themselves, that it is clear that they feel no confidence in the little that they do know; and it is because medicine is so imperfect that every half century we have a new quack, as he is termed, rising up, and beating the regular practitioners out of the field. I could tell a story about Morrison's pills which would surprise not a little, and all the parties are now alive to prove it; but instead of that, I will tell another which occurred in France, in which a quack medicine had a most wonderful and unusual effect, for it was the means of the *total destruction of a Banditti*, who had defied the Government of the country for many years. About twenty years ago,—I am not sure whether he still lives,—there was an irregular practitioner in France of the name of Le Roi. He was, by all accounts, the King of all Empirics, and the Emperor of all Quacks. He was more potent than the sovereign, and the *par l'ordre du Roi* of Government was insignificant, compared to the *par l'ordre du Roi* of this more potent personage. He did not publish his cures in *pamphlets*, but in large *quartos*. I have seen them myself, larger in size than an Ainsworth's dictionary. It so happened that an Englishman, who was afflicted with the *indescribables*, was recommended from every quarter to buy the medicines of Monsieur Le Roi. He did so, and his unknown complaint was removed. The consequence was, that the Englishman swore by Le Roi; and as he was proceeding on to Spain, he took with him a large supply of the doctor's medicines, that he might be prepared in case his complaint should return. All quack gentlemen take care that their medicines shall be palatable; no unwise precaution. I do not know a better dram than Solomon's Balm of Gilead. Old Solomon, by the bye, lived near Plymouth, and was very partial to the Navy. He kept an excellent table, and was very hospitable.

I recollect one day after the officers had drunk a very sufficient quantity of his claret and champagne, being a little elevated, they insisted upon Solomon bringing them out some Balm of Gilead as a finish, and they cleared off about two dozen one guinea bottles. The old gentleman made no objection to provide it as often as they called for more, and they separated; but the next day he sent them all their bills in for the said Balm of Gilead, observing, that although they were welcome to his wine and table, that he must be paid for his medicine. But to proceed.

The Englishman travelled with the king's messenger; most of his baggage had been sent on, but he would not part with his medicine, and this was all in the vehicle with himself. As they passed the Pyrenees they were stopped by the banditti, who dragged them out of the carriage, after shooting the postilion, and made them lie with their faces on the ground, with guards over them, while they rifled the carriage. They soon came to the packages of medicine, and observing that *Le Roi* was upon all the bottles, and knowing that they had possession of a king's messenger, they imagined that this was some liquor sent as a present to the King of Spain; they tasted it, and found that, like other quack medicines, it was very strong and very good.

Each man took his bottle, drank the king's health, and mirth and revelry took place, until they had consumed all that the Englishman had brought with him. Now there is a great difference between taking a table-spoonful, and six or seven bottles per man; and so it proved, for they had hardly finished the last case before they found that the medicine acted very powerfully as a cathartic; the whole banditti were simultaneously attacked with a most violent cholera; they disappeared one by one; at last the guards could contain themselves no longer, and they went off too. The two prisoners, perceiving this, rose from the ground, mounted the horses and galloped off as fast as they could. They gave notice to the authorities of the first town they arrived at, not four miles distant, and a large body of cavalry were sent out immediately. The effects of the medicine had been so violent that the whole of the banditti were found near to the spot where they had drunk the king's health, in such a state of suffering and exhaustion that they could make no efforts to escape, and were all secured, and eventually hung.

Chapter Thirty Nine

Lausanne.

I recollect some one saying, that in walking out you should never look up in the air, but always on the ground, as, by the former practice, you were certain never to find any thing, although you might by the latter. So if you will not enter into conversation, you are not likely to obtain much information; whereas if you do, you will always chance to obtain some, even from the quarters the least promising. I was seated on the box of the carriage, with the Swiss *voiturier*—and asked him, "If it were not a lucrative profession?"

"It may appear so to you, sir," replied he, "from the price paid for the horses, but it is not so. All we gain, is in five months in the year; the seven months of winter, we have to feed our horses without employment for them, that is, generally speaking."

"But have you no employment for them in the winter?"

"Yes, we put them into the waggons and draw wood and stone, which about pays their expenses. If you are known and trusted, you will be employed to transport wine, which is more profitable; but that *voiturier* who can find sufficient employment for his horses during the winter to pay their keeping, considers himself very fortunate."

"When you do make money, what do you do with it?"

"If we can buy a bit of land we do, but most people, if they can, buy a house, which pays better. I prefer land."

"There is not much territory in Switzerland, and land is not often for sale. Everybody cannot buy land. What do the others do?"

"Lock the money up in their chests."

"But do you never put your money in the foreign funds?"

"Yes, the rich do and those who understand it. We have a few very rich people in Switzerland, but, generally speaking, the people do not like to part with their money, and they keep it by them."

"I was told by a Frenchman at Basle, that there was a great deal of bullion lying idle in Switzerland?"

"He told you very true, sir; there is an enormous quantity of it, if collected together. Those are Jews," continued he, pointing to a *char-à-banc* passing.

"Have you many of those in Switzerland? I should think not."

"No, sir, we do not allow them. One or two families are perhaps permitted in a large town, but no more. We are a small country, and if we were to allow the Jews to settle here, we should soon have too large a population to support. By their customs, they may marry at any age, and they never go into the field, and work at the plough."

"But may not you marry at any age, and when you please?"

"No, sir; we have good laws in that respect, and it prevents the population increasing too fast. I belong to a commune (parish); if I wish to marry, I must first prove that all my debts are paid, and all my father's debts, and then the commune will permit the Curé to marry me."

"All your father's debts as well as your own?"

"That is to say, all the debts he may have incurred to the commune. Suppose my father had been a poor man and unable to work, the commune would have let him want for nothing; but in supplying him they would have incurred an expense, that must be repaid by his family before any of the sons are allowed to marry. In the same way, when my father died, although he received no assistance from the commune, he left little or nothing. The commune clothed and educated me till I was able to gain my own livelihood. Since I have done well, I have repaid the debt; I now may marry if I choose."

"But cannot you evade this law?"

"No, sir. Suppose I was at Berne, and wished to marry a woman who belonged to another commune as well as myself. The banns must be published three times in my parish, three times in her parish, and three times at Berne."

"But suppose you married in a foreign country?"

"If a Swiss marries in a foreign country, and has no debts to prevent his marrying, he must write home to the heads of the commune, stating his intention, and his banns will then be published in the commune, and a license sent him to marry. But if, having debts of your own or your father's, you marry without giving notice, you are then no longer belonging to the commune, and if you come back in distress, you will be conveyed to the confines of the republic, and advised to seek the parish of your wife in her country. If you are out of Switzerland with your wife, every child that you have born you must give notice of by letter to the commune, that it may be properly registered; and if you omit so doing, those children have no claim on their return."

Such was the result of our conversation, and I repeat it for the benefit of those who occupy themselves with our internal legislation.

I have been searching a long while for liberty, but I can find her nowhere on this earth: let me be allegorical. If all the world are still in love with the name of Liberty, how much more were all the world in love with the nymph herself when she first made her appearance on earth. Every one would possess her, and every one made the attempt, but Liberty was not to be caught. How was it possible without her destruction? After being harassed all over the world, and finding that she never was allowed to take breath, she once more fled from her pursuers, and, as they seized her garments, with the spring of the chamois she burst away, and bounding from the world, saved herself in Ether, where she remains to this day. Her dress was, however, left behind, and was carried home in triumph. It is, however, composed of such slippery materials as its former owner, and it escapes as it pleases from one party to another. It is this dress of Liberty which we now reverence as the goddess herself, and whatever is clothed with it for the time receives the same adoration as would have been offered up to the true shrine. Even Despotism, when in a very modest mood, will clothe herself in the garb of Liberty.

Now there is really a sort of petty despotism in these *free* cantons, which would be considered very offensive in England. What would an English farmer say, if he was told that he could not commence his harvest without the permission of Government? Yet such is the case in Switzerland, where there is a heavy fine if any one commences his vintage before the time prescribed by the authorities. Your grapes may be ripe, and be spoiled; you have to choose between that alternative, or paying a fine, which reduces your profits to *nil*. The reason given for this is that there are so many petty proprietors holding half and quarter acres of vineyards mixed together and not separated by a wall or fence, that if one began first he would rob the vineyard of the other—not arguing much for the Swiss honesty, which has become so proverbial.

The case of the vintage laws is peculiarly hard this season upon the small proprietors. The vintage has been late, and winter has now set in, all at once. After weather like summer, we are now deep in snow, and the thermometer below the freezing point. Few of the small proprietors have wine-presses; they have to wait until those who have them have got in their vintage, and then they borrow them. The consequence is, that the small proprietors are always the last to gather their grapes, and now they have been overtaken by the weather, and they will lose most of their harvest. Had they been permitted to pick their grapes at their own time, they might have used the presses, and have finished before the large vineyards had commenced.

From the inquiries I have made, it appears that the vineyards of Switzerland pay very badly. Land is at a very high price here, in the Canton de Vaud; 300 or 400 pounds per acre is not thought dear (600 pounds have been given); and in the best seasons a vineyard will not yield 10 pounds per acre. The wine is very indifferent, and requires to be kept for years to become tolerable.

But the Swiss are wedded to their vineyards; and although, if they laid down the land in pasture, they would gain twice as much, they prefer the speculation of the wine-press, which fails at least three times out of four.

The office of public executioner or Jack Ketch of a canton in Switzerland, as well as in many parts of Germany, is very appropriately endowed. He has a right to all animals who die a natural death, with their skins, hoofs, etcetera, and this, it is said, brings in a fair revenue, if attended to. Executions are so uncommon in Switzerland, that Jack Ketch would starve if he was not thus associated with death. When an execution does take place he is well paid; they say the sum he receives is upwards of twenty pounds; but it must be remembered that he does not hang, he decapitates, and this requires some address: the malefactor is seated in a chair, not laid down with his head on the block.

An execution took place at Berne when I was last in Switzerland; the criminal, after he was seated in the chair, was offered a cup of coffee, and as he was drinking it, the executioner, with one blow of his heavy sword, struck his head clear off; for a second or two the blood flew up like a fountain: the effect was horrid.

An Englishman at Lausanne had a very favourite Newfoundland dog, which died. He was about to bury it, when the executioner interfered and claimed the skin; and it was not until he had submitted to the demands of this official gentleman, that he was permitted to bury his favourite in a whole skin. Only imagine, half a dozen old dowagers of Park Lane, whose puffy lap-dogs were dead in their laps, bargaining for their darlings with Jack Ketch, because they wish to have them stuffed; and Jack's extortion raising his demands, in proportion to the value apparently placed upon the defunct favourites. Talking about lap-dogs, one of the best stories relative to these creatures is to be found in Madame de Crequey's Memoirs. A Madame de Blot, a French dandysette, if the term may be used, who considered her own sex as bound to be ethereal, and would pretend that the wing of a lark was more than sufficient for her sustenance during the twenty-four hours, had one of the smallest female spaniels that was ever known. She treated her like a human being, and when she went out to a party, used to desire her lady's maid to read the animal a comedy in five acts, to amuse it during her absence. It so happened that a fat priest, who was anxious for the protection of Madame de Blot, called to pay his respects. Madame de Blot made a sign to him, without speaking, to take his seat upon a large fauteuil. No sooner had the priest lowered down his heavy carcass into the chair, than he felt something struggling under him, and a little recollection told him that it must be the little spaniel. That it was all over with the spaniel was clear, and that if her mistress had discovered his accident, it was equally clear that it was all over with him, as far as the patronage of Madame de Blot was concerned. The priest showed a remarkable degree of presence of mind upon this trying occasion. He rose himself up a little from his chair and plumped down, so as to give the poor little spaniel her *coup de grâce*, and then entered into conversation with Madame de Blot. During the conversation he contrived by degrees to cram the dog, tail and all, into his capacious coat pockets. As soon as it was fairly out of sight, he rose, bade adieu to Madame de Blot, and backed out of the room with as great respect as if he was in the presence of royalty, much to the satisfaction of Madame de Blot, who was delighted at such homage, and little thought why the good priest would not turn his back to her. The story says, that the Madame de Blot never could find out what had become of her little dog.

Chapter Forty

Lausanne.

What a continual strife there is between literary men! I can only compare the world of authors to so many rats drowning in a tub, forcing each other down to raise themselves, and keep their own heads above water. And yet they are very respectable, and a very useful body of men, also, in a politico-economical sense of the word, independent of the advantages gained by their labours, by the present and the future; for their capital is *nothing* except brains, and yet they contrive to find support for themselves and thousands of others. It is strange when we consider how very few, comparatively speaking, are the number of authors, how many people are supported by them.

There are more than a thousand booksellers and publishers in the three kingdoms, all of whom rent more than a thousand houses, paying rent and taxes; support more than a thousand families, and many thousand clerks, as booksellers alone. Then we have to add the paper manufacturers, the varieties of bookbinders, printing-ink manufacturers, iron pens, and goose quills. All of which are subservient to and dependent upon these comparatively few heads.

What a *train* an author has! unfortunately for him it is too long. There are too many dependent upon him, and, like some potentates, the support of his state eats his whole revenue, leaving him nothing but bread and cheese and fame. Some French writer has said, "La littérature est le plus noble des loisirs, mais le dernier de tous les métiers;" and so it is, for this one reason, that according as an author's wants are cogent, so he is pressed down by the publisher. Authors and publishers are natural enemies, although they cannot live without each other. If an author is independent of literature, and has a reputation, he bullies the publisher: he is right; he is only revenging the insults contumely heaped upon those whom the publishers know to be in their power, and obliged to submit to them. Well, every dog has his day, and the time will come when I and others, having swam too long, shall find younger and fresher competitors, who will, like the rats, climb on our backs, and we shall sink to the bottom of the tub of oblivion. Now, we must drive on with the stream; the world moves on so fast, that there is no stopping. In these times, "Si on n'avance pas, on recule."

How the style of literature changes! Even now I perceive an alteration creeping on, which will last for a time. We are descending to the homely truth of Tenier's pictures.

Every work of fiction now is "sketched from nature;" the palaces, the saloon, all the elegancies of high life are eschewed, and the middle and vulgar classes are the subjects of the pencil. But this will not last long. It is the satiety of refinement on the part of the public which for a short time renders the change palatable.

I was yesterday informed that a celebrated author wished to be introduced to me. I was ashamed to say that I had never heard his name. The introduction took place, and there was a sort of patronising air on the gentleman's part, which I did not approve of. I therefore told him very frankly that I was not aware of the nature of his literary labours, and requested to know what were his works. He had *abridged* something, and he had written a *commentary* upon another thing!—just the employment fit for some old gentleman who likes still to puddle a little with ink. One could write a commentary upon any thing. One of my children is singing a nursery song, now I'll write a commentary on it in the shape of notes:—

Pussy cat, pussy cat, where have you been?
I've been to London to see the new queen.
Pussy cat, pussy cat, what did you there?
Hunted a titty mouse under the chair.

Now for a commentary:—

This simple nursery rhyme is in the familiar style of question and answer, which is always pleasing; and it is remarkable that two excellent moral lessons are to be found in so few words.

The child who sings it may be supposed to repeat the words without comprehending their full meaning; but although such may be the case, still it is most important that even the rhymes put into the infantine lips should afford an opportunity to those who watch over their welfare to point out to them on a proper occasion the instruction which they contain. In the first line, the term pussy cat may be considered tautological, as pussy and cat both refer to the same animal; but if so, it is allowable, as pussy may be considered as the christian name and cat as the surname of the animal. It is to be presumed that the cat addressed is young, for it evidently was at play, and old cats do not play. Otherwise it would not have been necessary to repeat her name, to call her attention to the question. The cat answers in few words, as if not wishing to be interrupted, that she has been to London to see the new queen. What queen of England may be referred to, it is impossible to positively ascertain; but as she says the new queen, we have a right to suppose that it must refer to the accession of a queen to the throne of England. We have here to choose between three, — Elizabeth, Mary, and Anne; and for many reasons, particularly as the two last were married, we are inclined to give the preference to the first, the word *new* having, for the sake of the metre, been substituted for virgin. Certain it is that a married woman cannot be considered as *new*, although she may not be old. We therefore adhere to our supposition that this rhyme was composed at the accession of the great Elizabeth. And here we may observe, that the old adage "that a cat may look at the king" is fully corroborated, for pussy says expressly that she has been to see the new queen, pointing out, that as the sun shines upon all alike, so the sun of royalty, in a well-administered government, will equally dispense its smiles upon all who approach to bask in them; and that even a cat is not considered as unworthy to look upon that gracious majesty who feels that it is called to rule over so many millions, for the purpose of making them happy.

It would appear as if the cat continued to play with her ball, or whatever else might have been its amusements, after having answered the first question; for, on the second question being put, her attention is obliged to be again roused by the repetition of her name. She is asked what she did there, and the reply is, that she hunted a titty mouse under the chair. There is a wonderful effect in this last line, which fully gives us at once the nature and disposition of the cat, and a very excellent moral lesson. The cat calls the mouse a *titty* mouse, a term of endearment applied to the very animal that she was putting in bodily fear. It is well known how cats will play with a mouse in the most graceful way; you would almost imagine, from the manner in which it is tossed so lightly and so elegantly, allowed to escape and then caught again, that it was playing with it in all amity, instead of prolonging its miseries and torturing it, previously to its ultimate destruction.

It is in reference to this peculiar character of the cat, that she is made to use the fond diminutive appellation of titty mouse.

The moral contained in this last line hardly needs to be pointed out to our intelligent readers. A cat goes to court, she enters the precincts of a palace, at last she is in the presence of royalty, not as usual in the kitchen, or the cellar, or the attics, or on the roofs, where cats do most congregate, but actually stands in the presence of royalty; and what does she do? Notwithstanding the awe which it may be naturally supposed she is inspired with, notwithstanding the probable presence of noble lords and ladies, forgetful of where she is, and in whose presence she stands, seeing a mouse under the chair, she can no longer control the powerful instincts of her nature; and forgetting that the object of her journey was to behold royalty, she no longer thinks of any thing but hunting the titty mouse under the chair. What a lesson is here taught to the juvenile sexes that we should never attempt to force ourselves above our proper situations in society, and that in so doing we soon prove how much we are out of our place, and how our former habits and pursuits will remain with us, and render us wholly unfit for a position to which we ought never to have aspired.

Chapter Forty One

Lausanne.

After all, there is more sympathy in this world than we would suppose, and it is something to find that, in the turmoil and angry war of opinion and interest, nations as well as parties can lay down their weapons for a time, and offer one general and sincere tribute to genius. In these exciting times, we hear of revolutions in Spain and Portugal, deaths of crowned men, with indifference, but a shock as astounding as that of an earthquake in the city of Peru was felt throughout Europe when the numerous periodicals spread the unexpected intelligence that the gifted Malibran was no more, that in the fulness of her talent and her beauty, just commencing the harvest ripe and abundant, produced by years of unremitting labour, in which art had to perfect nature, she had been called away to the silent tomb, and that voice which has electrified so many thousands was mute for ever. Poor Malibran! she had had but a niggard portion of happiness in this world, although she procured so much pleasure to others. A brutal father, from whom she received but blows, who sold her to a dotard, who would have sold her again would she have consented! until her late marriage, toiling for others, without one object in the world on whom to throw her warm affections. I remember one day when we were talking of seasickness, I observed that the best remedy was beating the sufferer: she shook her head.

"No," said she; "that will not cure it, or surely I should have been cured when I crossed the Atlantic with my father."

Those who knew Malibran only as a performer did not know enough of her; they should have known her in society, and in domestic life. She was the *ne plus ultra* of genius in a woman; one moment all sunshine, the next a cloud would come over her expressive features; changeable as the wind, but in every change delightful, for she never disguised a thought. Six weeks—but six short weeks, and I saw her at Brussels at her country house, whither she had retired after the fatigues of the season. How impressive must be her death. Had she sickened and died at Brussels, the shock would have been great, for it is a shock when youth, beauty, and talent are so suddenly mowed down; but she died, as it were, on the stage. Admiring and applauding thousands had been listening to her magical powers, thousands more waiting to hear her at the other festivals; all eyes were upon her, all expectation upon tiptoe, when death, like a matador, comes in, strikes his victim, bows sarcastically to the audience, and retires. A thousand sermons, and ten thousand common deaths could not have produced so effective a moral lesson as the untimely fate of Malibran. There is but one parallel to it, and the effect of it was tremendous. It was that of Mr Huskisson, on the opening of the Manchester Railroad. This is the second homily read to the good people of Liverpool and Manchester. Peace be with her, although her body is not permitted to be at rest.

The more I see of the Swiss and Switzerland, the more is my opinion confirmed as to the strongest feature in the national character being that of avarice. The country is poetry, but the inhabitants are the prose of human existence. Not a chalet but looks as the abode of innocence and peace; but whether you scale the beetling rock, or pause upon the verdant turf which encircles their picturesque habitations, the demon appears like Satan in the garden of Eden. The infant, radiant as love, extends its little hand for money; the adult, with his keen grey eye, searches into you to ascertain in what manner he may overreach you. Avarice rules over the beautiful country of Helvetia.

The prevailing foible of a nation is generally to be found in the proverbs of the country and of those adjacent. The Genevese appear to have the credit of excelling the Swiss generally: they say here, "Il faut trois Juifs pour faire un Baslois, et trois Baslois pour faire un Génévois."

Again:—

"Si un Génévois se jette par la fenêtre, suivez le? Il y aura pour gagner."

It was, however, a very neat answer given by a Swiss to a Frenchman, who asserted that the French fought for honour, and the Swiss for money.

"C'est vrai," replied the Swiss, "chacun se bat pour cela que lui manque."

The Swiss have abolished titles, they have crushed their nobility; but human nature will prevail; and they seek distinction by other channels; every one who has the least pretention to education or birth looks out for employment under government; and you can hardly meet with a well-dressed person in the streets who is not a magistrate, inspector, *directeur*, or *employé* in some way or the other, although the emoluments are little or nothing. The question has been brought forward as to trial by jury being introduced, and, strange to say, the majority are opposed to it as not being suitable to the Swiss. The reason they give is, that as all respectable people hold offices under Government, and are thereby excused from serving, that there will be nobody but the lower classes to sit as jurors. It is very difficult to obtain evidence in a Swiss court of justice; and this arises from the dislike of the Swiss to give evidence; as, by so doing, they may make enemies, and their own interests may be injured. This is completely the character of the Swiss. When I visited Switzerland in my younger days, I used my eyes only, and I was delighted; now that I visit it again, when years have made me reflect and inquire more, I am disappointed. The charm is dissolved, the land of liberty appears to me to be a land of petty tyranny in the Government, and of extreme selfishness in the individuals; even the much-vaunted fidelity of the Swiss seems not to have arisen from any other than mercenary motives. Indeed, there is something radically wrong—however faithful they may be to their employers, or however they may be brave and talented—in the hearts of those who volunteer for hire and pay to kill their fellow creatures. I could not put my trust in such men in private life, although I would in the service for which they have hired themselves.

Do the faults of this people arise from the peculiarity of their constitutions, or from the nature of their Government? To ascertain this, one must compare them with those who live, under similar institutions.

I must go to America, that's decided.

Chapter Forty Two

South West and by West three-quarters West

Jack Littlebrain was, physically considered, as fine grown, and moreover as handsome a boy as ever was seen, but it must be acknowledged that he was not very clever. Nature is, in most instances, very impartial; she has given plumage to the peacock, but, as every one knows, not the slightest ear for music. Throughout the feathered race it is almost invariably the same; the homeliest clad are the finest songsters. Among animals the elephant is certainly the most intelligent, but, at the same time he cannot be considered as a beauty. Acting upon this well ascertained principle, nature imagined, that she had done quite enough for Jack when she endowed him with such personal perfection; and did not consider it was at all necessary that he should be very clever; indeed, it must be admitted, not only that he was not very clever, but (as the truth must be told) remarkably dull and stupid. However, the Littlebrains have been for a long while a well-known, numerous, and influential family, so that, if it were possible that Jack could have been taught anything, the means were forthcoming: he was sent to every school in the country; but it was in vain. At every following vacation, he was handed over from the one pedagogue to the other, of those whose names were renowned for the Busbian system of teaching by stimulating both ends: he was horsed every day and still remained an ass, and at the end of six months, if he did not run away before that period was over, he was invariably sent back to his parents as incorrigible and unteachable. What was to be done with him? The Littlebrains had always got on in the world, somehow or another, by their interest and connections; but here was one who might be said to have no brains at all. After many pros and cons, and after a variety of consulting letters had passed between the various members of his family, it was decided that, as his maternal uncle, Sir Theophilus Blazers, GCB, was at that time second in command in the Mediterranean, he should be sent to sea under his command; the Admiral, having in reply to a letter on the subject, answered that it was hard indeed if he did not lick him into some shape or another; and that, at all events, he'd warrant that Jack should be able to box the compass before he had been three months nibbling the ship's biscuit; further, that it was very easy to get over the examination necessary to qualify him for lieutenant, as a turkey and a dozen of brown stout in the boat with him on the passing day, as a present to each of the passing captains, would pass him, even if he were as incompetent as a camel (or, as they say at sea, a cable), to pass through the eye of a needle; that having once passed, he would soon have him in command of a fine frigate, with a good nursing first lieutenant; and that if he did not behave himself properly, he would make his signal to come on board of the flag-ship, take him into the cabin, and give him a sound horsewhipping, as other admirals have been known to inflict upon their own sons under similar circumstances. The reader must be aware that, from the tenour of Sir Theophilus's letter, the circumstances which we are narrating must have occurred some fifty years ago.

When Jack was informed that he was to be a midshipman, he looked up in the most innocent way in the world, (and innocent he was, sure enough,) turned on his heels, and whistled as he went for want of thought. For the last three months he had been at home, and his chief employment was kissing and romping with the maids, who declared him to be the handsomest Littlebrain that the country had ever produced. Our hero viewed the preparations made for his departure with perfect indifference, and wished everybody good bye with the utmost composure. He was a happy, good-tempered fellow, who never calculated, because he could not; never decided, for he had not wit enough to choose; never foresaw, although he could look straight before him; and never remembered, because he had no memory. The line, "If ignorance is bliss, 'tis folly to be wise," was certainly made especially for Jack; nevertheless he was not totally deficient: he knew what was good to eat or drink, for his taste was perfect, his eyes were very sharp, and he could discover in a moment if a peach was ripe on the wall; his hearing was quick, for he was the first in the school to detect the footsteps of his pedagogue; and he could smell anything savoury nearly a mile off, if the wind lay the right way. Moreover, he knew that if he put his fingers in the fire that he would burn himself; that knives cut severely; that birch tickled, and several other little axioms of this sort which are generally ascertained by children at an early age, but which Jack's capacity had not received until at a much later date. Such as he was, our hero went to sea: his stock in his sea-chest being very abundant, while his stock of ideas was proportionably small.

We will pass over all the trans-shipments of Jack until he was eventually shipped on board the Mendacious, then lying at Malta with the flag of Sir Theophilus Blazers at the fore—a splendid ship, carrying 120 guns, and nearly 120 midshipmen of different calibres. (I pass over captain, lieutenant, and ship's company, having made mention of her most valuable qualifications.) Jack was received with a hearty welcome by his uncle, for he came in pudding-time, and was invited to dinner; and the Admiral made the important discovery, that if his nephew was a fool in other points, he was certainly no fool at his knife and fork. In a short time his messmates found out that he was no fool at his fists, and his knock-down arguments ended each disputation. Indeed, as the French would say, Jack was perfection in the *physique,* although so very deficient in the *morale.*

But if Pandora's box proved a plague to the whole world. Jack had his individual portion of it, when he was summoned to *box* the compass by his worthy uncle Sir Theophilus Blazers; who in the course of six months discovered that he could not make his nephew box it in the three, which he had warranted in his letter; every day our hero's ears were boxed, but the compass never. It required all the cardinal virtues to teach him the cardinal points during the forenoon, and he made a point of forgetting them before the sun went down. They attempted it (and various were the teachers employed to drive the compass into Jack's head) his head drove round the compass; and try all he could, Jack never could compass it. It appeared, as some people are said only to have one idea, as if Jack could only have one *point* in his head at a time, and *to* that point he would stand like a well-broken pointer. With him the wind never changed till the next day. His uncle pronounced him to be a fool, but that did not hurt his nephew's feelings; he had been told so too often already.

I have said that Jack had a great respect for good eating and drinking, and, moreover, was blessed with a good appetite: every person has his peculiar fancies, and if there was anything which more titillated the palate and olfactory nerves of our hero, it was a roast goose with sage and onions. Now it so happened, that having been about seven months on board of the Mendacious, Jack had one day received a summons to dine with the Admiral, for the steward had ordered a roast goose for dinner, and knew not only that Jack was partial to it, but also that Jack was the Admiral's nephew, which always goes for something on board of a flag-ship. Just before they were sitting down to table, the Admiral wishing to know how the wind was, and having been not a little vexed with the slow progress of his nephew's nautical acquirements, said, "Now, Mr Littlebrain, go up, and bring me down word how the wind is; and mark me, as, when you are sent, nine times out of ten you make a mistake, I shall now bet you five guineas against your dinner, that you make a mistake this time: so now be off and we will soon ascertain whether you lose your dinner or I lose my money. Sit down, gentlemen, we will not wait for Mr Littlebrain."

Jack did not much admire this bet on the part of his uncle, but still less did he like the want of good manners in not waiting for him. He had just time to see the covers removed, to scent a whiff of the goose, and was off.

"The Admiral wants to know how the wind is, sir," said Jack to the officer of the watch.

The officer of the watch went to the binnacle, and setting the wind as nearly as he could, replied, "Tell Sir Theophilus that it is *South West and by West three-quarters West.*"

"That's one of those confounded long points that I never can remember," cried Jack, in despair.

"Then you'll 'get goose,' as the saying is," observed one of the midshipmen.

"No; I'm afraid that I sha'n't get any," replied Jack, despondingly. "What did he say, South West and by North three-quarters East?"

"Not exactly," replied his messmate, who was a good-natured lad, and laughed heartily at Jack's version. "South West and by West three-quarters West."

"I never can remember it," cried Jack. "I'm to have five guineas if I do, and no dinner if I don't: and if I stay here much longer, I shall get no dinner at all events, for they are all terribly peckish, and there will be none left."

"Well, if you'll give me one of the guineas, I'll show you how to manage it," said the midshipman.

"I'll give you two, if you'll only be quick and the goose a'nt all gone," replied Jack.

The midshipman wrote down the point from which the wind blew, at full length, upon a bit of paper, and pinned it to the rim of Jack's hat. "Now," said he, "when you go into the cabin, you can hold your hat so as to read it, without their perceiving you."

"Well, so I can; I never should have thought of that," said Jack.

"You hav'n't wit enough," replied the midshipman.

"Well I see no wit in the compass," replied Jack.

"Nevertheless, it's full of point," replied the midshipman: "now be quick."

Our hero's eyes served him well, if his memory was treacherous and as he entered the cabin door he bowed over his hat very politely and said, as he read it off, "South West and by West three-quarters West," and then he added, without reading at all, "if you please, Sir Theophilus."

"Steward," said the Admiral, "tell the officer of the watch to step down."

"How's the wind, Mr Growler?"

"South West and by West three-quarters West," replied the officer.

"Then, Mr Littlebrain, you have won your five guineas, and may now sit down and enjoy your dinner."

Our hero was not slow in obeying the order, and ventured, upon the strength of his success, to send his plate twice for goose. Having eaten their dinner, drunk their wine, and taken their coffee, the officers, at the same time, took the hint which invariably accompanies the latter beverage, made their bows and retreated. As Jack was following his seniors out of the cabin, the Admiral put the sum which he had staked into his hands, observing, that "it was an ill wind that blew nobody good."

So thought Jack, who, having faithfully paid the midshipman the two guineas for his assistance, was now on the poop keeping his watch, as midshipmen usually do; that is, stretched out on the signal lockers, and composing himself to sleep after the most approved fashion, answering the winks of the stars by blinks of his eyes, until at last he shut them to keep them warm. But, before he had quite composed himself, he thought of the goose and the five guineas. The wind was from the same quarter, blowing soft and mild; Jack laid in a sort of reverie, as it fanned his cheek, for the weather was close and sultry.

"Well," muttered Jack to himself, "I do love that point of the compass, at all events, and I think that I never shall forget South West and by West three-quarters West. No I never—never liked one before, though—"

"Is that true?" whispered a gentle voice in his ear; "do you love 'South West and by West three-quarters West,' and will you, as you say, never forget her?"

"Why, what's that?" said Jack, opening his eyes, and turning half round on his side.

"It's me—'South West and by West three-quarters West,' that you say you love."

Littlebrain raised himself and looked round;—there was no one on the poop except himself and two or three of the after-guard, who were lying down between the guns.

"Why, who was it that spoke?" said Jack, much astonished.

"It was the wind you love, and who has long loved you," replied the same voice; "do you wish to see me?"

"See you,—see the wind?—I've been already sent on that message by the midshipmen," thought Jack.

"Do you love me as you say, and as I love you?" continued the voice.

"Well, I like you better than any other point of the compass, and I'm sure I never thought I should like one of them," replied Jack.

"That will not do for me; will you love only me?"

"I'm not likely to love the others," replied Jack, shutting his eyes again; "I *hate* them all."

"And love me?"

"Well, I do love you, that's a fact," replied Jack, as he thought of the goose and the five guineas.

"Then look round, and you shall see me," said the soft voice.

Jack, who hardly knew whether he was asleep or awake, did at this summons once more take the trouble to open his eyes, and beheld a fairy female figure, pellucid as water, yet apparently possessing substance; her features were beautifully soft and mild, and her outline trembled and shifted as it were, waving gently to and fro. It smiled sweetly, hung over him, played with his chestnut curls, softly touched his hips with her own, passed her trembling fingers over his cheeks, and its warm breath appeared as if it melted into his. Then it grew more bold,—embraced his person, searched into his neck and collar, as if curious to examine him.

Jack felt a pleasure and gratification which he could not well comprehend: once more the charmer's lips trembled upon his own, now remaining for a moment, now withdrawing, again returning to kiss and kiss again, and once more did the soft voice put the question,—"Do you love me?"

"Better than goose," replied Jack.

"I don't know who goose may be," replied the fairy form, as she tossed about Jack's waving locks; "you must love only me; promise me that before I am relieved."

"What, have you got the first watch, as well as me?" replied Jack.

"I am on duty just now, but I shall not be so long. We southerly winds are never kept long in one place; some of my sisters will probably be sent here soon."

"I don't understand what you talk about," replied Jack. "Suppose you tell me who you are, and what you are, and I'll do all I can to keep awake; I don't know how it is, but I've felt more inclined to go to sleep since you have been fanning me about, than I did before."

"Then I will remain by your side while you listen to me. I am, as I told you, a wind—"

"That's puzzling," said Jack, interrupting her.

"My name is 'South West and by West three-quarters West.'"

"Yes, and a very long name it is. If you wish me to remember you, you should have had a shorter one."

This ruffled the wind a little, and she blew rather sharp into the corner of Jack's eye,—however, she proceeded,—

"You are a sailor, and of course you know all the winds on the compass by name."

"I wish I did; but I don't," replied Littlebrain, "I can recollect you, and not one other."

Again the wind trembled with delight on his lips, and she proceeded:— "You know that there are thirty-two points on the compass, and these points are divided into quarters; so that there are, in fact, 128 different winds."

"There are more than I could ever remember; I know that," said Jack.

"Well, we are in all 128. All the winds which have northerly in them, are coarse and ugly; all the southern winds are pretty."

"You don't say so?" replied our hero.

"We are summoned to blow, as required, but the hardest duty generally falls to the northerly winds, as it should do, for they are the strongest; although we southerly winds can—blow hard enough when we choose. Our characters are somewhat different. The most unhappy in disposition, and I may say, the most malevolent, are the north and easterly winds; the North West winds are powerful, but not unkind; the South East winds vary, but, at all events, we of the South West are considered the mildest and most beneficent. Do you understand me?"

"Not altogether. You're going right round the compass, and I never could make it out, that's a fact. I hear what you say, but I cannot promise to recollect it; I can only recollect South West and by West three-quarters West."

"I care only for your recollecting me; if you do that, you may forget all the rest. Now you see we South Wests are summer winds, and are seldom required but in this season; I have often blown over your ship these last three months, and I always have lingered near you, for I loved you."

"Thank you—now go on, for seven bells have struck sometime, and I shall be going to turn in. Is your watch out?"

"No, I shall blow for some hours longer. Why will you leave me—why wo'n't you stay on deck with me?"

"What, stay on deck after my watch is out! No, if I do, blow me! We midshipmen never do that—but I say, why can't you come down with me, and turn in my hammock; it's close to the hatchway, and you can easily do it."

"Well, I will, upon one promise. You say that you love me, now I'm very jealous, for we winds are always supplanting one another. Promise me that you will never mention any other wind in the compass but me, for if you do, they may come to you, and if I hear of it I'll blow the masts out of your ship, that I will."

"You don't say so?" replied Jack, surveying her fragile, trembling form.

"Yes, I will, and on a lee shore too; so that the ship shall go to pieces on the rocks, and the Admiral and every soul on board her be drowned."

"No, you wouldn't, would you?" said our hero, astonished.

"Not if you promise me. Then I'll come to you and pour down your windsails, and dry your washed clothes as they hang on the rigging, and just ripple the waves as you glide along, and hang upon the lips of my dear love, and press him in my arms. Promise me, then, on no account ever to recollect or mention any other wind but me."

"Well, I think I may promise that," replied Jack, "I'm very clever at forgetting; and then you'll come to my hammock, won't you, and sleep with me? you'll be a nice cool bedfellow these warm nights."

"I can't sleep on my watch as midshipmen do; but I'll watch you while you sleep, and I'll fan your cheeks, and keep you cool and comfortable, till I'm relieved."

"And when you go, when will you come again?"

"That I cannot tell—when I'm summoned; and I shall wait with impatience, that you may be sure of."

"There's eight bells," said Jack, starting up; "I must go down and call the officer of the middle watch; but I'll soon turn in, for my relief is not so big as myself, and I can thrash him."

Littlebrain was as good as his word; he cut down his relief; and then thrashed him for venturing to expostulate. The consequence was, that in ten minutes he was in his hammock, and "South West and by West three-quarters West" came gently down the hatchway, and rested in his arms. Jack soon fell fast asleep, and when he was wakened up the next morning by the quarter-master, his bedfellow was no longer there. A mate inquiring how the wind was, was answered by the quartermaster that they had a fresh breeze from the North North West, by which Jack understood that his sweetheart was no longer on duty.

Our hero had passed such a happy night with his soft and kind companion, that he could think of nothing else; he longed for her to come again, and, to the surprise of everybody, was now perpetually making inquiries as to the wind which blew. He thought of her continually; and in fact was as much in love with "South West and by West three-quarters West" as he possibly could be. She came again—once more did he enjoy her delightful company; again she slept with him in his hammock, and then, after a short stay, she was relieved by another.

We do not intend to accuse the wind of inconstancy, as that was not her fault; nor of treachery, for she loved dearly; nor of violence, for she was all softness and mildness; but we do say, that "South West and by West three-quarters West" was the occasion of Jack being very often in a scrape, for our hero kept his word; he forgot all other winds, and, with him, there was no other except his dear "South West and by West three-quarters West." It must be admitted of Jack, that, at all events, he showed great perseverance, for he stuck to his point.

Our hero would argue with his messmates, for it is not those who are most capable of arguing who are most fond of it; and, like all arguers not very brilliant, he would flounder and diverge away right and left, just as the flaws of ideas came into his head.

"What nonsense it is your talking that way," would his opponent say; "why don't you come to the point?"

"And so I do," cried Jack.

"Well, then, what is your point?"

"South West and by West three-quarters West," replied our hero.

Who could reply to this? But in every instance, and through every difficulty, our hero kept his promise, until his uncle Sir Theophilus was very undecided, whether he should send him home to be locked up in a Lunatic Asylum, or bring him on in the service to the rank of post-captain. Upon mature consideration, however, as a man in Bedlam is a very useless member of society, and a tee-total non-productive, whereas a captain in the navy is a responsible agent, the Admiral came to the conclusion, that Littlebrain must follow up his destiny.

At last, Jack was set down as the greatest fool in the ship, and was pointed out as such. The ladies observed, that such might possibly be the case, but at all events he was the handsomest young man in the Mediterranean fleet. We believe that both parties were correct in their assertions.

Time flies—even a midshipman's time, which does not fly quite so fast as his money—and the time came for Mr Littlebrain's examination. Sir Theophilus, who now commanded the whole fleet, was almost in despair. How was it possible that a man could navigate a ship, with only one quarter point of the compass in his head?

Sir Theophilus scratched his wig; and the disposition of the Mediterranean fleet, so important to the country, was altered according to the dispositions of the captains who commanded the ships. In those days, there were martinets in the service; officers who never overlooked an offence, or permitted the least deviation from strict duty; who were generally hated, but at the same time were most valuable to the service. As for his nephew passing his examination before any of those of the first or second, or even of the third degree, the Admiral knew that it was impossible. The consequence was, that one was sent away on a mission to Genoa, about nothing; another to watch for vessels never expected, off Sardinia; two more to cruise after a French frigate which had never been built: and thus, by degrees, did the Admiral arrange, so as obtain a set of officers sufficiently pliant to allow his nephew to creep under the gate which barred his promotion, and which he never could have vaulted over. So the signal was made—our hero went on board—his uncle had not forgotten the propriety of a little *douceur* on the occasion; and, as the turkeys were all gone, three couple of geese were sent in the same boat, as a present to each of the three passing captains. Littlebrain's heart failed him as he pulled to the ship; even the geese hissed at him, as much as to say, "If you were not such a stupid ass, we might have been left alive in our coops." There was a great deal of truth in that remark, if they did say so.

Nothing could have been made more easy for Littlebrain than his examination. The questions had all been arranged beforehand; and some kind friend had given him all the answers written down. The passing captains apparently suffered from the heat of the weather, and each had his hand on his brow, looking down on the table at the time that Littlebrain gave his answers, so that of course they did not observe that he was reading them off. As soon as Littlebrain had given his answer, and had had sufficient time to drop his paper under the table, the captains felt better and looked up again.

There were but eight questions for our hero to answer. Seven had been satisfactorily got through; then came the eighth, a very simple one:— "What is your course and distance from Ushant to the Start?" This question having been duly put, the captains were again in deep meditation, shrouding their eyes with the palms of their hands.

Littlebrain had his answer—he looked at the paper. What could be more simple than to reply?—and then the captains would have all risen up, shaken him by the hand, complimented him upon the talent he had displayed, sent their compliments to the commander-in-chief, and their thanks for the geese. Jack was just answering, "North—"

"Recollect your promise!" cried a soft voice, which Jack well recollected.

Jack stammered—the captains were mute—and waited patiently.

"I must say it," muttered Jack.

"You shan't," replied the little Wind.

"Indeed I must," said Jack, "or I shall be turned back."

The captains, surprised at this delay and the muttering of Jack, looked up, and one of them gently inquired if Mr Littlebrain had not dropped his handkerchief or something under the table! And then they again fixed their eyes upon the green cloth.

"If you dare, I'll never see you again," cried "South West and by West three-quarters West,"—"never come to your hammock,—but I'll blow the ship on shore, every soul shall be lost, Admiral and all; recollect your promise!"

"Then I shall never pass," replied Jack.

"Do you think that any other point in the compass shall pass you except me?—never! I am too jealous for that. Come now, dearest!" and the Wind again deliciously trembled upon the lips of our hero, who could no longer resist.

"South West and by West three-quarters West," exclaimed Jack firmly.

"You have made a slight mistake, Mr Littlebrain," said one of the captains. "*Look* again—I meant to say, *think again*."

"South West and by West three-quarters West," again repeated Jack.

"Dearest, how I love you!" whispered the soft Wind.

"Why, Mr Littlebrain," said one of the captains—for Jack had actually laid the paper down on the table—"what's in the wind now?"

"She's obstinate," replied Jack.

"You appear to be so, at all events," replied the captain. "Pray try once more."

"I have it!" thought Jack, who tore off the last answer from his paper. "I gained five guineas by that plan once before." He then handed the bit of paper to the passing captain: "I believe that's right, sir," said our hero.

"Yes, that is right; but could you not have said it instead of writing it, Mr Littlebrain?"

Jack made no reply; his little sweetheart pouted a little, but said nothing; it was an evasion which she did not like. A few seconds of consultation then took place, as a matter of form. Each captain asked of the other if he was perfectly satisfied as to Mr Littlebrain's capabilities, and the reply was in the affirmative; and they were perfectly satisfied, that he was either a fool or a madman. However, as we have had both in the service by way of precedent, Jack was added to the list, and the next day was appointed lieutenant.

Our hero did his duty as lieutenant of the forecastle; and as all the duty of that officer is, when hailed from the quarterdeck, to answer, "*Ay, ay, sir,*" he got on without making many mistakes. And now he was very happy; no one dared to call him a fool except his uncle; he had his own cabin, and many was the time, that his dear little "South West and by West three-quarters West" would come in by the scuttle, and nestle by his side.

"You won't see so much of me soon, dearest," said she one morning, gravely.

"Why not, my soft one?" replied Jack.

"Don't you recollect that the winter months are coming on?"

"So they are," replied Jack. "Well, I shall long for you back."

And Jack did long, and long very much, for he loved his dear wind and the fine weather which accompanied her. Winter came on and heavy gales and rain, and thunder and lightning; nothing but double-reefed top-sails, and wearing in succession; and our hero walked the forecastle, and thought of his favourite wind. The North East winds came down furiously, and the weather was bitter cold. The officers shook the rain and spray off their garments when their watch was over, and called for grog.

"Steward, a glass of grog," cried one; "and let it be strong."

"The same for me," said Jack; "only, I'll mix it myself."

Jack poured out the rum till the tumbler was half full.

"Why, Littlebrain," said his messmate, "that is a dose; that's what we call a regular *Nor-wester*."

"Is it?" replied Jack. "Well then, Nor-westers suit me exactly, and I shall stick to them like cobblers' wax."

And during the whole of the winter months our hero showed a great predilection for Nor-westers.

It was in the latter end of February that there was a heavy gale; it had blown furiously from the northward for three days, and then it paused and panted as if out of breath—no wonder! And then the wind shifted, and shifted again, with squalls and heavy rain, until it blew from every quarter of the compass.

Our hero's watch was over, and he came down and called for a "Nor-wester" as usual.

"How is the wind now?" asked the first lieutenant the master, who came down dripping wet.

"South South West, but drawing now fast to the Westward," said old Spunyarn.

And so it was; and it veered round until "South West and by West three-quarters *West*," with an angry gust, came down the sky-light, and blowing strongly into our hero's ear, cried,—

"Oh, you false one!"

"False!" exclaimed Jack. "What! you here, and so angry too? What's the matter?"

"What's the matter!—do you think I don't know? What have you been doing over since I was away, comforting yourself during my absence with *Nor-westers*?"

"Why, you an't jealous of a Nor-wester, are you?" replied Littlebrain. "I confess, I'm rather partial to them."

"What! this to my face!—I'll never come again, without you promise me that you will have nothing to do with them, and never call for one again. Be quick—I cannot stay more than two minutes; for it is hard work now, and we relieve quick—say the word."

"Well, then," replied Littlebrain, "you've no objection to *half-and-half*?"

"None in the world; that's quite another thing, and has nothing to do with the wind."

"It has, though," thought Jack, "for it gets a man in the wind; but I won't tell her so; and," continued he, "you don't mind a raw nip, do you?"

"No—I care for nothing except a Nor-wester."

"I'll never call for one again," replied Jack; "it is but making my grog a little stronger; in future it shall be *half-and-half*."

"That's a dear! Now I'm off—don't forget me;" and away went the wind in a great hurry.

It was about three months after this short visit, the fleet being off Corsica, that our hero was walking the deck, thinking that he soon should see the object of his affections, when a privateer brig was discovered at anchor a few miles from Bastia. The signal was made for the boats of the fleet to cut her out; and the Admiral, wishing that his nephew should distinguish himself somehow, gave him the command of one of the finest boats. Now Jack was as brave as brave could be; he did not know what danger was; he hadn't wit enough to perceive it, and there was no doubt but he would distinguish himself. The boats went on the service. Jack was the very first on board, cheering his men as he darted into the closed ranks of his opponents. Whether it was that he did not think that his head was worth defending, or that he was too busy in breaking the heads of others to look after his own this is certain, that a tomahawk descended upon it with such force as to bury itself in his skull (and his was a thick skull too). The privateer's men were overpowered by numbers, and then our hero was discovered, under a pile of bodies, still breathing heavily. He was hoisted on board, and taken into his uncle's cabin: the surgeon shook his head when he had examined that of our hero.

"It must have been a most tremendous blow," said he to the Admiral, "to have penetrated—"

"It must have been, indeed," replied the Admiral, as the tears rolled down his cheeks; for he loved his nephew.

The surgeon having done all that his art would enable him, left the cabin to attend to the others who were hurt; the Admiral also went on the quarter-deck, walking to and fro for an hour in a melancholy mood. He returned to the cabin, and bent over his nephew; Jack opened his eyes.

"My dear fellow," said the Admiral, "how's your head now?"

"*South West and by West three-quarters West*," faintly exclaimed our hero, constant in death, as he turned a little on one side and expired.

It was three days afterwards, as the fleet were on a wind, making for Malta, that the bell of the ship tolled, and a body, sewed up in a hammock and covered with the Union Jack, was carried to the gangway by the Admiral's bargemen. It had been a dull cloudy day, with little wind; the hands were turned up, the officers and men stood uncovered; the Admiral in advance with his arms folded, as the chaplain read the funeral service over the body of our hero,—and as the service proceeded, the sails flapped, for the wind had shifted a little; a motion was made, by the hand of the officer of the watch, to the man at the helm to let the ship go off the wind, that the service might not be disturbed, and a mizzling soft rain descended. The wind had shifted to our hero's much loved *point*, his fond mistress had come to mourn over the loss of her dearest, and the rain that descended were the tears which she shed at the death of her handsome but not over-gifted lover.

Chapter Forty Three

III-Will

Dramatis Personae.

Mr **Cadaverous** , *An old miser, very rich and very ill.*

Edward , *A young lawyer without a brief.*

Mr Haustus Gumarabic , *Apothecary.*

Seedy , *Solicitor.*

Thomas Montague, John Montague , Nephews to Mr Cadaverous.

James Sterling, William Sterling , nephews twice removed to Mr Cadaverous.

Clementina Montagu , Niece to Mr Cadaverous.

Mrs Jellybags , Housekeeper and nurse.

Act One

Scene.—*A sick room.*—Mr **Cadaverous** *in an easy chair asleep, supported by cushions, wrapped up in his dressing-gown, a night-cap on his head.*—*A small table with phials, gallipots, etcetera.*—*Mrs Jellybags seated on a chair close to the table.*

(Mrs *Jellybags looks at* Mr Cadaverous , *and then comes forward.*) He sleeps yet—the odious old miser! Mercy on me, how I do hate him,—almost as much as he loves his money! there's one comfort, he cannot take his money-bags with him, and the doctor says that he cannot last much longer. Ten years have I been his slave—ten years have I been engaged to be married to Sergeant Major O'Callaghan of the Blues—ten years has he kept me waiting at the porch of Hymen,—and what thousands of couples have I seen enter during the time! Oh dear! its enough to drive a widow mad. I think I have managed it;—he has now quarrelled with all his relations, and Dr Gumarabic intends this day to suggest the propriety of his making his last will and testament. (Mr *Cadaverous , still asleep, coughs.*) He is waking, (*Looks at him.*) No, he is not. Well, then, I shall wake him, and give him a draught, for, after such a comfortable sleep as he is now in, he might last a whole week longer. (*Goes up to* Mr Cadaverous , *and shakes him.*)

Mr Cad. (starting up.) Ugh ugh! ugh! *(coughs violently.)* Oh! Mrs Jellybags, I'm so ill. Ugh! ugh!

Jel. My dear, dear sir! now don't say so. I was in hopes, after such a nice long sleep you would have found yourself so much better.

Cad. Long sleep! oh dear!—I'm sure I've not slept ten minutes.

Jel. (aside.) I know that. *(Aloud.)* Indeed, my dear sir, you are mistaken. Time passes very quick when we are fast asleep. I have been watching you and keeping the flies off. But you must now take your draught, my dear sir, and your pill first.

Cad. What! more pills and more draughts! Why, there's no end to them.

Jel. Yes, there will be, by and by, my dear sir. You know Doctor Gumarabic has ordered you take one pill and one draught every half hour.

Cad. And so I have—never missed one for the last six weeks—woke up for them day and night. I feel very weak—very weak, indeed! Don't you think I might eat something, my dear Mrs Jellybags?

Jel. Eat, my dear Mr Cadaverous!—how can you ask me, when you know that Doctor Gumarabic says that it would be the death of you?

Cad. Only the wing of a chicken,—or a bit of the breast—

Jel. Impossible!

Cad. A bit of dry toast, then; any thing, my dear Mrs Jellybags. I've such a gnawing—Ugh! ugh!

Jel. My dear sir, you would die if you swallowed the least thing that's nourishing.

Cad. I'm sure I shall die if I do not. Well, then, a little soup—I should like that very much indeed.

Jel. Soup! it would be poison, my dear sir! No, no. You must take your pill and your draught.

Cad. Oh dear! oh dear!—Forty-eight pills and forty-eight draughts every twenty-four hours!—not a wink of sleep day or night.

Jel. (soothingly.) But it's to make you well, you know, my dear Mr Cadaverous. Come, now. *(Hands him a pill and some water in a tumbler.)*

Cad. The last one is hardly down yet;—I feel it sticking half-way. Ugh! ugh!

Jel. Then wash them both down at once. Come, now, 'tis to make you well, you know.

Cadaverous takes the pill with a wry face, and coughs it up again.

Cad. Ugh! ugh! There—it's up again. Oh dear! oh dear!

Jel. You must take it, my dear sir. Come, now, try again.

Cad. (*coughing.*) My cough is so bad. (*Takes the pill.*) Oh, my poor head! Now I'll lie down again.

Jel. Not yet, my dear Mr Cadaverous. You must take your draught;—it's to make you well, you know.

Cad. What! another draught? I'm sure I must have twenty draughts in my inside, besides two boxes of pills!

Jel. Come, now—it will be down in a minute.

(*Cadaverous takes the wine-glass in his hand, and looks at it with abhorrence.*)

Jel. Come, now.

(*Cadaverous swallows the draught, and feels very sick, puts his handkerchief to his mouth, and, after a time, sinks back in the chair quite exhausted, and shuts his eyes.*)

Jel. (*aside.*) I wish the doctor would come. It's high time that he made his will.

Cad. (*drawing up his leg.*) Oh! oh! oh!

Jel. What's the matter, my dear Mr Cadaverous.

Cad. Oh! such pain!—oh! rub it, Mrs Jellybags.

Jel. What, here, my dear sir? (*Rubs his knee.*)

Cad. No, no!—Not there!—Oh, my hip!

Jel. What, here? (*Rubs his hip.*)

Cad. No, no!—higher—higher! Oh, my side!

Jel. What, here? (*Rubs his side.*)

Cad. No!—lower!

Jel. Here? (*Rubbing.*)

Cad. No!—higher!—Oh, my chest!—my stomach! Oh dear!—oh dear!

Jel. Are you better now, my dear sir?

Cad. Oh dear! oh! I do believe that I shall die! I've been a very wicked man, I'm afraid.

Jel. Don't say so, Mr Cadaverous. Every one but your nephews and nieces say that you are the best man in the world.

Cad. Do they? I was afraid that I had not been quite so good as they think I am.

Jel. I'd like to hear any one say to the contrary. I'd tear their eyes out,—that I would.

Cad. You are a good woman, Mrs Jellybags; and I shall not forget you in my will.

Jel. Don't mention wills, my dear sir. You make me so miserable. (*Puts her handkerchief to her eyes.*)

Cad. Don't cry, Mrs Jellybags. I won't talk any more about it. (*Sinks back exhausted.*)

Jel. (*wiping her eyes.*) Here comes Dr Gumarabic.

Enter **Gumarabic**

Gum. Good morning, Mistress Jellybags. Well, how's our patient?—better?—heh?

(Mrs *Jellybags shakes her head.*)

Gum. No: well, that's odd. (*Goes up to* Mr *Cadaverous* .) Not better, my dear sir?—don't you feel stronger?

Cad. (*faintly.*) Oh, no!

Gum. Not stronger! Let us feel the pulse. (Mrs *Jellybags hands a chair, and Gumarabic sits down, pulls out his watch, and counts.*) Intermittent—135—well, now—that's very odd! Mrs Jellybags, have you adhered punctually to my prescriptions?

Jel. Oh yes, sir, exactly.

Gum. He has eaten nothing?

Cad. Nothing at all.

Gum. And don't feel stronger? Odd—very odd! Pray, has he had any thing in the way of drink? Come, Mrs Jellybags, no disguise,—tell the truth;—no soup—warm jelly—heh?

Jel. No, sir; upon my word, he has had nothing.

Gum. Humph?—and yet feels no stronger? Well, that's odd!—Has he taken the pill every half-hour?

Jel. Yes, sir, regularly.

Gum. And feels no better! Are you sure that he has had his draught with his pill?

Jel. Every time, sir.

Gum. And feels no better! Well, that's odd!—very odd, indeed! (*Rises and comes forward with* Mrs *Jellybags* .) We must throw in some more draughts, Mrs Jellybags; there is no time to be lost.

Jel. I am afraid he's much worse, sir.

Gum. I am not at all afraid of it, Mrs Jellybags,—I am sure of it;—it's very odd,—but the fact is, that all the physic in the world won't save him; but still he must take it,—because—physic was made to be taken.

Jel. Very true, sir. (*Whispers to Gumarabic* .)

Gum. Ah! yes;—very proper. (*Going to* Mr *Cadaverous* .) My dear sir, I have done my best; nevertheless, you are ill,—very ill,—which is odd,—very odd! It is not pleasant,—I may say, very unpleasant,—but if you have any little worldly affairs to settle,—will to make,—or a codocil to add, in favour of your good nurse, your doctor, or so on,—it might be as well to send for your lawyer;—there is no saying, but, during my practice, I have sometimes found that people die. After all the physic you have taken, it certainly is odd—very odd—very odd, indeed;—but you might die to-morrow.

Cad. Oh dear!—I'm very ill.

Jel. (*sobbing.*) Oh dear! oh dear!—he's very ill.

Gum. (*comes forward, shrugging up his shoulders.*) Yes; he is ill—very ill;— to-morrow, dead as mutton! At all events he has not died for want of physic. We must throw in some more draughts immediately;—no time to be lost. Life is short,—but my bill will be long—very long!

(*Exit as scene closes.*)

Act 2

Scene 1 .—Enter Clementina , with a letter in her hand.

Clem. I have just received a letter from my dear Edward: he knows of my uncle's danger, and is anxious to see me. I expect him immediately. I hope he will not be seen by Mrs Jellybags as he comes in, for she would try to make more mischief than than she has already. Dear Edward! how he loves me! (*Kisses the letter.*)

Enter **Edward**

Edw. My lovely, my beautiful, my adored Clementina! I have called upon Mr Gumarabic, who tells me that your uncle cannot live through the twenty-four hours, and I have flown here, my sweetest, dearest, to—to—

Clem. To see me, Edward: surely there needs no excuse for coming?

Edw. To reiterate my ardent, pure, and unchangeable affection, my dearest Clementina to assure you, that in sickness or in health, for richer or for poorer, for better or for worse, as they say in the marriage ceremony, I am yours till death us do part.

Clem. I accept the vow, dearest Edward. You know too well my heart for me to say more.

Edw. I do know your heart, Clementina, as it is,—nor do I think it possible that you could change;—still, sometimes—that is for a moment when I call to mind that, by your uncle's death, as his favourite niece, living with him for so many years, you may soon find yourself in possession of thousands,—and that titled men may lay their coronets at your feet,—then, Clementina—

Clem. Ungenerous and unkind!—Edward, I almost hate you. Is a little money, then, to sway my affections? Shame, Edward, shame on you! Is such your opinion of my constancy? (*Weeps.*) You must judge me by your own heart.

Edw. Clementina! dearest Clementina!—I did!—but rather—that is,—I was not in earnest;—but when we value any object as I value you,—it may be forgiven, if I feel at times a little jealous;—yes, dearest, jealous!

Clem. 'Twas jealousy then, Edward, which made you so unkind? Well, then, I can forgive that.

Edw. Nothing but jealousy, dearest! I cannot help, at times, representing you surrounded by noble admirers,—all of them suing to you,—not for yourself, but for your money, tempting you with their rank;—and it makes me jealous, horribly jealous! I cannot compete with lords, Clementina,—a poor barrister without a brief.

Clem. I have loved you for yourself, Edward. I trust you have done the same toward me.

Edw. Yes; upon my soul, my Clementina!

Clem. Then my uncle's disposition of his property will make no difference in me. For your sake, my dear Edward, I hope he will not forget me. What's that? Mrs Jellybags is coming out of the room. Haste, Edward;—you must not be seen here. Away, dearest!—and may God bless you.

Edw. (*kisses her hand.*) Heaven preserve my adored, my matchless, ever-to-be-loved Clementina.

(*Exeunt separately.*)

Scene 2.—The sick room—Mr Cadaverous, *lying on sofa-bed*—Mr Seedy, *the lawyer, sitting by his side, with papers on the table before him.*

Seedy. I believe now, sir, that every thing is arranged in your will according to your instructions. Shall I read it over again; for although signed and witnessed, you may make any alteration you please by a codicil.

Cad. No, no. You have read it twice, Mr Seedy, and you may leave me now. I am ill, very ill, and wish to be alone.

Seedy (folds up his papers and rises.) I take my leave, Mr Cadaverous, trusting to be long employed as your solicitor.

Cad. Afraid not, Mr Seedy. Lawyers have no great interest in heaven. Your being my solicitor will not help me there.

Seedy (coming forward as he goes out.) Not a sixpence to his legal adviser! Well, well! I know how to make out a bill for the executors.

(Exit Seedy, and enter Mrs Jellybags*.)*

Jel. (with her handkerchief to her eyes.) Oh dear! oh dear! oh, Mr Cadaverous, how can you fatigue and annoy yourself with such things as wills?

Cad. (faintly.) Don't cry, Mrs Jellybags. I've not forgotten you.

Jel. (sobbing.) I can't—help—crying. And there's Miss Clementina,— now that you are dying,—who insists upon coming in to see you.

Cad. Clementina, my niece, let her come in, Mrs Jellybags; I feel I'm going fast,—I may as well take leave of every body.

Jel. (sobbing.) Oh dear! oh dear! You may come in, Miss.

Enter **Clementina**

Clem. My dear uncle, why have you, for so many days, refused me admittance? Every morning have I asked to be allowed to come and nurse you, and for more than three weeks have received a positive refusal.

Cad. Refusal! Why I never had a message from you.

Clem. No message! Every day I have sent, and every day did Mrs Jellybags reply that you would not see me.

Cad. (faintly.) Mrs Jellybags,—Mrs Jellybags—

Clem. Yes, uncle; it is true as I stand here;—and my brother Thomas has called almost every day, and John every Sunday, the only day he can leave the banking-house; and cousins William and James have both been here very often.

Cad. Nobody told me! I thought every one had forgotten me. Why was I not informed, Mrs Jellybags?

Jel. (*in a rage.*) Why, you little, story-telling creature, coming here to impose upon your good uncle! You know that no one has been here—not a soul;—and as for yourself, you have been too busy looking after a certain gentleman ever to think of your poor uncle;—that you have;—taking advantage of his illness to behave in so indecorous a manner. I would have told him every thing, but I was afraid of making him worse.

Clem. You are a false, wicked woman!

Jel. Little impudent creature,—trying to make mischief between me and my kind master, but it won't do. (*To Clementina aside.*) The will is signed, and I'll take care he does not alter it;—so do your worst.

Cad. (*faintly.*) Give me the mixture, Mrs —

Clem. I will, dear uncle. (*Pours out the restorative mixture in a glass.*)

Jel. (*going back.*) You will, Miss,—indeed! but you shan't.

Clem. Be quiet, Mrs Jellybags;—allow me at least to do something for my poor uncle.

Clem. Give me the mix—

Jel. (*prevents Clementina from giving it, and tries to take it from her.*) You shan't, Miss!—You never shall.

Cad. Give me the —

(Mrs *Jellybags and Clementina scuffle, at last Clementina throws the contents of the glass into* Mrs *Jellybags's face.*)

Clem. There, then!—since you will have it.

Jel. (*in a rage.*) You little minx!—I'll be revenged for that. Wait a little till the will is read,—that's all;—See if I don't bundle you out of doors,—that I will.

Clem. As you please, Mrs Jellybags; but pray give my poor uncle his restorative mixture.

Jel. To please you?—Not I! I'll not give him a drop till I think proper. Little, infamous, good-for-nothing—

Cad. Give me—oh!

Jel. Saucy—man-seeking—

Clem. Oh! as for that, Mrs Jellybags, the big sergeant was here last night—I know that. Talk of men indeed!

Jel. Very well, Miss!—very well! Stop till the breath is out of your uncle's body—and I'll beat you till your's is also.

Cad. Give—oh!

Clem. My poor uncle! He will have no help till I leave the room—I must go. Infamous woman! *Exit.*

Cad. Oh!

Jel. I'm in such a rage!—I could tear her to pieces!—the little!—the gnat! Oh, I'll be revenged! Stop till the will is read, and then I'll turn her out into the streets to starve. Yes! yes! the will!—the will! (*Pauses and pants for breath.*) Now, I recollect the old fellow called for his mixture. I must go and get some mere. I'll teach her to throw physic in my face.

(*Goes out and returns with a phial—pours out a portion, and goes up to* Mr Cadaverous *.*)

Jel. Here, my dear Mr Cadaverous. Mercy on me!—Mr Cadaverous!—why, he's fainted!—Mr Cadaverous! (*Screams.*) Lord help us!—why, he's dead! Well now, this sort of thing does give one a shock, even when one has longed for it. Yes, he's quite dead! (*Coming forward.*) So, there's an end of all his troubles—and, thank Heaven! of mine also. Now for Sergeant-major O'Callaghan, and—love! Now for Miss Clementina, and—revenge? But first the will!—the will!

Curtain drops

Act 3

Mrs Jellybags

Oh dear!—this is a very long morning. I feel such suspense—such anxiety; and poor Sergeant-major O'Callaghan is quite in a perspiration! He is drinking and smoking down in the kitchen to pass away the time, and if the lawyer don't come soon, the dear man will be quite fuddled. He talks of buying a farm in the country. Well, we shall see; but if the Sergeant thinks that he will make ducks and drakes of my money, he is mistaken. I have not been three times a widow for nothing—I will have it all settled upon myself; that must and shall be, or else—no Sergeant O'Callaghan for me!

Enter **Clementina**

So, here you are, Miss. We'll wait till the will is read, and then we shall see who is mistress here.

Clem. I am as anxious as you, Mrs Jellybags. You may have wheedled my poor uncle to make up the will in your favour; if so, depend upon it, I shall expect nothing from your hands.

Jel. I should rather think not, Miss. If I recollect right, you threw the carminative mixture in my face.

Clem. And made you blush for the first time in your life.

Jel. I shall not blush to slam the door in your face.

Clem. Rather than be indebted to you, I would beg my bread from door to door.

Jel. I expect that you very soon will.

Enter **Edward**

Edw. My dearest Clementina, I have come to support you on this trying occasion.

Jel. And ascertain how matters stand, before you decide upon marrying, I presume, Mr Edward.

Edw. Madam, I am above all pecuniary considerations.

Jel. So everybody says, when they think themselves sure of money.

Edw. You judge of others by yourself.

Jel. Perhaps I do—I certainly do expect to be rewarded for my long and faithful services.

Clem. Do not waste words upon her, my dear.—You have my solemn promise; nothing shall change my feeling towards you.

Jel. That may be; but did it never occur to you, Miss, that the gentleman's feelings might alter?

Edw. Detestable wretch!

(*Hands Clementina to a chair on the right, and sits by her. Enter Nephews John , Thomas , William , and James , all with white pocket-handkerchiefs in their hands—they take their seats two right and two left.*)

Jel. (*aside.*) Here they all come, like crows that smell carrion. How odious is the selfishness of this world! But here is Mr Gumarabic. How do you do, Sir? (*Curtsies with a grave air.*)

Gum. Very well, I thank you, Mrs Jellybags. Can't say the—same of all my patients. Just happened to pass by—thought I would step in and hear the will read—odd, that I should pop in at the time—very odd. Pray, may I ask, my dear Mrs Jellybags, were you present at the making of the will?

Jel. No, my dear sir; my nerves would not permit me.

Gum. Nerves!—odd, very odd! Then you don't know how things are settled?

Jel. No more than the man in the moon, my dear sir.

Gum. Man in the moon!—odd comparison that from a woman!—very odd! Hope my chance won't prove all moonshine.

Jel. I should think not, my dear sir; but here comes Mr Seedy, and we shall know all about it.

(*Enter* Mr *Seedy* —Mrs *Jellybags* , *all courtesy, waves her hand to a chair in the centre, with a table before it.* Mr *Seedy sits down, pulls the will out of his pocket, lays it on the table, takes out his snuff-box, takes a pinch, then his handkerchief, blows his nose, snuffs the candles, takes his spectacles from his waistcoat pocket, puts them on, breaks the seals, and bows to the company:* Mrs *Jellybags has taken her seat on the left next to him, and* Dr *Gumarabic by her side.* Mrs *Jellybags sobs very loud, with her handkerchief to her face.*)

Seedy . Silence, if you please.

(Mrs *Jellybags stops sobbing immediately.*)

Edw. (*putting his arm round Clementina's waist.*) My dearest Clementina!

(Mr *Seedy hems twice, and then reads,—*)

"The last Will and Testament of Christopher Cadaverous, Gentleman, of Copse horton, in the County of Cumberland.

"I, Christopher Cadaverous, being at this time in sound mind, do hereby make my last will and testament.

"First, I pray that I may be forgiven all my manifold sins and wickedness, and I do beg forgiveness of all those whom I may have injured unintentionally or otherwise; and at the same time do pardon all those who may have done me wrong, even to John Jones, the turnpike man, who unjustly made me pay the threepenny toll twice over on Easter last, when I went up to receive my dividends.

"My property, personal and real, I devise to my two friends, Solomon Lazarus, residing at Number 3, Lower Thames-street, and Hezekiah Flint, residing at Number 16, Lothbury, to have and to hold for the following uses and purposes:—

"First, to my dearly beloved niece, Clementina Montagu, I leave the sum of one hundred and fifty pounds, three and a half per cent consols, for her sole use and benefit, to be made over to her, both principal and interest, on the day of her marriage." (*Edward withdraws his arm from Clementina's waist—turns half round from her, and falls back in his chair with a pish!*)

"To my nephew, Thomas Montagu, I leave the sum of nineteen pounds nineteen shilling and sixpence—having deducted the other sixpence to avoid the legacy duty."

(*Thomas turns from the lawyer with his face to the front of the stage; crossing his legs.*)

"To my nephew, John Montagu, I leave also the sum of nineteen pounds nineteen shillings and sixpence."

(*John turns away in the same manner.*)

"To my nephew, once removed, James Stirling, I leave the sum of five pounds to purchase a suit of mourning."

(*James turns away as the others.*)

"To my nephew, once removed, William Stirling, I leave the sum of five pounds to purchase a suit of mourning."

(*William turns away as the others.*)

"To my kind and affectionate housekeeper, Mrs Martha Jellybags—"

(Mrs *Jellybags sobs loudly, and cries* "Oh dear! Oh dear!")

Mr *Seedy* . Silence, if you please. (*Reads.*)

"In return for all her attention to me during my illness, and her ten years' service, I leave the whole of my—"

(Mr *Seedy having come to the bottom of the page lays down the will, takes out his snuff-box, takes a pinch, blows his nose, snuffs the candles, and proceeds.*)

"I leave the whole of my wardrobe, for her entire use and disposal; and also my silver watch with my key and seal hanging to it.

"And having thus provided for—"

(Mrs *Jellybags , who has been listening attentively, interrupts* Mr *Seedy in great agitation.*)

Jel. Will you be pleased to read that part over again?

Seedy . Certainly, ma'am. "I leave the whole of my wardrobe, and also my silver watch, with the key and seal hanging to it."

(Mrs *Jellybags screams, and falls back in a swoon on her chair—no one assists her.*)

"And having thus provided for all my relations, I do hereby devise the rest of my property to the said Solomon Lazarus and Hezekiah Flint, to have and to hold for the building and endowment of an hospital for diseases of the heart, lights, liver, and spleen, as set off by the provisions in the schedule annexed to my will as part and codicil to it."

Seedy . Would the relations like me to read the provisions?

Omnes . No! no! no!

(Mr *Seedy is about to fold up the papers.*)

Gum. I beg your pardon, sir, but is there no other codicil?

Seedy . I beg your pardon, Mr Gumarabic, I recollect now there is one relative to you.

Gum. (*nods his head.*) I thought so.

(Seedy *reads*)

"And whereas I consider that my apothecary, Mr Haustus Gumarabic, hath sent in much unnecessary physic, during my long illness—it is my earnest request that my executors will not fail to tax his bill."

Gum. (*rises and comes forward.*) Tax my bill!—well that is odd, very odd! I may as well go and look after my patients. (*Exit.*)

(James *and* William *come forward*)

James . I say, Bill, how are you off for a suit of mourning?

Will. Thanky for nothing, Jem. If the old gentleman don't go to heaven until I put it on, he will be in a very bad way. Come along, it's no use staying here.

(John *and* Thomas *come forward*)

John . I say, Tom, how are you off for nineteen pounds nineteen and six? Heh!

Thos. Let's toss and see which shall have both legacies. Here goes— heads or tails?

John . Woman for ever.

Thos. You've won, so there's an end of not only my expectations but realities. Come along, Mrs Jellybags must be anxious to look over her wardrobe.

John . Yes, and also the silver watch and the key and seal hanging to it. Good bye, Jemmy! Ha! ha!

(*Exeunt, laughing.*)

Clem. For shame, John. (*Turns to Edward* .) My dear Edward, do not appear so downcast. I acknowledge that I am myself much mortified and disappointed—but we must submit to circumstances. What did I tell you before this will was read?—that nothing could alter my feelings towards you, did I not?

Edw. (*with indifference.*) Yes.

Clem. Why then annoy yourself, my dear Edward?

Edw. The confounded old junks!

Clem. Nay, Edward, recollect that he is dead—I can forgive him.

Edw. But I won't. Has he not dashed my cup of bliss to the ground? Heavens! what delightful anticipations I had formed of possessing you and competence—all gone!

Clem. All gone, dear Edward?

(Mrs *Jellybags* , *who has been sitting very still, takes her handkerchief from her eyes and listens.*)

Edw. Yes, gone!—gone for ever! Do you imagine, my ever dear Clementina, that I would be so base, so cruel, so regardless of you and your welfare, to entrap you into marriage with only one hundred and fifty pounds! No, no!—judge me better. I sacrifice myself—my happiness—all for you!—banish myself from your dear presence, and retire to pass the remainder of my existence in misery and regret, maddened with the feeling that some happier mortal will obtain that dear hand, and will rejoice in the possession of those charms which I had too fondly, too credulously, imagined as certain to be mine.

(*Takes out his handkerchief and covers his face; Clementina also puts her handkerchief to her face and weeps. Mrs Jellybags nods her head ironically.*)

Clem. Edward!

Edw. My dear, dear Clementina!

Clem. You won't have me?

Edw. My honour forbids it. If you knew my feelings—how this poor heart is racked!

Clem. Don't leave me, Edward. Did you not say that for richer or for poorer, for better or for worse, you would be mine, till death did us part?

Edw. Did I!

Clem. You know you did, Edward.

Edw. It's astonishing how much nonsense we talk when in love. My dearest Clementina, let us be rational. We are almost without a sixpence. There is an old adage, that when poverty comes in at the door, love flies out of the window. Shall I then make you miserable! No! no! Hear me, Clementina. I will be generous. I now absolve you from all your vows. You are free. Should the time ever come that prosperity shine upon me, and I find that I have sufficient for both of us of that dross which I despise, then will I return, and, should my Clementina not have entered into any other engagement, throw my fortune and my person at her feet. Till then, dearest Clementina, farewell!

Clem. (*sinking into a chair sobbing.*) Cruel Edward! Oh, my heart will break!

Edw. I can bear it myself no longer. Farewell! farewell! (*Exit.*)

Jel. (*coming forward.*) Well, this is some comfort.—(*To Clementina .*) Did I not tell you, Miss, that if you did not change your mind, others might?

Clem. Leave me, leave me.

Jel. No, I shan't; I have as good a right here as you, at all events. I shall stay, Miss.

Clem. (*rising.*) Stay then—but I shall not. Oh, Edward! Edward! (*Exit, weeping.*)

Jel. (*alone.*) Well, I really thought I should have burst—to be forced not to allow people to suppose that I cared, when I should like to tear the old wretch out of his coffin to beat him. *His* wardrobe! If people knew his wardrobe as well as I do, who have been patching at it these last ten years— not a shirt or a stocking that would fetch sixpence! And as for his other garments, why a Jew would hardly put them into his bag! (*Crying.*) Oh dear! oh dear! After all, I'm just like Miss Clementina; for Sergeant O'Callaghan, when he knows all this, will as surely walk off without beat of drum, as did Mr Edward—and that too with all the money I have lent him. Oh these men! these men!—whether they are living or dying there is nothing in them but treachery and disappointment! When they pretend to be in love, they only are trying for your money; and even when they make their wills, they leave to those behind them nothing but *ill-will.*

(*Exit, crying, off the stage as the curtain falls.*)

Chapter Forty Four

The Sky-Blue Domino

It was a flue autumnal evening; I had been walking with a friend until dusk on the Piazza Grande, or principal square in the town of Lucca. We had been conversing of England, our own country, from which I had then banished myself for nearly four years, having taken up my residence in Italy to fortify a weak constitution, and having remained there long after it was requisite for my health from an attachment to its pure sky, and the *dolce far niente* which so wins upon you in that luxurious climate. We had communicated to each other the contents of our respective letters arrived by the last mail; had talked over politics, great men, acquaintances, friends and kindred; and, tired of conversation, had both sank into a pleasing reverie as we watched the stars twinkling above us, when my friend rose hastily and bid me good night.

"Where are you going, Albert?" inquired I.

"I had nearly forgotten I had an appointment this evening. I promised to meet somebody at the Marquesa di Cesto's masquerade."

"Pshaw! are you not tired of these things?" replied I; "that eternal round of black masks and dominos of all colours; heavy harlequins, fools and clowns by nature wearing their proper dresses there, and only in masquerade when out of it; nuns who have no holiness in their ideas, friars without a spice of religion, ugly Venuses, Dianas without chastity, and Hebes as old as your grandmother."

"All very true, Herbert, and life itself is masquerade enough; but the fact is, that I have an appointment: it is of importance, and I must not fail."

"Well, I wish you more amusement than I have generally extracted from these burlesque meetings," replied I. "Adieu, and may you be successful!" And Albert hastened away.

I remained another half hour reclining on the bench, and then returned to my lodgings. My servant Antonio lighted the candle and withdrew. On the table lay a note; it was an invitation from the Marquesa. I threw it on one side and took up a book, one that required reflection and deep examination; but the rattling of the wheels of the carriages as they whirled along past my window would not permit me to command my attention. I threw down the book; and taking a chair at the window, watched the carriages full of masks as they rolled past, apparently so eager in the pursuit of pleasure. I was in a cynical humour. What fools, thought I, and yet what numbers will be there; there will be an immense crowd; and what can be the assignation which Albert said was of such consequence? Such was my reflection for the next ten minutes, during which at least fifty carriages and other vehicles had passed in review before me.

And then I thought of the princely fortune of the Marquesa, the splendid palazzo at which the masquerade was given, and the brilliant scene which would take place.

"The Grand Duke is to be there, and everybody of distinction in Lucca. I have a great mind to go myself."

A few minutes more elapsed. I felt that I was lonely, and I made up my mind that I would go. I turned from the window and rang the bell.

"Antonio, see if you can procure me a domino, a dark-coloured one if possible; and tell Carlo to bring the carriage round as soon as he can."

Antonio departed, and was away so long that the carriage was at the door previous to his return.

"Signor, I am sorry, very, very sorry; but I have run to every shop in Lucca, and there is nothing left but a sky-blue domino, which I have brought with me."

"Sky-blue! why, there will not be two sky-blue dominos in the whole masquerade: I might as well tell my name at once, I shall be so conspicuous."

"You are as well hidden under a sky-blue domino as a black one, Signor, if you choose to keep your own secrets," observed Antonio.

"Very true," replied I, "give me my mask."

Enshrouding myself in the sky-blue domino, I went down the stairs, threw myself into the carriage, and directed Carlo to drive to the palazzo of the Marquesa.

In half an hour we arrived at the entrance-gates of the Marquesa's superb country seat. From these gates to the palazzo, a sweep of several hundred yards, the avenue though which the driver passed was loaded with variegated lamps, hanging in graceful festoons from branch to branch; and the notes of music from the vast entrance-hall of the palazzo floated through the still air. When I arrived at the area in front of the flight of marble steps which formed the entrance of the palazzo, I was astonished at the magnificence, the good taste, and the total disregard of expense which were exhibited. The palazzo itself appeared like the fabric built of diamonds and precious stones by the genii who obeyed the ring and lamp of Aladdin, so completely was its marble front hidden with a mass of many-coloured lamps, the reflection from whose galaxy of light rendered it bright as day for nearly one hundred yards around; various mottoes and transparencies were arranged in the walks nearest to the palazzo; and then all was dark, rendered still darker from the contrast with the flood of light which poured to a certain distance from the scene of festivity. Groups of characters and dominos were walking to and fro in every direction; most of them retracing their steps when they arrived at the sombre walks and alleys, some few pairs only continuing their route where no listeners were to be expected.

This is an animating scene, thought I, as the carriage stopped, and I am not sorry that I have made one of the party. As soon as I had descended, I walked up the flight of marble steps which led to the spacious hall in which the major part of the company were collected. The music had, for a moment, ceased to play; and finding that the perfume of the exotics which decorated the hall was too powerful, I was again descending the steps, when my hand was seized and warmly pressed by one in a violet-coloured domino.

"I am so glad that you are come; we were afraid that you would not. I will see you again directly," said the domino; and it then fell back into the crowd and disappeared.

It immediately occurred to me that it was my friend Albert who spoke to me. "Very odd," thought I, "that he should have found me out!" And again I fell into the absurdity of imagining that because I had put on a conspicuous domino, I was sure to be recognised. "What can he want with me? We must be in some difficulty, some unexpected one, that is certain." Such were my reflections as I slowly descended the steps, occasionally pausing for a moment on one, as I was lost in conjecture, when I was again arrested by a slight slap on the shoulder. I looked round: it was a female; and although she wore her half-mask, it was evident that she was young, and I felt convinced that she was beautiful.

"Not a word," whispered she, putting her finger to her lip; "follow me." Of course I followed: who could resist such a challenge?

"You are late," said the incognito, when we had walked so far away from the palazzo as to be out of hearing of the crowd.

"I did not make up my mind to come until an hour ago," replied I.

"I was so afraid that you would not come. Albert was sure that you would, he was right. He told me just now that he had spoken to you."

"What! was that Albert in the rose-coloured domino?"

"Yes; but I dare not stay now—my father will be looking for me. Albert is keeping him in conversation. In half an hour he will speak to you again. Has he explained to you what has occurred?"

"Not one word."

"If he has not had time—and I doubt if he will have, as he must attend to the preparations—I will write a few lines, if I can, and explain, or at least tell you what to do; but I am so harassed, so frightened! We do indeed require your assistance. Adieu!" So saying, the fair unknown tripped hastily away.

"What the deuce is all this?" muttered I, as I watched her retreating figure. "Albert said that he had an appointment, but he did not make me his confidant. It appears that something which has occurred this night occasions him to require my assistance. Well, I will not fail him."

For about half an hour I sauntered up and down between the lines of orange-trees which were dressed up with variegated lamps, and shed their powerful fragrance in the air: I ruminated upon what might be my friend's intentions, and what might be the result of an intrigue carried on in a country where the stiletto follows Love so close through all the mazes of his labyrinth, when I was again accosted by the violet-coloured domino.

"Hist!" whispered he, looking carefully round as he thrust a paper into my hand; "read this after I leave you. In one hour from this be you on this spot. Are you armed?"

"No," replied I; "but Albert—"

"You may not need it; but nevertheless take this,—I cannot wait." So saying, he put a stiletto into my hand, and again made a hasty retreat.

It had been my intention to have asked Albert what was his plan, and further why he did not speak English instead of Italian, as he would have been less liable to be understood if overheard by eavesdroppers; but a little reflection told me that he was right in speaking Italian, as the English language overheard would have betrayed him, or at least have identified him as a foreigner.

"A very mysterious affair this!" thought I; "but, however, this paper will, I presume, explain the business. That there is a danger in it is evident, or he would not have given me this weapon;" and I turned the stiletto once or twice to the light of the lamp next to me, examining its blade, when, looking up, I perceived a black domino standing before me.

"It is sharp enough, I warrant," said the domino; "you have but to strike home. I have been waiting for you in the next walk, which I thought was to be our rendezvous. Here is a paper which you will fasten to his dress. I will contrive that he shall be here in an hour hence by a pretended message. After his death you will put this packet into his bosom;—you understand. Fail not: remember the one thousand sequins; and here is my ring, which I will redeem as soon as your work is done. The others will soon be here. The pass-word is 'Milano.' But I must not be seen here. Why a sky-blue domino? it is too conspicuous for escape;" and as I received from him the packet and ring, the black domino retreated through the orange grove which encircled us.

I was lost in amazement: there I stood with my hands full—two papers, a packet, a stiletto, and a diamond ring!

"Well," thought I, "this time I am most assuredly taken for somebody else—for a bravo I am not. There is some foul work going on, which perhaps I may prevent."

"But why a sky-blue domino?" said he.

I may well ask the same question. "Why the deuce did I come here in a sky-blue domino, or any domino at all?"

I put the ring on my finger, the stiletto and packet in my bosom, and then hastened away to the garden on the other side of the palazzo, that I might read the mysterious communication put into my hands by my friend Albert; and as I walked on, my love for admiration led me away so as to find myself pleased with the mystery and danger attending upon the affair; and feeling secure, now that I had a stiletto in my bosom for my defence, I resolved that I would go right through it until the whole affair should be unravelled.

I walked on till I had gained the last lamp on the other side of the palazzo. I held up to its light the mysterious paper: it was in Italian, and in a woman's handwriting.

"We have determined upon flight, as we cannot hope for safety here, surrounded as we are by stilettoes on every side. We feel sure of pardon as soon as the papers which Albert received by this day's mail, and which he will entrust to you when you meet again, are placed in my father's hands. We must have your assistance in removing our treasure. Our horses are all ready, and a few hours will put us in safety; but we must look to you for following us in your carriage, and conveying for me what would prove so great an incumbrance to our necessary speed. When Albert sees you again, he will be able to tell you where it is deposited.

Follow us quick, and you will always have the gratitude of—

" *Viola* .

"PS. I write in great haste, as I cannot leave my father's side for a moment without his seeking for me."

"What can all this mean? Albert told me of no papers by this day's mail. Viola! I never heard him mention such a name. He said to me, 'Read this, and all will be explained.' I'll be hanged if I am not as much in the dark as ever! Follow them in my carriage with the treasure—never says where! I presume he is about to run off with some rich heiress. Confound this sky-blue domino! Here I am with two papers, a packet, a stiletto, and a ring; I am to receive another packet, and am to convey treasure. Well, it must solve itself—I will back to my post; but first let me see what is in this paper which I am to affix upon the man's dress after I have killed him." I held it up to the light, and read, in capital letters, "The reward of a traitor!" "Short and pithy," muttered I, as I replaced it in my pocket: "now I'll back to the place of assignation, for the hour must be nearly expired."

As I retraced my steps, I again reverted to the communication of Viola— "Surrounded as we are by stilettoes on every side!" Why, surely Albert cannot be the person that I am required by the black domino to despatch; and yet it may be so—and others are to join me here before the hour is passed. A thought struck me: whoever the party might be whose life was to be taken, whether Albert or another, I could save him.

My reverie was again broken by a tap on the shoulder.

"Am I right? What is the pass-word?"

"Milano!" replied I, in a whisper.

"All's right, then—Giacomo and Tomaso are close by—I will fetch them."

The man turned away, and in a minute re-appeared with two others, bending as they forced their way under the orange-trees.

"Here we all are, Felippo," whispered the first. "*He* is to be here in a few minutes."

"Hush!" replied I, in a whisper, and holding up to them the brilliant ring which sparkled on my finger.

"Ah, Signor, I cry your mercy," replied the man, in a low voice; "I thought it was Felippo."

"Not so loud," replied I, still in a whisper. "All is discovered, and Felippo is arrested. You must away immediately. You shall hear from me to-morrow."

"Corpo di Bacco! Where, Signor? at the old place?"

"Yes away—now, and save yourselves."

In a few seconds the desperate men disappeared among the trees, and I was left alone.

"Slaves of the Ring, you have done my bidding at all events, this time," thought I, and I looked at the ring more attentively. It was a splendid solitaire diamond, worth many hundred crowns. "Will you ever find your way back to our lawful owner?" was the question in my mind when Albert made his appearance in his violet-coloured domino.

"'Twas imprudent of you to send me the paper by the black domino," said he, hastily. "Did I not tell you that I would be here in an hour? We have not a moment to spare. Follow me quickly, and be silent."

I followed—the paper which Albert referred to needed no explanation; it was, indeed, the only part of the whole affair which I comprehended. He led the way to about three hundred yards of the path through the wood.

"There," said he, "in that narrow avenue, you will find my faithful negro with his charge. He will not deliver it up without you show him this ring." And Albert put a ring upon my finger.

"But, Albert,"—my mind misgave me—Albert never had a faithful negro to my knowledge; it must be some other person who had mistaken me for his friend,—"I am afraid," continued I—

"Afraid!—let me not hear you say that. You never yet knew fear," said he, interrupting me. "What have you to fear between this and Pisa? Your own horses will take you there in three hours. But here's the packet, which you must deliver yourself. Now that you know where the negro is, return to the palazzo, deliver it into his own hands, requesting his immediate perusal. After that do not wait a moment, but hasten here to your charge. While the Grand Duke is reading it I will escape with Viola."

"I really cannot understand all this," said I, taking the packet.

"All will be explained when we meet at Pisa. Away, now; to the Grand Duke—I will go to the negro and prepare him for your coming."

"But allow me—"

"Not a word more, if you love me," replied the violet-coloured domino, who, I was now convinced, was not Albert; it was not his voice—there was a mystery and a mistake; but I had become so implicated that I felt I could not retreat without sacrificing the parties, whoever they might be.

"Well," said I, as I turned back to the palazzo, "I must go on now; for, as a gentleman and man of honour, I cannot refuse. I will give the packet to the Grand Duke, and I will also convey his treasure to Pisa, Confound this sky-blue domino!"

As I returned to the palazzo, I was accosted by the black domino.

"Milano!" replied I.

"Is all right, Felippo?" said he, in a whisper.

"All is right, Signor," was my answer.

"Where is he?"

I pointed with my finger to a clump of orange-trees.

"And the paper and packet?"

I nodded my head.

"Then you had better away — I will see you to-morrow."

"At the old place, Signor?"

"Yes," replied the black domino, cutting into a cross-path, and disappearing.

I arrived at the palazzo, mounted the steps, forced my way through the crowd, and perceived the Grand Duke in an inner saloon, the lady who had accosted me leaning on his arm. It then occurred to me that the Grand Duke had an only daughter, whose name was Viola. I entered the saloon, which was not crowded, and walking boldly up to the Grand Duke, presented the packet, requesting that his Highness would give it his immediate attention. I then bowed, and hastened away, once more passed through the thronged hall, and gained the marble steps of the palazzo.

"Have you given it?" said a low voice close to me.

"I have," replied I; "but, Signor —"

"Not a word, Carlo: hasten to the wood, if you love me." And the violet-coloured domino forced his way into the crown which filled the hall.

"Now for my journey to Pisa," said I. "Here I am, implicated in high treason, perhaps, in consequence of my putting on a sky-blue domino. Well, there's no help for it."

In a few minutes I had gained the narrow avenue, and having pursued it about fifty yards, perceived the glaring eyes of the crouched negro. By the starlight, I could just distinguish that he had a basket, or something like one, before him.

"What do you come for, Signor?" said the negro, rising on his feet.

"For what has been placed under your charge; here is the ring of your master."

The negro put his fingers to the ring and felt it, that he might recognise it by its size and shape.

"Here it is, Signor," said he, lifting up the basket gently, and putting it into my arms. It was not heavy, although somewhat cumbrous from its size.

"Hark! Signor, there is confusion in the palazzo. You must be quick, and I must not be seen with you." And away darted the negro like lightning through the bushes.

I also hastened away with the basket (contents unknown), for it appeared to me that affairs were coming to a crisis. I heard people running different ways, and voices approaching me. When I emerged from the narrow avenue, I perceived several figures coming down the dark walk at a rapid pace, and, seized with a sort of panic, I took to my heels. I soon found that they were in pursuit, and I increased my speed. In the gloom of the night, I unfortunately tripped over a stone, and fell with the basket to the ground; and then the screams from within informed me that the treasure intrusted to my safe keeping was a child. Fearful that it was hurt, and forgetting, for the time, the danger of being captured, I opened the lid, and examined its limbs, while I tried to pacify it; and while I was sitting down in my sky-blue domino, thus occupied in hushing a baby, I was seized by both shoulders, and found myself a prisoner.

"What is the meaning of this rudeness, Signors?" said I, hardly knowing what to say.

"You are arrested by order of the Grand Duke," was the reply.

"I am arrested!—why?—I am an Englishman!"

"That makes no difference; the orders are to arrest all found in the garden in sky-blue dominos."

"Confound the sky-blue domino!" thought I, for the twentieth time at least. "Well, Signora, I will attend you; but first let me try to pacify this poor frightened infant."

"Strange that he should be found running away with a child at the same time that the Lady Viola has disappeared!" observed one of my captors.

"You are right, Signora," replied I; "it is very strange; and what is more strange is, that I can no more explain it than you can. I am now ready to accompany you. Oblige me by one of you carrying the basket while I take care of the infant."

In a few minutes we had arrived at the palazzo. I had retained my mask, and I was conducted through the crowd into the saloon into which I had previously entered when I delivered the packet to the Grand Duke.

"There he is! there he is!" was buzzed through the crowd in the hall. "Holy Virgin! he has a child in his arms! *Bambino bellissimo!*" Such were the exclamations of wonder and surprise as they made a lane for my passage, and I was in the presence of the Grand Duke, who appeared to be in a state of great excitement.

"It is the same person!" exclaimed the Duke. "Confess! are you not the party who put a packet into my hands about a quarter of an hour since?"

"I am the person, your Highness," replied I, as I patted and soothed the frightened child.

"Who gave it you?"

"May it please your Highness, I do not know."

"What child is that?"

"May it please your Highness, I do not know."

"Where did you get it?"

"Out of that basket, your Highness."

"Who gave you the basket?"

"May it please your Highness, I do not know."

"You are trifling with me. Let him be searched."

"May it please your Highness, I will save them that trouble, if one of the ladies will take the infant. I have received a great many presents this evening, all of which I will have the honour of displaying before your Highness."

One of the ladies held out her arms to the infant, who immediately bent from mine toward her, naturally clinging to the other sex as its friend in distress.

"In the first place, your Highness, I have this evening received this ring," taking off my finger the one given by the party in a violet-coloured domino, and presenting it to him.

"And from whom?" said his Highness, instantly recognising the ring.

"May it please your Highness, I do not know. I have also received another ring, your Highness," continued I, taking off the ring given me by the black domino.

"And who gave you this?" interrogated the Duke, again evidently recognising it.

"May it please your Highness, I do not know. Also, this stiletto, but from whom, I must again repeat, I do not know. Also, this packet, with directions to put it into a dead man's bosom."

"And you are, I presume, equally ignorant of the party who gave it to you?"

"Equally so, your Highness; as ignorant as I am of the party who desired me to present you with the other packet which I delivered. Here is also a paper I was desired to pin upon a man's clothes after I had assassinated him."

"Indeed!—and to this, also, you plead total ignorance?"

"I have but one answer to give to all, your Highness, which is, I do not know."

"Perhaps, Sir, you do not know your own name or profession," observed his Highness, with a sneer.

"Yes, your Highness," replied I, taking off my mask, "that I do know. I am an Englishman, and, I trust, a gentleman, and a man of honour. My name is Herbert; and I have more than once had the honour to be a guest at your Highness's entertainments."

"Signor, I recognise you," replied the Grand Duke. "Let the room be cleared—I must speak with this gentleman alone."

When the company had quitted the saloon, I entered into a minute detail of the events of the evening, to which his Highness paid the greatest attention; and when I had finished, the whole mystery was unravelled to me by him, and with which I will now satisfy the curiosity of my readers.

The Grand Duke had one daughter, by name Viola, whom he had wished to marry to Rodolph, Count of Istria; but Viola had met with Albert, Marquis of Salerno, and a mutual attachment had ensued. Although the Grand Duke would not force his daughter's wishes and oblige her to marry Count Rodolph, at the same time he would not consent to her espousals with the Marquis Albert. Count Rodolph had discovered the intimacy between Viola and the Marquis of Salerno, and had made more than one unsuccessful attempt to get rid of his rival by assassination. After some time, a private marriage with the marquis had been consented to by Viola; and a year afterwards the Lady Viola retired to the country, and without the knowledge, or even suspicions, of her father, had given birth to a male child, which had been passed off as the offspring of one of the ladies of the court who was married, and to whom the secret had been confided.

At this period the secret societies, especially the *Carbonari*, had become formidable in Italy, and all the crowned heads and reigning princes were using every exertion to suppress them. Count Rodolph was at the head of these societies, having joined them to increase his power, and to have at his disposal the means of getting rid of his rival. Of this the Marquis of Salerno had received intimation, and for some time had been trying to obtain proof against the count; for he knew that if once it was proved, Count Rodolph would never be again permitted to appear in the state of Lucca. On the other hand, Count Rodolph had been making every arrangement to get rid of his rival, and had determined that it should be effected at this masquerade.

The Marquis of Salerno had notice given him of this intention, and also had on that morning obtained the proof against Count Rodolph, which he was now determined to forward to the Grand Duke; but, aware that his assassination by the *Carbonari* was to be attempted, and also that the wrath of the Grand Duke would be excessive when he was informed of their private marriage, he resolved to fly with his wife to Pisa, trusting that the proofs of Count Rodolph being connected with the *Carbonari*, and a little time, would soften down the Grand Duke's anger. The marquis had arranged that he should escape from the Duke's dominions on the night of the masquerade, as it would be much easier for his wife to accompany him from thence than from the Grand Duke's palace, which was well guarded; but it was necessary that they should travel on horseback, and they could not take their child with them. Viola would not consent that it should be left behind; and on this emergency he had written to his friend, the Count d'Ossore, to come to their assistance at the masquerade, and, that they might recognise him, to wear a sky-blue domino, a colour but seldom put on. The Count d'Ossore had that morning left his town mansion on a hunting excursion, and did not receive the letter, of which the Marquis and Viola were ignorant. Such was the state of affairs at the time that I put on the sky-blue domino to go to the masquerade.

My first meeting with the marquis in his violet-coloured domino is easily understood: being in a sky-blue domino I was mistaken for the Count d'Ossore. I was myself led into the mistake by the Marquis Albert having the same Christian name as my English friend. The second meeting with the Count Rodolph, in the black domino, was accidental. The next walk had been appointed as the place of meeting with the *Carbonari* Felippo and his companions; but Count Rodolph, perceiving me examining my stiletto by the light of the lamp, presumed that I was Felippo, and that I had mistaken the one path for the other which had been agreed upon. The papers given to me by Count Rodolph were *Carbonari* papers, which were to be hid in the marquis's bosom after he had been assassinated, to make it appear that he had belonged I to that society, and by the paper affixed to his clothes, that he had been murdered by the agents of the society for having betrayed them. The papers which the marquis had requested me to give to the Grand Duke were the proofs of Count Rodolph's belonging to the secret society; and with the papers was enclosed a letter to the Grand Duke, in which they I acknowledged their secret union. And now, I believe, the reader will comprehend the whole of this mysterious affair.

After all had been explained, I ventured to ask his Highness if he would permit me to fulfil my promise of taking the child to its mother, as I considered it a point of honour that I should keep my engagement, the more so, as the delay would occasion the greatest distress to his daughter; and I ventured to add, that I trusted his Highness would pardon what could not now be remedied, and that I should have the satisfaction of being the bearer of such pleasing intelligence to his daughter and the marquis.

The Grand Duke paced the room for a minute, and then replied, "Signor Herbert, I feel so disgusted with the treachery and baseness of Count Rodolph, that I hardly need observe, if my daughter were free he never should espouse her; indeed, he will have immediate orders to quit the state. You have been instrumental in preserving the life of the Marquis of Salerno, who is my son-in-law, and as matters now stand, I am indebted to you. Your dismissal of the bravoes, by means of the count's ring, was a masterly stroke. You shall have the pleasure of taking my forgiveness to my daughter and her husband; but as for the child, it may as well remain here. Tell Viola I retain it as a hostage for the quick return of its mother."

I took my leave of his Highness, and hastened to Pisa, where I soon found out the retreat of the marquis and his wife. I sent up my name, requesting immediate admittance, as having a message from the Grand Duke. I found them in great distress. The Count d'Ossore had returned late on the night of the masquerade, found the letter, hastened to the Marquesa de Cesto's, and had arrived just after the elopement had been discovered. He immediately followed them to Pisa, when an explanation took place, and they discovered that they had been communicating with some unknown person, by whom they had, in all probability, been betrayed.

It would be difficult to portray their astonishment and joy when I entered into a detail of what had occurred, and wound up with the message from the Grand Duke; and I hardly need add, now that I wind up my story, that the proofs of gratitude I received from the marquis and his wife, during my subsequent residence in Italy, left me no occasion to repent that I had gone to the masquerade of the Marquesa de Cesto, in a *Sky-Blue Domino* .

Chapter Forty Five

Modern Town Houses

I have often thought, when you consider the difference of comfort between houses built from sixty to a hundred years back, in comparison with the modern edifices, that the cry of the magician in "Aladdin," had he called out "new houses," instead of "new lamps," for old ones, would not have appeared so very absurd. It was my good fortune, for the major part of my life, to occupy an ancient house, built, I believe, in the reign of Queen Elizabeth. My father lived in it before I was in existence: I was born in it, and it was bequeathed to me. It has since been my misfortune to have lived three years in one of the modern-built houses; and although I have had my share of the ills to which we all are heir, I must date my real unhappiness from the first month after I took possession. With your permission, I will enter into my history, as it may prove a warning to others, who will not remember the old proverb of *"Let well alone."*

I am a married man, with six children; my three eldest are daughters, and have now quitted a school, near Portman-Square, to which my wife insisted upon my sending them, as it was renowned for finishing young ladies. Until their return to domiciliate themselves under my roof, I never heard a complaint of my house, which was situated at Brompton. It was large, airy, and comfortable, with excellent shrubberies, and a few acres of land; and I possessed every comfort and even luxury which could be rationally required, my wife and daughters having their carriage, and in every respect my establishment being that of a gentleman.

I had not, however, taken my daughters from school more than two months, before I was told that we were "living out of the world," although not a mile and a half from Hyde Park Corner; and, to my surprise, my wife joined in the cry; it was always from morn to night, "We might do this but, we cannot do this because, we are quite out of the world." It was too far to dine out in town; too far for people to come and dine with us; too far to go to the play, or the opera; too far to drive in the park; too far even to walk in Kensington Gardens. I remonstrated, that we had managed to dine out, to receive visitors, and to enjoy all other amusements very well for a considerable number of years, and that it did not appear to me that

Brompton had walked away from London, on the contrary, that London was making rapid advances towards Brompton; but it would not do,—all day the phrase rang in my ears, "out of the world," until I almost began to wish that I was out too. But it is no use having the best of an argument when opposed to women. I had my choice, either to give up my house, and take another in London, or to give up my peace. With an unwilling sigh, I at last consented to leave a place dear to me, from long association and many reminiscences; and it was arranged that Brompton Hall was to be let, or sold, and that we were to look out immediately for a house in some of the squares in the metropolis. If my wife and daughters found that the distance from London was too far for other purposes, at all events it was not too far for house-hunting. They were at it incessantly week after week; and, at last, they fixed upon one in the neighbourhood of Belgrave-Square, which, as they repeated, possessed all the cheerfulness and fresh air of the country, all the advantages of a town residence. The next day I was to be dragged to see it, and give my opinion; at the same time, from the commendations bestowed upon it previous to my going, I felt assured that I was expected to give their opinion, and not my own.

The next day, accordingly, we repaired thither, setting off immediately after breakfast, to meet the surveyor and builder, who was to be on the spot. The house in question was one of a row just building, or built, whitened outside, in imitation of stone. It was Number 2. Number 1 was finished; but the windows still stained with the drippings of the whitewash and colouring. Number 2, the one in question, was complete; and, as the builder asserted, ready for immediate occupation. Number 3 was not so far advanced. As for the others, they were at present nothing but carcasses, without even the front steps built to them; and you entered them by a drawbridge of planks.

The builder stood at the front door, and bowed most respectfully. "Why," observed I, looking at the piles of mortar, lime, and bricks, standing about in all directions, "we shall be smothered with dust and lime for the next two years."

"Don't be alarmed, sir," replied the builder; "every house in the row will be finished before the winter. We really cannot attend to the applications for them."

We entered the house.

"Is not the entrance handsome?" observed my wife; "so neat and clean."

To this I had not a reply to make; it certainly did look neat and clean.

We went into the dining-room. "What a nice room," exclaimed my eldest daughter. "How many can we dine in this room?"

"Um!" replied I; "about twelve, I suppose, comfortably."

"Dear me!" observed the builder; "you have no notion of the size of the house; rooms are so deceiving, unfurnished. You may sit down twenty with ease; I'll appeal to the lady. Don't you think so, ma'am?"

"Yes, I do," replied my wife.

After that we went over the drawing-rooms, bed-rooms, and attics.

Every bed-room was apportioned by my wife and daughters, and the others were allotted to the servants; and that in the presence of the builder, who took good note of all that passed.

The kitchen was admired; so were the pantry, scullery, coal-hole, dust-hole, etcetera; all so nice and clean; so compact; and, as the builder observed, not a nail to drive anywhere.

"Well, my dear, what do you think now? isn't it a charming house?" said my wife, as we re-ascended into the dining-parlour.

"It's a very nice house, my dear; but still it requires a little consideration," replied I.

"Consideration, my dear?" replied my wife; "what! now that you have gone over it?"

"I am afraid that I cannot give you very long, sir," observed the builder; "there are two other parties after the house, and I am to give them an answer by two o'clock."

"Mr Smithers told me the same yesterday," whispered my wife.

"What did you say the rent was, Mr Smithers?"

"Only 200 pounds per annum."

"Any ground-rent?"

"Only 27 pounds 10 shillings."

"And the taxes?"

"Oh, they will be a mere trifle."

"The rent appears to me to be very high."

"High, my dear sir! consider the situation, the advantages. We can't build them fast enough at that price. But of course, sir, you best know," replied he, carelessly walking towards the window.

"Take it; my dear," said my wife.

"You must take it, papa."

"Pray take it, papa."

"Mr Whats-your-name, I beg your pardon—"

"Smithers, sir," said the builder, turning round.

"Pray, Mr Smithers, what term of lease do you let at?"

"Seven, fourteen, or twenty-one, at the option of either party, sir."

"I should have no objection to take it for three years."

"Three years, my dear sir!—that would be doing yourself an injustice. You would lose half the value of your fixtures provided you left—and then the furniture. Depend upon it, sir, if you once get into it, you will never wish to leave it."

"That may or not be," replied I; "but I will not take it for more than three years. The town-air may not agree with me; and if, as you say, people are so anxious to take the houses, of course it can make no difference to you."

"I'm afraid, sir, that for so short a time—"

"I will not take it for longer," replied I, rising up, glad of an excuse to be off.

"Oh, papa!"

"My dear Mr B—."

"On that point," replied I, "I will not be overruled. I will not take a lease for more than three years, with the right of continuing, if I please."

The builder perceived that I was in earnest.

"Well, sir," replied he, "I hardly know what to say; but rather than disappoint the ladies, I will accept you as a tenant for three years certain."

"Confound the fellow!" thought I; but I was pinned, and there was an end of the matter. Mr Smithers pulled out paper and ink; two letters of agreement were written upon a small deal table, covered with blotches of various coloured paints; and the affair was thus concluded.

We got into the carriage and drove home, my wife and daughters in ecstasies, and I obliged to appear very well satisfied, that I might not damp their spirits; yet I must say that although the house appeared a very nice house, I had my forebodings.

"At all events," thought I, "the lease is only for three years;" and thus I consoled myself.

The next day the whole house was in commotion. I believe my wife and daughters were up at daybreak. When I went into the breakfast room,

I discovered that the pictures had been taken down, although there was no chance of their being hung up for many weeks at least, and every thing was in preparation for packing up. After breakfast my wife set off for town to order carpets and curtains, and did not come home till six o'clock, very tired with the fatigues of the day. She had also brought the measure of every grate, to ascertain what fenders would suit; the measure of the bed-rooms and attics, to remodel the carpets; for it was proposed that Brompton Hall should be disposed of, the new occupier taking at a valuation what furniture might be left. To this I appeared to consent; but was resolved in my own mind that, if taken, it should only be for the same term of years as my new lease. I will pass over a month of hurry, bustle, and confusion; at the end of which I found myself in our new habitation. It was completely furnished, with the exception of the drawing-room carpet, which had not been laid down, but was still in a roll tied up with packthread in the middle of the room. The cause of this I soon understood from my wife. It was always the custom, she said, to give a house-warming upon entering a new house, and she therefore proposed giving a little dance. To this, as it would please her and my daughters, I raised no objection.

I have always observed, that what is proposed as a little dance invariably ends in a great one; for from the time of proposing till the cards are about, it increases like a snowball; but that arises, perhaps, from the extreme difficulty of knowing when to draw the line between friends and acquaintances. I have also observed that when your wife and daughters intend such a thing, they always obtain permission for the ball first, and then tack on the supper afterwards; commencing with a mere stand-up affair,—sandwiches, cakes, and refreshments,—and ending with a regular sit-down affair, with Gunter presiding over all. The music from two fiddles and a piano also swells into Collinet's band, verifying the old adage, "In for a penny, in for a pound." But to all this I gave my consent; I could afford it well, and I liked to please my wife and daughters. The ball was given, and this house-warming ended in house-breaking; for just before the supper-quadrille, as it was termed, when about twenty-four young ladies and gentlemen were going the grand ronde, a loud noise below, with exclamations and shrieks, was heard, and soon afterwards the whole staircase was smothered with dust.

"What *is* the matter?" cried my wife, who had passed to the landing-place on the stairs before me.

"Ma'am," said one of Mr Gunter's men, shaking the lappets of his blue coat, which were covered with white dust, "the whole ceiling of the dining-room has come down!"

"Ceiling come down!" screamed my wife.

"Yes, ma'am," replied our own servant; "and the supper and supper-tables are all smashed flat with the weight on it."

Here was a catastrophe. My wife hastened down, and I followed. Sure enough the weight of mortar had crushed all beneath it—all was chaos and confusion. Jellies, blancmanges, pâtés, cold roasts, creams, trifles,—all in one mass of ruin, mixed up with lime, horse-hair, plaster of Paris, and stucco. It wore all the appearance of a Swiss avalanche in miniature.

"Good heavens, how dreadful!" exclaimed my wife.

"How much more so if there had been people in the room," replied I.

"What could be the cause of it!" exclaimed my wife.

"These new houses, sir, won't bear dancing in," observed Mr Gunter's head man.

"So it appears," replied I.

This unfortunate accident was the occasion of the party breaking up: they knew that there was no chance of supper, which they had looked forward to; so they put on their shawls and departed, leaving us to clear up the wreck at our leisure. In fact, as my daughters declared, it quite spoiled the ball as well as the supper.

The next morning I sent for Mr Smithers, who made his appearance, and showed him what had taken place.

"Dear me, I'm very sorry; but you had too many people above stairs—that is very clear."

"Very clear, indeed, Mr Smithers. We had a ball last night."

"A ball, sir! Oh, then no wonder."

"No wonder! What! do you mean to say that balls are not to be given?"

"Why, really, sir, we do not build private houses for ball-rooms—we could not, sir; the price of timber just now is enormous, and the additional strength required would never pay us."

"What then! do you mean to say that there are no balls to be given in London?"

"Oh no, sir!—certainly not; but you must be aware that few people do. Even our aristocracy hire Willis's rooms for their balls. Some of the old houses, indeed, such as Devonshire House, may do for such a thing."

"But, Mr Smithers, I expect you will make this ceiling good."

"Much obliged to you, sir, for giving me the preference—I will do it as reasonable as anybody," replied Mr Smithers, bowing. "I will order my workmen directly—they are only next door."

For a fortnight we were condemned to dine in the back dining-room; and after that Mr Smithers sent in a bill which cost me more than the ball and supper.

So soon as all was right again, I determined that I would hang up my pictures; for I had been accustomed to look at them for years, and I missed them. I sent for a carpenter, and gave him directions.

"I have the middle now, sir, exactly," said the man, standing on the high steps; "but," continued he, tapping with his hammer, "I can't find wood."

"Can't find wood!"

"No, sir," replied the man, tapping as far as he could reach from right to left; "nothing to nail to, sir. But there never is no wood in these new-built houses."

"Confound your new houses!" exclaimed I.

"Well, it is very provoking, my dear!" exclaimed my wife.

"I suppose that their new houses are not built for pictures any more than for balls," replied I; and I sighed. "What must be done?"

"I think, sir, if you were to order brass rods to be fixed from one corner to the other, we might find means to fasten them," observed the carpenter; "but there's no wood, that's certain."

"What the devil is the house built of then?" exclaimed I.

"All lath and plaster, sir," replied the man, tapping right and left.

At a heavy expense I procured the rods, and at last the pictures were hung up.

The next annoyance that we had was a very bad smell, which we found to proceed from the drains; and the bricklayers were sent for. All the drains were choked, it appeared, from their being so very narrow; and after having up the whole basement, at the expense of 40 pounds, that nuisance was abated.

We now had two months' repose, and I was in hopes that things would go on more comfortably; but one day I overheard a conversation between my wife and daughters, as I passed by the door of the room, which I must candidly acknowledge gave me satisfaction.

"It's really very awkward, mamma—one don't know where to put anything: there's not a cupboard or stow-hole in the whole house—not even a store-room."

"Well, it is so, my dear; I wonder we did not observe it when we looked over it. What a nice set of cupboards we had at Brompton Hall."

"Oh! yes—I wish we had them here, mamma. Couldn't we have some built?"

"I don't like to speak to your papa about it, my dear; he has already been put to such expense, what with the ceiling and the drains."

"Then don't, mamma; papa is really very good-natured."

The equinoxes now came on, and we had several gales of wind, with heavy rain—the slates blew off and rattled up and down all night, while the wind howled round the corner of the square. The next morning complaints from all the attic residents; one's bed was wetted quite through with the water dropping through the ceiling—another had been obliged to put a basin on the floor to catch the leak—all declared that the roof was like a sieve. Sent again for Mr Smithers, and made a complaint.

"This time, Mr Smithers," said I, with the lease in my hand, "I believe you will acknowledge these are landlord's repairs."

"Certainly, sir, certainly," exclaimed Mr Smithers; "I shall desire one of my men to look to it immediately; but the fact is, with such heavy gales, the slates must be expected to move a little. Duchesses and countesses are very light, and the wind gets underneath them."

"Duchesses and countesses very light!" exclaimed my wife; "what do you mean?"

"It's the term we give to slates, madam," replied he; "we cannot put on a heavy roof with a brick-and-a-half wall. It would not support one."

"*Brick-and-a-half* wall!" exclaimed I;—"surely, Mr Smithers, that's not quite safe with a house so high."

"Not quite safe, my dear sir, if it were a single house; but," added he, "in a row, one house supports another."

"Thank Heaven," thought I, "I have but a three-years' lease, and six months are gone already."

But the annoyances up to this period were internal; we now had to experience the external nuisances attending a modern-built house.

"Number 1 is taken, papa, and they are getting the furniture in," said my eldest daughter one day; "I hope we shall have nice neighbours. And

William told Mary that Mr Smithers told him, when he met him in the street, that he was now going to fit up Number 3 as fast as he could."

The report was true, as we found from the report of the carpenters' hammers for the next three or four weeks. We could not obtain a moment's sleep except in the early part of the night, or a minute's repose to our ears during the day. The sound appeared as if it was *in* our house instead of next door; and it commenced at six o'clock in the morning, and lasted till seven in the evening. I was hammered to death; and, unfortunately, there was a constant succession of rain, which prevented me going out to avoid it. I had nothing to do but to watch my pictures, as they jumped from the wall with the thumps of the hammers. At last Number 3 was floored, wainscotted, and glazed, and we had a week's repose.

By this time Number 1 was furnished, and the parties who had taken it came in. They were a gouty old gentleman, and his wife, who, report said, had once been his cook. My daughters' hopes of pleasant neighbours were disappointed. Before they had been in a week, we found ourselves at issue: the old gentleman's bed was close to the partition-wall, and in the dead of the night we could distinctly hear his groans and also his execrations and exclamations, when the fit came on him. My wife and daughters declared that it was quite horrible, and that they could not sleep for them.

Upon the eighth day there came a note:— "Mrs Whortleback's compliments to Mr and Mrs —, and begs that the young people will not play on the piany, as Mr Whortleback is very ill with the gout."

Now, my daughters were proficients on the piano, and practised a great deal. This note was anything but satisfactory: to play when the old gentleman was ill would be barbarous,—not to play was to deprive ourselves of our greatest pleasure.

"Oh dear! how very disagreeable," cried my daughters.

"Yes, my dear; but if we can hear his groans, it's no wonder that he can hear the piano and harp: recollect the wall is only a brick and a half thick."

"I wonder music don't soothe him," observed the eldest.

Music is a mockery to a man in agony. A man who has been broken on the wheel would not have his last hours soothed by the finest orchestra. After a week, during which we sent every day to inquire after Mr Whortleback's health, we ventured to resume the piano and harp; upon which the old gentleman became testy, and sent for a man with a trumpet, placing him in the balcony, and desiring him to play as much out of tune as possible whenever the harp and piano sounded a note. Thus were we at open hostility with our only neighbour; and, as we were certain if my daughters touched their instruments, to have the trumpet blowing discord for an hour or two either that day or the next, at last the piano was unopened, and the harp remained in its case. Before the year closed, Number 3 became tenanted; and here we had a new annoyance. It was occupied by a large family; and there were four young ladies who were learning music. We now had our annoyance: it was strum, strum, all day long; one sister up, another down; and every one knows what a bore the first lessons in music are to those who are compelled to hear them. They could just manage to play a tune, and that eternal tune was ringing in our ears from morning to night. We could not send our compliments, or blow a trumpet. We were forced to submit to it. The nursery also being against the partition wall, we had the squalls and noise of the children on the one side, added to groans and execrations of the old gentleman on the other.

However, custom reconciled us to everything, and the first vexation gradually wore off. Yet I could not help observing that when I was supposed not to be in hearing, the chief conversation of my wife, when her friends called upon her, consisted of a description of all the nuisances and annoyances that we suffered; and I felt assured that she and my daughters were as anxious to return to Brompton Hall as I was. In fact, the advantages which they had anticipated by their town residence were not realised. In our situation, we were as far off from most of our friends, and still farther from some than we were before, and we had no longer the same amusements to offer them. At our former short distance from town, access was more easy to those who did not keep a carriage, that is, the young men; and those were the parties who, of course, my wife and daughters cared for most. It was very agreeable to come down with their portmanteaus,—enjoy the fresh air and green lanes of the country for an afternoon,—dine, sleep, and breakfast, and return the next morning by conveyances which passed us every quarter of an hour; but to dine with us in — Square, when the expense of a hackney-coach there and back was no trifle, and to return at eleven o'clock at night, was not at all agreeable. We found that we had not so much society, nor were we half so much courted, as at Brompton Hall. This was the bitterest blow of all, and my wife and daughters would look out of the windows and sigh; often a whole day passed without one friend or acquaintance dropping in to relieve its monotony.

We continued to reside there, nevertheless, for I had made up my mind that the three years would be well spent if they cured my wife and daughters of their town mania; and although anxious, as I am sure they were, to return, I never broached the matter, for I was determined that the cure should be radical. Numbers 4, 5, 6, 7, and 8, were finished the next year, and, by the persuasions of Mr Smithers, were taken by different parties in the spring. And now we had another nuisance. Nothing but eternal rings at the bell. The man-servant grumbled, and was behind with his work; and when scolded, replied that there was no time for any thing, that when cleaning his knives and plate the bell was rung, and he was obliged to wash himself, throw on his jacket, and go up to answer the front door; that the bell was not rung for us, but to find out where some new-comer lived, and to ascertain this they always rang at the house which appeared the longest inhabited. There was no end to the ringing for some months, and we had three servants who absolutely refused to stay in so bad a place. We had also to contend with letters and notes in the same way, brought to us at haphazard: "Does Mr So-and-so live here?" — "No, he does not." — "Then pray where does he?" This was interminable, and not five minutes in the day passed without the door-bell being rung. For the sake of not changing my servants I was at last put to the expense of an extra boy for no other purpose but to answer the constant applications at the door. At last we had remained there for two years and nine months, and then my wife would occasionally put the question whether I intended to renew the lease; and I naturally replied that I did not like change.

Then she went upon another tack; observed that Clara did not appear well for some time, and that she thought that she required country air; but, in this, I did not choose to agree with her.

One day I came home, and, rubbing my hands as if pleased, said, "Well, at last I've an offer for Brompton Villa for a term of seven years, — a very fair offer and good tenants, — so that will now be off my hands."

My wife looked mortified, and my daughters held down their heads.

"Have you let it, papa?" said one of my daughters, timidly.

"No, not yet; but I am to give an answer to-morrow morning."

"It requires consideration, my dear," replied my wife.

"Requires consideration!" said I. "Why, my dear, the parties have seen the house, and I have been trying to let it these three years. I recollect when I took this house I said it required consideration, but you would not allow any such thing."

"I'm sure I wish we had," said Clara.

"And so do I."

"The fact is, my dear," said my wife, coming round to the back of my chair, and putting her arms round my neck, "we all wish to go back to Brompton."

"Yes, yes, papa," added my daughters, embracing me on each side.

"You will allow, then, that I was right in not taking a lease for more than three years."

"Yes: how lucky you were so positive!"

"Well, then, if that is the case, we will unfurnish this house, and, as soon as you please, go back to Brompton Hall."

I hardly need observe that we took possession of our old abode with delight, and that I have had no more applications for a change of residence, or have again heard the phrase that we were living "out of the world."

Chapter Forty Six

The Way To Be Happy

Cut your coat according to your cloth, is an old maxim and a wise one; and if people will only square their ideas according to their circumstances, how much happier might we all be! If we only would come down a peg or two in our notions, in accordance with our waning fortunes, happiness would be always within our reach. It is not what we have, or what we have not, which adds or subtracts from our felicity. It is the longing for more than we have, the envying of those who possess that more, and the wish to appear in the world of more consequence than we really are, which destroy our peace of mind, and eventually lead to ruin.

I never witnessed a man submitting to circumstances with good humour and good sense, so remarkably as in my friend Alexander Willemott. When I first met him, since our school days, it was at the close of the war: he had been a large contractor with Government for army clothing and accoutrements, and was said to have realised an immense fortune, although his accounts were not yet settled. Indeed it was said that they were so vast, that it would employ the time of six clerks, for two years, to examine them, previous to the balance sheet being struck. As I observed, he had been at school with me, and, on my return from the East Indies, I called upon him to renew our old acquaintance, and congratulate him upon his success.

"My dear Reynolds, I am delighted to see you. You must come down to Belem Castle; Mrs Willemott will receive you with pleasure, I'm sure. You shall see my two girls."

I consented. The chaise stopped at a splendid mansion, and I was ushered in by a crowd of liveried servants. Every thing was on the most sumptuous and magnificent scale. Having paid my respects to the lady of the house, I retired to dress, as dinner was nearly ready, it being then half-past seven o'clock. It was eight before we sat down. To an observation that I made, expressing a hope that I had not occasioned the dinner being put off, Willemott replied, "On the contrary, my dear Reynolds, we never sit down until about this hour. How people can dine at four or five o'clock, I cannot conceive. I could not touch a mouthful."

The dinner was excellent, and I paid the encomiums which were its due.

"Do not be afraid, my dear fellow—my cook is an *artiste extraordinaire*—a regular *Cordon Bleu*. You may eat any thing without fear of indigestion. How people can live upon the English cookery of the present day, I cannot conceive. I seldom dine out, for fear of being poisoned. Depend upon it, a good cook lengthens your days, and no price is too great to insure one."

When the ladies retired, being alone, we entered into friendly conversation. I expressed my admiration of his daughters, who certainly were very handsome and elegant girls.

"Very true; they are more than passable," replied he. "We have had many offers, but not such as come up to my expectations. Baronets are cheap now-a-days, and Irish lords are nothings; I hope to settle them comfortably. We shall see. Try this claret; you will find it excellent, not a headache in a hogshead of it. How people can drink port, I cannot imagine."

The next morning he proposed that I should rattle round the park with him. I acceded, and we set off in a handsome open carriage, with four greys, ridden by postilions at a rapid pace. As we were whirling along, he observed, "In town we must of course drive but a pair, but in the country I never go out without four horses. There is a spring in four horses which is delightful; it makes your spirits elastic, and you feel that the poor animals are not at hard labour. Rather than not drive four, I would prefer to stay at home."

Our ride was very pleasant, and in such amusements passed away one of the most pleasant weeks that I ever remembered. Willemott was not the least altered—he was as friendly, as sincere, as open-hearted, as when a boy at school. I left him, pleased with his prosperity, and acknowledging that he was well deserving of it, although his ideas had assumed such a scale of magnificence.

I went to India when my leave expired, and was absent about four years. On my return, I inquired after my friend Willemott, and was told that his circumstances and expectations had been greatly altered. From many causes, such as a change in the Government, a demand for economy, and the wording of his contracts having been differently rendered from what Willemott had supposed their meaning to be, large items had been struck out of his balance sheet, and, instead of being a millionaire, he was now a gentleman with a handsome property. Belem Castle had been sold, and he now lived at Richmond, as hospitable as ever, and was considered a great addition to the neighbourhood. I took the earliest opportunity of going down to see him.

"Oh, my dear Reynolds, this is really kind of you to come without invitation. Your room is ready, and bed well aired, for it was slept in three nights ago. Come—Mrs Willemott will be delighted to see you."

I found the girls still unmarried, but they were yet young. The whole family appeared as contented and happy, and as friendly, as before. We sat down to dinner at six o'clock; the footman and coachman attended. The dinner was good, but not by the *artiste extraordinaire*. I praised everything.

"Yes," replied he, "she is a very good cook; she unites the solidity of the English with the delicacy of the French fare; and, altogether, I think it a *decided improvement*. Jane is quite a treasure." After dinner, he observed, "Of course you know I have sold Belem Castle, and reduced my establishment. Government have not treated me fairly, but I am at the mercy of Commissioners, and a body of men will do that which, as individuals, they would be ashamed of. The fact is, the odium is borne by no one in particular, and it is only the sense of shame which keeps us honest, I am afraid. However, here you see me, with a comfortable fortune, and always happy to see my friends, especially my old schoolfellow. Will you take *port* or claret; the port is very fine, and so is the claret. By the by, do you know— I'll let you into a family secret; Louisa is to be married to a Colonel Willer— an *excellent* match! It has made us all happy."

The next day we drove out, not in an open carriage as before, but in a chariot and with a *pair of horses*.

"These are handsome horses," observed I.

"Yes," replied he, "I am fond of good horses; and, as I only keep a pair, I have the best. There is a certain degree of pretension in *four horses*, I do not much like—it appears as if you wished to overtop your neighbours."

I spent a few very pleasant days, and then quitted his hospitable roof. A severe cold, caught that winter, induced me to take the advice of the physicians, and proceed to the South of France, where I remained two years. On my return, I was informed that Willemott had speculated, and had been unlucky on the Stock Exchange; that he had left Richmond, and was now living at Clapham. The next day I met him near the Exchange.

"Reynolds, I am happy to see you. Thompson told me that you had come back. If not better engaged, come down to see me; I will drive you down at four o'clock, if that will suit."

It suited me very well, and, at four o'clock, I met him according to appointment at a livery stables over the Iron Bridge. His vehicle was ordered out, it was a phaeton drawn by two long-tailed ponies—altogether a very neat concern. We set off at a rapid pace.

"They step out well, don't they? We shall be down in plenty of time to put on a pair of shoes by five o'clock, which is *our dinner-time*. Late dinners don't agree with me—they produce indigestion. Of course, you know that Louisa has a little boy."

I did not; but congratulated him.

"Yes, and has now gone out to India with her husband. Mary is also engaged to be married—a very *good* match—a Mr Rivers, in the law. He has been called to the bar this year, and promises well. They will be a little pinched at first, but we must see what we can do for them."

We stopped at a neat row of houses, I forget the name, and, as we drove up, the servant, the only man-servant, came out, and took the ponies round to the stable, while the maid received my luggage, and one or two paper-bags, containing a few extras for the occasion. I was met with the same warmth as usual by Mrs Willemott. The house was small, but very neat; the remnants of former grandeur appeared here and there, in one or two little articles, favourites of the lady. We sat down at five o'clock to a *plain* dinner, and were attended by the footman, who had rubbed down the ponies and pulled on his livery.

"A good plain cook is the best thing, after all," observed Willemott. "Your fine cooks won't condescend to roast and boil. Will you take some of this sirloin, the under-cut is excellent. My dear, give Mr Reynolds some Yorkshire pudding."

When we were left alone after dinner, Willemott told me, very unconcernedly, of his losses.

"It was my own fault," said he; "I wished to make up a little sum for the girls, and risking what they would have had, I left them almost pennyless. However, we can always command a bottle of port and a beef-steak, and *what more* in this world can you have? Will you take port or white?—I have no claret to offer you."

We finished our port, but I could perceive no difference in Willemott. He was just as happy and as cheerful as ever. He drove me to town the next day. During our drive, he observed, "I like ponies, they are so little trouble; and I prefer them to driving one horse in this vehicle, as I can put my wife and daughters into it. It's selfish to keep a carriage for yourself alone, and one horse in a four-wheeled double chaise appears like an imposition upon the poor animal."

I went to Scotland, and remained about a year. On my return, I found that my friend Willemott had again shifted his quarters. He was at Brighton; and having nothing better to do, I put myself in the "Times," and arrived at the Bedford Hotel. It was not until after some inquiry, that I could find out his address. At last I obtained it, in a respectable but not fashionable part of this overgrown town. Willemott received me just as before.

"I have no spare bed to offer you, but you must breakfast and dine with us every day. Our house is small, but it's very comfortable, and Brighton is a very convenient place. You know Mary is married. A good place in the courts was for sale, and my wife and I agreed to purchase it for Rivers. It has reduced us a little, but they are very comfortable. I have retired from business altogether; in fact, as my daughters are both married, and we have enough to live upon, what can we wish for more? Brighton is very gay, and always healthy; and, as for carriage and horses, they are no use here—there are *flies* at every corner of the streets."

I accepted his invitation to dinner. A parlour-maid waited, but everything, although very plain, was clean and comfortable.

"I have still a bottle of wine for a friend, Reynolds," said Willemott, after dinner; "but, for my part, I prefer *whisky-toddy*—it agrees with me better. Here's to the health of my two girls, God bless them, and success to them in life!"

"My dear Willemott," said I, "I take the liberty of an old friend, but I am so astonished at your philosophy, that I cannot help it. When I call to mind Belem Castle, your large establishment, your luxuries, your French cook, and your stud of cattle, I wonder at your contented state of mind under such a change of circumstances."

"I almost wonder myself, my dear fellow," replied he. "I never could have believed, at that time, that I could live happily under such a change of circumstances; but the fact is, that, although I have been a contractor, I have a good conscience; then, my wife is an excellent woman, and provided she sees me and her daughters happy, thinks nothing about herself; and, further, I have made it a rule, as I have been going down hill, to find reasons why I should be thankful, and not discontented. Depend upon it, Reynolds, it is not a loss of fortune which will affect your happiness, as long as you have peace and love at home."

I took my leave of Willemott and his wife, with respect as well as regard; convinced that there was no pretended indifference to worldly advantages; that it was not, that the grapes were sour, but that he had learned the whole art of happiness, by being contented with what he had, and by "cutting his coat according to his cloth."

Chapter Forty Seven

How to Write a Fashionable Novel

(*Scene—Chamber in Lincoln's Inn.* **Arthur Ansard** *at a briefless table, tête-à-tête with his wig on a block. A casts a disconsolate look upon his companion, and soliloquises.*)

Yes, there you stand, "partner of my toils, my feelings, and my fame." We do not *suit*, for we never gained a *suit* together. Well, what with reporting for the bar, writing for the Annuals and the Pocket-books, I shall be able to meet all demands, except those of my tailor; and, as his bill is most characteristically long, I think I shall be able to make it stretch over till next term, by which time I hope to fulfil my engagements with Mr C, who has given me an order for a fashionable novel, written by a "nobleman." But how I, who was never inside of an aristocratical mansion in my life, whose whole idea of Court is comprised in the Court of King's Bench, am to complete my engagement, I know no more than my companion opposite, who looks so placidly stupid under my venerable wig. As far as the street door, the footman and carriage, and the porter, are concerned, I can manage well enough; but as to what occurs within doors I am quite abroad. I shall never get through the first chapter; yet that tailor's bill must be paid. (*Knocking outside.*) Come in, I pray.

Enter **Barnstaple**

B. Merry Christmas to you, Arthur.

A. Sit down, my dear fellow; but don't mock me with merry Christmas. He emigrated long ago. Answer me seriously: do you think it possible for a man to describe what he never saw?

B (putting his stick up to his chin.) Why, 'tis possible; but I would not answer for the description being quite correct.

A. But suppose the parties who read it have never seen the thing described?

B. Why then it won't signify whether the description be correct or not.

A. You have taken a load off my mind; but still I am not quite at ease. I have engaged to furnish C with a fashionable novel.

B. What do you mean to imply by a fashionable novel?

A. I really can hardly tell. His stipulations were, that it was to be a "fashionable novel in three volumes, each volume not less than three hundred pages."

B. That is to say, that you are to assist him in imposing on the public.

A. Something very like it, I'm afraid; as it is further agreed that it is to be puffed as coming from a highly talented nobleman.

B. You should not do it, Ansard.

A. So conscience tells me, but my tailor's bill says Yes; and that is a thing out of all conscience. Only look here.

Displays a long bill.

B. Why, I must acknowledge, Ansard, that there is some excuse. One needs must, when the devil drives; but you are capable of better things.

A. I certainly don't feel great capability in this instance. But what can I do? The man will have nothing else—he says the public will read nothing else.

B. That is to say, that because one talented author astonished the public by style and merits peculiarly his own, and established, as it were, a school for neophites, his popularity is to be injured by contemptible imitators. It is sufficient to drive a man mad, to find that the tinsel of others, if to be purchased more cheaply, is to be pawned upon the public instead of his gold; and more annoying still, that the majority of the public cannot appreciate the difference between the metal and the alloy. Do you know, Ansard, that by getting up this work, you really injure the popularity of a man of great talent?

A. Will he pay my tailor's bill!

B. No; I dare say he has enough to do to pay his own. What does your tailor say?

A. He is a staunch reformer, and on March the 1st he declares that he will have the bill, the whole bill, and nothing but the bill—carried to my credit. Mr C, on the 10th of February, also expects the novel, the whole novel, and nothing but the novel, and that must be a fashionable novel. Look here, Barnstaple. (*Shows his tailor's bill*).

B. I see how it is. He "pays your poverty, and not your will."

A. And, by your leave, I thus must pay my bill (*bowing*).

B. Well, well, I can help you: nothing more difficult than to write a good novel, and nothing more easy than to write a bad one. If I were not above the temptation, I could pen you a dozen of the latter every ordinary year, and thirteen, perhaps, in the bissextile. So banish that Christmas cloud from your brow; leave off nibbling your pen at the wrong end, and clap a fresh nib to the right one. I have an hour to spare.

A. I thank you: that spare hour of yours may save me many a spare day. I'm all attention—proceed.

B. The first point to be considered is the *tempus*, or time; the next the *locus*, or place; and lastly the *dramatis personae* and thus, chapter upon chapter, will you build a novel.

A. Build!

B. Yes, build; you have had your dimensions given, the interior is left to your own decoration. First, as to the opening. Suppose we introduce the hero in his dressing-room. We have something of the kind in Pelham; and if we can't copy his merits, we must his peculiarities. Besides, it always is effective: a dressing-room or boudoir of supposed great people, is admitting the vulgar into the arcana, which they delight in.

A. Nothing can be better.

B. Then, as to time; as the hero is still in bed, suppose we say four o'clock in the afternoon?

A. In the morning, you mean.

B. No; the afternoon. I grant you that fashionable young men in real life get up much about the same time as other people; but in a fashionable novel your real exclusive never rises early. The very idea makes the tradesman's wife lift up her eyes. So begin. "It was about thirty-three minutes after four, *post meridian*—."

A. Minute—to a minute!

B. "That the Honourable Augustus Bouverie's finely chiselled—"

A. Chiselled!

B. Yes; great people are always chiselled; common people are only cast.—"Finely chiselled head was still recumbent upon his silk-encased pillow. His luxuriant and Antinous-like curls were now confined in *papillotes* of the finest satin paper, and the *tout ensemble* of his head—"

A. Tout ensemble!

B. Yes; go on.—"Was gently compressed by a caul of the finest network, composed of the threads spun from the beauteous production of the Italian worm."

A. Ah! now I perceive—a silk nightcap. But why can't I say at once a silk nightcap?

B. Because you are writing a fashionable novel.—"With the forefinger of his gloved left hand—"

A. But he's not coming in from a walk—he's not yet out of bed.

B. You don't understand it.—"Gloved left hand he applied a gentle friction to the portal of his right eye, which unclosing at the silent summons, enabled him to perceive a repeater studded with brilliants, and ascertain the exact minute of time, which we have already made known to the reader, and at which our history opens."

A. A very grand opening indeed!

B. Not more than it ought to be for a fashionable novel.—"At the sound of a silver *clochette,* his faithful Swiss valet Coridon, who had for some time been unperceived at the door, waiting for some notice of his master, having thrown off the empire of Somnus, in his light pumps, covered with beaver, moved with noiseless step up to the bedside, like the advance of eve stealing over the face of nature."

A. Rather an incongruous simile.

B. Not for a fashionable novel.—"There he stood, like Taciturnity bowing at the feet of proud Authority."

A. Indeed, Barnstaple, that is too *outré.*

B. Not a whit: I am in the true "Cambysis' vein."—"Coridon having softly withdrawn the rose-coloured gros de Naples bed-curtains, which by some might have been thought to have been rather too extravagantly fringed with the finest Mechlin lace, exclaimed with a tone of tremulous deference and affection, '*Monsieur a bien dormi?*' 'Coridon,' said the Honourable Augustus Bouverie, raising himself on his elbow in that eminently graceful attitude for which he was so remarkable when reclining on the ottomans at Almacks—"

A. Are you sure they have ottomans there?

B. No; but your readers can't disprove it.—"'Coridon,' said he, surveying his attendant from head to foot, and ultimately assuming a severity of countenance, 'Coridon, you are becoming gross, if not positively what the people call *fat.*' The Swiss attendant fell back in graceful astonishment three steps, and arching his eyebrows, extending his inverted palms forward, and raising his shoulders above the apex of his head, exclaimed, '*Pardon, milor, j'en aurais un horreur parfait.*' 'I tell you,' replied our gracefully recumbent hero, 'that it is so, Coridon; and I ascribe it to your partiality for that detestable wine called Port. Confine yourself to Hock and Moselle, sirrah: I fear me, you have a base hankering after mutton and beef. Restrict yourself to salads, and do not sin even with an omelette more than once a week. Coridon must be visionary and diaphanous, or he is no Coridon for me. Remove my night-gloves, and assist me to rise: it is past four o'clock, and the sun must have, by this time, sufficiently aired this terrestrial globe.'"

A. I have it now; I feel I could go on for an hour.

B. Longer than that, before you get him out of his dressing-room. You must make at least five chapters before he is apparelled, or how can you write a fashionable novel, in which you cannot afford more than two incidents in the three volumes? Two are absolutely necessary for the editor of the Gazette to extract as specimens, before he winds up an eulogy. Do you think that you can proceed now for a week, without my assistance?

A. I think so, if you will first give me some general ideas. In the first place, am I always to continue in this style?

B. No; I thought you knew better. You must throw in patches of philosophy every now and then.

A. Philosophy in a fashionable novel?

B. Most assuredly, or it would be complained of as trifling; but a piece, now and then, of philosophy, as unintelligible as possible, stamps it with deep thought. In the dressing-room, or boudoir, it must be occasionally Epicurean; elsewhere, especially in the open air, more Stoical.

A. I'm afraid that I shall not manage that without a specimen to copy from. Now I think of it, Eugene Aram says something very beautiful on a starry night.

B. He does: it is one of the most splendid pieces of writing in our language. But I will have no profanation, Arthur;—to your pen again, and write. We'll suppose our hero to have retired from the crowded festivities of a ball-room at some lordly mansion in the country, and to have wandered into a churchyard, damp and dreary with a thick London fog. In the light dress of fashion, he throws himself on a tombstone. "Ye dead!" exclaims the hero, "where are ye? Do your disembodied spirits now float around me, and, shrouded in this horrible veil of nature, glare unseen upon vitality? Float ye upon this intolerable mist, in yourselves still more misty and intolerable? Hold ye high jubilee to-night? or do ye crouch behind these monitorial stones, gibbering and chattering at one who dares thus to invade your precincts? Here may I hold communion with my soul, and, in the invisible presence of those who could, but dare not to reveal. Away! it must not be."

A. What mustn't be?

B. That is the mystery which gives the point to his soliloquy. Leave it to the reader's imagination.

A. I understand. But still the Honourable Augustus cannot lie in bed much longer, and I really shall not be able to get him out without your assistance. I do not comprehend how a man can get out of bed *gracefully*; he must show his bare legs, and the alteration of position is in itself awkward.

B. Not half so awkward as you are. Do you not feel that he must not be got out of bed at all — that is, by description.

A. How then?

B. By saying nothing about it. Recommence as follows: — "'I should like the bath at seventy-six and a half, Coridon,' observed the Honourable Augustus Bouverie, as he wrapped his embroidered dressing gown round his elegant form, and sank into a *chaise longue*, wheeled by his faithful attendant to the fire." There, you observe, he is out of bed, and nothing said about it.

A. Go on, I pray thee.

A. "'How is the bath perfumed?' *'Eau de mille fleurs.'* *'Eau de mille fleurs*! Did not I tell you last week that I was tired of that villainous compound? It has been adulterated till nothing remains but its name. Get me another bath immediately *à la violette*; and, Coridon, you may use that other scent, if there is any left, for the poodle; but observe, only when *you* take him an airing, not when he goes with *me.'"*

A. Excellent! I now feel the real merits of an exclusive; but you said something about dressing-room, or in-door philosophy.

B. I did; and now is a good opportunity to introduce it. Coridon goes into the ante-chamber to renew the bath, and of course your hero has met with a disappointment in not having the bath to his immediate pleasure. He must press his hands to his forehead. By-the-by, recollect that his forehead, when you describe it, must be high and white as snow: all aristocratical foreheads are — at least, are in a fashionable novel.

A. What! the women's and all?

B. The heroine's must be; the others you may lower as a contrast. But to resume with the philosophy. He strikes his forehead, lifts his eyes slowly up to the ceiling, and drops his right arm as slowly down by the side of the *chaise longue*; and then in a voice so low that it might have been considered a whisper, were it not for its clear and brilliant intonation, he exclaims—

A. Exclaims in a whisper!

B. To be sure; you exclaim mentally, why should you not in a whisper?

A. I perceive—your argument is unanswerable.

B. Stop a moment; it will run better thus:— "The Honourable Augustus Bouverie no sooner perceived himself alone, than he felt the dark shades of melancholy ascending and brooding over his mind, and enveloping his throbbing heart in their—their *adamantine* chains. Yielding to the overwhelming force, he thus exclaimed, 'Such is life—we require but one flower, and we are offered noisome thousands—refused that we wish, we live in loathing of that not worthy to be received—mourners from our cradle to our grave, we utter the shrill cry at our birth, and we sink in oblivion with the faint, wail of terror. Why should we, then, ever commit the folly to be happy?'"

A. Hang me, but that's a poser!

B. Nonsense! hold your tongue; it is only preparatory to the end. "Conviction astonishes and torments—destiny prescribes and falsifies—attraction drives us away—humiliation supports our energies. Thus do we recede into the present, and shudder at the Elysium of posterity."

A. I have written all that down, Barnstaple; but I cannot understand it, upon my soul!

B. If you had understood one particle, that particle I would have erased. This is your true philosophy of a fashionable novel, the extreme interest of which consists in its being unintelligible. People have such an opinion of their own abilities, that if they understood you, they would despise you; but a dose like this strikes them with veneration for your talents.

A. Your argument is unanswerable; but you said that I must describe the dressing-room.

B. Nothing more easy; as a simile, compare it to the shrine of some favoured saint in a richly-endowed Catholic church. Three tables at least, full of materials in methodised confusion—all tending to the beautification of the human form divine. Tinted perfumes in every variety of cut crystal receivers, gold and silver. If at a loss, call at Bayley and Blew's, or Smith's in Bond Street. Take an accurate survey of all you see, and introduce your whole catalogue. You cannot be too minute. But, Arthur, you must not expect me to write the whole book for you.

A. Indeed I am not so exorbitant in my demands upon your good-nature; but observe, I may get up four or five chapters already with the hints you have given me, but I do not know how to move, such a creation of the brain—so ethereal, that I fear he will melt away; and so fragile, that I am in terror lest he fall to pieces. Now only get him into the breakfast-room for me, and then I ask no more for the present. Only dress him, and bring him *down stairs.*

B. There again you prove your incapability. Bring him down stairs! Your hero of a fashionable novel never ascends to the first floor. Bed-room, dressing-room, breakfast-room, library, and boudoir, all are upon a level. As for his dressing, you must only describe it as perfect when finished; but not enter into a regular detail, except that, in conversation with his valet, he occasionally asks for something unheard-of, or fastidious to a degree. You must not walk him from one chamber to another, but manage it as follows:— "It was not until the beautiful airs of the French clock that decorated the mantel-piece had been thrice played, with all their variations, that the Honourable Augustus Bouverie entered his library, where he found his assiduous Coridon burning an aromatic pastille to disperse the compound of villainous exhalations arising from the condensed metropolitan atmosphere. Once more in a state of repose, to the repeated and almost affecting solicitations of his faithful attendant, who alternately presented to him the hyson of Pekoe, the bohea of Twankay, the fragrant berry from the Asiatic shore, and the frothing and perfumed decoction of the Indian nut, our hero shook his head in denial, until he at last was prevailed upon to sip a small liqueur glass of *eau sucré.*" The fact is, Arthur, he is in love—don't you perceive? Now introduce a friend, who rallies him—then a resolution to think no more of the heroine—a billet on a golden salver—a counter resolution—a debate which equipage to order—a decision at last—hat, gloves, and furred great coat—and by that time you will have arrived to the middle of the first volume.

A. I perceive; but I shall certainly stick there without your assistance.

B. You shall have it, my dear fellow. In a week I will call again, and see how you get on. Then we'll introduce the heroine; that, I can tell you, requires some tact—*au revoir.*

A. Thanks, many thanks, my dear Barnstaple. Fare you well.

*Exit **Barnstaple** .*

A (looking over his memoranda.) — It will do! (*Hopping and dancing about the room.*) Hurrah! my tailor's bill will be paid after all!

Part II

Mr Arthur Ansard's Chambers as before. Mr Ansard . with his eyes fixed upon the wig block, gnawing the feather end of his pen. The table, covered with sundry sheets of foolscap, show strong symptoms of the Novel progressing.

Ansard (*solus*)

Where is Barnstaple? If he do not come soon, I shall have finished my novel without a heroine. Well, I'm not the first person who has been foiled by a woman. (*Continues to gnaw his pen in a brown study.*)

Barnstaple enters unperceived, and slaps Ansard on the shoulder. The latter starts up.

B. So, friend Ansard, making your dinner off your pen: it is not every novel-writer who can contrive to do that even in anticipation. Have you profited by my instructions?

A. I wish I had. I assure you that this light diet has not contributed, as might be expected, to assist a heavy head, and one feather is not sufficient to enable my genius to take wing. If the public knew what dull work it is to write a novel, they would not be surprised at finding them dull reading. *Ex nihilo nihil fit.* Barnstaple, I am at the very bathos of stupidity.

B. You certainly were absorbed when I entered, for I introduced myself.

A. I wish you had introduced another personage with you—you would have been doubly welcome.

B. Who is that?

A. My heroine. I have followed your instructions to the letter. My hero is as listless as I fear my readers will be, and he is not yet in love. In fact, he is only captivated with himself. I have made him dismiss Coridon.

B. Hah! how did you manage that?

A. He was sent to ascertain the arms on the panel of a carriage. In his eagerness to execute his master's wishes, he came home with a considerable degree of perspiration on his brow, for which offence he was immediately put out of doors.

B. Bravo—it was unpardonable—but still—

A. O! I know what you mean—that is all arranged; he has an annuity of one hundred pounds per annum.

B. My dear Ansard, you have exceeded my expectations; but now for the heroine.

A. Yes, indeed; help me — for I have exhausted all my powers.

B. It certainly requires much tact to present your heroine to your readers. We are unfortunately denied what the ancients were so happy to possess, — a whole *cortège* of divinities that might be summoned to help any great personage in, or the author out of, a difficulty; but since we cannot command their assistance, like the man in the play who forgot his part, we will do without it. Now, have you thought of nothing new, for we must not plagiarise even from fashionable novels?

A. I have thought — and thought — and can find nothing new, unless we bring her in in a whirlwind: that has not yet been attempted.

B. A whirlwind! I don't know — that's hazardous. Nevertheless, if she were placed on a beetling cliff, overhanging the tempestuous ocean, lashing the rocks with its wild surge; of a sudden, after she has been permitted to finish her soliloquy, a white cloud rising rapidly and unnoticed — the sudden vacuum — the rush of mighty winds through the majestic and alpine scenery — the vortex gathering round her — first admiring the vast efforts of nature; then astonished; and, lastly, alarmed, as she finds herself compelled to perform involuntary gyrations, till at length she spins round like a well-whipped top, nearing the dangerous edge of the precipice. It is bold, and certainly quite novel — I think it will do. Portray her delicate little feet, peeping out, pointing downwards, the force of the elements raising her on her tip toes, now touching, now disdaining the earth. Her dress expanded wide like that of Herbelé in her last and best pirouette — round, round she goes — her white arms are tossed frantically in the air. Corinne never threw herself into more graceful attitudes. Now is seen her diminishing ankle — now the rounded symmetry — mustn't go too high up though — the wind increases — her distance from the edge of the precipice decreases — she has no breath left to shriek — no power to fall — threatened to be ravished by the wild and powerful god of the elements — she is discovered by the Honourable Augustus Bouverie, who has just finished his soliloquy upon another adjacent hill. He delights in her danger — before he rushes to her rescue, makes one pause for the purpose of admiration, and another for the purpose of adjusting his shirt collar.

A. The devil he does!

B. To be sure. The hero of a fashionable novel never loses caste. Whether in a storm, a whirlwind, up to his neck in the foaming ocean, or tumbling down a precipice, he is still the elegant and correct Honourable Augustus Bouverie. To punish you for your interruption, I have a great mind to make him take a pinch of snuff before he starts. Well—he flies to her assistance—is himself caught in the rushing vortex, which prevents him from getting nearer to the lady, and, despite of himself, takes to whirling in the opposite direction. They approach—they recede—she shrieks without being heard—holds out her arms for help—she would drop them in despair, but cannot, for they are twisted over her head by the tremendous force of the element. One moment they are near to each other, and the next they are separated; at one instant they are close to the abyss, and the waters below roar in delight of their anticipated victims, and in the next a favouring change of the vortex increases their distance from the danger—there they spin—and there you may leave them, and commence a new chapter.

A. But is not all this naturally and physically impossible?

B. By no means; there is nothing supernatural in a whirlwind, and the effect of a whirlwind is to twist everything round. Why should the heroine and the Honourable Augustus Bouverie not be submitted to the laws of nature? besides, we are writing a fashionable novel. Wild and improbable as this whirlwind may appear, it is within the range of probability: whereas, that is not at all adhered to in many novels—witness the drinking scene in —, and others equally *outrées*, in which the author, having turned probability out of doors, ends by throwing possibility out of the window—leaving folly and madness to usurp their place—and play a thousand antics for the admiration of the public, who, pleased with novelty, cry out "How fine!"

A. Buy the book, and laud the author.

B. Exactly. Now, having left your hero and heroine in a situation peculiarly interesting, with the greatest nonchalance, pass over to the continent, rave on the summit of Mont Blanc, and descant upon the strata which compose the mountains of the Moon in Central Africa. You have been philosophical, now you must be geological. No one can then say that your book is light reading.

A. That can be said of few novels. In most of them even smoke assumes the ponderosity of lead.

B. There is a metal still heavier, which they have the power of creating—gold—to pay a dunning tailor's bill.

A. But after being philosophical and geological, ought one not to be a little moral.

B. Pshaw! I thought you had more sense. The great art of novel-writing is to make the vices glorious, by placing them in close alliance with redeeming qualities. Depend upon it, Ansard, there is a deeper, more heartfelt satisfaction that mere amusement in novel-reading; a satisfaction no less real, because we will not own it to ourselves; the satisfaction of seeing all our favourite and selfish ideas dressed up in a garb so becoming, that we persuade ourselves that our false pride is proper dignity, our ferocity courage, our cowardice prudence, our irreligion liberality, and our baser appetites, mere gallantry.

A. Very true, Barnstaple; but really I do not like this whirlwind.

B. Well, well! I give it up then: it was your own idea. We'll try again. Cannot you create some difficulty or dilemma, in which to throw her, so that the hero may come to her rescue with *éclat.*

A. Her grey palfrey takes fright.

B. So will your readers; stale—quite stale!

A. A wild bull has his horns close to her, and is about to toss her.

B. As your book would be!—away with contempt. Vapid—quite vapid!

A. A shipwreck—the waves are about to close over her.

B. Your book would be closed at the same moment—worn out—quite worn out.

A. In the dead of the night, a fire breaks out—she is already in the midst of the flames—

B. Where your book would also be by the disgusted reader—worse and worse.

A. Confound it—you will not allow me to expose her to earth, air, fire, or water. I have a great mind to hang her in her garters, and make the hero come and cut her down.

B. You might do worse—and better.

A. What—hang myself?

B. That certainly would put an end to all your difficulties. But, Ansard, I think I can put your heroine in a situation really critical and eminently distressing, and the hero shall come to her relief, like the descent of a god to the rescue of a Greek or Trojan warrior.

A. Or of Bacchus to Ariadne in her distress.

B. Perhaps a better simile. The consequence will be, that eternal gratitude in the bosom of the maiden will prove the parent of eternal love, which eternity of passion will of course until they are married.

A. I'm all attention.

B. Get up a splendid dinner party for their first casual meeting. Place the company at table.

A. Surely you are not going to choke her with the bone of a chicken.

B. You surely are about to murder me, as Sampson did the Philistines—

A. With the jaw-bone of a fashionable novel-writer, you mean.

B. Exactly. But to proceed:— they are seated at table; can you describe a grand dinner?

A. Certainly, I have partaken of more than one.

B. Where?

A. I once sat down three hundred strong at the Freemasons' Tavern.

B. Pshaw! a mere hog feed.

A. Well, then, I dined with the late lord mayor.

B. Still worse. My dear Ansard, it is however of no consequence. Nothing is more difficult to attain, yet nothing is more easy to describe, than a good dinner. I was once reading a very fashionable novel by a very fashionable bookseller, for the author is a mere nonentity, and was very much surprised at the accuracy with which a good dinner was described. The mystery was explained a short time afterwards, when casually taking up Eustache Eude's book in Sams's library, I found that the author had copied it out exactly from the injunctions of that celebrated gastronome. You can borrow the book.

A. Well, we will suppose that done; but I am all anxiety to know what is the danger from which the heroine is to be rescued.

B. I will explain. There are two species of existence—that of mere mortal existence, which is of little consequence, provided, like Caesar, the hero and heroine die decently: the other is of much greater consequence, which is fashionable existence. Let them once lose caste in that respect, and they are virtually dead, and one mistake, one oversight, is a death-blow for which there is no remedy, and from which there is no recovery. For instance, we will suppose our heroine to be quite confounded with the appearance of our hero—to have become *distraite, rêveuse*—and, in short, to have lost her recollection and presence of mind. She has been assisted to *filet de soles*. Say that the only sauce ever taken with them is *au macédoine*—this is offered to her, and, at the same time, another, which to eat with the above dish would be unheard of. In her distraction she is about to take the wrong sauce—

actually at the point of ruining herself for ever and committing suicide upon her fashionable existence, while the keen grey eyes of Sir Antinous Antibes, the arbiter of fashion, are fixed upon her. At this awful moment, which is for ever to terminate her fashionable existence, the Honourable Augustus Bouverie, who sits next to her, gently touches her *séduisante* sleeve— blandly smiling, he whispers to her that the *other* is the sauce *macédoine*. She perceives her mistake, trembles at her danger, rewards him with a smile, which penetrates into the deepest recesses of his heart, helps herself to the right sauce, darts a look of contemptuous triumph upon Sir Antinous Antibes, and, while she is dipping her sole into the sauce, her soul expands with gratitude and love.

A. I see, I see. Many thanks; my heroine is now a fair counterpart of my hero.

> "Ah, sure a pair were never seen,
> So justly form'd to meet by nature."

B. And now I'll give you another hint, since you appear grateful. It is a species of clap-trap in a novel, which always takes—to wit, a rich old uncle or misanthrope, who, at the very time that he is bitterly offended and disgusted with the hero, who is in awkward circumstances, pulls out a pocketbook and counts down, say fifteen or twenty thousand pounds in bank notes, to relieve him from his difficulties. An old coat and monosyllables will increase the interest.

A. True. (*sighing.*) Alas! there are no such uncles in real life; I wish there were.

B. I beg your pardon; I know no time in which *my uncle* forks out more bank notes than at present.

A. Yes, but it is for value, or more than value, received.

B. That I grant; but I am afraid it is the only "uncle" left now; except in a fashionable novel. But you comprehend the value of this new auxiliary.

A. Nothing can be better. Barnstaple, you are really —, but I say no more. If a truly great man cannot be flattered with delicacy, it must not be attempted at all; silence then becomes the best tribute. Your advice proves you to be truly great. I am silent, therefore you understand the full force of the oratory of my thanks.

B (bowing.) Well, Ansard, you have found out the cheapest way of paying off your bills of gratitude I ever heard of. "Poor, even in thanks," was well said by Shakespeare; but you, it appears, are rich, in having nothing at all wherewith to pay. If you could transfer the same doctrine to your tradesmen, you need not write novels.

A. Alas! my dear fellow, mine is not yet written. There is one important feature, nay, the most important feature of all—the style of language, the diction—on that, Barnstaple, you have not yet doctrinated.

B (pompously.) When Demosthenes was asked what were the principal attributes of eloquence, he answered, that the first was action; on being asked which was the second, he replied, action; and the third, action; and such is the idea of the Irish *mimbers* in the House of Commons. Now there are three important requisites in the diction of a fashionable novel. The first, my dear fellow, is—flippancy; the second, flippancy; and flippancy is also the third. With the dull it will pass for wit, with some it will pass for scorn,—and even the witty will not be enabled to point out the difference, without running the risk of being considered invidious. It will cover every defect with a defect still greater; for who can call small beer tasteless when it is sour, or dull when it is bottled and has a froth upon it?

A. The advice is excellent; but I fear that this flippancy is as difficult to acquire an the tone of true eloquence.

B. Difficult! I defy the writers of the silver-fork school to write out of the style flippant. Read but one volume of —, and you will be saturated with it; but if you wish to go to the fountain-head, do as have done most of the late fashionable novel-writers, repair to their instructors—the lady's-maid, for flippancy in the vein *spirituelle!* to a London footman for the vein critical; but, if you wish a flippancy of a still higher order, at once more solemn and more empty, which I would call the vein political, read the speeches of some of our members of Parliament. Only read them, I wish no man so ill an to inflict upon him the torture of hearing them—read them, I say, and you will have taken the very highest degree in the order of inane flippancy.

A. I see it at once. Your observations are as true as they are severe. When we would harangue geese, we must condescend to hiss; but still, my dear Barnstaple, though you have fully proved to me that in a fashionable novel all plot is unnecessary, don't you think there ought to be a catastrophe, or sort of a kind of an end to the work, or the reader may be brought up short, or as the sailors say, "all standing," when he comes to the word "Finis," and exclaim with an air of stupefaction—"And then—"

B. And then, if he did, it would be no more than the fool deserved. I don't know whether it would not be advisable to leave off in the middle of a sentence, of a word, nay of a syllable, if it be possible: I am sure the winding-up would be better than the lackadaisical running-down of most of the fashionable novels. Snap the mainspring of your watch, and none but an ass can expect you to tell by it what it is o'clock; snap the thread of your narrative in the same way, and he must be an unreasonable being who would expect a reasonable conclusion. Finish thus, in a case of delicate distress; say, "The Honourable Mr Augustus Bouverie was struck in a heap with horror. He rushed with a frantic grace, a deliberate haste, and a graceful awkwardness, and whispered in her ear these dread and awful words, 'IT IS TOO LATE!'" Follow up with a — and Finis.

A. I see; the fair and agitated reader will pass a sleepless night in endeavouring to decipher the mutilated sentence. She will fail, and consequently call the book delightful. But should there not have been a marriage previously to this happy awful climax?

B. Yes; everything is arranged for the nuptials—carriages are sent home, jewellery received but not paid for, dresses all tried on, the party invited— nay, assembled in the blue-and-white drawing-room. The right reverend my lord bishop is standing behind the temporary altar—he has wiped his spectacles and thumbed his prayer-book—all eyes are turned towards the door, which opens not—the bride faints, for the bridegroom cometh not— he's not "i' the vein"—a something, as like nothing as possible, has given him a disgust that is surmountable—he flings his happiness to the winds, though he never loved with more outrageous intensity than at the moment he discards his mistress; so he fights three duels with the two brothers and father. He wounds one of the young men dangerously, the other slightly; fires his pistol in the air when he meets her father—for how could he take the life of him who gave life to his adored one? Your hero can always hit a man just where he pleases—vide every novel in Mr C's collection. The hero becomes misanthropical, the heroine maniacal. The former marries an antiquated and toothless dowager, as an escape from the imaginary disgust he took at a sight of a matchless woman; and the latter marries an old brute, who threatens her life every night, and puts her in bodily fear every morning, as an indemnity in full for the loss of the man of her affections. They are both romantically miserable; and then comes on your tantalising scenes of delicate distress, and so the end of your third volume, and then finish without any end at all. *Verb. sap. sat.* Or, if you like it better, kill the old dowager of a surfeit, and make the old brute who marries the heroine commit suicide; and, after all these unheard-of trials, marry them as fresh and beautiful as ever.

A. A thousand thanks. Your *verba* are not thrown to a *sap*. Can I possibly do you any favour for all this kindness?

B. Oh, my dear fellow! the very greatest. As I see yours will be, at all points, a most fashionable novel, do me the inestimable favour *not* to ask me *to read it.*

Chapter Forty Eight

How to Write a Book of Travels

Mr Ansard's *Chambers*

Ansard. (alone.) Well, I thought it hard enough to write a novel at the dictate of the bibliopolist; but to be condemned to sit down and write my travels—travels that have never extended farther than the Lincoln's Inn Coffee House for my daily food, and a walk to Hampstead on a Sunday. These travels to be swelled into Travels up the Rhine in the year 18—. Why, it's impossible. O that Barnstaple were here, for he has proved my guardian angel! Lazy, clever dog!

Enter **Barnstaple**

Barnstaple. Pray, my dear Ansard, to whom did you apply that last epithet?

Ansard. My dear Barnstaple, I never was more happy to see you. Sit down, I have much to tell you, all about myself and my difficulties.

Barnstaple. The conversation promises to be interesting to me, at all events.

Ansard. Everything is interesting to true friendship.

Barnstaple. Now I perceive that you do want something. Well, before you state your case, tell me, how did the novel go off?

Ansard. Wonderfully well. It was ascribed to Lord G—: the bait took, and 750 went off in a first edition, and the remainder of the copies printed went off in a second.

Barnstaple. Without being reprinted?

Ansard. Exactly. I was surprised at my success, and told my publisher so; but he answered that he could sell an edition of any trash he pleased.

Barnstaple. That was not flattering.

Ansard. Not very; but his bill was honoured, and that consoled me. However, to proceed to business—he has given me another order—A Journey up the Rhine, in two volumes, large octavo, in the year 18—. Now, Barnstaple, what's to be done?

Barnstaple. Write it, to be sure.

Ansard. But you well know I have never been out of England in my life.

Barnstaple. Never mind, write it.

Ansard. Yes, it's very well to say write it; but how the devil am I to write it? Write what I have never seen—detail events which never occurred—describe views of that which I have not even an idea—travel post in my old arm-chair. It's all very well to say write it, but tell me, how.

Barnstaple. I say again, write it, and pocket the money. Ansard, allow me to state that you are a greenhorn. I will make this mountain of difficulties vanish and melt away like snow before the powerful rays of the sun. You are told to write what you have never seen; but if you have not, others have, which will serve your purpose just as well. To detail events which have never occurred—invent them, they will be more amusing. Describe views, etcetera, of which you are ignorant—so are most of your readers; but have we not the art of engraving to assist you? To travel post in your arm-chair—a very pleasant and a very profitable way of travelling, as you have not to pay for the horses and postilions, and are not knocked to pieces by continental roads. Depend upon it, the best travels are those written at home, by those who have never put their foot into the Calais packet-boat.

Ansard. To me this is all a mystery. I certainly must be a greenhorn, as you observe.

Barnstaple. Why, Ansard, my dear fellow, with a book of roads and a gazetteer, I would write a more amusing book of travels than one half which are now foisted on the public. All you have to do is to fill up the chinks.

Ansard. All I want to do is to fill up the chinks in my stomach, Barnstaple; for, between you and me, times are rather queer.

Barnstaple. You shall do it, if you will follow my advice. I taught you how to write a fashionable novel; it will be hard, indeed, if I cannot send you up the Rhine. One little expense must be incurred—you must subscribe a quarter to a circulating library, for I wish that what you do should be well done.

Ansard. Barnstaple, I will subscribe to—anything.

Barnstaple. Well, then, since you are so reasonable, I will proceed. You must wade through all the various "Journeys on the Rhine," "Two Months on the Rhine," "Autumns on the Rhine," etcetera, which you can collect. This you will find the most tiresome part of your task. Select one as your guide, one who has a reputation; follow his course, not exactly—that I will explain afterwards—and agree with him in every thing, generally speaking. Praise his exactitude and fidelity, and occasionally quote him; this is but fair; after you rob a man (and I intend you shall rifle him most completely), it is but decent to give him kind words. All others you must abuse, contradict, and depreciate. Now, there is a great advantage in so doing: in the first place, you make the best writer your friend—he forgets your larcenies in your commendation of him, and in your abuse of others. If his work be correct, so must yours be; he praises it everywhere—perhaps finds you out, and asks you to dine with him.

Ansard. How should I ever look at his injured face?

Barnstaple. On the contrary, he is the obliged party—your travels are a puff to his own.

Ansard. But, Barnstaple, allowing that I follow this part of your advice, which I grant to be very excellent, how can I contradict others, when they may be, and probably are, perfectly correct in their assertions?

Barnstaple. If they are so, virtue must be its own reward. It is necessary that you write a book of travels, and all travellers contradict each other—ergo, you must contradict, or nobody will believe that you have travelled. Not only contradict, but sneer at them.

Ansard. Well, now do explain how that is to be done.

Barnstaple. Nothing more simple: for instance, a man measures a certain remarkable piece of antiquity—its length is 747 feet. You must measure it over again, and declare that he is in error, that it is only 727. To be sure of your being correct, measure it *twice* over, and then convict him.

Ansard. But surely, Barnstaple, one who has measured it is more likely to be correct than one who has not.

Barnstaple. I'll grant you that he is correct to half an inch—that's no matter. The public will, in all probability, believe you, because you are the last writer, and because you have *decreased* the dimensions. Travellers are notorious for amplification, and if the public do not believe you, let them go and measure it themselves.

Ansard. A third traveller may hereafter measure it, and find that I am in the wrong.

Barnstaple. Ten to one if you are not both in the wrong; but what matter will that be? your book will have been sold.

Ansard. Most true, O king! I perceive now the general outline, and I feel confident that, with your kind assistance, I may accomplish it. But, Barnstaple, the beginning is everything. If I only had the first chapter as a start, I think I could get on. It is the *modus* that I want—the style. A first chapter would be a key-note for the remainder of the tune, with all the variations.

Barnstaple. Well, then, take up your pen. But before I commence, it may be as well to observe, that there is a certain method required, even in writing travels. In every chapter you should have certain landmarks to guide you. For instance, enumerate the following, and select the works from which they may be obtained, so as to mix up the instructive with the amusing. Travelling—remarks on country passed through—anecdote—arrival at a town—churches—population—historical remarks—another anecdote—eating and drinking—natural curiosities—egotism—remarks on the women (never mind the men)—another anecdote—reflections—an adventure—and go to bed. You understand, Ansard, that in these memoranda you have all that is required; the rule is not to be followed absolutely, but generally. As you observed, such is to be the tune, but your variations may be infinite. When at a loss, or you think you are dull, always call in a grisette, and a little mystery; and, above all, never be afraid of talking too much about yourself.

Ansard. Many, many thanks; but now, my dear Barnstaple, for the first chapter.

Barnstaple. Let your style be flowery—I should say florid—never mind a false epithet or two in a page, they will never be observed. A great deal depends upon the first two pages—you must not limp at starting; we will, therefore, be particular. Take your pen.

(*Barnstaple muses for a while, and then continues.*)

"A severe cough, which refused to yield even to the balmy influence of the genial spring of 18—, and threatened a pulmonary complaint, induced me to yield to the reiterated persuasions of my physicians to try a change of air, as most likely to ward off the threatened danger. Where to direct my steps was the difficult point to ascertain. Brighton, Torquay, Cromer, Ilfracombe, had all been visited and revisited. At either of these fashionable resorts I was certain to fall in with a numerous acquaintance, whose persuasions would have induced me to depart from that regularity of diet and of rest, so imperiously insisted upon by my medical advisers. After much cogitation, I resolved upon a journey up the Rhine, and to escape the ruthless winter of our northern clime in the more genial land of history."

Ansard. Land of history—I presume you mean Italy; but am I to go there?

Barnstaple. No, you may recover, and come back again to skate upon the Serpentine, if you please. You observe, Ansard, I have not made you a fellow with 50 pounds in his pocket, setting out to turn it into 300 pounds by a book of travels. I have avoided mention of Margate, Ramsgate, Broadstairs, and all common watering-places; I have talked of physicians in the plural; in short, no one who reads that paragraph, but will suppose that you are a young man of rank and fortune, to whom money is no object, and who spends hundreds to cure that which might be effected by a little regularity, and a few doses of ipecacuanha.

Ansard. I wish it were so. Nevertheless, I'll travel *en grand seigneur*—thats more agreeable even in imagination, than being rumbled in a *"diligence."*

Barnstaple. And will produce more respect for your work, I can assure you. But to proceed. Always, when you leave England, talk about *hospitality.* The English like it. Have you no relations or friends in whose opinion you wish to stand well? Public mention in print does wonders, especially with a copy handsomely bound "from the author."

Ansard. Really, Barnstaple, I do not know any one. My poor mother is in Cumberland, and that is not *en route.* I have a maternal uncle of the name of Forster, who lives on the road—a rich, old, miserly bachelor; but I can't say much for his hospitality. I have called upon him twice, and he has never even asked me to dinner.

Barnstaple. Never mind. People like being praised for a virtue which they do not possess—it may prove a legacy. Say, then, that you quitted the hospitable roof of your worthy and excellent-hearted relation, Mr Forster and felt—

Ansard. Felt how?

Barnstaple. How—why you felt, as he wrung your hand, that there was a sudden dissolution of the ties of kindred and affection.

Ansard. There always has been in that quarter, so my conscience is so far clear.

Barnstaple. You arrive at Dovor (mind you spell it Dovor)—go to bed tired and reflective—embark early the next morning—a rough passage—

Ansard. And sea-sick, of course?

Barnstaple. No, Ansard; there I'll give you a proof of my tact—you shan't be sea-sick.

Ansard. But I'm sure I should be.

Barnstaple. All travellers are, and all fill up a page or two with complaints, *ad nauseam*—for that reason sick you shall not be. Observe— to your astonishment you are not sea-sick: the other passengers suffer dreadfully; one young dandy puffs furiously at a cigar in bravado, until he sends it over the side, like an arrow from the blow-pipe of a South American Indian. Introduce a husband with a pretty wife—he jealous as a dog, until he is sick as a cat—your attentions—she pillowed on your arms, while he hangs over the lee gunwale—her gratitude—safe arrival at Calais—sweet smiles of the lady—sullen deportment of the gentleman—a few hints—and draw the veil. Do you understand?

Ansard. Perfectly. I can manage all that.

Barnstaple. Then when you put your foot on shore, you must, for the first time, *feel sea-sick.*

Ansard. On shore?

Barnstaple. Yes; reel about, not able to stand—every symptom as if on board. Express your surprise at the strange effect, pretend not to explain it, leave that to medical men, it being sufficient for you to state the *fact.*

Ansard. The *fact!* O Barnstaple!

Barnstaple. That will be a great hit for a first chapter. You reverse the order of things.

Ansard. That I do most certainly. Shall I finish the first chapter with that *fact?*

Barnstaple. No. Travellers always go to bed at the end of each chapter. It is a wise plan, and to a certain degree it must be followed. You must have a baggage adventure—be separated from it—some sharp little urchin has seized upon your valise—it is nowhere to be found—quite in despair— walk to the Hotel d'Angleterre, and find that you are met by the landlord and garçons, who inform you that your carriage is in the remise, and your rooms ready—ascend to your bedroom—find that your baggage is not only there, but neatly laid out—your portmanteau unstrapped—your trunk uncorded—and the little rascal of a commissaire standing by with his hat in his hand, and a smile *de malice,* having installed *himself* as your *domestique de place*—take him for his impudence—praise the *"Cotelettes* and the *vin de Beaune"*—wish the reader good night, and go to bed. Thus ends the first chapter.

(*Ansard gets up and takes Barnstaple's hand, which he shakes warmly without speaking. Barnstaple smiles and walks out. Ansard is left hard at work at his desk.*)

Arthur Ansard in his Chambers, solus, with his pen in his hand.

Ansard. Capital! that last was a *hit.* It has all the appearance of reality. To be sure, I borrowed the hint, but that nobody will be able to prove. (*Yawns.*) Heigho! I have only got half way on my journey yet, and my ideas are quite exhausted. I am as much worn out and distressed as one of the German post-horses which I described in my last chapter. (*Nods, and then falls fast asleep.*)

Barnstaple taps at the door; receiving no answer, he enters.

Barnstaple. So—quite fast. What can have put him to sleep? (*Reads the manuscript on the table.*) No wonder, enough to put anybody to sleep apparently. Why, Ansard!

Ansard. (*starting up, still half asleep.*) Already? Why, I've hardly shut my eyes. Well, I'll be dressed directly; let them get some *café* ready below. Henri, did you order the hind-spring to be repaired! (*Nods again with his eyes shut.*)

Barnstaple. Hallo! What now, Ansard, do you really think that you are travelling?

Ansard. (*waking up*). Upon my word, Barnstaple, I was so dreaming. I thought I was in my bed at the Hotel de Londres, after the fatiguing day's journey I described yesterday. I certainly have written myself into the conviction that I was travelling post.

Barnstaple. All the better—you have embodied yourself in your own work, which every writer of fiction ought to do; but they can seldom attain to such a desideratum. Now, tell me, how do you get on?

Ansard. Thank you—pretty well. I have been going it with four post-horses these last three weeks.

Barnstaple. And how far have you got?

Ansard. Half way—that is, into the middle of my second volume. But I'm very glad that you're come to my assistance, Barnstaple; for to tell you the truth, I was breaking down.

Barnstaple. Yes, you said something about the hind-spring of your carriage.

Ansard. That I can repair without your assistance; but my spirits are breaking down. I want society. This travelling post is dull work. Now, if I could introduce a companion—

Barnstaple. So you shall. At the next town that you stop at, buy a *Poodle*.

Ansard. A *Poodle*! Barnstaple? How the devil shall I be assisted by a poodle?

Barnstaple. He will prove a more faithful friend to you in your exigence, and a better companion than one of your own species. A male companion, after all, is soon expended, and a female, which would be more agreeable, is not admissible. If you admit a young traveller into your carriage—what then? He is handsome, pleasant, romantic, and so forth; but you must not give his opinions in contradiction to your own, and if they coincide, it is superfluous. Now, a poodle is a dog of parts, and it is more likely that you fall in with a sagacious dog than with a sagacious man. The poodle is the thing; you must recount your meeting, his purchase, size, colour, and qualifications, and anecdotes of his sagacity, vouched for by the landlord, and all the *garçons* of the hotel. As you proceed on your travels, his attachment to you increases, and wind up every third chapter with "your faithful Mouton."

Ansard. Will not all that be considered frivolous?

Barnstaple. Frivolous! by no means. The frivolous will like it, and those who may have more sense, although they may think that Mouton does not at all assist your travelling researches, are too well acquainted with the virtues of the canine race, and the attachment insensibly imbibed for so faithful an attendant, not to forgive your affectionate mention of him. Besides it will go far to assist the verisimilitude of your travels. As for your female readers, they will prefer Mouton even to you.

Ansard. All-powerful and mighty magician, whose wand of humbug, like that of Aaron's, swallows up all others, not excepting that of divine Truth, I obey you! Mouton shall be summoned to my aid: he shall flourish, and my pen shall flourish in praise of his endless perfections. But, Barnstaple, what shall I give for him?

Barnstaple. (*thinks awhile.*) Not less than forty louis.

Ansard. Forty louis for a poodle!

Barnstaple. Most certainly; not a sou less. The value of any thing in the eyes of the world is exactly what it costs. Mouton, at a five-franc piece, would excite no interest; and his value to the reader will increase in proportion to his price, which will be considered an undeniable proof of all his wonderful sagacity, with which you are to amuse the reader.

Ansard. But in what is to consist his sagacity?

Barnstaple. He must do everything but speak. Indeed, he must so far speak as to howl the first part of "Lieber Augustin."

Ansard. His instinct shall put our boasted reason to the blush. But—I think I had better not bring him home with me.

Barnstaple. Of course not. In the first place, it's absolutely necessary to kill him, lest his reputation should induce people to seek him out, which they would do, although, in all probability, they never will his master. Lady Cork would certainly invite him to a literary *soirée*. You must therefore kill him in the most effective way possible, and you will derive the advantage of filling up at least ten pages with his last moments—licking your hand, your own lamentations, violent and inconsolable grief on the part of Henri, and tanning his skin as a memorial.

Ansard. A beautiful episode, for which receive my best thanks. But, Barnstaple, I have very few effective passages as yet. I have remodelled several descriptions of mountains, precipices, waterfalls, and such wonders of the creation—expressed my contempt and surprise at the fear acknowledged by other travellers, in several instances. I have lost my way twice—met three wolves—been four times benighted—and indebted to lights at a distance for a bed at midnight, after the horses have refused to proceed. All is incident, and I am quite hard up for description. Now, I have marked down a fine passage in —'s work—a beautiful description of a cathedral with a grand procession. (*Reads*.) "What with the effect of the sun's brightest beams upon the ancient glass windows—various hues reflected upon the gothic pillars—gorgeousness of the procession—sacerdotal ornaments—tossing of censers—crowds of people—elevation of the host, and sinking down of the populace *en masse*." It really is a magnificent line of writing, and which my work requires. One or two like that in my book would do well to be quoted by impartial critics, before the public are permitted to read it. But here, you observe, is a difficulty. I dare not borrow the passage.

Barnstaple. But you shall borrow it—you shall be even finer than he is, and yet he shall not dare to accuse you of plagiarism.

Ansard. How is that possible, my dear Barnstaple? I am all impatience.

Barnstaple. His description is at a certain hour of the day. All you have to do is to portray the scene in nearly the same words. You have as much right to visit a cathedral as he has, and as for the rest—here is the secret. You must visit it at *night*. Instead of "glorious beams," you will talk of "pale melancholy light;" instead of "the stained windows throwing their various hues upon the gothic pile," you must "darken the massive pile, and light up the windows with the silver rays of the moon." The glorious orb of day must give place to thousands of wax tapers—the splendid fret—work of the roof you must regret was not to be clearly distinguished—but you must be in ecstasies with the broad light and shade—the blaze at the altar—solemn hour of night—feelings of awe—half a Catholic—religious reflections, etcetera. Don't you perceive?

Ansard. I do. Like the rest of my work, it shall be all *moonshine*. It shall be done, Barnstaple; but have you not another idea or two to help me with?

Barnstaple. Have you talked about cooks?

Ansard. As yet, not a word.

Barnstaple. By this time you ought to have some knowledge of gastronomy. Talk seriously about eating.

Ansard. (*writes.*) I have made a memo.

Barnstaple. Have you had no affront?

Ansard. Not one.

B. Then be seriously affronted—complain to the burgomaster, or mayor, or commandant, whoever it may be—they attempt to bully—you are resolute and firm as an Englishman—insist upon being righted—they must make you a thousand apologies. This will tickle the national vanity, and be read with interest.

Ansard. (*writes.*) I have been affronted. Anything else which may proceed from your prolific brain, Barnstaple?

Barnstaple. Have you had a serious illness?

Ansard. Never complained even of a headache.

Barnstaple. Then do everything but die—Henri weeping and inconsolable—Mouton howling at the foot of your bed—kick the surgeons out of the room—and cure yourself with three dozen of champagne.

Ansard. (*writes.*) Very sick—cured with three dozen of champagne—I wish the illness would in reality come on, if I were certain of the cure *gratis*. Go on, my dear Barnstaple.

Barnstaple. You may work in an episode here—delirium—lucid intervals—gentle female voice—delicate attentions—mysterious discovery from loquacious landlady—eternal gratitude—but no marriage—an apostrophe—and all the rest left to conjecture.

Ansard. (*writes down.*) Silent attentions—conjecture—I can manage that, I think.

Barnstaple. By the bye, have you brought in Madame de Staël?

Ansard. No—how the devil am I to bring her in?

Barnstaple. As most other travellers do, by the head and shoulders. Never mind that, so long as you bring her in.

Ansard. (*writes*). Madame de Staël by the shoulders—that's not very polite towards a lady. These hints are invaluable; pray go on.

Barnstaple. Why, you have already more hints this morning than are sufficient for three volumes. But, however, let me see. (*Barnstaple thinks a little*). Find yourself short of cash.

Ansard. A sad reality, Barnstaple. I shall write this part well, for truth will guide my pen.

Barnstaple. All the better. But to continue—no remittances—awkward position—explain your situation—receive credit to any amount—and compliment your countrymen.

Ansard. (writes.) Credit to any amount—pleasing idea. But I don't exactly perceive the value of this last hint, Barnstaple.

Barnstaple. All judicious travellers make it a point, throughout the whole of their works, to flatter the nation upon its wealth, name, and reputation in foreign countries; by doing so you will be read greedily, and praised in due proportion. If ever I were to write my travels into the interior of Africa, or to the North Pole, I would make it a point to discount a bill at Timbuctoo, or get a cheque cashed by the Esquimaux, without the least hesitation in either case. I think now, that what with your invention, your plagiarism, and my hints, you ought to produce a very effective Book of Travels; and with that feeling I shall leave you to pursue your Journey, and receive, at its finale, your just reward. When we meet again, I hope to see you advertised.

Ansard. Yes, but not exposed, I trust. I am *incognito*, you know.

Barnstaple. To be sure, that will impart an additional interest to your narrative. All the world will be guessing who you may be. Adieu, voyageur. (*Exit Barnstaple .*)

Ansard. And Heaven forfend that they should find me out! But what can be done? In brief, I cannot get a brief, and thus I exercise my professional acquirements how I can, proving myself as long-winded, as prosy perhaps, and certainly as lying, as the more fortunate of my fraternity.

Chapter Forty Nine

How to Write a Romance

Mr Arthur Ansard , standing at his table, selecting a steel pen from a card on which a dozen are ranged up, like soldiers on parade.

I must find a regular *graver* to write this chapter of horrors. No goose quill could afford me any assistance. Now then. Let me see—(*Reads, and during his reading Barnstaple comes in at the door behind him, unperceived.*) "At this most monstrously appalling sight, the hair of Piftlianteriscki raised slowly the velvet cap from off his head, as if it had been perched upon the rustling quills of some exasperated porcupine—(I think that's new)—his nostrils dilated to that extent that you might, with ease, have thrust a musket bullet into each—his mouth was opened so wide, so unnaturally wide, that the corners were rent asunder, and the blood slowly trickled down each side of his bristly chin—while each tooth loosened from its socket with individual fear.—Not a word could he utter, for his tongue, in its fright, clung with terror to his upper jaw, as tight as do the bellies of the fresh and slimy soles, paired together by some fisherwoman; but if his tongue was paralysed, his heart was not—it throbbed against his ribs with a violence which threatened their dislocation from the sternum, and with a sound which reverberated through the dark, damp subterrene—" I think that will do. There's *force* there.

Barnstaple. There is, with a vengeance. Why, what is all this?

Ansard. My dear Barnstaple, you here! I'm writing a romance for B—. It is to be supposed to be a translation.

Barnstaple. The Germans will be infinitely obliged to you; but, my dear fellow, you appear to have fallen into the old school—that's no longer in vogue.

Ansard. My orders are for the old school. B— was most particular on that point. He says that there is a re-action—a great re-action.

Barnstaple. What, on literature? Well, he knows as well as any man. I only wish to God there was in everything else, and we could see the good old times again.

Ansard. To confess the truth, I did intend to have finished this without saying a word to you. I wished to have surprised you.

Barnstaple. So you have, my dear fellow, with the few lines I have heard. How the devil are you to get your fellow out of that state of asphyxia?

Ansard. By degrees—slowly—very slowly—as they pretend that we lawyers go to heaven. But I'll tell you what I have done, just to give you an idea of my work. In the first place, I have a castle perched so high up in the air, that the eagles, even in their highest soar, appear but as wrens below.

Barnstaple. That's all right.

Ansard. And then it has subterraneous passages, to which the sewers of London are a mere song; and they all lead to a small cave at high-water mark on the sea-beach, covered with brambles and bushes, and just large enough at its entrance to admit of a man squeezing himself in:

Barnstaple. That's all right. You cannot be too much underground; in fact, the two first, and the best part of the third volume, should be wholly in the bowels of the earth, and your hero and heroine should never *come to light* until the last chapter.

Ansard. Then they would never have been born till then, and how could I marry them? But still I have adhered pretty much to your idea; and, Barnstaple, I have such a heroine—such a love—she has never seen her sweetheart, yet she is most devotedly attached, and has suffered more for his sake than any mortal could endure.

Barnstaple. Most heroines generally do.

Ansard. I have had her into various dungeons for three or four years, on black bread and a broken pitcher of water—she has been starved to death—lain for months and months upon wet straw—had two brain fevers—five times has she risked violation, and always has picked up, or found in the belt of her infamous ravishers, a stiletto, which she has plunged into their hearts, and they have expired with or without a groan.

Barnstaple. Excellent: and of course comes out of her dungeons each time as fresh, as sweet, as lovely, as pure, as charming, and as constant as ever.

Ansard. Exactly; nothing can equal her infinite variety of adventure, and her imperishable beauty and unadhesive cleanliness of person; and, as for lives, she has more than a thousand cats'. After nine months' confinement in a dungeon, four feet square, when it is opened for her release, the air is perfumed with the ambrosia which exhales from her sweet person.

Barnstaple. Of course it does. The only question is, what ambrosia smells like. But let me know something about your hero.

Ansard. He is a prince and a robber.

Barnstaple. The two professions are not at all incompatible. Go on.

Ansard. He is the chief of a band of robbers, and is here, there and everywhere. He fills all Europe with terror, admiration, and love.

Barnstaple. Very good.

Ansard. His reasons for joining the robbers are, of course, a secret (and upon my word they are equally a secret to myself); but it is wonderful the implicit obedience of his men, and the many acts of generosity of which he is guilty. I make him give away a great deal more money than his whole band ever take, which is so far awkward, that the query may arise in what way he keeps them together, and supplies them with food and necessaries.

Barnstaple. Of course with *IOUs* upon his princely domains.

Ansard. I have some very grand scenes, amazingly effective; for instance, what do you think, at the moment after the holy mass has been performed in Saint Peter's at Rome, just as the pope is about to put the sacred wafer into his mouth and bless the whole world, I make him snatch the wafer out of the pope's hand, and get clear off with it.

Barnstaple. What for, may I ask?

Ansard. That is a secret which I do not reveal. The whole arrangement of that part of the plot is admirable. The band of robbers are disguised as priests, and officiate, without being found out.

Barnstaple. But isn't that rather sacrilegious?

Ansard. No; it appears so to be, but he gives his reasons for his behaviour to the pope, and the pope is satisfied, and not only gives him his blessing, but shows him the greatest respect.

Barnstaple. They must have been very weighty reasons.

Ansard. And therefore they are not divulged.

Barnstaple. That is to say, not until the end of the work.

Ansard. They are never divulged at all; I leave a great deal to the reader's imagination—people are fond of conjecture. All they know is, that he boldly appears, and demands an audience. He is conducted in, the interview is private, after a sign made by our hero, and at which the pope almost leaps off the chair. After an hour he comes out again, and the pope bows him to the very door. Every one is astonished, and, of course, almost canonise him.

Barnstaple. That's going it rather strong in a Catholic country. But tell me, Ansard, what is your plot?

Ansard. Plot; I have none.

Barnstaple. No plot!

Ansard. No plot, and all plot. I puzzle the reader with certain materials. I have castles and dungeons, corridors and creaking doors, good villains and bad villains. Chain armour and clank of armour, daggers for gentlemen, and stilettoes for ladies. Dark forests and brushwood, drinking scenes, eating scenes, and sleeping scenes — robbers and friars, purses of gold and instruments of torture, an incarnate devil of a Jesuit, a handsome hero, and a lovely heroine. I jumble them all together, sometimes above, and sometimes underground, and I explain nothing at all.

Barnstaple. Have you nothing supernatural?

Ansard. O yes! I've a dog whose instinct is really supernatural, and I have two or three visions, which may be considered so, as they tell what never else could have been known. I decorate my caverns and dungeons with sweltering toads and slimy vipers, a constant dropping of water, with chains too ponderous to lift, but which the parties upon whom they are riveted, clang together as they walk up and down in their cells, and soliloquise. So much for my underground scenery. Above, I people the halls with pages and ostrich feathers, and knights in bright armour, a constant supply of generous wine, and goblets too heavy to lift, which the knights toss off at a draught, as they sit and listen to the minstrel's music.

Barnstaple. Bravo, Ansard, bravo. It appears to me that you do not want assistance in this romance.

Ansard. No, when I do I have always a holy and compassionate friar, who pulls a wonderful restorative or healing balm, out of his bosom. The puffs of Solomon's Balm of Gilead are a fool to the real merits of my pharmacopoeia contained in a small vial.

Barnstaple. And pray what may be the title of this book of yours, for I have known it take more time to fix upon a title than to write the three volumes.

Ansard. I call it *The Undiscovered Secret,* and very properly so too, for it never is explained. But if you please, I will read you some passages from it. I think you will approve of them. For instance, now let us take this, in the second volume. You must know, that Angelicanarinella (for that is the name of my heroine) is thrown into a dungeon not more than four feet square, but more than six hundred feet below the surface of the earth. The ways are so intricate, and the subterranean so vast, and the dungeons so numerous, that the base Ethiop, who has obeyed his master's orders in confining her, has himself been lost in the labyrinth, and has not been able to discover what dungeon he put her in. For three days he has been looking for it, during which our heroine has been without food, and he is still searching and scratching his woolly head in despair, as he is to die by slow torture, if he does not reproduce her—for you observe, the chief who has thrown her into his dungeon is most desperately in love with her.

Barnstaple. That of course; and that is the way to prove romantic love— you ill treat—but still she is certainly in a dilemma, as well as the Ethiop.

Ansard. Granted; but she talks like the heroine of a romance. Listen. (*Ansard reads.*) "The beauteous and divinely moulded form of the angelic Angelicanarinella pressed the dank and rotten straw which had been thrown down by the scowling, thick-lipped Ethiop for her repose—she, for whom attendant maidens had smoothed the Sybaritic sheet of finest texture, under the elaborately carved and sumptuously gilt canopy, the silken curtains, and the tassels of the purest dust of gold."

Barnstaple. Tassels of dust of gold! only figuratively, I suppose.

Ansard. Nothing more. "Each particular straw of this dank, damp bed was elastic with delight, at bearing such angelic pressure; and, as our heroine cast her ineffably beaming eyes about the dark void, lighting up with their effulgent rays each little portion of the dungeon, as she glanced them from one part to another, she perceived that the many reptiles enclosed with her in this narrow tomb, were nestling to her side, their eyes fixed upon her in mute expressions of love and admiration. Her eclipsed orbs were each, for a moment, suffused with a bright and heavenly tear, and from the suffusion threw out a more brilliant light upon the feeling reptiles who paid this tribute to her undeserved sufferings. She put forth her beauteous hand, whose 'faint tracery'—(I stole that from Cooper)—whose faint tracery had so often given to others the idea that it was ethereal, and not corporeal, and lifting with all the soft and tender handling of first love a venerable toad, which smiled upon her, she placed the interesting animal so that it could crawl up and nestle in her bosom, 'Poor child of dank, of darkness, and of dripping,' exclaimed she, in her flute-like notes, 'who sheltereth thyself under the wet and mouldering wall, so neglected in thy form by thy mother Nature, repose awhile in peace where princes and nobles would envy thee, if they knew thy present lot. But that shall never be; these lips shall never breathe a tale which might endanger thy existence; fear not, therefore, their enmity, and as thou slowly creepest away thy little round of circumscribed existence, forget me not, but shed an occasional pearly tear to the memory of the persecuted, the innocent Angelicanarinella!'" What d'ye think of that?

Barnstaple. Umph! a very warm picture certainly; however, it is natural. You know, a person of her consequence could never exist without a little *toadyism.*

Ansard. I have a good many subterraneous soliloquies, which would have been lost for ever, if I did not bring them up.

Barnstaple. That one you have just read is enough to make everybody else bring up.

Ansard. I rather plume myself upon it.

Barnstaple. Yes, it is a feather in your cap, and will act as a feather in the throat of your readers.

Ansard. Now I'll turn over the second volume, and read you another *morceau*, in which I assume the more playful vein. I have imitated one of our modern writers, who must be correct in her language, as she knows all about heroes and heroines. I must confess that I've cribbed a little.

Barnstaple. Let's hear.

Ansard. "The lovely Angelicanarinella *pottered* for some time about this fairy chamber, then 'wrote journal.' At last, she *threw herself down on the floor*, pulled out the miniature, *gulped* when she looked at it, and then *cried herself to sleep.*"

Barnstaple. Pottered and *gulped!* What language do you call that?

Ansard. It's all right, my dear fellow. I understand that it is the refined slang of the modern boudoir, and only known to the initiated.

Barnstaple. They had better keep it entirely to their boudoirs. I should advise you to leave it all out.

Ansard. Well, I thought that one who was so very particular, must have been the standard of perfection herself.

Barnstaple. That does not at all follow.

Ansard. But what I wish to read to you is the way in which I have managed that my secret shall never be divulged. It is known only to four.

Barnstaple. A secret known to four people! You must be quick then.

Ansard. So I am, as you shall hear; they all meet in a dark gallery, but do not expect to meet any one but the hero, whom they intend to murder, each one having, unknown to the others, made an appointment with him for that purpose, on the pretence of telling him the great secret. Altogether the scene is well described, but it is long, so I'll come at once to the *dénouement.*

Barnstaple. Pray do.

Ansard. "Absenpresentini felt his way by the slimy wall, when the breath of another human being caught his ear: he paused, and held his own breath. 'No, no,' muttered the other, 'the *secret of blood and gold* shall remain with me alone. Let him come, and he shall find death.' In a second, the dagger of Absenpresentini was in the mutterer's bosom:— he fell without a groan. 'To me alone the secret of blood and gold, and with me it remains,' exclaimed Absenpresentini. 'It does remain with you,' cried Phosphorini, driving his dagger into his back:— Absenpresentini fell without a groan, and Phosphorini, withdrawing his dagger, exclaimed, 'Who is now to tell the secret but me?' 'Not you,' cried Vortiskini, raising up his sword and striking at where the voice proceeded. The trusty steel cleft the head of the abandoned Phosphorini, who fell without a groan. 'Now will I retain the secret of blood and gold,' said Vortiskini, as he sheathed his sword. 'Thou shalt,' exclaimed the wily Jesuit, as he struck his stiletto to the heart of the robber, who fell without a groan. 'With me only does the secret now rest, by which our order might be disgraced; with me it dies,' and the Jesuit raised his hand. 'Thus to the glory and the honour of his society does Manfredini sacrifice his life.' He struck the keen-pointed instrument into his heart, and died without a groan. 'Stop,' cried our hero."

Barnstaple. And I agree with your hero: stop, Ansard, or you'll kill me too—but not without a groan.

Ansard. Don't you think it would act well?

Barnstaple. Quite as well as it reads; pray is it all like this?

Ansard. You shall judge for yourself. I have half killed myself with writing it, for I chew opium every night to obtain ideas. Now again—

Barnstaple. Spare me, Ansard, spare me; my nerves are rather delicate; for the remainder I will take your word.

Ansard. I wish my duns would do the same, even if it were only my washerwoman; but there's no more tick for me here, except this old watch of my father's, which serves to remind me of what I cannot obtain from others—time; but, however, there is a time for all things, and when the time comes that my romance is ready, my creditors will obtain the *ready.*

Barnstaple. Your only excuse, Ansard.

Ansard. I beg your pardon. The public require strong writing now-a-days. We have thousands who write well, and the public are nauseated with what is called *good writing.*

Barnstaple. And so they want something bad, eh? Well, Ansard, you certainly can supply them.

Ansard. My dear Barnstaple, you must not disparage this style of writing—it is not bad—there is a great art in it. It may be termed writing intellectual and ethereal. You observe, that it never allows probabilities or even possibilities to stand in its way. The dross of humanity is rejected: all the common wants and grosser feelings of our natures are disallowed. It is a novel which is all mind and passion. Corporeal attributes and necessities are thrown on one side, as they would destroy the charm of perfectability. Nothing can soil, or defile, or destroy my heroine; suffering adds lustre to her beauty, as pure gold is tried by fire: nothing can kill her, because she is all mind. As for my men, you will observe when you read my work—

Barnstaple. When I do!

Ansard. Which, of course, you will—that they also have their appetites in abeyance; they never want to eat, or drink, or sleep—are always at hand when required, without regard to time or space. Now there is a great beauty in this description of writing. The women adore it because they find their sex divested of those human necessities, without which they would indeed be angels! the mirror is held up to them, and they find themselves perfect— no wonder they are pleased. The other sex are also very glad to dwell upon female perfectability, which they can only find in a romance, although they have often dreamt of it in their younger days.

Barnstaple. There is some truth in these remarks. Every milliner's girl, who devours your pages in bed by the half-hour's light of tallow stolen for the purpose, imagines a strong similarity between herself and your Angelicanarinella, and every shop-boy measuring tape or weighing yellow soap will find out attributes common to himself and to your hero.

Ansard. Exactly. As long as you draw perfection in both sexes, you are certain to be read, because by so doing you flatter human nature and self-love, and transfer it to the individual who reads. Now a picture of real life—

Barnstaple. Is like some of Wouvermans' best pictures, which will not be purchased by many, because his dogs in the foreground are doing exactly what all dogs will naturally do when they first are let out of their kennels.

Ansard. Wouvermans should have known better, and made his dogs better mannered if he expected his pictures to be hung up in the parlour of refinement.

Barnstaple Very true.

Ansard. Perhaps you would like to have another passage or two.

Barnstaple. Excuse me: I will imagine it all. I only hope, Ansard, this employment will not interfere with your legal practice.

Ansard. My dear Barnstaple, it certainly will not, because my legal practice cannot be interfered with. I have been called to the bar, but find no employment in my calling. I have been sitting in my gown and wig for one year, and may probably sit a dozen more before I have to rise to address their lordships. I have not yet had a guinea brief. My only chance is to be sent out as judge to Sierra Leone, or perhaps to be made a commissioner of the Court of Requests.

Barnstaple. You are indeed humble in your aspirations. I recollect the time, Ansard, when you dreamt of golden fame, and aspired to the woolsack—when your ambition prompted you to midnight labour, and you showed an energy—

Ansard. (*putting his hands up to his forehead, with his elbows on the table.*) What can I do, Barnstaple? If I trust to briefs, my existence will be but brief— we all must live.

Barnstaple. I will not reply as Richelieu did to a brother author, "Je ne vois pas la nécessité;" but this I do say, that if you are in future to live by supplying the public with such nonsense, the shorter your existence the better.

Chapter Fifty

The Legend Of The Bell Rock

There was a grand procession through the streets of the two towns of Perth and Dundee. The holy abbots, in their robes, walked under gilded canopies, the monks chanted, the censers were thrown, flags and banners were carried by seamen, lighted tapers by penitents; Saint Antonio, the patron of those who trust to the stormy ocean, was carried in all pomp through the streets; and, as the procession passed, coins of various value were thrown down by those who watched it from the windows, and, as fast as thrown were collected by little boys dressed as angels, and holding silver vessels to receive the largesses. During the whole day did the procession continue, and large was the treasure collected in the two towns. Every one gave freely, for there were few, indeed none, who, if not in their own circle, at least among their acquaintances, had to deplore the loss of some one dear to them, or to those they visited, from the dangerous rock which lay in the very track of all the vessels entering the Firth of Tay.

These processions had been arranged, that a sufficient sum of money might be collected to enable them to put in execution a plan proposed by an adventurous and bold young seaman, in a council held for the purpose, of fixing a bell on the rock, which could be so arranged that the slightest breath of wind would cause the hammer of it to sound, and thus, by its tolling, warn the mariner of his danger; and the sums given were more than sufficient. A meeting was then held, and it was unanimously agreed that Andrew M'Clise should be charged with the commission to go over to Amsterdam, and purchase the bell of a merchant residing there, whom Andrew stated to have one in his possession, which, from its fine tone and size, was exactly calculated for the purport to which it was to be appropriated.

Andrew M'Clise embarked with the money, and made a prosperous voyage. He had often been at Amsterdam, and had lived with the merchant, whose name was Vandermaclin; and the attention to his affairs, the dexterity and the rapidity of the movements of Andrew M'Clise, had often elicited the warmest encomiums of Mynheer Vandermaclin; and many evenings had Andrew M'Clise passed with him, drinking in moderation their favourite scheedam, and indulging in the meditative merschaum. Vandermaclin had often wished that he had a son like Andrew M'Clise, to whom he could leave his property, with the full assurance that the heap would not be scattered, but greatly added to.

Vandermaclin was a widower. He had but one daughter, who was now just arrived at an age to return from the pension to her father's house, and take upon herself the domestic duties. M'Clise had never yet seen the beautiful Katerina.

"And so, Mynheer M'Clise," said Vandermaclin, who was sitting in the warehouse on the ground-floor of his tenement, "you come to purchase the famous bell of Utrecht; with the intention of fixing it upon that rock, the danger of which we have so often talked over after the work of the day has been done? I, too, have suffered from that same rock, as you well know; but still I have been fortunate. The price will be heavy; and so it ought to be, for the bell itself is of no small weight."

"We are prepared to pay it, Mynheer Vandermaclin."

"Nevertheless, in so good a cause, and for so good a purport, you shall not be overcharged. I will say nothing of the beauty of the workmanship, or even of the mere manufacture. You shall pay but its value in metal; the same price which the Jew Isaacs offered me for it but four months ago. I will not ask what a Jew would ask, but what a Jew would give, which makes no small difference. Have you ten thousand guilders?"

"I have, and more."

"That is my price, Mynheer M'Clise, and I wish for no more; for I, too, will contribute my share to the good work. Are you content, and is it a bargain?"

"It is; and the holy abbots will thank you on vellum, Mynheer Vandermaclin, for your generosity."

"I prefer the thanks of the bold seamen to those of the idle churchmen; but, never mind, it is a bargain. Now, we will go in; it is time to close the doors. We will take our pipes, and you shall make the acquaintance of my fair daughter, Katerina."

At the time we are speaking of, M'Clise was about six-and-twenty years of age; he was above the middle size, elegant in person, and with a frankness and almost nobility in his countenance, which won all who saw him.

His manners were like those of most seamen, bold, but not offensively so. His eye was piercing as an eagle's; and it seemed as if his very soul spoke from it. At the very first meeting between him and the daughter of Vandermaclin, it appeared to both as if their destinies were to unite them.

They loved not as others love, but with an intensity which it would be impossible to portray; but they hardly exchanged a word. Again and again they met; their eyes spoke, but nothing more. The bell was put on board the vessel, the money had been paid down, and M'Clise could no longer delay. He felt as if his heart-strings were severed as he tore himself away from the land where all remained that he coveted upon earth. And Katerina, she too felt as if her existence was a blank; and as the vessel sailed from the port, she breathed short; and when not even her white and lofty topgallant sail could be discovered as a speck, she threw herself on her couch and wept. And M'Clise as he sailed away, remained for hours leaning his cheek on his hand, thinking of, over and over again, every lineament and feature of the peerless Katerina.

Two months passed away, during which M'Clise was busied every ebb of the tide in superintending the work on the rock. At last, all was ready; and once more was to be beheld a gay procession; but this time it was on the water. It was on a calm and lovely summer's morn, that the abbots and the monks, attended by a large company of the authorities, and others, who were so much interested in the work in hand, started from the shore of Aberbrothwick in a long line of boats, decorated with sacred and with other various banners and devices. The music floated along the water, and the solemn chants of the monks were for once heard where never yet they had been heard before, or ever will again. M'Clise was at the rock, in a small vessel purposely constructed to carry the bell, and with sheers to hang it on the supports imbedded in the solid rock. The bell was in its place, and the abbot blessed the bell; and holy water was sprinkled on the metal, which was for the future to be lashed by the waves of the salt sea. And the music and the chants were renewed; and as they continued, the wind gradually rose, and with the rising of the wind the bell tolled loud and deep. The tolling of the bell was the signal for return, for it was a warning that the weather was about to change, and the procession pulled back to Aberbrothwick, and landed in good time; for in one hour more, and the rocky coast was again lashed by the waves, and the bell tolled loud and quick, although there were none there but the sea-gull, who screamed with fright as he wheeled in the air at this unusual noise upon the rock, which, at the ebb he had so often made his resting-place.

M'Clise had done his work; the bell was fixed; and once more he hastened with his vessel to Amsterdam. Once more was he an inmate of Vandermaclin's house; once more in the presence of the idol of his soul. This time they spoke; this time their vows were exchanged for life and death. But Vandermaclin saw not the state of their hearts. He looked upon the young seamen as too low, too poor, to be a match for his daughter; and as such an idea never entered his head, so did he never imagine that he would have dared to love. But he was soon undeceived; for M'Clise frankly stated his attachment, and demanded the hand of Katerina; and, at the demand, Vandermaclin's face was flushed with anger.

"Mynheer M'Clise," said he, after a pause, as if to control his feelings; "when a man marries, he is bound to show that he has wherewithal to support his wife; to support her in that rank, and to afford her those luxuries to which she has been accustomed in her father's house. Show me that you can do so, and I will not refuse you the hand of Katerina."

"As yet, I have not," replied M'Clise; "but I am young and can work; I have money, and will gain more. Tell me what sum do you think that I should possess to warrant my demanding the hand of your daughter?"

"Produce twelve thousand guilders, and she is yours," replied the merchant.

"I have but three thousand," replied M'Clise.

"Then, think no more of Katerina. It is a foolish passion, and you must forget it. And, Mynheer M'Clise, I must not have my daughter's affections tampered with. She must forget you; and that can only be effected by your not meeting again. I wish you well, Mynheer M'Clise, but I must request your absence."

M'Clise departed from the presence of the merchant, bowed down with grief and disappointment. He contrived that a letter, containing the result of his application, should be put in the hands of Katerina. But Vandermaclin was informed of this breach of observance, and Katerina was sent to a convent, there to remain until the departure of her lover; and Vandermaclin wrote to his correspondent at Dundee, requesting that the goods forwarded to him might not be sent by the vessel commanded by M'Clise.

Of this our young captain received information. All hope was nearly gone; still he lingered, and delayed his departure. He was no longer the active, energetic seaman; he neglected all, even his attire.

M'Clise knew in which convent his fair Katerina had been immured; and often would he walk round its precincts, with the hope of seeing her, if it were but for a moment, but in vain. His vessel was now laden, and he could delay no longer. He was to sail the next morning; and once more did the unhappy young man take his usual walk to look at those walls which contained all that was dear to him on earth. His reverie was broken by a stone falling down to his feet; he took it up; there was a small piece of paper attached to it with a silken thread. He opened it; it was the handwriting of Katerina, and contained but two words—"*The Bell.*"

The bell! M'Clise started; for he immediately comprehended what was meant. The whole plan came like electricity through his brain. Yes; then there was a promise of happiness. The bell was worth ten thousand guilders; that sum had been offered, and would now be given by Isaacs the Jew. He would be happy with his Katerina; and he blessed her ingenuity for devising the means. For a minute or two he was transported; but the reaction soon took place. What was he about to attempt? sacrilege—cruelty. The bell had been blessed by the holy church; it had been purchased by holy and devout alms. It had been placed on the rock to save the lives of his brother seamen; and were he to remove it, would he not be responsible for all the lives lost? Would not the wail of the widow, and the tears of the orphan, be crying out to Heaven against him? No, no! never! The crime was too horrible; and M'Clise stamped upon the paper, thinking he was tempted by Satan in the shape of woman; but when woman tempts, man is lost. He recalled the charms of Katerina; all his repugnance was overcome; and he resolved that the deed should be accomplished, and that Katerina should be gained, even if he lost his soul.

Andrew M'Clise sailed away from Amsterdam, and Katerina recovered her liberty. Vandermaclin was anxious that she should marry: and many were the suitors for her hand, but in vain. She reminded her father, that he had pledged himself, if M'Clise counted down twelve thousand guilders, that she should be his wife; and to that pledge she insisted that he was bound fast. And Vandermaclin after reasoning with her, and pointing out to her that twelve thousand guilders was a sum so large, that M'Clise might not procure until his old age, even if he were fortunate, acknowledged that such was his promise, and that he would, like an honest man, abide by it, provided that M'Clise should fulfil his part of the agreement in the space of two years; after which he should delay her settlement no longer. And Katerina raised her eyes to heaven, and whispered, as she clasped her hands, "The Bell." Alas! that we should invoke Heaven when we would wish to do wrong: but mortals are blind, and none so blind as those who are impelled by passion.

It was in the summer of that year that M'Clise had made his arrangements: having procured the assistance of some lawless hands, he had taken the advantage of a smooth and glassy sea and a high tide to remove the bell on board his own vessel; a work of little difficulty to him, as he had placed it there, and knew well the fastenings. He sailed away for Amsterdam, and was permitted by Heaven to arrive safe with his sacrilegious freight. He did not, as before, enter the canal opposite to the house of Vandermaclin, but one that ran behind the habitation of the Jew Isaacs. At night, he went into the house, and reported to the Jew what he had for sale; and the keen grey eyes of the bent-double little Israelite sparkled with delight, for he knew that his profit would be great. At midnight the bell was made fast to the crane, and safely deposited in the warehouse of the Jew, who counted out the ten thousand guilders to the enraptured M'Clise, whose thoughts were wholly upon the possession of his Katerina, and not upon the crime he had committed.

But, alas! to conceal one crime, we are too often obliged to be guilty of even deeper; and thus it was with Andrew M'Clise. The people who had assisted, upon the promise of a thousand guilders being divided among them, now murmured at their share, and insisted upon an equal division of the spoils, or threatened with an immediate confession of the black deed.

M'Clise raved, and cursed, and tore his hair; promised to give them the money as soon as he had wedded Katerina; but they would not consent. Again the devil came to his assistance, and whispered how he was to act: he consented. The next night the division was to be made. They met in his cabin; he gave them wine, and they drank plentifully; but the wine was poisoned, and they all died before the morning. M'Clise tied weights to their bodies, and sunk them in the deep canal; broke open his hatches, to make it appear that his vessel had been plundered; and then went to the authorities denouncing his crew as having plundered him, and escaped. Immediate search was made, but they were not to be found; and it was supposed that they had escaped in a boat.

Once more M'Clise, whose conscience was seared, went to the house of Vandermaclin, counted down his twelve thousand guilders, and claimed his bride; and Vandermaclin, who felt that his daughter's happiness was at stake, now gave his consent. As M'Clise stated that he was anxious to return to England, and arrange with the merchants whose goods had been plundered, in a few days the marriage took place; and Katerina clasped the murderer in her arms. All was apparent joy and revelry; but there was anguish in the heart of M'Clise, who, now that he had gained his object, felt that it had cost him much too dear, for his peace of mind was gone for ever. But Katerina cared not; every spark of feeling was absorbed in her passion, and the very guilt of M'Clise but rendered him more dear; for was it not for her that he had done all this? M'Clise received her portion, and hasted to sail away; for the bodies were still in the canal, and he trembled every hour lest his crime should be discovered. And Vandermaclin bade farewell to his daughter: and, he knew not why, but there was a feeling he could not suppress, that they never should meet again.

"Down—down below, Katerina! this is no place for you," cried M'Clise, as he stood at the helm of the vessel. "Down, dearest, down, or you will be washed overboard. Every sea threatens to pour into our decks; already have we lost two men. Down, Katerina! down, I tell you."

"I fear not; let me remain with you."

"I tell you, down!" cried M'Clise, in wrath; and Katerina cast upon him a reproachful look, and obeyed.

The storm was at its height; the sun had set, black and monstrous billows chased each other, and the dismasted vessel was hurried on towards the land. The wind howled, and whistled sharply at each chink in the bulwarks of the vessel. For three days had they fought the gale, but in vain. Now, if it continued, all chance was over; for the shore was on their lee, distant not many miles. Nothing could save them, but gaining the mouth of the Firth of Tay, and then they could bear up for Dundee. And there was a boiling surge, and a dark night, and roaring seas, and their masts were floating far away; and M'Clise stood at the helm, keeping her broadside to the sea: his heart was full of bitterness, and his guilty conscience bore him down, and he looked for death, and he dreaded it; for was he not a sacrilegious murderer, and was there not an avenging God above?

Once more Katerina appeared on deck, clinging for support to Andrew.

"I cannot stay below. Tell me, will it soon be over?"

"Yes," replied M'Clise, gloomily; "it will soon be over with all of us."

"How mean you? you told me there was no danger."

"I told you falsely; there is death soon, and damnation afterwards; for you I have lost my soul!"

"Oh! say not so."

"I say it. Leave me, leave me, woman, or I curse thee."

"Curse me, Andrew? Oh, no! Kiss me, Andrew; and if we are to perish, let us expire in each other's arms."

"'Tis as well; you have dragged me to perdition. Leave me, I say, for you have my bitter curse."

Thus was his guilty love turned to hate, now that death was staring him in the face.

Katerina made no reply. She threw herself on the deck, and abandoned herself to her feeling of bitter anguish. And as she lay there, and M'Clise stood at the helm, the wind abated; the vessel was no longer borne down as before, although the waves were still mountains high. The seamen on board rallied; some fragments of sail were set on the remnants of the masts, and there was a chance of safety. M'Clise spoke not, but watched the helm. The wind shifted in their favour; and hope rose in every heart. The Firth of Tay was now open, and they were saved! Light was the heart of M'Clise when he kept away the vessel, and gave the helm up to the mate. He hastened to Katerina, who still remained on the deck, raised her up, whispered comfort and returning love; but she heard not—she could not forget—and she wept bitterly.

"We are saved, dear Katerina!"

"Better that we had been lost!" replied she, mournfully.

"No, no! say not so, with your own Andrew pressing you to his bosom."

"Your bitter curse!"

"'Twas madness—nothing—I knew not what I said." But the iron had entered into her soul. Her heart was broken.

"You had better give orders for them to look out for the Bell Rock," observed the man at the helm to M'Clise.

The Bell Rock! M'Clise shuddered, and made no reply. Onward went the vessel, impelled by the sea and wind: one moment raised aloft, and towering over the surge; at another, deep in the hollow trough, and walled in by the convulsed element. M'Clise still held his Katerina in his arms, who responded not to his endearments, when a sudden shock threw them on the deck. The crashing of the timbers, the pouring of the waves over the stern, the heeling and settling of the vessel, were but the work of a few seconds. One more furious shock,—she separates, falls on her beam ends, and the raging seas sweep over her.

M'Clise threw from him her whom he had so madly loved, and plunged into the wave. Katerina shrieked, as she dashed after him, and all was over.

When the storm rises, and the screaming sea-gull seeks the land, and the fisherman hasten his bark towards the beach, there is to be seen, descending from the dark clouds with the rapidity of lightning, the form of Andrew M'Clise, the heavy bell to which he is attached by the neck, bearing him down to his doom.

And when all is smooth and calm, when at the ebbing tide, the wave but gently kisses the rock, then by the light of the silver moon, the occupants of the vessels which sail from the Firth of Tay, have often beheld the form of the beautiful Katerina, waving her white scarf as a signal that they should approach, and take her off from the rock on which she is seated. At times, she offers a letter for her father, Vandermaclin; and she mourns and weeps as the wary mariners, with their eyes fixed on her, and with folded arms, pursue their course in silence and in dread.

Chapter Fifty One

Moonshine

Those who have visited our West India possessions must have often been amused with the humour and cunning which occasionally appear in a negro more endowed than the generality of his race, particularly when the master also happens to be a humourist. The swarthy servitor seems to reflect his patron's absurdities; and having thoroughly studied his character, ascertains how far he can venture to take liberties without fear of punishment.

One of these strange specimens I once met with in a negro called Moonshine, belonging to a person equally strange in his own way, who had, for many years, held the situation of harbour-master at Port Royal, but had then retired on a pension, and occupied a small house at Ryde, in the Isle of Wight. His name was Cockle, but he had long been addressed as Captain Cockle; and this brevet rank he retained until the day of his death. In person he was very large and fat—not unlike a cockle in shape: so round were his proportions, and so unwieldy, that it appeared much easier to roll him along from one place to another, than that he should walk. Indeed, locomotion was not to his taste: he seldom went much farther than round the small patch of garden which was in front of his house, and in which he had some pinks and carnations and chrysanthemums, of which he was not a little proud. His head was quite bald, smooth, and shining white; his face partook of a more roseate tint, increasing in depth till it settled into an intense red at the tip of his nose. Cockle had formerly been a master of a merchant-vessel, and from his residence in a warm climate had contracted a habit of potation, which became confirmed during the long period of his holding his situation at Port Royal. He had purchased Moonshine for three hundred dollars, when he was about seven years old, and, upon his return to England, had taken him with him.

Moonshine was very much attached to his master, very much attached to having his own way, and was, farther, very much attached to his master's grog bottle.

The first attachment was a virtue: the second human nature; and the third, in the opinion of old Cockle, a crime of serious magnitude. I very often called upon Captain Cockle, for he had a quaint humour about him which amused; and, as he seldom went out, he was always glad to see any of his friends. Another reason was, that I seldom went to the house without finding some entertainment in the continual sparring between the master and the man. I was at that time employed in the Preventive Service, and my station was about four miles from the residence of Cockle. One morning I stalked in, and found him, as usual, in his little parlour on the ground-floor.

"Well, Cockle, my boy, how are you?"

"Why, to tell you the truth, Bob, I'm all wrong. I'm on the stool of repentance; to wit, on this easy chair, doing penance, as you perceive, in a pair of duck trousers. Last night I was half-seas over, and tolerably happy; this morning I am high and dry, and intolerably miserable. Carried more sail than ballast last night, and lost my head; this morning I've found it again, with a pig of ballast in it, I believe. All owing to my good nature."

"How is that, Cockle?"

"Why, that Jack Piper was here last night; and rather than he should drink all the grog and not find his way home, I drank some myself—he'd been in a bad way if I had not, poor fellow!—and now, you see, I'm suffering all from good nature. Easiness of disposition has been my ruin, and has rounded me into this ball, by wearing away all my sharp edges, Bob."

"It certainly was very considerate and very kind of you, Cockle, especially when we know how much you must have acted at variance with your inclinations."

"Yes, Bob, yes, I am the milk punch of human kindness. I often cry— when the chimney smokes; and sometimes—when I laugh too much. You see, I not only give my money, as others will do, but, as last night, I even give my head to assist a fellow-creature. I could, however, dispense with it for an hour or two this morning."

"Nay, don't say that; for although you might dispense with the upper part, you could not well get on without your mouth, Cockle."

"Very true, Bob; a chap without a mouth would be like a ship without a companion hatch;—talking about that, the combings of my mouth are rather dry—what do you say, Bob, shall we call Moonshine?"

"Why it's rather broad daylight for Moonshine."

"He's but an eclipse—a total eclipse, I may say. The fact is, my head is so heavy, that it rolls about on my shoulders; and I must have a stiffener down my throat to prop it it up. So Moonshine, shine out, you black-faced rascal!"

The negro was outside, cleaning his knives:— he answered, but continued at his work.

"How me shine, Massa Cockle, when you neber gib me *shiner*?"

"No: but I'll give you a *shinner* on your lower limb, that shall make you feel planet-struck, if you don't show your ugly face," replied Cockle.

"Massa Cockle, you full of dictionary dis marning."

"Come here, sir!"

"Why you so parsonal dis marning, sar," replied Moonshine, rubbing away at the knifeboard—"my face no shine more dan your white skull widout hair."

"I pulled one out, you scoundrel, every time you stole my grog, and now they are all gone.—Hairs; what should I do with heirs when I've nothing to leave," continued Cockle, addressing me—"hairs are like rats, that quit a ship as soon as she gets old. Now, Bob, I wonder how long that rascal will make us wait. I brought him home and gave him his freedom—but give an inch and he takes an ell. Moonshine, I begin to feel angry—the tip of my nose is red already."

"Come directly, Massa Cockle."

Moonshine gave two more rubs on the board, and then made his appearance.

"You call me, sar?"

"What's the use of calling you, you black rascal?"

"Now sar, dat not fair—you say to me, Moonshine, always do one thing first—so I 'bey order and finish knives—dat ting done, I come and 'bey next order."

"Well, bring some cold water and some tumblers."

Moonshine soon appeared with the articles, and then walked out of the room, grinning at me.

"Moonshine, where are you going, you thief?—when did you ever see me drink cold water, or offer it to my friend?"

"Neber see you drink it but once, and den you tipsy, and tink it gin; but you very often gib notin but water to your friends, Massa Cockle."

"When, you scoundrel?"

"Why, very often you say dat water quite strong enough for me."

"That's because I love you, Moonshine. Grog is a sad enemy to us."

"Massa Cockle real fine Christian—he lub him enemy," interrupted Moonshine, looking at me.

"At all events, I'm not ashamed to look mine enemy in the face—so hand us out the bottle."

Moonshine put the bottle on the table.

"Now, Bob," said Cockle, "what d'ye say to a *seven bell-er*? Why, hallo! what's become of all the grog?"

"All drank last night, Massa Cockle," replied Moonshine.

"Now, you ebony thief, I'll swear that there was half a bottle left when I took my last glass; for I held the bottle up to the candle to ascertain the ullage."

"When you go up tairs, Massa Cockle, so help me Gad! not one drop left in de bottle."

"Will you take your oath, Moonshine, that you did not drink any last night?"

"No, Massa Cockle, because I gentleman, and neber tell lie—me drink, because you gib it to me."

"Then I must have been drunk indeed. Now, tell me, how did I give it to you?—tell me every word which passed."

"Yes, Massa Cockle, me make you recollect all about it. When Massa Piper go away, you look at bottel and den you say, "Fore I go up to bed, I take one more glass for *coming* up.'—Den I say, "Pose you do, you nebber be able to *go up*.' Den you say, 'Moonshine, you good fellow (you always call me good fellow when you want me), you must help me.' You drink you grog—you fall back in de chair, and you shut first one eye, and den you shut de oder. I see more grog on the table: so I take up de bottel and I say, 'Massa Cockle, you go up stairs?' and you say, 'Yes, yes—directly.' Den I hold de bottel up and say to you, 'Massa, shall I help you?' and you say, 'Yes, you must *help* me.' So den I take one glass of grog, 'cause you tell me to help you."

"I didn't tell you to help yourself though, you scoundrel!"

"Yes, Massa, when you tell me to help you with de bottel, I 'bey order, and help myself. Den, sar, I waits little more, and I say, 'Massa now you go up 'tairs,' and you start up and you wake, and you say, 'Yes, yes;' and den I hold up and show you bottel again, and I say, 'Shall I *help* you massa?' and den you say 'Yes.' So I 'bey order again, and take one more glass. Den you open mouth and you snore—so I look again and I see one little glass more in bottel, and I call you, 'Massa Cockle, Massa Cockle,' and you say, 'high—high!'—and den you head fall on you chest, and you go sleep again—so den I call again and I say; 'Massa Cockle, here one lilly more drop, shall I drink it?' and you nod you head on you bosom, and say noting—so I not quite sure, and I say again, 'Massa Cockle, shall I finish this lilly drop?' and you nod you head once more. Den I say, 'all right,' and I say, 'you very good helt, Massa Cockle;' and I finish de bottel. Now, Massa, you ab de whole tory, and it all really for true."

I perceived that Cockle was quite as much amused at this account of Moonshine's as I was myself, but he put on a bluff look.

"So, sir, it appears that you took advantage of my helpless situation, to help yourself."

"Massa Cockle, just now you tell Massa Farren dat you drink so much, all for good nature Massa Piper—I do same all for good nature."

"Well, Mr Moonshine, I must have some grog," replied Cockle, "and as you helped yourself last night, now you must help me;—get it how you can, I give you just ten minutes—"

"'Pose you give gib me ten shillings, sar," interrupted Moonshine, "dat better."

"Cash is all gone. I havn't a skillick till quarter-day, not a shot in the locker till Wednesday. Either get me some more grog, or you'll get more kicks than halfpence."

"You no ab money—you no ab tick—how I get grog, Massa Cockle? Missy O'Bottom, she tells me, last *quarter* day, no pay *whole* bill, she not *half* like it; she say you great deceiver, and no trust more."

"Confound the old hag! Would you believe it, Bob, that Mrs Rowbottom has wanted to grapple with me these last two years—wants to make me landlord of the Goose and Pepper-box, taking her as a fixture with the premises. I suspect I should be the goose and she the pepper-box;—but we never could shape that course. In the first place, there's too much of her; and, in the next, there's too much of me. I explained this to the old lady as well as I could; and she swelled up as big as a balloon, saying, that, when people were really *attached*, they never *attached* any weight to such trifling obstacles."

"But you must have been sweet upon her, Cockle?"

"Nothing more than a little sugar to take the nauseous taste of my long bill out of her mouth. As for the love part of the story, that was all her own. I never contradict a lady, because it's not polite; but since I explained, the old woman has huffed, and won't trust me with half a quartern—will she, Moonshine?"

"No, sar: when I try talk her over, and make promise, she say dat *all moonshine*. But, sar, I try 'gain—I tink I know how." And Moonshine disappeared, leaving us in the dark as to what his plans might be.

"I wonder you never did marry, Cockle," I observed.

"You would not wonder if you knew all. I must say, that once, and once only, I was very near it. And to whom do you think it was—a woman of colour."

"A black woman?"

"No: not half black, only a quarter—what they call a quadroon in the West Indies. But, thank Heaven! she refused me."

"Refused you? hang it, Cockle, I never thought that you had been refused by a woman of colour."

"I was, though. You shall hear how it happened. She had been the quadroon wife (you know what that means) of a planter of the name of Guiness; he died, and not only bequeathed her her liberty, but also four good houses in Port Royal, and two dozen slaves. He had been dead about two years, and she was about thirty, when I first knew her. She was very rich, for she had a good income and spent nothing, except in jewels and dress to deck out her own person, which certainly was very handsome, even at that time, for she never had had any family. Well, if I was not quite in love with her, I was with her houses and her money; and I used to sit in her verandah and talk sentimental. One day I made my proposal. 'Massa Cockle,' said she, 'dere two ting I not like; one is, I not like your name. 'Pose I 'cept your offer, you must change you name.'

"'Suppose you accept my offer, Mistress Guiness, you'll change your name. I don't know how I am to change mine,' I replied.

"'I make 'quiry, Massa Cockle, and I find that by act and parliament you get another name.'

"'An act of parliament!' I cried.

"'Yes, sar; and I pay five hundred gold Joe 'fore I hear people call me Missy Cockle—dat *shell* fish,' said she, and she turned up her nose.

"'Humph!' said I, 'and pray what is the next thing which you wish?'

"'De oder ting, sar, is, you no ab *coat am arms*, no ab seal to your watch, with bird and beast 'pon 'em; now 'pose you promise me dat you take oder name, and buy um coat am arms; den, sar, I take de matter into 'sideration.'

"'Save yourself the trouble, ma'am,' said I, jumping up; 'my answer is short—I'll see you and your whole generation hanged first!'

"Well, that was a very odd sort of a wind-up to a proposal; but here comes Moonshine."

The black entered the room, and put a full bottle down on the table.

"Dare it is, sar," said he, grinning.

"Well, done, Moonshine, now I forgive you; but how did you manage it?"

"Me tell you all de tory, sar—first I see Missy O'Bottom, and I say, 'How you do, how you find himsel dis marning? Massa come, I tink, by an bye, but he almost fraid,' I said. She say, 'What he fraid for?' He tink you angry— not like see him—no lub him any more: he very sorry, very sick at 'art—he very much in lub wid you."

"The devil you did!" roared Cockle; "now I shall be bothered again with that old woman; I wish she was moored as a buoy to the Royal George."

"Massa no hear all yet. I say, 'Miss O'Bottom, 'pose you no tell?' 'I tell.'—'Massa call for clean shirt dis morning, and I say, it no clean shirt day, sar;' he say, 'Bring me clean shirt;' and den he put him on clean shirt and he put him on clean duck trowsers, he make me brush him best blue coat. I say, 'What all dis for, massa?' He put him hand up to him head, and he fetch him breath and say—'I fraid Missy O'Bottom, no hear me now—I no hab courage;' and den he sit all dress ready, and no go. Den he say, 'Moonshine, gib me one glass grog, den I hab courage.' I go fetch bottle, and all grog gone—not one lilly drop left; den massa fall down plump in him big chair, and say, 'I neber can go.' 'But,' say Missy O'Bottom, 'why he no send for some?' "'Cause,' I say, 'quarter-day no come—money all gone.'—Den say she, 'If you poor massa so *very* bad, den I trust you one bottel—you gib my compliments and say, I very appy to see him, and stay at home,'—Den I say, 'Missy O'Bottom pose massa not come soon as he take one two glass grog cut my head off.' Dat all, sar."

"That's all, is it? A pretty scrape you have got me into, you scoundrel! What's to be done now?"

"Why, let's have a glass of grog first, Cockle," replied I, "we've been waiting a long while for it, and we'll then talk the matter over."

"Bob, you're sensible, and the old woman was no fool in sending the liquor—it requires *Dutch* courage to attack such a Dutch-built old schuyt;

let's get the cobwebs out of our throats, and then we must see how we can get out of this scrape. I expect that I shall pay 'dearly for my whistle' this time I wet mine. Now, what's to be done, Bob?"

"I think that you had better leave it to Moonshine," said I.

"So I will.—Now, sir, as you have got me into this scrape, you must get me out of it.—D'ye hear?"

"Yes, Massa Cockle, I tink—but no ab courage."

"I understand you, you sooty fellow—here, drink this, and see if it will brighten up your wits. He's a regular turnpike, that fellow, every thing must pay toll."

"Massa Cockle, I tell Missy O'Bottom dat you come soon as you hab two glass grog; 'pose you only drink one."

"That won't do, Moonshine, for I'm just mixing my second; you must find out something better."

"One glass grog, massa, gib no more dan one tought—dat you ab—"

"Well, then, here's another.—Now recollect, before you drink it, you are to get me out of this scrape; if not, you get into a scrape, for I'll beat you as—as white as snow."

"'Pose you no *wash* nigger white, you no *mangle* him white, Massa Cockle," added Moonshine.

"The fellow's *ironing* me, Bob, ar'n't he?" said Cockle, laughing. "Now, before you drink, recollect the conditions."

"Drink first, sar, make sure of dat," replied Moonshine, swallowing off the brandy; "tink about it afterwards.—Eh! I ab it," cried Moonshine, who disappeared, and Cockle and I continued in conversation over our grog, which to sailors is acceptable in any one hour in the twenty-four. About ten minutes afterwards Cockle perceived Moonshine in the little front garden. "There's that fellow, Bob; what is he about?"

"Only picking a nosegay, I believe," replied I, looking out of the window.

"The rascal, he must be picking all my chrysanthemums. Stop him, Bob."

But Moonshine vaulted over the low pales, and there was no stopping him. It was nearly an hour before he returned; and when he came in, we found that he was dressed out in his best, looking quite a dandy, and with some of his master's finest flowers, in a large nosegay, sticking in his waistcoat.

"All right, sar, all right; dat last glass grog gib me fine idee; you neber ab more trouble bout Missy O'Bottom."

"Well, let's hear," said Cockle.

"I dress mysel bery 'pruce, as you see, massa. I take nosegay."

"Yes, I see that, and be hanged to you."

"Neber mind, Massa Cockle. I say to Missy O'Bottom, 'Massa no able come, he very sorry, so he send me;' 'well,' she say, 'what you ab to say, sit down, Moonshine, you very nice man.' Den I say, 'Massa Cockle lub you very much, he tink all day how he make you appy; den he say, Missy O'Bottom very fine 'oman, make very fine wife.' Den Missy O'Bottom say, "Top a moment,' and she bring a bottel from cupboard, and me drink something did make 'tomach feel really warm; and den she say, 'Moonshine, what you massa say?' den I say, massa say, 'You fine 'oman, make good wife;' but he shake um head, and say, 'I very old man, no good for noting; I tink all day how I make her appy, and I find out—Moonshine, you young man, you 'andsome feller, you good servant, I not like you go away, but I tink you make Missy O'Bottom very fine 'usband; so I not care for myself, you go to Missy O'Bottom, and tell I send you, dat I part wid you, and give you to her for 'usband.'"

Cockle and I burst out laughing. "Well, and what did Mrs Rowbottom say to that?"

"She jump up, and try to catch me hair, but I bob my head, and she miss; den she say, 'You filthy black rascal, you tell you massa, 'pose he ever come here, I break his white bald pate; and 'pose you ever come here, I smash you woolly black skull.'—Dat all, Massa Cockle; you see all right now, and I quite dry wid talking."

"All right! do you call it. I never meant to quarrel with the old woman; what d'ye think, Bob—is it all right?"

"Why, you must either have quarrelled with her, or married her, that's clear."

"Well, then, I'm clear of her, and so it's all right. It a'n't every man who can get out of matrimony by sacrificing a nosegay and two glasses of grog."

"Tree glasses, Massa Cockle," said Moonshine.

"Well, three glasses; here it is, you dog, and its dog cheap, too. Thank God, next Wednesday's quarter day. Bob, you must dine with me—cut the service for to-day."

"With all my heart," replied I, "and I'll salve my conscience by walking the beach all night; but, Cockle, look here, there is but a drop in the bottle, and you have no more. I am like you, with a clean swept hold. You acknowledge the difficulty?"

"It stares me in the face, Bob; what must be done?"

"I'll tell you—in the first place, what have you for dinner?"

"Moonshine, what have we got for dinner?"

"Dinner, sar?—me not yet tink about dinner. What you like to eat, sar?"

"What have we got in the house, Moonshine?"

"Let me see, sar? first place, we ab very fine piece picklum pork; den we have picklum pork; and den—let me tink—den we ab, we ab picklum pork, sar."

"The long and the short of it is, Bob, that we have nothing but a piece of pickled pork; can you dine off that?"

"Can a duck swim, Cockle!"

"Please, sar, we ab plenty pea for *dog baddy*," said Moonshine.

"Well, then, Cockle, as all that is required is to put the pot on the fire, you can probably spare Moonshine, after he has done that, and we will look to the cookery; start him off with a note to Mr Johns, and he can bring back a couple of bottles from my quarters."

"Really dat very fine tought, Massa Farren; I put in pork, and den I go and come back in one hour."

"That you never will, Mr Moonshine; what's o'clock now? mercy on us, how time flies in your company, Cockle, it is nearly four o'clock; it will be dark at six."

"Neber mind, sar, me always ab *moonshine* whereber I go," said the black, showing his teeth.

"It will take two hours to boil the pork, Bob; that fellow has been so busy this morning that he has quite forgot the dinner."

"All you business, Massa Cockle."

"Very true; but now start as soon as you can, and come back as soon as you can; here's the note."

Moonshine took the note, looked at the direction, as if he could read it, and in a few minutes was seen to depart.

"And now, Cockle," said I, "as Moonshine will be gone some time, suppose you spin us a yarn to pass away the time."

"I'll tell you what, Bob, I am not quite so good at that as I used to be. I've an idea that when my pate became bald, my memory oozed away by insensible perspiration."

"Never mind, you must have something left, you can't be quite empty."

"No, but my tumbler is; so I'll just fill that up, and then I'll tell you how it was that I came to go to sea."

"The very thing that I should like to hear, above all others."

"Well, then, you must know that, like cockles in general, I was born on the sea-shore, just a quarter of a mile out of Dover, towards Shakespeare's Cliff. My father was a fisherman by profession, and a smuggler by practice, all was fish that came to his net; but his cottage was small, he was supposed to be very poor, and a very bad fisherman, for he seldom brought home many; but there was a reason for that, he very seldom put his nets overboard. His chief business lay in taking out of vessels coming down Channel, goods which were shipped and bonded for exportation, and running them on shore again. You know, Bob, that there are many articles which are not permitted to enter even upon paying duty, and when these goods, such as silks, etcetera, are seized or taken in prizes, they are sold for exportation. Now, it was then the custom for vessels to take them on board in the river, and run them on shore as they went down Channel, and the fishing-boats were usually employed for this service; my father was a well-known hand for this kind of work, for not being suspected, he was always fortunate; of course, had he once been caught, they would have had their eyes upon him after he had suffered his punishment. Now the way my father used to manage was this: there was a long tunnel-drain from some houses used as manufactories, about a hundred yards above his cottage, which extended out into the sea at low-water mark, and which passed on one side of our cottage. My father had cut from a cellar in the cottage into the drain, and as it was large enough for a man to kneel down in, he used to come in at low-water with his coble, and make fast the goods, properly secured from the wet and dirt in tarpaulin bags, to a rope, which led from the cellar to the sea through the drain. When the water had flowed sufficiently to cover the mouth of the drain, he then threw the bags overboard, and, securing the boat, went to the cottage, hauled up the articles, and secured them too; d'ye understand? My father had no one to assist him but my brother, who was a stout fellow, seven years older than myself, and my mother, who used to give a helping hand when required; and thus did he keep his own counsel, and grow rich; when all was right, he got his boat over into the harbour, and having secured her, he came home as innocent as a lamb. I was then about eight or nine years old, and went with my father and brother in the coble, for she required three hands, at least, to manage her properly, and like a tin-pot, although not very big, I was very useful. Now it so happened that my father had notice that a brig, laying in Dover harbour, would sail the next day, and that she had on board of her a quantity of lace and silks, purchased at the Dover custom-house for exportation, which he was to put on shore again to be sent up to London. The sending up to London we had nothing to do with; the agent at Dover managed all that; we only left the articles at his house, and then received the money on the nail. We went to the harbour, where we found the brig hauling out, so we made all haste to get away before her. It blew fresh from the northward and eastward, and there was a good deal of sea running. As we were shoving out, the London agent, a jolly little round-faced fellow, in black clothes, and a bald white head, called to us, and said that he wanted to board a vessel in the offing, and asked whether we would take him. This was all a ruse, as he intended to go on board of the brig with us to settle matters, and then return in the pilot boat. Well, we hoisted our jib, drew aft our foresheet, and were soon clear of the harbour; but we found that there was a devil of a sea running, and more wind than we bargained for; the brig came out of the harbour with a flowing sheet, and we lowered down the foresail to reef it—father and brother busy about that, while I stood at the helm, when the agent said to me, 'When do you mean to make a voyage?' 'Sooner than father thinks for,' said I, 'for I want to see the world.' It was sooner than I *thought for* too, as you shall hear. As soon as the brig was well out, we ran down to her, and with some difficulty my father and the agent got on board, for the sea was high and cross, the tide setting against the wind; my brother and I were left in the boat to follow in the wake of the brig; but as my brother was casting off the rope forward, his leg caught in the bight, and into the sea he went; however, they hauled him on board, leaving me alone in the coble. It was not of much consequence, as I could manage to follow before the wind under easy sail, without assistance: so I kept her in the wake of the brig, both of us running nearly before it at the rate of five miles an hour, waiting till my father should have made up his packages, of a proper size to walk through the tunnel drain.

"The Channel was full of ships, for the westerly winds had detained them for a long time. I had followed the brig about an hour, when the agent went on shore in a pilot boat, and I expected my father would soon be ready; then the wind veered more towards the southward, with dirt: at last it came on foggy, and I could hardly see the brig, and as it rained hard, and blew harder, I wished that my father was ready, for my arms ached with steering the coble for so long a while. I could not leave the helm, so I steered on at a black lump, as the brig looked through the fog: at last the fog was so thick that I could not see a yard beyond the boat, and I hardly knew how to steer. I began to be frightened, tired, and cold, and hungry I certainly was. Well, I steered on for more than an hour, when the fog cleared up a little, and to my joy I saw the stern of the brig just before me. I expected that she would round-to immediately, and that my father would praise me for my conduct; and, what was still more to the purpose, that I should get something to eat and drink. But no: she steered on right down Channel, and I followed for more than an hour, when it came on to blow very hard, and I could scarcely manage the boat—she pulled my little arms off. The weather now cleared up, and I could make out the vessel plainly; when I discovered that it was not the *brig*, but a bark which I had got hold of in the fog, so that I did not know what to do; but I did as most boys would have done in a fright,—I sat down and cried; still, however, keeping the tiller in my hand, and steering as well as I could. At last. I could hold it no longer; I ran forward, let go the fore and jib haul-yards, and hauled down the sails; drag them into the boat I could not, and there I was, like a young bear adrift in a washing-tub. I looked around, and there were no vessels near; the bark had left me two miles astern, it was blowing a gale from the SE, with a heavy sea—the gulls and sea-birds wheeling and screaming in the storm. The boat tossed and rolled about so that I was obliged to hold on, but she shipped no water of any consequence, for the jib in the water forward had brought her head to wind, and acted as a sort of floating anchor. At last I lay down at the bottom of the boat and fell asleep. It was daylight before I awoke, and it blew harder than ever; and I could just see some vessels at a distance, scudding before the gale, but they could hardly see me. I sat very melancholy the whole day, shedding tears, surrounded by nothing but the roaring waves. I prayed very earnestly: I said the Lord's Prayer, the Belief, and as much of the Catechism as I could recollect. I was wet, starving, and miserably cold. At night I again fell asleep from exhaustion. When morning broke, and the sun shone, the gale abated, and I felt more cheered; but I was now ravenous from hunger, as well as choking from thirst, and was so weak that I could scarcely stand. I looked round me every now and then, and in the afternoon saw a large vessel standing right for me; this gave me courage and strength. I stood up and waved my hat, and they saw me—the sea was still running very high, but the wind had gone down. She rounded-to so as to bring me under her lee. Send a boat she could not, but the sea bore her down upon me, and I was soon close to her. Men in the chains were ready with ropes, and I knew that this was my only chance. At last, a very heavy sea bore her right down upon the boat, lurching over on her beam ends, her main chains struck the boat and sent her down, while I was seized by the scruff of the neck by two of the seamen, and borne aloft by them as the vessel returned to the weather-roll. I was safe. And, as soon as they had given me something to eat, I told my story. It appeared that she was an East India-man running down Channel, and not likely to meet with anything to scud me back again. The passengers, especially the ladies, were very kind to me: and as there was no help for it, why, I took my first voyage to the *East Indies.*"

"And your father and your brother?"

"Why, when I met them, which I did about six years afterwards, I found that they had been in much the same predicament, having lost the coble, and the weather being so bad that they could not get on shore again. As there was no help for it, they took their first voyage to the *West Indies;* so there was a dispersion of an united family—two went west, one went east, coble went down, and mother, after waiting a month or two, and supposing father dead, went off with a soldier. All dispersed by one confounded gale of wind from the northward and eastward, so that's the way that I went to sea, Bob. And now it's time that Moonshine was back."

But Moonshine kept us waiting for some time: when he returned it was then quite dark, and we had lighted candles, anxiously waiting for him; for not only was the bottle empty, but we were very hungry. At last we heard a conversation at the gate, and Moonshine made his appearance with the two bottles of spirits, and appeared himself to be also in high spirits. The pork and peas-pudding soon were on the table. We dined heartily, and were sitting over the latter part of the first bottle in conversation, it being near upon the eleventh hour, when we heard a noise, at the gate—observed some figures of men, who stayed a short time and then disappeared. The door opened, and Moonshine went out. In a few seconds he returned, bringing in his arms an anker of spirits, which he laid on the floor, grinning so wide that his head appeared half off. Without saying a word, he left the room and returned with another.

"Why, what the devil's this?" cried Cockle.

Moonshine made no answer, but went out and in until he had brought six ankers in, one after another, which he placed in a row on the floor. He then shut the outside door, bolted it, came in, and seating himself on one of the tubs, laughed to an excess which compelled him to hold his sides; Cockle and I looking on in a state of astonishment.

"Where the devil did all this come from?" cried Cockle, getting out of his easy chair. "Tell me, sir, or by—"

"I tell you all, Massa Cockle:— you find me better friend dan Missy O'Bottom. Now you hab plenty, and neber need scold Moonshine 'pose he take lilly drap. I get all dis present to you, Massa Cockle."

Feeling anxious, I pressed Moonshine to tell his story.

"I tell you all, sar. When I come back wid de two bottle I meet plenty men wid de tubs: dey say, 'Hollo there, who be you?' I say, 'I come from station: bring massa two bottel, and I show um.' Den dey say, 'Where you massa?' and I say, 'At um house at Ryde'—(den dey tink dat you my massa, Massa Farren)—so dey say, 'Yes, we know dat, we watch him dere, but now you tell, so we beat you dead.' Den I say, 'What for dat; massa like drink, why you no gib massa some tub, and den he neber say noting, only make fuss some time, 'cause of Admirality.' Den dey say, 'You sure of dat?' and I say, 'Quite sure massa neber say one word.' Den dey talk long while; last, dey come and say, 'You come wid us and show massa house.' So two men come wid me, and when dey come to gate I say, 'Dis massa house when he live at Ryde, and dere you see massa;'—and I point to Massa Cockle, but dey see Massa Ferran—so dey say. 'All very good; tree, four hour more, you find six tub here; tell you massa dat every time run tub, he alway hab six;' den dey go way, den dey come back, leave tub; dat all, massa."

"You rascal!" exclaimed I, rising up, "so you have compromised me; why I shall lose my commission if found out."

"No, sar; nobody wrong but de smuggler; dey make a lilly mistake; case you brought to court-martial, I give evidence, and den I clear you."

"But what must we do with the tubs, Cockle?" said I, appealing to him.

"Do Bob?—why they are a present—a very welcome one, and a very handsome one into the bargain. I shall not *keep* them, I pledge you my word; let that satisfy you—they shall be *fairly entered*."

"Upon that condition, Cockle," I replied, "I shall of course not give information against you." (I knew full well what he meant by saying he would not *keep* them.)

"*How* I do, Massa Cockle," said Moonshine, with a grave face; "I take um to the Custom-house to-night or to-morrow morning."

"To-morrow, Moonshine," replied Cockle; "at present just put them out of sight."

I did not think it prudent to make any further inquiries; but I afterwards discovered that the smugglers, true to their word, and still in error, continued to leave six tubs in old Cockle's garden whenever they succeeded in running a cargo, which, notwithstanding all our endeavours, they constantly did. One piece of information I gained from this affair, I found that the numbers of the cargoes which were run compared to those which were seized during the remainder of the time I was on that station, was in the proportion of ten to one. The cargoes run were calculated by the observations of old Cockle, who, when I called upon him, used to say very quietly, "I shouldn't wonder if they did not run a cargo last night, Bob, in spite of all your vigilance—was it very dark?"

"On the contrary," replied I, looking at the demure face of the negro; "I suspect it was *Moonshine.*"